SCARE TACTICS

Scare Tactics

A NOVEL

David Milofsky

Also by David Milofsky

A Message from Carnegie
A Milwaukee Inheritance
Where I'm Living Now (stories)
Managed Care
A Friend of Kissinger
Color of Law
Eternal People
Playing From Memory

Once More, To Jeanie

Democracy's a very fragile thing...As soon as you stop being responsible to it and allow it to turn into scare tactics, it's something else. It may be an inch away from totalitarianism.

—Sam Shepard

Hell is a truth seen too late.

—Thomas Hobbes

Prologue: Summer, 1953

It was a bad time. Not the worst maybe because you had the Depression which for some reason people were now calling The Great Depression, even if there was nothing great about it, when children were served dirt sandwiches for lunch, the sky cracked for lack of rain, men left home to ride empty boxcars rather than face their families without jobs and despite the alphabet agencies of the so-called New Deal, poverty hung in the air like humidity and caused everyone's shoulders to sag. The only solution was war which ended the Depression but brought in its place rationing, a raging black market and an endless procession of body bags from Europe, the Pacific and points in between. And even after that, after the latest war to end all wars, things didn't really improve. London had been reduced to a gravel pit and in gratitude for his leadership, the voters tossed Churchill out at the first opportunity. The allies divided up Europe with everyone getting a piece of the pie except of course the Germans who, having lost again, were left to starve in peace. Refugees from the death camps and ruined cities filled makeshift camps set up by the international agencies who had nothing else to offer. And then for the coup de grace, Truman dropped bombs on Hiroshima and Nagasaki, ushering in what came to be known as the atomic era which finally made the Japanese stop their end of the war but stopped also the lives of thousands of people who'd been living in those cities minding their own business.

You'd think everyone would have had enough by now, but once the world war was over and the boys came home with medals and missing appendages, ready to start finally the life they'd thought they were fighting for, taking a job or buying some hurriedly constructed house in Levittown, the daily papers were reporting about yet another war in Korea. New Draft notices were going out and the military was preparing for an attack on Alaska. Even more ominous was what came to be known as the Cold War which when you looked at it wasn't that different from the old war except now no one wore uniforms to tell you which side they were on. Instead, the enemy was invisible and everywhere; spies were in the government, the army, next door, at the store, around the corner and in less obvious places you hadn't thought to look. Everyone suspected everyone because those commies were tricky and what's more, they were on the move, coming to your town, your block, next door. All of which made it important to elect a five-star general as president even if he had no experience in politics and really little interest in the whole thing. He'd managed D-Day so how hard could running the country be?

The House Committee on UnAmerican Activities had been instituted in the forties and was doing its part diligently to ferret out spies, holding hearings, swearing in revolutionaries and sympathizers. And now a local boy, just back from the war with medals he'd made for himself had come in with Eisenhower and started his own committee to investigate, though he wasn't sure what exactly. He'd look around and see what he could see. For Tailgunner Joe, everyone was a potential source, a possible witness. Keep those letters coming, the Senator said, and the people responded. They informed on neighbors, business partners, friends or former friends or just someone they saw on the street who walked funny. The tension divided the country like never before, even during the Depression or the war when at least we'd all been on the same side. Families were split and Sunday dinner became impossible. The guy at the next desk was a suspect. What did you see, what do you know? Put it on a card and send it in, McCarthy wanted to know. Fear was everywhere, like the polio that terrified every mother; and like the disease, this spread through the air, radioactive, scouring the fields and cities equally, dividing the country with surgical acuity. It was unlike anything we had ever known. Everything was different now.

One

MADISON

Nine o'clock and the night was black as pitch which made it impossible for Edgeworth to find the last devilled egg his wife had packed for the picnic. He was sitting on an army blanket with his son, fingering the wool with his hands, but the sky was a vast rug wrapped around the world. Fireworks would bleach the air for a moment before everything went black again. Yellow banana shapes and scarlet arrows lit up the sky as the darkened shapes of neighbors shifted back and forth to get a better look. Ed never got this. How could there be a bad view of the sky? He could smell the animal shit from the zoo back there in the dark and even the odor of dead alewives from the lake beyond, but this didn't help him find the egg.

Every few minutes there was a new explosion cutting up the sky and the concussion would reverberate inside Ed's head as if someone had stuck a knife in his ear and hollowed out his skull. The War wasn't so long gone that he didn't still feel every explosion, actually any loud noise, a car backfiring on the street, Janey's Mixmaster, as putting him back on the beach in Anzio shrinking away from German bombers. He'd gone over to St. Mary's with this, and the doctors gave his condition some long name Ed couldn't remember but there was no cure, so it didn't really matter.

For a moment he wished his wife were there with them tonight, not that she would have been any help. She was no fan of picnics, didn't like sitting on the grass, the mosquitoes buzzing around. And lately she wasn't much of a fan of Ed either. She said she was tired of hearing about the war and thought he was making too much of the headaches and ringing in his ears, even after the doctors brought her in to explain. Janey didn't like doctors either; she acted as if it was all some kind of conspiracy to make her sympathetic to her husband and she wasn't having any. Get over it, was the total of Janey's advice and Ed wished he could take it. But really it wasn't just this, wasn't one thing or another; it was everything between them, their life together, which would have made it harder to locate had they been trying to do so. Overall, it was just easier not to have her there, easier for both of them.

Now Ed put his hands to his ears to drown out the noise and avoided looking overhead. He was only there for the kid, after all. Little Ed got a kick out of the fireworks, actually liked the explosions, the bright lights and other families sitting together on the grass in the dark. And the big American Flag they lit up at the end thrilled him. If it wasn't for the boy, Ed could easily have skipped the whole thing.

"Excuse me, sir," a voice to his left said. It seemed amazing that he'd heard with all that was going on but when Ed turned, he saw a young guy with a butch haircut and a tie over his short-sleeved shirt kneeling on the edge of his blanket. Who wears a tie to the fireworks in Vilas Park, Ed wondered, but he tried to be polite to everyone.

"You talking to me?"

The kid held out a clipboard with something typed on it. "Would you be willing to sign this?" he asked. "I'm Jim Simmons from the *Herald*."

"I used to carry the *Herald* out home in Dane," Ed said irrelevantly, remembering early morning trips on his bike the big wire basket loaded with papers as he rode from farm to farm and in the village. This kid looked like a paper boy, but he seemed to be a reporter. Ed squinted at the clipboard, but he had taken off his glasses to rest his eyes. Near-sighted since childhood, Ed had never liked the damned things and did without them when it was possible. Even he could see the sky without glasses.

His head was still ringing from the noise but that wasn't this kid's fault "Let me see that," he said. Ed took the clipboard in his hand, fished the glasses out of his pocket and examined it closely. Then he looked up at the reporter.

"This is part of the Bill of Rights," he said. Ed had never gotten past high school, but he knew the Bill of Rights and the Constitution.

The reporter nodded. "That's right. So will you sign it?"

Ed didn't know why they'd want signatures on the Bill of Rights. He guessed it was some new kind of petition that was going around, but what the hell. "Sure," he said. "I'll sign that. We've never been closer to losing what they stand for than we are today. Anyway, I live on Madison Street, so I've almost got to sign it, don't I?"

Ed expected the kid to laugh, but he didn't respond so Ed wrote his name at the bottom of the page. It was blank otherwise. "You should really get some other names on this, son," he said.

"I've asked over a hundred people tonight," Simmons said. "Everyone else turned me down. Someone told me to get this commie crap out of here and another lady thought it was something from the Russians. I showed it to a guy who said he was a lawyer, and he said the Bill of Rights wasn't even in the Constitution. You're the only one I've found who was willing to sign."

Ed looked more closely at the reporter who was sweating and seemed to shake sitting on his haunches in front of him. He felt a slight tremor and wondered if he should have held back like everyone else. In the army he had learned not to volunteer but how much damage could approving the Bill of Rights do? It made no sense that anyone would refuse to sign off on that.

"Sonofabitch," Ed said. "Russian propaganda, imagine that. What's got everyone so damned scared?" he asked, knowing the answer to his question.

"You tell me," Simmons said, shaking his head. "But thanks anyway. Now I can go back to the office and write the story. You made my night."

Ed watched the kid make his way out of the park in the night and wondered what the world was coming to. A wind had come up over the lake and he shivered in his short-sleeved shirt. The Bill of Rights was now Russian propaganda. If he hadn't heard it, he wouldn't have believed it.

Ed was in the kitchen the next morning, eating his grapefruit with the new spoon his wife had bought when Janey announced, "You're in the paper" and held up the *Herald*. She was standing next to the stove, hip cocked in the pink housecoat she wore in the morning and Ed could tell from her look that she was annoyed about something.

He ignored this because recently Janey had been pissed off about a lot of things and Ed had decided it was best just to wait and hope it would blow over. Instead, he focused on the grapefruit. Ed couldn't get the spoon to work. Why they shouldn't just use a knife to section the grapefruit like they always used to do he didn't know. But he wasn't going to fight Janey about this; they had enough trouble as it was. "Yeah?" he said now not looking at the paper she was holding up. "Why?"

"They quoted you," Janey said, holding up the paper close to her face. "They called you Edgeworth. Did you sign something, write a letter?"

Damn, he'd spent years getting people to call him Ed and now this, he thought irrelevantly. Fucking Edgeworth. It was his mother who dreamed up the fancy name, saw it in a magazine and thought it would give him some class, but it had been nothing but a pain in the ass his whole life. "Yeah," he said. "I signed the Bill of Rights because this reporter asked me to. Made no sense, but why not? So what?"

"Well, apparently you're the only one who did," Janey said, gesturing at the paper with an eggbeater. She handed the sheet to him. "Could you just tell me why you had to go and stick your neck out like that?"

The story quoting him had made the front page under the headline "4ᵗʰ of July Celebrants Afraid to Sign the Declaration and Bill of Rights." A sub-head read: 'Petition' Turned Down by 111 out of 112 Persons."

Beneath that was a story with Simmons' byline which said Ed was the only man with "the courage to sign" and quoted Ed saying, "What are they all scared of?"

He looked up at his wife and said, "I didn't stick anything out. It was the goddamned Bill of Rights. Who wouldn't sign that?"

Janey shrugged, "The paper says one hundred and eleven people wouldn't. But it's your funeral. Yell at me all you want and you're still in the paper. I've got laundry to do."

Then she was gone. First thing in the morning and he needed this?

As if they didn't have enough things to fight about. Stick my neck out, he thought. Crazy. That wasn't him in any way. So why did he do it, sign the damned thing? He wouldn't have admitted it to Janey but now he wasn't sure. In general, he avoided anything that might lead to conflict, no matter what it was. He didn't belong to a political party. Growing up on the farm in Dane he never even joined 4-H. There wasn't time for any of that just trying to make a living during the Depression. Then there was the War. He met Janey when he was on leave for before shipping out and went to a dance at the VFW where she'd come down from Mineral Point for the night. They'd had a great day together and then he was gone, sure he'd never see her again.

When Ed was overseas, he had figured he might go to college under the G.I. Bill if he survived. But as it turned out, he had a family to support right away so instead he'd taken a six-week insurance course at the tech school and had been working at the same agency ever since. He'd done well enough there to buy a fixer-upper near the Stadium and a used Plymouth, both of which he could work on himself on weekends. One thing about growing up on a farm, Ed could fix almost anything with a motor. On weekends, the guy down at the Phillips station on the corner would let him use his lift and in his spare time, Ed rebuilt the carburetor on the Plymouth along with replacing the brake drums and the shocks which had the body scraping the pavement when he drove. The station owner was impressed enough to offer him a job as a mechanic, but Ed said he'd rather stay where he was. When he took the time to think about it, Ed considered himself to be doing okay. Not great, but okay. And he wasn't done yet, not even thirty. There was time. But stick his neck out? Why would he ever do that?

Ed dropped Ed Jr off at summer school and thought some of the kids waiting in line gave him the gimlet eye but who knows with kids anymore? He put it out of his mind and continued driving downtown to his office. Summer school had been Janey's idea too. The kid hadn't done well the year before, and they almost held him back, so this was supposed to give him a boost. When Ed was a boy there was no school or summer camp; all he did was work on the farm and later when he'd washed dishes at the diner in town. But Janey said they should want something better for Ed jr. maybe even send him to college some day and Ed couldn't really argue with this.

The University had spread out enough in recent years that there was a minor traffic jam on Johnson Street, but Ed still got to work in plenty of time. He was sitting at his desk by nine when a secretary came by and said the boss wanted to talk to him. He was a fairly new guy, new to Ed anyway, transferred in from Omaha, and they hadn't really had a chance to talk yet. Ed didn't know what this was about but figured he'd better find out, so he got up from his desk and walked down the hall.

Bob DiPietro was the guy's name. Ed was Irish but he had nothing against Italians like he had nothing against the Polacks or the Jews or anyone else. He figured that was what they were fighting for over there in Europe.

"Come on in," DiPietro said, waving him to a seat. Then he smiled and held up the newspaper. "A little pink, are we, Ed?"

"Pink?" Ed said. "What the hell are you talking about?"

"Take it easy," DiPietro said. "Says here you're a radical, the only one to sign on this petition at the park last night during the fireworks." He was smiling to show he wasn't completely serious, but Ed had a funny feeling that he was.

"It's nothing," Ed said feeling himself growing hot. "It's that reporter down to the paper trying to sell copies, that's all. He ambushed me when I was down at Vilas with my kid."

DiPietro nodded. "Okay, I get it," he said. "But I'd appreciate you being a little more careful. Our clients read the papers too."

Ed just looked at the guy. He was twenty-three too young to be in the War but a college grad with a business degree so he was the boss and Ed worked for him. It was the way of the world. "Careful about what exactly? It wasn't even really a petition, for Christ's sake. I signed on to the Bill of Rights," Ed said. "I'd do that every day of the week. You've heard of it, right? It's in the Constitution, right up front there?"

DiPietro shrugged in a way that made Ed wonder if he really had heard of the Bill of Rights, much less read it but the manager gave nothing away. He puffed out his cheeks and shrugged. "Fine with me, but point being other people might think it meant something else, signing on when no one else will, see what I mean? There must have been some reason no one else at the park was willing to go along last night. You'd agree with that, wouldn't you, Ed?"

Ed knew the smart thing to do at this point was to smile and walk away, say, sure he'd watch it in the future, but something stopped him. "I'll tell you why they wouldn't sign," Ed said, "the reporter told me. They thought it was Russian propaganda, that's why. The Bill of Rights. Can you believe that? It's that goddamned McCarthy. He's got everyone scared to walk across the street. Anyway, yes, I signed the paper, but so what? Is it really that important? I mean, what am I doing here?"

DiPietro nodded in a careful way that made Ed sorry he'd brought up the Senator. For all he knew, DiPietro had voted for him. "Scared to walk across the street, Ed? I don't know," the manager said. "That's above my pay grade. But look, do me a favor." DiPietro got up and walked around his desk. He was a little guy with a crewcut. DiPietro's head came up to Ed's armpits but now he put his hand on Ed's shoulder and patted it, as if he was his father confessor or something. "Just don't sign anything else, okay?"

Then he let Ed go back to work, but the memory of the meeting stayed in Ed's mind all day. There was something menacing in what DiPietro had said, maybe not a warning, exactly, but something like it. Watch yourself, don't do it again, sign, whatever. Be careful. Ed thought maybe that was advice he'd be wise to follow but there was something inside him pushing back on this. He hadn't done anything wrong; he had nothing to apologize for and he wasn't going to give on this. It seemed important though he wasn't sure why.

Oddly enough, Ed had met the senator, if you could call shaking hands meeting someone. He was out at the Shorewood Shopping Center on University Avenue buying ice skates for Ed junior when he saw a crowd gathered in the corner. When he elbowed his way inside, he found McCarthy signing pictures of himself in an airplane wearing a flight jacket. It looked posed and Ed suspected the guy had never gotten near a bomber but what did he know? Anyway, he got in line and when his turn came the senator offered his hand and Ed took it. McCarthy didn't really shake like a man but gave only his fingers which were as cold as macaroni in his grip.

McCarthy wasn't tall but wide somehow and wore a wrinkled tan suit with his tie pulled away from his collar. He was a guy who looked uncomfortable in his clothes and had a bad comb-over with a few greasy hairs arranged over a mostly bald head.

"Hey, buddy," McCarthy said, licking spittle off his lips. "Thanks for coming down." They shook hands again and then Ed was swept away by the crowd.

That was the extent of Ed's involvement in politics up to that point. He always took the time to vote, even if he seldom bothered to research the candidates or the issues. Which made calling him a commie sympathizer now almost comical. Ed had never known a communist, never went to meetings if there even were meetings like that in Dane. Sometimes, he would go down to the VFW post for a beer and he belonged to a bowling league on Tuesdays at the Capital Bowl. No reds there.

And once he got married, there wasn't even much time for all of that. Yet even if DiPietro calling him on the carpet irritated him, Ed figured the guy had to do it or thought he had to and wasn't happy about him having his name in the paper. He figured the uproar over the Vilas Park story would die down soon enough but even though he hadn't changed the way he thought about it, he regretted the uproar a simple thing like signing had caused. A little pink, Di Pietro had said. Jesus!

He decided to go home for lunch, just to get away from the office and was surprised to find his wife there making tuna fish. "You were all anyone could talk about today at the store," Janey said. "Everyone was asking me about it."

"Asking you about what?"

"What do you think, whether you're a communist or maybe a sympathizer."

"The people you work with at the Ben Franklin asked you about this?"

"They're not stupid, Ed. They can read. I just wish for once you had kept quiet about that."

"For once? What are you talking about? When did anything like this happen before?"

"It doesn't matter," Janey said. "It's happened now."

"People have too much time on their hands," Ed said. "I'm no communist. You know better than that."

Janey shrugged expressively. "Maybe so, but I guess we don't want communists everywhere around Madison, do we?"

"Jesus, Janey," Ed said. "I don't know. I wouldn't know a communist from Ron Ruggles across the street and neither would you. I'll tell you this, though, when we were fighting the Nazis, the Russians were right there with us and they lost as many men as we did. I guess communists were all right then."

"Okay," Janey said. "I wasn't in the War but what about the Rosenbergs? Those Jews they killed for giving out secrets and being spies? Or all these movie stars they had up on the tv in front of that committee."

Ed had only a vague memory of the Rosenberg trial. He remembered seeing a couple of young boys, their kids, he supposed, standing outside the courthouse somewhere in New York. "I don't know about the Rosenbergs or anyone else," Ed said. "But I'm not a spy. I do okay but let's face it, I'm nobody when it comes to all that. All I did was sign a copy of the Bill of Rights at a 4th of July celebration. If that means I'm a communist, then fine, I'm a fucking communist. Just like James Madison, who wrote the damned thing."

"Sure, Mr. Innocent. You didn't do anything and everyone else is wrong. Your trouble is you're too accommodating, that's how you got into trouble buying that wreck out back that you're spending every weekend fixing. You thought the salesman was your friend and now we've got a car that won't run. You try to please everyone but what about us? You didn't want to disappoint the reporter who asked you to sign the petition and now we've got the whole neighborhood thinking you're a spy. That's great, Ed. That's just great."

"Terrific," Ed said. "We start off talking about one thing and you throw in the whole kitchen sink. Thanks for lunch, Janey, even if I didn't eat it."

And with that Ed walked out of the room, breathing hard. He didn't know why Janey had to come down on him about this, or why she'd really care. Things hadn't been great between them lately, mostly because he knew she wanted another kid to keep Little Ed company. It was why she took the job down to the Ben Franklin, but money was still tight. They barely made it to the next paycheck when another set of bills would appear in the mailbox. Ed supposed it would be nice to have a larger family, but he was having trouble supporting the one he already had. He'd tried to explain this to Janey, but she didn't really seem to listen. People find ways to pay for the things they really want, she'd said, and that was where they left it, until today when suddenly, they were fighting about communism.

Movement distracted him. Ed looked out of his front window. There were some kids gathered in the front yard who ran away after they saw him. Something looked off so he opened the door and walked outside where he saw someone had written "Commie" in red paint on his front sidewalk. He took a deep breath and the sharp bite of the California Pepper tree he had planted stung his nostrils. His neighbors had told him not to plant it, that a tree like that wouldn't grow in Wisconsin and yet it had, bushing out above the Azaleas and American Holly along the sides of the yard. Now he felt a kinship with the pepper tree, a sense of partnership with the tree that wouldn't grow in hostile soil.

He looked up and down the street, but the kids were gone, if they were even the ones who'd painted the word on his walk. Everything was quiet now, ominous. "Jesus H. Christ," he said to himself. What would be next? Then he went in to find a mop and bucket to clean the walk.

A few days went by, and people didn't seem to mention or make jokes about the newspaper article as much anymore, but it had had its effect. DiPietro took him off the accounts he'd been working on and put him on a desk. His excuse was the accounting course Ed had taken at the voch school the year before, but Ed knew that wasn't the real reason. He thought he was good with people and liked to be out of the office, moving around making calls rather than sitting around with all the typists. He felt suddenly visible, like when he was a kid, and the teacher would send him to the principal, and everyone would be looking when he returned to class. He didn't like the feeling, like a rash on the back of his neck from the sun. People looked through him instead of making eye contact and he imagined they were talking about him when he wasn't looking. He responded by isolating himself. He stopped going out for lunch at Crandall's with the group and instead had Janey pack him a bag that he ate at his desk. Still, he knew a lot of it was in his head. The fact was he'd been a good earner for the agency and that had to be the most important thing. If he stayed calm and did whatever work they gave him, in time this would go away.

Ed had never thought of himself as being pugnacious or argumentative as a kid his mother had always cautioned him against fighting because he was so much bigger than the other boys and it had become an ingrained habit to hold his feelings inside. Despite this, he found himself feeling angry now. He knew there was nothing to the whole communist business but being accused and forced to defend himself got his back up.

He thought it should be no big deal that he had been willing to sign on at the park, yet it seemed as if it was. He remembered his dad saying, "Tall oaks from little acorns grow." This wasn't a tree or anything like one, but what might have started out as real concern about patriotism had led to wide-ranging suspicion about anyone who had different ideas. Which is where Ed found himself. For the tenth time today, he told himself to keep cool and mind his own business.

Ed worked all afternoon but felt the back of his neck still hot from all the people he imagined watching him as he walked away from the Square toward the bus. No matter what happened from now on, Ed felt the experience had changed him. He felt different inside, prickly, on his guard, but against what or who wasn't clear. What bothered him more was that when he got home, he found little Ed with a bloody nose.

"What's going on?" Ed said. His son had never been a fighter.

"Nothing," Edgeworth jr. said.

Ed nodded. "Must be something," he said. "Look at that nose."

Little Ed shrugged. "Some kids at school said you're a Red."

Ed felt like someone had pushed him into the wall. "What did you say to that?" he asked.

"Nothing," the boy said. "I hit one of them and he hit me back and then the principal got in the middle and stopped us."

This is how it goes, Ed thought. The adults pass on this crap to their kids who bring it to school. Now little Ed was suffering because of something his father had done. Instead of regretting it, however, Ed picked up the phone and called the school to make an appointment to see the principal, a tall man named H. Paul Sigman who wore wire-rimmed glasses and wanted everyone to call him Dr. Sigman.

The next morning Ed was in Sigman's office at nine. "Not working today, Mr. Malloy?" Sigman asked, his voice mellow and syrupy.

"I'm going in late," Ed said. "Not a problem."

Sigman nodded and motioned him toward a chair at the side of his desk. "I assume you're here because of the unpleasantness involving your son yesterday afternoon."

This made Ed bristle, but he was determined not to get upset. What good would that do? "My son wasn't the problem," he said.

Sigman nodded. "Yes, sorry. Let me rephrase that. One of the other boys had a problem with your son that resulted in unpleasantness."

Ed nodded. "It wasn't about anything Edgeworth did. If it was, I wouldn't be here. They got in a fight over something someone said to him about me."

"Yes," Sigman said. "That sounds right."

"Let me ask you," Ed said. "Were you in the War, Dr. Sigman?"

Sigman flushed and shook his head. "Unfortunately, I wasn't able to serve," he said. He indicated his glasses. "My eyes."

There were plenty of guys in Ed's unit that wore glasses, but he wasn't about to argue. People who wanted to get out of the war always found a way. "What I mean is I didn't watch my buddies die at Anzio to come back here and be called a Red or have other people tell their kids I am one."

"Now there's no reason to get excited," Sigman said, brushing his lapels. "After all, we have no control over what people tell their children."

"Actually, I think you have a lot of control," Ed said, his voice rising. "I'm always getting these messages home asking us to come in and volunteer for this committee or that or bring food to a bake sale or give money for a field trip."

"Yes," Sigman said. "School business."

Having made his point, Ed moved on, "Little Ed never had trouble with those kids before," he said.

Sigman nodded. "That's true. Edgeworth's a good boy, very well behaved, an excellent student. He's never been any sort of problem to me or his teachers."

They sat silently for a moment. Neither man mentioned the story in the newspapers, but it sat between them in the small office. Ed knew Sigman couldn't control any of the other parents and he wasn't really worried about what they might be saying about him except for the way it might affect his son. Where that was concerned, Sigman was the law here if there was a law in elementary school.

Ed cleared his throat. "But somehow, this very well-behaved boy, this very good student is all of a sudden getting in fights with other kids in the schoolyard and you've got nothing to say about that?"

Sigman nodded determinedly. "Yes, I see what you mean and of course you're right, Mr. Malloy. Everything that happens here is my responsibility so this is what I'm going to do. I'll have a talk with Edgeworth's teacher and with the other boys involved. And I'm also going to continue to keep an eye on the situation. I think that will take care of the whole matter. Does that sound satisfactory to you?"

"Let's hope that does take care of it," Ed said. "I don't like to come home from work and find my kid with blood on his face."

"Of course not," Sigman said rising from his desk to let Ed know the interview was over. "Let me see what I can do." The other man hesitated, as if he was considering his next move. Then he cleared his throat and added, "I will say, Mr. Malloy, that all of this had to start somewhere. Regardless of what people might have said to their children, they were reacting to something. You'd agree?"

"It's my fault?" Ed said. "If I hadn't signed the damned petition at the park the parents wouldn't have talked to their kids and the kids wouldn't have gotten into a fight with my son? Is that what you're saying?"

Sigman moved back in his seat. "No, I wouldn't put it that way exactly," he said carefully. "I wouldn't put it that baldly."

"Right," Ed said. And with that Ed was out of Sigman's office and on his way to the parking lot.

It had been a hell of a week. He'd become a celebrity, written up in the paper and now he was in trouble at work because of it. His wife was pissed off at him and his kid was getting beat up at school. You wondered what could be coming next, but Ed had a feeling he didn't really want to know.

Two

NEW YORK

Not that I'm a big reader of literature but I always agreed with something Mark Twain said about autobiographies: You can only tell the truth from the grave. I never got any farther than *Tom Sawyer* with Twain, but he was right about that. You've got a better chance of getting away with murder than being honest and speaking your mind. What I'm writing here is for the drawer until I've moved on; I won't be publishing it or even showing it to anyone else. That being so, if anything I say bothers you, too bad. Your problem's not with me. I'm not here.

If that's clear, okay, here we go. I don't know what you'd want to call this. A confession? Forget about it. Roy Cohn doesn't do confessions. I'd fight, hell, I'd die before I'd confess or apologize for anything. So, okay, no confession but maybe a memoir of that crazy time when I was working with Joe McCarthy, calling everyone from pencil pushers to generals on the carpet in order to track down communists working undercover in the government. And beyond memories, maybe a shot at finally setting the record straight after the hit job the press did on us back then. It's more than ten years ago now that I'm writing this, a decade that saw the country change, moving first one way and then the other and now we've got a guy running for president who'd make McCarthy himself look a little pink. Who knows, maybe all this will make people look at McCarthy and that time in a different way, a better way if you ask me.

If my name means anything to you, it's probably because before I worked for Joe's committee, I was part of the prosecution team that sent Ethel and Julius Rosenberg to the great hereafter for selling secrets to the Russians. That was my baptism in the fight against communism and despite the flack I got from liberal bleeding hearts and even my parents whining about the kids the Rosenbergs left behind, the truth is I was proud of what I did, proud then and proud now. One thing for sure, it was the only reason Joe McCarthy could have heard about me because you couldn't say we moved in the same circles.

Even so, it wasn't a huge surprise when I got the call. I was in a good place, in the *gribbones,* in the chicken fat, as my old man might have said. I was known around the city, both Uptown and down in the Village where I had three rooms on Charles Street, enough money to do whatever I wanted and a succession of young boys and girls looking for adventure moving through my place at odd hours. I might be in all the papers, but the thing about New York is no one really cared what I did on my own time. In a city of voyeurs, no one was watching or trying to catch me out. This had a freeing effect that I liked as a young man making my way around the city.

I knew all about Joe, of course, from reading Sokolsky's columns, but I wouldn't say I was paying close attention. At the time, I didn't really know if he was some kind of *potzer* raising hell about communists to get his name out or the real thing. The only way to tell for sure was to meet the guy and check him out in person, but I was busy and didn't know when that might happen. Turned out, it was sooner than I thought when I was invited to a party Sokolsky gave for the Senator after the Republicans won big in fifty-two.

I knew Sok through my dad and he called to say it would be worth my while to come down to the party. I didn't see it at the time. Like I said, things were good for me, and I wasn't looking around, but if Sok called, you'd be an idiot not to pay attention, so I went over to the Astor that afternoon. There were a lot of people there and McCarthy and I only shook hands but a week later his secretary called to ask if I'd like to come down to meet Joe. I didn't know what it was all about until Hoover told me McCarthy was looking for counsel for his sub-committee. I knew Hoover from the Rosenbergs' trial, and I knew he was always hot on the heels of anyone he thought was even vaguely pink. He said Joe McCarthy was the real thing and I should take the meeting.

McCarthy's role running the Sub-Committee on Investigations had started out as a kind of a joke chairmanship with no power. Joe had developed a following during the campaign, so leadership thought they had to give him something. Still, I understood that being asked to interview as his counsel was a semi-big deal.

Other than what I'd read in the papers McCarthy was a mystery to me. I knew he was from Wisconsin, but the truth was I wasn't quite sure where Wisconsin was. I had it mixed up in my mind with Minnesota and had to look at a map to figure out which was where. Even then the map I had didn't show McCarthy's hometown, a place called Little Chute which, you guessed it, was near Big Chute and that was near Appleton, which I'd also never heard of. I learned that he'd been a state judge after law school and then signed up for the marines even though judges were exempt from service. He'd supposedly won a medal during the War, though there was some question about how this happened and whether it was legitimate. Now he was starting his second term in the Senate and the word was he liked to play rough.

Other than this, I knew *bupkas* about the man I was about to go to work for, during what would turn out to be the most amazing fifteen months of my life. McCarthy had no pedigree, wouldn't even know what one was. Like me, he had an innate suspicion of the upper crust and a chip on his shoulder the size of Mount Everest. The whole world of Ivy League schools, private clubs, bespoke clothes and secret handshakes meant nothing to him. He was a small-town guy and proud of it. If Little Chute wasn't the middle of nowhere it was close enough but somehow Joe had the political smarts to make it out of there, beat a LaFollette in Wisconsin and now get named the head of a Senate committee when some of the old farts up there had been around for twenty years without getting named chair of anything. So even if my knowledge of the Senator was limited, I knew enough to give him some space, some respect. I knew that.

If McCarthy had been mostly unknown when he came to Washington, everyone had heard of him after the speech he gave in Wheeling, West Virginia in 1950 when he waved a paper in his hand that he said was a list of three hundred Reds he'd uncovered in the

State Department. No one remembers this now and you'd have to say Wheeling was a nowhere place in a nothing state. McCarthy had only ended up giving the speech when the locals couldn't find someone more important, but in the end it didn't matter. Waving that list in front of the screaming crowd was great theater and just like that Joe was on his way.

Every paper in the country ran the Wheeling story, but when the reporters asked to see the list of Communists, Joe told them it was classified. By the next week, McCarthy had revised the number of commies down to fifty or so and then he lost the list. God knows how many names there really were to begin with, if there were any, but that wasn't important. From that time on, McCarthy was in the headlines, and he loved it, had a gift for it. He'd invite the reporters into his room for drinks and bullshit with them right up until deadline. Most reporters are Democrats, so you'd think they'd be outraged by McCarthy's red baiting but no matter what they are politically, reporters love a story, and this guy was news. Every so often they'd get in a dig by calling him the "Junior" senator from Wisconsin in an article but since no one knew who the senior senator was this didn't matter. McCarthy was on the cover of *Time* and the front page of the New York *Times,* and you can't buy publicity like that.

Even so, I wouldn't have taken the train down to Washington that rainy morning in December except I had heard Bobby Kennedy was angling for the same position with McCarthy's sub-committee. I knew Bobby a little bit, didn't like him and just wanted to slap that little shit down. What I didn't know was that McCarthy was tight with Joe Kennedy, that bullshit Irish thing they have going on, *erin go bragh* and all that. Even Jack who was going to be the great liberal hero later on loved McCarthy and Joe was popular in Massachusetts which hadn't gone over to the Democrats yet. The family had him up to Hyannis Port to talk about it and Joe had even dated one of the Kennedy girls. The old man wanted Bobby for the job and while McCarthy didn't owe him exactly, Joe Kennedy usually got what he wanted.

Considering everything that went on later, I probably should have walked away, said fine, hire Bobby, what do I care? I wasn't even a Republican and I knew it would annoy my folks if I went to work for one. But ironically, I thought it could be a good thing if I crossed the line because half the assholes in this country think all Jews are commies thanks to the Rosenbergs. This being so, it made a kind of sense strategically to have me working for the chief red-hunter in the Senate. Not that I was particularly observant when it came to religion. Yom Kippur and maybe a seder every now and then, but that was it. To me being a Jew had nothing, or almost nothing to do with religion. It was a culture, I guess, the way you talked, carried yourself, walked down the street, what you liked to eat and drink. Same with the Italians and the Irish. Take a look and you can tell right away what a guy is, a New Yorker can anyway.

When I tried to explain some of this to my father, how working for McCarthy would be good for our people, he didn't want to hear it and I didn't really blame him. He was a judge, and the New York Democratic machine had gotten him the job. He'd pulled strings to get me into law school at Columbia and wanted me to find a job he and my mother would have considered more respectable. Something they could tell their friends about. When I called to let him know about the meeting with McCarthy, he hung up the phone. Not the first time I'd disappointed the old man, but what the hell, I went for the job interview anyway.

I wouldn't really have called McCarthy handsome. Rugged maybe, if you go for that sort of thing, but not handsome. He was around 5'10 with the elevators he said he wore because of all the shrapnel in his legs, which was a laugh because this guy was never near combat. His hair was thinning even when I met him, a few strands brushed across a bald dome. He could have worn a rug, but he chose to slick down his hair with the Wildroot Cream Oil he bought by the case because he thought it cured baldness. He had good shoulders maybe because of his boxing career at Marquette and the flushed cheeks and red nose of a guy that liked to drink. His eyes were small but smart and they were the key. Not that he was any kind of intellectual but sneaky smart, hard to fool, and not someone you really wanted to fuck with like Drew Pearson found out when he got knocked out in a restaurant cloakroom for writing that the Senator was a fag which was not something you even joked about then. Everyone else gave him a wide berth, a good thing because McCarthy weaved when he walked down the aisle like a guy trying to find his bearings on a ship.

It's not that my main purpose is to right wrongs here. McCarthy didn't care about that and neither did I. But there are some popular misimpressions that need to be addressed. McCarthy was never smooth and didn't pretend to be. He was rough-hewn, a country boy and proud of it. He had simple tastes and was never pompous regardless of his high position. He took his work seriously but never himself. Despite his pugnacious public appearance, in person he was warm and friendly to everyone. He didn't care about money or cars and never even owned an expensive watch. If he was your friend, he was your friend for life and would fight for you. What I'm trying to say is he was the total package; he was something.

The meeting was in McCarthy's Senate office. It was a big room with high windows that let in the faded sunlight of early winter. His eyes were already red at eight in the morning, and I could tell it had been a tough night. McCarthy was a drinking man in a town that liked to drink, and Joe never had trouble finding a friendly bartender or hangers-on willing to stay up all night with him. It was obvious right away that the Senator didn't care about clothes. He bought his suits off the rack at Penney's and his tie hung loose like a rag around his neck. I guessed it was a club tie or maybe an old school tie, but he never belonged to a club. Still, on this day he was wearing a pretty good pinstripe even if it looked like he'd slept in it. Bits of toilet paper were spread around his face like snow from when he'd cut himself shaving, a problem for drinkers whose hands shake in the morning. When he talked his tongue wagged back and forth as if it was on a rubber band. There were sweat circles under his arms and yellow bags of fat swam in his eyes.

Still, he was sharp in the way he looked at you, suspicious maybe, but sharp too. He had some papers arranged on a huge walnut desk, which was scarred with cigarette burns and marks from his shoes. I couldn't read the papers upside down, but they could have been about me. I'd never sent down a cv; I didn't even have one. My resume was I knew a guy who knew a guy, like that. In my world it was all word of mouth, the fact was that even at twenty-six, I could pick up the phone and make things happen. Ever since I was in high school, I'd made an art of hanging out with people who counted and that would only increase with age. What others said about me was what mattered, not where I went to school.

Anyway, now McCarthy glanced quickly at the papers as if he thought they were alive and might jump up suddenly and bite him. Then he shoved them violently aside, no longer a threat. I'd learn later that despite the bookcase in the corner, he never read anything, not even the morning papers. He wasn't a great listener either. Like many people, he heard what he wanted to hear, especially when it had to do with him. But he took a lot in anyway.

"Sok says you're a tough SOB," McCarthy began abruptly.

Sokolsky was my guy, I knew that he was the reason I was there that morning. As far as I could tell, he knew everyone worth knowing and had written about them in his column. Hanging with Sok as he moved through a restaurant in Manhattan was like trailing a hurricane, throwing people and tables in his wake as he moved along. For the rest, I'd grown up in a tough town but had never thrown a punch. At five foot eight and one hundred forty-eight pounds it would have been like committing suicide in my neighborhood. I moved around easily in my world but that was because I knew it and I was known.

"I'm not that tough," I said, though I was pleased Sokolsky had said I was.

"Not what Sok says," McCarthy said. "And Sok doesn't bullshit." He paused and looked up at the windows as if he was waiting for divine inspiration. It took long enough that I looked up there myself but there was nothing special to see. Then he was back, quickly, shifting in his chair trying to get comfortable. "Anyway, I'm the head of this investigations sub-committee and what I need is a guy who can kick some assess and get things moving."

He looked at me searchingly as if it was obvious what he was talking about but I had no idea, so I asked him what they were investigating.

McCarthy gave a big sigh at this, as if I was a moron but I didn't keep track of every goddamned committee in Washington. Most of them never did anything anyway so why bother? "Everyone knows State's full of fags and commies," McCarthy went on, "but now we got to go out and find them. This committee's going to investigate the whole damned thing."

I thought there was no need to mention I had a locker in a Downtown bathhouse where I played slap and tickle with boys on a regular basis, especially since the word on the street was that McCarthy himself could be a homo, but this kind of thing wasn't going to run in the respectable papers unless they had photos and that wasn't going to happen. From my point of view, it was a possibility. McCarthy wasn't married and didn't have any serious girlfriends. Who knew what the truth was? It occurred to me that I might be putting myself at risk by taking this job. Being with boys in New York was one thing, but no one knew me in Washington, and I could easily be outed if I ended up at the wrong parties. It was something to think about.

"I can probably do that," I said now.

"Probably?" McCarthy said in a mocking tone. "Probably ain't going to do it for me." I was to learn this kind of sarcasm was typical of him. He had no use for subtlety, disdained it, in fact. "I need a guy who knows for sure."

I smiled at this. I was really starting to like Joe. "Okay, Senator," I said. "Sorry, you're right. I can do this. I'm sure of it. No problem."

McCarthy nodded, a tight smile on his face. Then, "Okay, that's more like it." Then he paused and looked up at the windows again. "This is probably going to work out, but I got to talk to a few people," he said. I knew he meant he had to talk to Joe Kennedy about his son but didn't let on I knew. You always had to hold something back, not let the other guy know things if he didn't have to. After all, I didn't work for McCarthy yet. We were still negotiating. And if in the end, he picked that snotnose over me it would be his funeral, not mine.

I trusted my instincts and thought the meeting was going well but what I'd heard from Sok was that despite McCarthy's reputation as a killer, he had a hard time saying no to people, to anyone, about anything. This struck me as odd given the fact that he was ruining lives every day but those were lives he didn't care about, not lives of people he owed or might owe in the future. Then he surprised me. "Is there anything you need from me?"

This is not a question I was getting very often. My deal was to push push push and then maybe get lucky in the end, but if this senator was asking me, I thought I should come up with something. Anything, really. The salary was nothing so there was no point in asking for more money. "I've got a friend who might help us with that investigation," I said.

"A friend?" McCarthy looked suspicious. Who had friends? Not him, that was for sure. His whole world was tied up in a tight little ball. A few of the guys from Wisconsin, shitkickers like him, maybe a few women, his secretary. From what I'd heard he didn't even go to parties in Washington. He didn't have any friends in the Senate that was for sure.

"It's a guy I know named David Schine," I said quickly. "From Harvard, his father owns hotels, he's a smart guy."

"Harvard?" McCarthy's mouth turned down at this. He hated the establishment or what he thought of as the establishment for what he imagined had been done to him. He used that hatred as an engine to make him work harder. It was an essential part of how he'd gotten as far as he had. And there was nothing more establishment than Harvard. I regretted saying anything and immediately started backing and filling to make up for my mistake.

"Yeah, he went there, but that's all. It's not what he's about. He didn't belong to Porcellian or anything. It's just that he wrote a good pamphlet about communism. I met him through Sok who knows his old man and vouches for him. I think he could help us."

I didn't actually know if Schine was smart or not and the pamphlet was bullshit that he'd published himself, but McCarthy didn't need to know that. I'd been introduced to Dave at a private party at the Stork Club a few weeks before and we'd seen each other several times since then. What I actually knew was that he was handsome and that his family had an apartment in the Waldorf where I'd spent a couple of nights. I hadn't come down to Washington planning to mention him, but McCarthy had asked me what I wanted and since I felt obliged to say something Schine was the first thing that came to mind. I'd figure out later what to do with him if McCarthy said yes. How big a problem could that be?

"Anyway, he's loaded so he'll work for free," I said. "Maybe he could be a consultant or something."

McCarthy shrugged. His attitude toward money was like his attitude toward clothes, which was probably why he was always getting dunning letters from small town banks in Wisconsin. "Sok likes him?" he asked now, unwilling to let the thing go entirely.

"He's how I met Schine," I said, which was a lie. I'd never seen Sok at the Stork Club. It wasn't his kind of place. Winchell sure, but not Sok. "That and the pamphlet he wrote."

I could tell McCarthy wasn't excited about Schine, but I didn't care. He'd asked what I needed, and I decided on the spot I needed Dave even if I hadn't told him about it yet. Of course, if I'd known how much trouble I'd run into because of Dave I might have held off when McCarthy asked, but I didn't. It's like a lot of things you might do differently if you knew ahead of time how they'd turn out. But I've never been big on regrets. If you're wrong, screw it, and move on.

I heard church bells ringing out the hour and suddenly remembered it was Sunday though I was pretty sure Joe was skipping mass today. "Let me think about it," McCarthy said now. Then he heaved himself to his feet and straightened his jacket. I got up and we shook hands.

"So, I'll be hearing from you?"

McCarthy nodded but I could see I'd lost his attention. "I'll be in touch, or someone will," he said, waving in the direction of his outer office which had been empty when I walked in.

And that was the beginning.

Three

MADISON

Janey Cardy had modest desires. She wanted little more than to get out of Mineral Point and put some distance between herself and the life she had known growing up there. When the mines gave out in the thirties, her father had descended into alcoholism, like most of the men in town and she thought the boys in her high school would be the same, those that came back from the War anyway. Most of her girlfriends were married a year after graduation, if they could find a man, but Janey was determined to make a new path for herself which is why she was at the USO dance in Dodgeville that night where she met Edgeworth Malloy, looking big and handsome in his uniform. Janey was tall and thin and had towered over the boys in Mineral Point, so she was immediately drawn to this man. Edgeworth was standing off to the side of the room nursing a beer and looked like he wasn't going to move so Janey asked him to dance, and they ended up wrestling in the back seat of someone's car in the parking lot before he took her home and then re-joined his unit and shipped out a day later.

Janey knew enough not to pin her hopes on anyone in particular and Edgeworth wasn't the only man she met at the USO dances, not the only one she slept with either, but the list wasn't long and when she found herself pregnant, she decided it was up to her to decide who the father of her baby should be. She'd kept the names and addresses of all the boys she had met but liked the fact that Edgeworth hadn't pressed himself on her and so in the end she wrote to him to say that he had become a father to a baby boy whom she had named Edgeworth jr.

Ed didn't come home for another two years but when he did, they were married in City Hall and if he didn't seem delighted exactly with the way things had worked out, he didn't try to evade responsibility and Janey never found it necessary to tell him that had he died in Italy she had two or three other candidates she could have called upon.

Janey didn't consider herself devious in this regard, just realistic. She thought of herself as being like a persimmon, tough on the outside but sweet and fresh within. Even as a girl she had no intention of staying home and making pasties for her husband's lunch bucket or doing walking tours of Shakerag Street for tourists. It may have been good enough for her mother, but it wasn't for her and now Janey had the life she had always wanted. She took pride in her home and enjoyed sending her husband off to work in his suit and tie with the other men in the morning and then taking care of the house and their little boy the rest of the day. No one ever remarked on the fact that Little Ed was small for his size and didn't resemble Ed in his coloring. When they had another, Janey assumed that child would look different from them both, but people in Madison were too polite to remark on such things and she never mentioned it in conversation with her co-workers when she took a job after Little Ed started school. These things would work themselves out naturally.

Janey liked Madison, liked their neighborhood and the fact that she lived in the capital city of the state even if she seldom got anywhere near Capital Square. She even liked the University though she had little to do with it because she thought it added a certain tone to the city that it might otherwise have lacked. Money was tight but they were young, and she was confident in herself and in Ed. Things would improve over time. It was this that upset her about her husband's sudden notoriety. She knew Ed wasn't a dangerous radical, but she was sensitive to the fact that if enough people thought he was it could threaten the good life she'd built so carefully. Janey couldn't allow that to happen.

Things had gotten worse at the office. There was now wide space between Edgeworth's desk and the others around him, spreading like a lagoon with a few isolated islands spotted here and there. It had happened gradually, perhaps at night or over lunch hour but one day he noticed desks that had been a few feet away had moved. Ed had never been big on bull sessions with his co-workers or checking out pictures of the son-in-law or new grandchildren. There was a weekly card game he never attended and a bowling team that met on a night he didn't want to go out. He didn't think of himself as being unfriendly or anti-social; he'd just always kept to himself, no big hoorah for him, even when he played fullback on the football team and might have taken a cheerleader to the Homecoming Dance. These things weren't for him. That was it: mind your own business and I'll mind mine had always been his way but now he began to have second thoughts and wondered if he'd been wise in walling himself off from others. He had assumed if he worked and kept his head down, it would be enough, but the moving desks around him told another story. It wasn't a good sign.

There was no one in the office he could talk to and there was no way he'd get an honest answer anyway. Somehow the word had gone around that he was trouble; it was as if he had a contagious disease, and they were effecting a quarantine. When he tried to talk to Janey about this, she just threw her hands up and said he had created his own problem. That he didn't understand what he'd done, which was ridiculous. He was a working man, the first in his family out of overalls. How could he not know the importance of work?

"What are you scared of?" he asked her.

"What am I scared of?" Janey said. "Are you serious, Ed?" Your job's on the line. And we can't afford to lose that job."

"I haven't lost anything yet," Ed said, hoping his bravado would reassure her. "Besides, my reputation's more important than a paycheck."

Janey was disdainful. "Your reputation? Spare me. Who do you think you are? We're ordinary people. We don't have reputations. We can't worry about all that."

"Well, I do," Ed said. "You don't have to be rich living out in Maple Bluff to care about your reputation. If I don't care about it who's going to, Janey, will you tell me that?"

They didn't discuss it anymore but what Janey said had gotten to Ed. He didn't think he was really scared the way he was when bombs were dropping all around him, but DiPietro's questioning had affected him in another way. When he was overseas, he figured if he could only survive and get home, everything would be fine, even easy. Now he was finding reality was anything but easy. He wasn't sleeping at night, and his appetite had fallen off to the point that his suits were baggy on him. So not scared exactly, but something like that, something a lot like that.

The next morning Ed found a note from DiPietro on his desk when he came to work. He looked around quickly but saw only saw the backs of his co-workers. He read the note again: "Ed, please see me when you can. Thanks. DP"

He hadn't talked to DiPietro since the morning after the article appeared and he thought things had settled down, hoped they had. Now he imagined some *sub rosa* whispering campaign going on under the appearance of normality. He grabbed his suit coat off the hanger, checked himself quickly in the mirror on his desk and trudged down the hall to the boss' office.

The door was open and when DiPietro noticed him he beckoned with his arm. "Ed, come on in," he called out. "Take a seat, want coffee."

"I'm fine," Ed said. He was aware that he sounded defensive and tried to soften it a little. He held up the note. "You wanted to see me."

DiPietro pursed his lips. "Come on, Ed. It's not like that. Relax, not a big problem or anything. I just like to keep up with the troops, check in every now and then."

It always irritated Ed when a guy who never saw a fox hole in his life talked about his troops or his team or any other such thing he knew fuckall about. Without intending it, he was suddenly back in Italy, ducking, swiveling his head around, searching for cover. DiPietro looked alarmed and said, "You, okay there," Ed.

Ed straightened his shoulders and blew out some breath. "Sure, I'm okay," he said and smiled. "I'm here. What's up?"

DiPietro nodded his head, and Ed could see his scalp shining pink through his flat top "Right," the manager said. "Fine." Then he slid a single piece of paper across the desk without another saying another word.

Ed glanced at DiPietro questioningly. Then he looked down and started to read: "I am a loyal American. I swear that for the five years previous to this oath I have not advised or advocated the overthrow of the Government of the United State of America and that also I am not nor have I ever been or become a member or affiliated with any group, society or organization that has advised or advocated the overthrow of the Government of the United States of America...." There was more, but Ed understood. He knew about loyalty oaths and Truman's Program that came out after the War when everyone was scared the Russians were going to infiltrate the country and take over the government.

He raised his head from the paper and saw DiPietro looking at him expectantly, his small black eyes like bee bees. "What's this all about then?" he said.

"Just what it says, Ed," DiPietro said. "I think it's all pretty clear, self-explanatory. Keep on reading."

"I don't have to read anymore," Ed said, biting off his words. "I know what it says, and it's got nothing to do with me." He hesitated and took a deep breath. "No one asked me to sign anything when I was busting my ass in Italy trying not to get killed. No one over there asked me a goddamned thing about my loyalty. You were maybe in high school then, is that right?"

DiPietro hunched his shoulders and sighed. "I was hoping you weren't going to make this personal, Ed," he said. "And it doesn't matter where I was or where you were years ago."

"Personal?" Ed said. "It is personal if I've got to swear I'm loyal to this country. And as to where I was or you were, I've got an Honorable Discharge and a Purple Heart framed on my wall at home that says it does matter, that it actually matters a hell of a lot."

"Well, yes," DiPietro said quickly. "That's not what I meant to say. Of course, we all value and thank you for your service. No question about that. Absolutely no question at all."

Ed took another deep breath and looked at the floor which seemed to be coming up at him. Janey was always telling him to control himself if someone said something stupid about the War. She thought he'd been angry since he got home but he didn't see it, didn't see it at all. What was wrong with defending yourself if you needed to? He reminded himself that he worked for this guy and tried to soften his voice.

"Okay, so thanks for that. But then what's with calling me in here to look at this?" Ed gestured at the paper between them on the desk. "If you value my service so much, what am I doing here looking at this?"

"Oh, I wouldn't really call it a loyalty oath," DiPietro said carefully, pursing his lips. "Maybe more like something that just asserts your patriotism and loyalty to America. What's wrong with that?"

"I already told you, goddamnit," Ed said. "If I fought for my country for five years, risked my life and killed Germans I didn't know on the other side, that's enough. I shouldn't have to sign anything to prove my patriotism or whatever you want to call it." He gestured at the paper. "That's a loyalty oath right there is what that is and I'm not signing it." Ed was aware his hands were trembling and shoved them under the table. He had heard about people getting fired if they wouldn't sign these things, but that was in big government jobs in Washington, not for some podunk insurance agency in Wisconsin. Next thing you knew they'd be watching everything you did, what clubs you belonged to, keeping track of what you read, which movies you watched, checking to make sure you said correct things in the right way, parted your hair just so, wore a certain color of coat. Who knew how far it might go? They could even have you carrying around identity cards like they did over behind the Iron Curtain. Whatever happened to the right to have your own opinions and say what you liked in America?

DiPietro's face was blanched. It looked as if it had become narrower somehow, his scalp pinker. "I was really hoping you'd react differently to this, Ed," he said. "And I'd advise you to think this over very carefully. Talk about it with your wife, your pastor, your friends. I'm sure you'll re-evaluate it when you do that. I wouldn't want you to make any hasty decisions."

As if DiPietro really cared whether he thought things over or not. What a joke. Ed took a deep breath. He knew this prick wasn't worth fighting with; he should walk away but he couldn't stop himself from going on. "I'll do that but let me ask you one thing," he said, pointing at the paper lying inertly on the desk between them. "Are you asking everyone in the office to sign this?"

DiPietro sat back. He looked as if he'd taken a punch in the gut. "Now, Ed, you know I don't discuss personnel decisions with anyone other than the person involved. What other folks do or don't do isn't really any of your concern."

"Right," Ed said," but somehow it seems like everyone down here knows my business anyway; no one wants to sit next to me or have lunch and I'm at a desk instead of seeing clients like I always did before. So, you just answered my question. I need to sign a paper saying I'm loyal because some kid buttonholed me over by the park on the Fourth and then wrote it up in the *Herald*, is that just about it or am I missing something."

DiPietro ran his fingers over his scalp but sounded defeated when he responded. "I think we're done here, Ed. I'm trying to be fair but you're making it hard, I have to say. No one's asking you to do anything crazy no matter how you put it together. So just take that statement home with you today, talk it over with the wife and get it back to me signed when you can. No hurry."

But Ed didn't pick up the paper or reply. He just got to his feet and returned to his desk.

Janey had packed Ed a lunch but instead of eating in the office, he left the building on Fairchild Street and walked a half block over to the Capitol where he sat on a bench and ate. He'd always liked the grounds around the building even if he'd only gone inside once or twice when he walked all the way upstairs to the War Museum they had there and breathed in the musty smell of history.

Someone had told him the building had the biggest dome outside of the Capitol in Washington and Ed had no reason to doubt this even if it made no sense that a small state like Wisconsin would have gone in for such extravagance. Whether it was true or not, the building was beautiful, white and gleaming in the summer sunshine, and the park that circled it was well used with kids running around and bums sleeping off a drunk when Ed came by in the morning or in the afternoon on the way home from work. From where he sat, he could look straight down State Street and see the University on the hill a mile away. People would joke that the legislators wanted to keep an eye on the University, but Ed supposed it went the other way too.

When he was first out of the service, Ed thought about taking advantage of the G.I. Bill and going for a degree at the big U but there was no way to make it work financially with Janey and the baby needing his support. There were times he regretted this, and he could actually get angry if he thought about it much, but it did no good to go down that path and Ed knew it. Time went by, you made the decisions you did and that was your life. You were who you were. No one cared if you'd been the captain of the football team or fought for your country and seen your buddies shot down like dogs in some forgotten hellhole. No one cared and no one was going to care. The only thing to do was forget about it.

Ed threw what was left of his lunch into a garbage can. It was only one o'clock, but he was through for the day and decided to go home without checking back in at the office. No one likely gave a shit and if they did, too bad. He took off his suit jacket and folded it under his arm. Instead of going for the bus, he decided to walk down past the University. He could use the exercise and if he was lucky, maybe some of the brains down there would rub off on him. He damned sure could use them.

Regardless of the weather you could count on the college kids being out and around on the campus. As Ed walked up State Street, past the various shops that changed but somehow always seemed the same to him, whether selling tee shirts, books, oriental rugs or an alternative for lunch. There was a store that offered foundation garments for women as well as hats, a jewelry store, three bars standing next to each other, a barber shop, a delicatessen and a music store that advertised lessons along with the latest records which could be sampled in one of their listening booths along an inside wall.

Bascom Hill rose ahead of him as he walked and Ed was amazed, as always, at the sheer number of students who were out of class and how young they seemed even with a few older students that might be vets mixed in. It wasn't a great day for sunbathing, chilly for August, and rain had made the Hill muddy and less appealing than usual. Ed's mind went back again to the Italian campaign, and he wondered idly how many of these kids knew anything about what they'd gone through over there. He remembered being bogged down by the German artillery, covered with dirt and refuse, his ears ringing with gun fire and the smell of burned flesh in his nostrils. Looking again at the muddy Hill, Ed thought the Italian mud had been different than this, denser, dark as shit and smeared all over your pants and blouse. He remembered it as being like quicksand, holding you so tight your boots and socks came off in it, along with the occasional body part, a hand, or a foot of a dead

G.I. And then later the goddamned mud sticking to everything when you tried to clean up as if to remind you that this war wasn't really going away, wouldn't ever truly be ended.

At the top of the Hill was a statue of Lincoln looking down at everything beneath him. The legend was that he would rise from his chair whenever a virgin walked past but Abe wasn't getting up today. Although Ed had lived in Madison for years and had even gone to a few football games, he'd never actually been inside the University. Now, on a whim, he walked into a small Lannon stone building on the South Side of the Hill, appropriately named South Hall. A sign inside the door informed him that this was the oldest building on the Hill, the original home of the University back in the 19th Century. Inside, Ed saw a small woman in a print dress, her hair in a bun, sitting at a table. She looked up expectantly and immediately Ed felt self-conscious.

"Can I help you?" the woman asked. She wore frameless glasses and might have been thirty but seemed younger somehow.

"I'm sorry," Ed said. "I was just walking by. I'm not a student or anything, never been in a university building before, to tell the truth. I live in town," he added, as if this explained anything.

"Welcome then," the woman said. "I'm Susan Rozelle, one of the assistant deans. Is there anything I can show you?"

Ed wasn't really sure what a dean was, much less an assistant dean, but he instinctively liked the woman and wanted to keep the conversation going. "I don't think so. Like I said, I was just walking by."

"Are you by any chance a veteran?" Susan Rozelle asked.

"Hundred and first Airborne," Ed said and immediately felt stupid. What did this woman care where he served?

"Thank you for your service," Susan Rozelle said. "I ask because one of the programs I work with here is for veterans that might want to return to school. I assume you qualify for the G.I. Bill of Rights."

"I guess I do," Ed said. "I never really looked into it before; I got a family to support and had to go to work right after I got out of the service."

"Of course," Susan said. "That's why we have programs that allow you to continue at your job and still work for your degree at night or in the summer."

She made the whole thing sound so reasonable, even inevitable, that Ed wondered why he'd never thought about anything like this before. "I didn't know," he said lamely.

"Well, now you do," Susan said and smiled warmly. "Let me give you a few things to read over and then you can call me if you want to pursue any of this further."

Pursue was the kind of four-bit word that was unfamiliar to Ed or had been before this. "I'd like that," he said. And he left South Hall with an armful of brochures and a smile on his face. For fifteen minutes he hadn't thought at all of DiPietro, or the shit show his life seemed to have become.

Janey was in the kitchen when Ed got home. He poured himself a cup of coffee and sat down at the table under the window. The *Herald* was on the table, but Ed couldn't focus; the words seemed to swim in the black ink in front of him and he looked away.

"You're home early," Janey said. "It's not even three."

"I didn't feel like staying," Ed said. "I took my lunch and ate in Capitol Park and then walked home. It wasn't that hot."

Janey stopped what she was doing and turned to look at him. "Can you do that? Leave early?" He could hear anxiety in her voice, and it made his stomach sink. "Was something wrong?"

Ed didn't really want to discuss it with his wife. She'd been upset by the newspaper article and little Ed being bothered at school. That was enough, without this latest thing with DiPietro. It would blow over anyway and then what was the point? "I don't want to talk about it," Ed said. "Nothing I can't handle."

But Janey was sensitive to suggestion. "Handle what?" she said, her voice rising. She sat down across from him and smoothed the blue-checked waxcloth with her fingers. "Tell me what's going on, Ed."

Ed mimicked her, brushing the table for non-existent crumbs and sighed. "They want me to sign something, I don't know," he said. He felt the walls closing in, as if the air had been vacuumed out of the room.

"Sign what?"

"It's some kind of statement, you know, that I'm patriotic and all that. Like I said, I can handle it. Not a big deal, really."

Janey's eyes bored into him like lasers. She wasn't buying it. "You're home early, I can see you're worked up about something, so I'm guessing maybe it is a big deal no matter what you say. You need that job, Eddie, we do. You know that. So, if they want you to sign something, then sign it. What are you talking about anyway?"

"I just don't like it, that's all," Ed said. It was bad enough with DiPietro now he had his wife starting in on him and he felt cornered. "Whose side are you on?" he asked.

Janey flared up at this. "Whose side am I on? I'm on my side, our side, Little Ed's side. Don't be stupid, Ed. Who do you think you are anyway? You've got to come to your senses and step back from this. Signing that petition and getting in the paper was bad enough; if your boss is upset about this then you have to fall in line. You're not in charge at the agency, you just work there. They tell you to do something, you just do it. That's how it works. What do they want you to sign anyway?"

Ed saw Janey's hands were shaking. He knew she was mad, but he could see she was scared too. "Calm down," he said. "It's a statement, all right, saying I'm a patriotic American and all that, like a loyalty oath or something. You know what a loyalty oath is, right?"

"I read about them in the paper," Janey said. "But what's that got to do with you? Wasn't it about keeping Russian spies out of the government."

"Exactly," Ed said. "That's my point. I'm not Russian and I don't work for the government so why should I have to sign anything?"

"But they asked you to anyway," Janey said quietly. "Are they telling other people in the office to sign too?"

"I don't know," Ed said. "I asked but DiPietro wouldn't tell me. Said what other people were doing was none of my business, and he's right about that. This is up to me."

"Okay," Janey said, coming around to sit next to him at the table. "But you're going to sign it, aren't you? I mean, you have to."

"I don't have to, goddamn it," Ed said. "I did what I had to do for this country, and it ought to be enough. I went to the damned war and fought for five years. Watched my friends die shitty deaths and then helped to bury them. As far as I'm concerned that's the end of what I had to do." And with that he got up and went into his little den off the front entrance.

He lay down on the ratty couch they'd inherited from his parents. Janey had crocheted some covers for a couple of old pillows and now Ed put them under his head and looked up on the wall where Janey had framed his honorable discharge and service medals. What good was all that doing now, he wondered. He closed his eyes and tried to forget about it.

He knew Janey was right. Sign the damned oath and move on was the smart thing to do if that was all there was to it. And yet there was something in him that wanted to push back, maybe for the first time in his life. He'd always been a guy to toe the line, do what was expected and more, never a rebel, never one to raise hell or challenge authority. He wasn't timid or afraid to fight if it came to that, but he was lucky in being bigger than most of the other kids growing up, so he never had to.

Looking back, there just never seemed to be much that was worth getting excited about, at least to Ed. Even-tempered, Easy Ed, some of the kids had called him back in Dane when he was growing up. And yet now, Easy Ed wasn't easy at all. DiPietro's words kept echoing in his brain: Go home and think it over, DiPietro had said. Talk to your wife, your pastor, and Ed might even have done this if he had a pastor but it had been years since he'd seen the inside of a church.

He was restless and couldn't sleep. He got up and went outside, walked around the yard where the lilacs had already faded from violet to brown. He took a seat on a bench in the yard, which reminded him of the work that remained to be done. He needed to mow the grass, trim bushes, work on the little garden they'd put in last spring. He'd tried to get little Ed to help out, but the boy was hopeless when it came to yardwork and Janey would never push him.

He looked up at the house, yellow in the afternoon light. When he'd bought it three years before it had been a wreck. He got a sweetheart loan because the bank wanted to get it off its books and no one else would buy the place, but Ed liked the house the first time he saw it because it reminded him of the farmhouses of his youth. It still had a windmill in the side yard when they moved in, but the water went bad, and he had to dig a trench to the street to connect with city water. Then the coal furnace went out in the middle of the winter, and he moved Janey and Little Ed to a hotel while he got a new gas furnace installed in the basement. One of the dormers had collapsed into the attic and the lintels sagged as if they'd been browbeaten by nature, which Ed guessed is what had happened. Taking care of all this and painting occupied most of his free time for the first two years, but Ed never minded hard work and doing most of it himself saved money. There was still more to do, and he'd need a new room before long, but he'd made the house livable and in the process, he'd grown attached to it.

Not that Janey cared about any of this. She could go on about how he was failing them as a man and not working enough, but she had no appreciation for what he did. Now, she interrupted his thoughts when she raised the sash and called out that there was a phone call for him.

"Who is it?" Ed said, thinking it would be the office wondering where the hell he was. But Janey didn't answer and in time Ed got up, went back inside the house and picked up the phone.

"Mr. Malloy?"

"This is Ed Malloy. Who's this?"

"It's Jimmy Simmons, Mr. Malloy. How are you, sir?"

"Do I know you?" Ed said.

"Sorry, Jimmy Simmons, I'm a reporter with the *Herald*. Remember, we met at Vilas Park on the Fourth of July. I was just following up. "

Jesus, Ed thought. The kid in the park with the petition to sign. "Jimmy, that's your name? And you're that reporter?"

"Yes, Sir, that's me."

"You've got me in some trouble, Jimmy. Did you know that? I mean, your article did. In fact, it's been a real pain in the ass, pardon my French."

"That's okay, sir," Simmons said.

"It's not okay with me," Ed said. "Actually, it's not okay at all."

"That's not what I meant," Simmons said quickly. "I mean your language is okay. We hear everything down here. And I'm sorry if what I wrote caused you any trouble."

"Not just me," Ed said. "My kid got beat up in the schoolyard and someone painted "Commie" in red paint on the sidewalk in front of my house. Do you think that's okay, Jimmy?"

Simmons was quiet on the phone. Then he said. "No, that's definitely not okay. And I'm really sorry, Mr. Malloy. I never intended for that to happen."

It always annoyed Ed when people said things like that. As if there were no consequences for your actions as long as you hadn't intended for them to happen. But it wasn't this kid's fault. He took another deep breath. "Well, that's what happened," Ed said. "No matter what you intended."

"My editor liked the story," Simmons said. "I was going to go on with it, do a second story, a follow-up. He says people have a right to know."

Ed sighed. "Let me ask you something, Jimmy," he said. "Aren't reporters supposed to write about things that actually happen, like fires or wars or whatever?"

"Yes," Simmons said. "That's true."

"And yet this wasn't something that happened, was it? Not really. This was you going into the park and starting a story all by yourself, asking people to sign things when they were just out with their families enjoying themselves, maybe having a picnic, and then writing if they didn't want to sign your petition. Isn't that so?"

"I see what you're saying," Simmons said. "I kind of created a story and then wrote about it, is that it?"

The kid sounded crestfallen now and it made Ed feel bad. As far as he could tell Jimmy was well meaning and trying hard to do his job, just like Ed had tried to do his. He'd said that causing Ed trouble wasn't what he was trying to do, and Ed believed him, even if it didn't matter very much in the end. It wasn't going to help getting pissed off at him. It had been a lousy day, but it wasn't the reporter's fault.

"Mr. Malloy," Simmons said. "Are you still there?"

But Ed had said enough. "I'll talk to you later, Jimmy," he said. Then he hung up.

Four

NEW YORK

You didn't have to be a genius to figure my being a Jew was part of the reason McCarthy hired me. There was a general belief that most of the communists in the government were of the Hebrew persuasion and McCarthy wanted to back away from that idea. There was money in our community to be raised for future campaigns and he was smart enough to know he'd do well to cultivate that part of Washington drawn to Bernard Baruch and Hyman Rickover. Not that this was my crowd or that the Jewish grandees would have anything to do with me, but to McCarthy a Jew was pretty much a Jew, and he wasn't far wrong there. Anyway, if he was using me in this respect, I would be doing as much with him to get a role on a Senate committee. You could say we were using each other, or that it started that way, but over time things changed and we became something close to friends.

Dave Schine was a different matter and a different kind of Jew. Dave and I couldn't have been more dissimilar. He was tall and fair while I was short and dark complected. He had a relaxed, casual way about him while I was intense and argumentative. He wore expensive clothes well and had a *laissez faire* attitude that drew beautiful Gentile women like moths to a light. I was glad he did, too, because I tended to be struck dumb whenever I got close to blonde hair. Dave never exercised a day in his life and yet he always seemed to be fit and ate whatever he wanted. Meanwhile, I was a regular at the gym, dieted all the time and still couldn't get rid of the love handles around my waist.

While McCarthy and I were alike in resenting the upper classes, I had to admire the way Dave had put it to the Brahmins at Harvard, first by demanding a private room and then setting up a woman he described as his secretary in it to serve him after hours. Then if that wasn't enough, he cruised around Cambridge in a big black Packard with a driver and a radiophone. Most of all he didn't give a shit if it pissed people off, didn't care if he got tapped for a club and never bought into the rest of the elitist bullshit they were throwing around up there. He didn't study or make grades and at one point there was even a possibility he'd be thrown out of school, but this didn't worry Dave. He knew that no one with money ever really got dismissed from Harvard. A semester off, maybe, but that was it. The gentleman's C was coign of the realm there.

My situation was different. Where I grew up in the Bronx before my mother moved us to Park Avenue all the Jews played handball on the public courts, and I enjoyed the sweaty camaraderie of those games and hanging afterwards at a nearby deli where we argued about the Dodgers, the Yankees and the Giants. Most of the boys I knew growing up went to City College which was famous for breeding communists, but my parents wanted me to go uptown to Morningside Heights instead. Not that life for me was much different at Columbia than it would have been at City. Columbia was supposed to be an Ivy, and I guess it was, but you'd never mistake the campus life there for Yale or Princeton with their private societies and eating clubs. To me, Columbia seemed more like a streetcar college with a lot of the same Jewish boys I'd seen on the handball courts filling my classrooms.

By stressing our differences, I don't mean to say Dave Schine and I were like Mutt & Jeff, the cartoon couple popular at that time, but we were an odd pair and that was a large part of what made it work for me. I suppose I envied him his apparent *goyishness* and ability to move in that world. But what had he ever accomplished? Everything he had was handed to him. Was I in love with him as the geniuses in the Senate would later think? It wasn't that simple though I might have fantasized about lying next to his smooth back and broad chest in those big beds at the Waldorf, but it never went beyond that. Maybe I wanted to *be* him or like him at least. I certainly thought he was a good-looking man, but I didn't want to sleep with him. If I had, I'd say so. Why not? Like

I said before this is a pile of memories and I'm already history.

So, it wasn't love between Schine and me. We're clear there. It wasn't that kind of friendship, not really intimate at all. We didn't share deep secrets or late drunken nights. I was drawn to Dave because he was different. I'd never known anyone in the tribe like him and that's true even now. If you want to know, looking back I think I made a mistake bringing him down to Washington and busting my ass for him. Especially since Dave didn't even want the job. He had a nice life in New York and Harvard or not, he wasn't the most ambitious guy I ever met, then or later. I should have left the whole thing alone but backing off was never one of my talents.

"McCarthy wants me?" he said incredulously when I told him about my meeting with the senator over lunch in the Cub Room upstairs at the Stork Club. It was our usual place to meet in those days and often the owner would drop over if things were slow and sit with us for a while. The word was that Billingsley didn't like Jews, but I spent a lot of money at his place, so we got along fine.

"Sure," I said. "He read your pamphlet on communism. That was enough to make him interested right away." This was bullshit, of course. No one read Dave's pamphlet, which was full of mistakes, published by his family's company, and put in all their hotels for the enlightenment of their guests.

"Okay," Dave said doubtfully. "I guess that's kind of interesting, but what would I do down there?"

"It's a subcommittee on investigations," I said brightly. "We'll investigate. They're talking about Reds and faggots in the State Department and the rest of the government."

Dave remained unconvinced over a three-hour lunch during which he criticized my table manners and told me some books I should read. In time I got him to at least think about giving Washington a try. A week later I got a call from Schine saying he'd accept our offer.

After that, we fell into a pattern. He'd come down on Monday, stay at the Statler and have lunch with me and McCarthy at the Carroll Arms. When Dave felt like it, he showed up at the office, which was okay because no one was quite sure who was working for who. The Senate Office Building where most staffers had their offices was packed. McCarthy had thirty people working for him and most of them were housed in closets down in the basement, which wasn't going to work for Schine and me.

I told McCarthy we needed room to work, and Joe let me lease space in an office building a block away. I ordered a lot of furniture, which pissed some people off, but Joe didn't care. Beyond this, the Senator didn't give me much direction or tell me what I was supposed to be doing. To say he wasn't attentive to detail is to understate it by a thousand. You'd see him in the morning for ten minutes over coffee, he'd throw out some ideas about the international threat of communism and then he'd be off somewhere leaving you to figure out what to do next.

"You're supposed to be an idea man," Joe said at one of our meetings early on. "Why I hired you. So, figure it out. Get some ideas on where to start."

While this was going on, I was also familiarizing myself with my new territory, when you got down to it, almost a different country with its own customs and rules. The Senator was busy, and I didn't really want him leading me around by the nose anyway. McCarthy and I would meet to catch up when it suited him and that was good enough for me. The rest of the time I'd be working through letters that had come into the office from various sources. If you read the papers, you'd think McCarthy was just a crank, but the truth was he'd become kind of a folk hero. Letters arrived by the bushel daily and I was amazed at the number of people who were regularly feeding McCarthy tips on the communists hiding undercover in government. I also got regular briefings from J. Edgar Hoover who invited me to look over any FBI documents that he thought might be interesting to me.

For the first few months most of my time was spent selecting out the few promising leads sent in by the lunatics. Before meeting McCarthy, I might have thought he was an opportunist looking for an issue to ride to the top, and although he was ambitious, I quickly saw he was sincere. For him, the battle with communism was not only a crusade but something he thought represented a real threat to the country.

By the time he hired me, McCarthy had already been attacking Truman and his administration for his whole first term and he didn't see Eisenhower as much of an improvement, even if Ike had run on the promise of rooting communists out of high places.

"That's the thing about generals," McCarthy said. "They're throwing them back at the Officers Club while the rest of us are out there doing the fighting."

This of course was vainglorious since McCarthy had been an officer in the Marines and kept far away from any actual fighting. But Joe wasn't a man for nuances, and he was also critical of Eisenhower's secretary of state, John Foster Dulles. "Don't forget," he said. "Dulles was a fan of Alger Hiss before he got put away. He'd like people to forget about all that. State's a problem, Roy, a big problem."

Occasionally, McCarthy would round back to the differences in our backgrounds. On one occasion he told me his campaign manager, a Wisconsin lawyer named Van Susteran didn't like New Yorkers and thought I was rude. "Well, maybe not rude," McCarthy said, hedging a bit, "but too abrupt, know what I mean."

I did. "Look, Senator," I said, "When we first met, you told me you wanted a tough guy and even if I'm not that tough, I grew up in the Bronx and New York's a tough town. One thing I learned when I was a kid was you don't get along in that world by arguing about which fork to use. Where I come from, people go for what they want and, my opinion, if someone's upset by that, too bad."

McCarthy laughed out loud and patted me on the shoulder. "Good line," he said. "I'll tell Van you said that about the forks."

"You tell him whatever you want, Senator. But that's the truth." I wasn't going to let some small town lawyer affect my standing with McCarthy.

McCarthy was still smiling. "Take it easy," he said. "Van's an old friend. He'll be fine once he gets to know you." Then he got serious. "The next big thing we need to do is look at the International Information Agency and the Voice of America," he said. "That's what I want you to be thinking about now."

"Anything in particular?" I was aware that the VOA was part of the International Information Agency but beyond that, my knowledge of the service was sketchy, and I didn't know what McCarthy was going for exactly. Obviously, the IIA was supposed to be anti-communist and reached most of the people in Europe. I also knew that the VOA had grown to the point that it was the biggest radio service in the world except for the BBC and Radio Moscow. So what was the problem?

McCarthy shook his head. "Everything," he said. "Their radio goes out all over the world and they're supposed to be putting out good news about America. But Sok's getting stuff from a group over there that a bunch of subversives have infiltrated the network. If these guys are pink and that's slanting the broadcasts the other way, it's giving comfort to the enemy.

"Subversives in the radio network?"

"Bet your ass," McCarthy said. "They're everywhere." McCarthy leaned over and said in a hoarse whisper, "Look, I know, no one cares about the radio, but the deal is we start small with VOA and build to hearings looking at the State Department and the Army. If we're going to nail those bastards, we have to put together a good resume, get some momentum going."

It was a process, but I hadn't given McCarthy much credit for being a strategist, if only because he seemed to shoot from the hip. But I was new to all this and trying to catch up with McCarthy as he went along, which wasn't easy. I wanted to present myself as a guy in the know even if I really knew almost nothing about what I was doing. "Okay," I said. "We'll look into it."

"See that you do," McCarthy said. "A guy named Paul Deac is our contact in Europe and he's sent us a shitload of material to check out. Look at their staff, their libraries and everything else they do. We'll be having hearings later in the spring, so we've got to be ready for that."

"Libraries?" I asked. I had heard about the radio, but this was news to me.

McCarthy nodded. "They've got them in cultural centers attached to all our embassies, books and magazines, newspapers by Americans in English for anyone who wants them. That's okay, but we want them to have the right books."

"Damned right," I said more emphatically than I felt. I was making this up as I went along and was still afraid that McCarthy would figure out I was all talk and go back to Bobby Kennedy to make his dad happy. The idea that we maintained libraries for Americans looking for entertainment during a slow night in Paris or Rome seemed pretty harmless. I had no idea which McCarthy would think were the right books, but I thought I knew someone who would. An idea was taking shape. "Maybe that's something Schine and I could look into."

But McCarthy's mind was already elsewhere. That was the way he was, head on a swivel, always looking around, waving at someone across the room, drumming with his fingers on the table. "Got to go," he said, getting up. "We'll talk about this more next time."

I knew Sok and Winchell and a few others had been running columns about communist infiltration at the Voice of America so that gave me a place to start. Since McCarthy had brought it up, I figured it wouldn't hurt for Dave and me to hold our own interviews with people working at the Information Agency and the Voice. Their headquarters were on Fifty-Seventh St. in New York, so once we got going it would make more sense to go to them rather than bringing their people down to Washington.

I could have rented space for the interviews or gone to the IIA offices, but I didn't want to be on their turf. In the end, we decided to run at least some of the interviews out of Dave's apartment in the Waldorf Towers, so before you knew it, we had all these IIA bigwigs waiting their turn in the dining room, wondering what dirt we'd come up with on them. There was something delicious about holding their feet to the fire when most of the people we talked to were probably my father's age. Not that our interviews were all about intimidation or embarrassing bureaucrats, but it was in there no question.

Going to work for McCarthy put me in bad odor with my parents, their friends and some bleeding hearts who were moved by the Rosenbergs. It wasn't that I didn't care about my parents or their friends but to me, it was simple: you want to stay out of trouble don't sell out your country to the Russians. I thought anyone who'd been involved with the communists, anyone who went to a meeting or had a card, even if it was ten years ago, was fair game. Who knew how far that crap went? Put it another way, I had respect for the other side too and understood that most of these leftists were serious people, dedicated to what they were doing, not college kids playing a radical game for a semester or two.

I also knew the Russians weren't going to let go of people they'd spent time recruiting and training. It was our job to find them, and they weren't going to make it easy. The way I saw it, this was a fight, maybe to the death. If someone jumped off a building or walked in front of a car when he was about to come before McCarthy's committee, that was likely proof that the guy wasn't as pure as he claimed to be. The world's not a pleasant place, at least not my world.

I wouldn't say I was running scared, but I'd put myself out there in a foreign environment where I wasn't known, and I felt the pressure increasing daily. The way I dealt with this was to work harder and stay later. The only relaxation I got was going to the gym where I worked out three times a week with a trainer. I had a few flirtatious encounters in the locker room with men who frequented the place, but I was determined to stay away from that, the risk of exposure was too great. I felt safe indulging my tastes in New York where no one cared what I did, but in Washington I imagined the cameras were always on and every microphone was live.

From the outside, committee hearings in Washington seem both more and less dramatic than they really are. The big rooms and stagey setting always seemed more for show than substance to me and the committee members more concerned with getting their names in the paper than finding anything substantial. The witnesses were little more than props even if their careers could be affected by their testimony.

For our committee, the VOA hearings were mostly table setting, a prelude for bigger things to follow. The whole thing was something like a symphony, with this first set of hearings the first movement, introducing themes and leitmotifs that could be repeated later. There were likely to be few revelations here. We were warming up, trying out a few things.

The hearings were held at a courthouse downtown in Foley Square which was familiar territory for me. The room was large with tall ceilings but still seemed close with the television lights, the reporters and the audience nearly on top of us. The smell of wet wool was in the air mixed with the aroma of ladies' perfume and pomade. I felt the audience crowded behind me even if we had a table to ourselves in the front. It was like being inside a cave with the walls moving ever closer. It made me uncomfortable enough that I had to constantly move around swiveling my head to see who was behind me in the room, who had changed seats.

I knew my way around the courtroom, but it was the first time I'd sat at a table with the Senator or watched him operate. It was a good way, a public way, to get to know McCarthy and I was immediately impressed with the way he handled himself. He could turn a witness better than any lawyer I've seen in twenty years of practicing law with some pretty smart guys.

The first issues we dealt with were the placement of VOA radio transmitters in America but before we lulled everyone into unconsciousness, Joe got to the heart of the matter, the fact that the VOA had dismantled its Hebrew desk, supposedly because very few listeners spoke Hebrew. I was Jewish but like most Jews I forgot what Hebrew I knew after my bar mitzvah and hadn't needed it since. I doubted there was much of an audience for a Hebrew radio broadcast, but McCarthy saw something here worth pursuing.

The order to close down the Hebrew section had been given by a man named Reed Harris, whom I'd known slightly in New York. Years before, he'd been involved with the Young Communist League when they were defending a Marxist professor at Columbia. Harris had supposedly given all that up long ago, but McCarthy wasn't convinced he'd reformed. Joe was an absolutist when it came to communism. Once a communist, always a communist was the way he saw it. Joe had our table piled high with an intimidating amount of paper as well as two large briefcases that he always carried with him. I'd never seen him take anything out of the cases, but he liked to shuffle through the papers to intimidate witnesses.

Harris was slightly stooped with gray hair and wire-rimmed glasses that he frequently took off to clean on his tie. He'd brought his wife with him but during the three days we had him, he never turned to her or even seemed aware that she was there. To me, he seemed less worried than pre-occupied, as if we were keeping him from some important meeting. This of course only served to piss McCarthy off.

In any case, Joe jumped right in without any niceties. "Mr. Harris," he said. "Do you consider yourself to be a good American, a patriotic American."

"I do, Mr. Chairman," Harris said tartly. "I always have."

"And yet you were a member of the Communist Party and tried to get Marxist professors hired at Columbia."

"No, that's not correct," Harris said quickly. "I wasn't involved in hiring but I did try to stop them from firing professors because of their political beliefs," Here he paused, polished his glasses again and then inspected them in the light from the tall windows.

This made McCarthy smile. I imagined him licking his lips, a wolf contemplating a meeting with a lamb. He waited a moment and then said, "And those political beliefs were Marxist, isn't that correct?"

"Yes, Mr. Chairman," Harris said. "In that particular case, they were."

"I see. Then you defended other professors who weren't Marxists as well as those who were?" McCarthy said.

"Well, no," Harris said, "because those weren't the professors who were being attacked, but I hope I'd defend anyone whose political beliefs might lead to them losing their jobs."

"Fine," McCarthy said, "but regardless of who you say you'd defend in other circumstances if the situation came up, for the record and our purposes, the professors you actually did defend were Marxists."

"Yes, sir, that's correct." Harris said. "But I have to say, this was more than twenty years ago."

McCarthy nodded and shuffled some papers. I noticed his knee jumping up and down under the table. I had the thought that he might be nervous, something that hadn't occurred to me before. It was Harris who was under the gun, after all. Now, McCarthy looked up and said, "Mr. Harris, you say you consider yourself a loyal American, but didn't you also write a book attacking the great all-American sport of football."

This came out of nowhere but that was McCarthy. It was the equivalent of what they call a no-look pass in basketball designed to surprise the defender. But I knew what he was talking about. In the Thirties, Harris had written a book called *Big Football* in which he essentially said college football players were paid gladiators, not students. No one I knew had read it but apparently McCarthy had and that was what mattered.

"I didn't attack football," Harris protested. "What I said was that universities had professionalized it and that the people who played football were more like hired guns than students."

"I think you called them 'privileged mugs," McCarthy said. "Is that true?"

"You seem to be one of the few people in America who actually read that book," Harris said. "I'd be flattered if I didn't think you were using it to try to wring my neck very skillfully."

McCarthy smiled. "Maybe I just like football and its place in American life," he said. Then he looked back at his note and continued. "In that same book didn't you also attack marriage, the American Legion and what you call conformity but which some of us would call the American way?"

Harris was sweating now. "Sir, I wrote that book in just a few weeks a long time ago. I swear that I support and believe in marriage. I have kids at home and attend church regularly."

"Does your wife know that you wrote a book attacking marriage," McCarthy asked. He was having fun now, a slight smile on his lips.

"I don't know," Harris said, looking sideways at his wife whose expression hadn't changed. "We've never discussed it."

"Well," McCarthy said, nodding at Mrs. Harris, "she'll know now." He hesitated, then dived in once more. "Going back to the business about the Hebrew Desk," he said. "That was your decision to close it down, is that correct, Mr. Harris."

"Yes, sir," Harris said.

"Would you call yourself an antisemite?" McCarthy said now.

"Of course not," Harris said. "That's a fantastic thing to say. Very unfair."

Probably because I was Jewish, McCarthy then asked me to take over the questioning, though I hadn't been prepped on this. I was to learn this was McCarthy's style. He might interrupt in the middle of something I was saying and take over the questioning or as in the present instance, become bored and just stop mid-sentence, leaving me holding the bag. But he was looking at me expectantly now as if he wanted me to levitate or something. I could feel the room behind me pressing forward so I cleared my throat and picked up the questioning.

"All right, you say you're not antisemitic," I began, "that's very good, just what we'd expect of a person in your high position. And yet you made a point of closing only the Hebrew Language desk rather than some others. Can you enlarge on that for us?"

"It was a financial decision," Harris said. "Our budget is limited, and, in my judgement, other areas were more crucial to our mission."

"Your judgement?" This sounded a little grandiose to me since this guy was little more than a paper pusher at the agency.

"Yes," Harris said, sounding a bit prissy now. "That's what I get paid to do. Make decisions, difficult ones that someone has to make?"

I looked down at my notes, but this was strictly for show as I had written nothing on the pad before coming into the hearing. Not knowing exactly where I was going, I said, "Hebrew, of course, is the national language of Israel? Do you have Jewish friends in Israel? Have you been there?"

"No," Harris said. "I hope to go in the future. Of course, I have many Jewish friends here in New York."

"But you're not Jewish yourself?"

"I'm not, as you know very well, sir."

"Well, then, did you ask any of your many Jewish friends here in New York what they thought of your decision to close down the Hebrew desk?" I asked.

"I did not," Harris said. "Nor did I consult them about any of the dozens of other decisions I've made as Deputy Director."

I leaned over and whispered, "I'm done with this guy, Senator."

Joe smiled and said, "Okay, but I'm not."

McCarthy took over, pressing Harris on the difference between his political beliefs now and in the Thirties, and managed to get in a few digs about Acheson and Truman, mentioning Alger Hiss in the bargain.

"That man has nothing to do with me," Harris said. "How could you bring up something so irrelevant to this discussion?"

McCarthy shrugged. "I'm not so sure about that. He was a government employee, just like you, had ties with the communists as you did."

"Just like thousands of other people you've tried to smear with your innuendo," Harris said angrily. The hearing dragged on for another hour or so, but serious damage had been done, and Harris resigned his position with the VOA a few weeks later.

In the end, despite McCarthy's attacks, the VOA was able to go on mostly unchanged under new leadership. The hearings began to lose their juice after we dealt with Harris and we finally let them go, choosing to concentrate on other things. Looking back, I wouldn't say the VOA sessions were a complete success, but they were a beginning for Joe and the Committee, maybe the end of the first movement. Also, I'd learned some things about my boss. I was impressed by his intelligence and ability to think quickly and re-direct his questions if something surprising came up.

With the hearings behind us, I was set to look at the overseas libraries which looked to be more important in the long term. I'd done more research since McCarthy told me to look into them and their staffers. By the time Schine and I got on the plane for Germany in April I knew where we were going and what we were looking for.

I'd never been to Europe but while we were over there, we didn't spend any time sightseeing. Instead, as soon as we landed, we went to the office of the American High Commission in Bonn and started asking questions. The director was a man who'd written a communist play some years earlier and refused to answer any questions, saying we should bring him in front of the Committee if we wanted to grill him. He eventually got his wish and may have been sorry for it but at this point he felt justified in pushing back on us and McCarthy. This scene repeated itself in Frankfurt at the America House where we were greeted by a junior official named Burton, who wasn't much older than I was.

While Burton and I talked, Schine started making his way through the library stacks, but when I noticed a large pile of newspapers and magazines off to the side. I asked if there were any anti-communist magazines.

"I'm not sure what you're looking for," Burton said. "We have *Time* magazine. Is that anti-communist?"

"Not in my book," I said. "What about the American Legion magazine?"

"We don't have that," the man said. "I don't think there are many American veterans living in Bonn, so it didn't seem to make sense to include it in the collection."

"Even though we have a major army base here?" I said, which made the guy step back. "What about *The Freeman* then? I'd call that a solid anti-communist magazine."

"No, I don't think so." Burton seemed pleased with his answer, or he might have simply been pleased to have an answer and show he knew something about his own collection.

I was determined not to let this smart ass show me up. "Or *The Stars & Stripes*?" I asked. "There may not be many vets but there are a lot of active servicemen in Germany. Surely you have that here."

This made Bruton uncomfortable. "I'm sorry," he said. "Let me make some notes and I'll see about ordering some of these things."

"You do that," I said. "By the way, where do you keep all the communist books since you say you've got none that are anti-communist?"

"Oh, we don't have a section for communist books," Burton said, laughing nervously. "We wouldn't go out of our way to order anything like that."

"Is that right?"

At this point, Schine came out of the stacks with an armload of books he'd gathered. "Isn't this information center supposed to show America in a good light?" Dave asked innocently.

"Well, we hope so," Bruton said.

"Who ordered all the Dashiell Hammett, a known communist author then?" Dave held up a few books for inspection. I didn't know who Hammett was or what he might have written, but later he'd do time courtesy of HUAC for being a communist. We had nothing to do with the House Committee and never sent anyone to jail for anything, but I'll admit we had some interests in common.

"And what about this?" Dave said now. Burton looked at the books, trying to decipher what Dave was holding up, though he clearly had no idea what was in his library.

"Sinclair Lewis," David said. "Another communist, a man who turned down the greatest literary prize a writer could earn."

"Really?" Burton said. "I didn't know." As if to explain his ignorance, he added, "I should tell you that actually I haven't been here very long."

"*It Couldn't Happen Here*," Dave read a title of one of the books he'd brought back. Do you think that's an appropriate novel to demonstrate what's good about America?"

"I really couldn't say," Burton replied. He was beginning to sweat under Dave's questions, but I was silently congratulating myself on bringing Schine along. There were some people who'd suggested he was a lightweight and I might have been among them before the trip, but it was something to watch him take this embassy lackey down.

"I see you've also got works by Dreiser, Stephen Crane and Frank Norris," Dave went on. "Not to mention Upton Sinclair, John Dos Passos, Ring Lardner and James Wechsler, all critics of our country. And what about Richard Wright and Langston Hughes, more authors that hate America."

Burton tried to make a comeback by saying, "If you could just suggest some other authors, as Mr. Cohn suggested magazines, I could make notes and see if we could get some books by them."

But Schine was ready for this. "I haven't gone to the trouble of making a list, but some that come to mind are Booth Tarkington, Edgar Guest, Zane Grey, Edna Ferber and Pearl Buck. All good Americans who love their country."

I had no idea whether this was true or not, but it didn't matter. Burton was looking anxiously for the exit, and I was congratulating myself on a job well done. I didn't think much of the Ivy League, but you can't beat a Harvard education. Whoever heard of all these writers? But the point had been made because they were clearly news to Burton too. If he didn't know who was in his collection, who was stocking the library, the CP?

When he was through with the books, Dave was ready to move on to magazines, but we'd made our point and after a few hours, we went to a press conference the embassy had organized with the reporters who were following our trip, most of whom seemed intent on embarrassing us. Someone had given them copies of Dave's pamphlet on communism and they made a big deal about a few typos. One even asked Dave if it was true that he had a large collection of cigar bands, which was bullshit but I was used to dealing with writers and Dave wasn't, so he just sat there turning red with anger without saying a word.

More important was that the people from the embassy were trying to make us look bad and even screwed things up with the hotel by giving Dave and me a double room. I wasn't going to let that pass. "What do you think that we're from, State?" I said. I wasn't going to let them get off implying that Dave and I were faggots.

"An innocent mistake," Bruton said. "Very sorry. We'll fix it."

"Innocent my ass," I said, pointing at him. "I've got your name. I'm the wrong man to fuck with. Remember that."

After Bonn, we took off first for Vienna where we stayed for a couple of days looking into leads we'd gotten about communists who'd gone underground and wanted to talk to us about the VOA. After wandering around the backstreets behind the link road and paying money to a couple of dirty panhandlers with bad English, we knew as much as we had when we started. Why McCarthy had wanted me to talk to these idiots I'll never know but he was the boss, so we went wherever he told us to go.

No one asked why McCarthy had sent a couple of Jews over to look at the information centers, but even if neither Dave nor I were religious, it was impossible to be in Hitler's hometown and not think about what this visit would have been like ten years earlier. We were fortunate in that neither of our families had been involved in what came to be called the Holocaust. Our people came earlier, to escape the Czar, but you'd have to be brain-dead not to think of Nazis in long black overcoats walking the dark streets in Vienna. The War was less than a decade over and without concentrating on it consciously, whenever I met a German, in the street or in the hotel, I found myself wondering where he had been during Kristallnacht or when Jesse Owens came over and kicked Hitler's ass in the Olympics.

People have short memories. Mention the War to someone in Europe and a cloudy look comes into their eyes as if it was decades ago. Every Frenchman will tell you he was with the Free French, hiding out with DeGaulle, which you know is bullshit. There's also a tendency to ignore the fact that Hitler was popularly elected before he started killing off his enemies. Walking around Vienna, I found myself looking over my shoulder, wondering if there were remnants of the party lurking in the backstreets, like those Japanese soldiers that turn up every now and then in the jungle, unaware the War is over. No one ever said anything about the Nazis to me directly during the trip, but I couldn't help but wonder where they'd all gone. I couldn't get out of Vienna fast enough.

The rest was the kind of European tour I'd never had or even thought about having. Places like Belgrade, Athens, Frankfort and Paris were only names to me before that trip, so in a way I suppose I should be grateful, despite the roasting we got from the press. What's more, I couldn't really disagree with the reporters who wrote articles saying the idea of sending a couple of privileged kids over to question diplomats in foreign capitals was an arrogant thing to do, but in the end that didn't amount to much.

After our stops in Europe, we flew to London where there was another hit squad of reporters waiting for us at Heathrow who seemed mainly interested in asking about Dave's background. We fenced with them for a while but after a week out of the country I'd had more than enough of the working press or the part of it that had decided to follow us to Europe. You keep hearing about the peoples' "right to know" but so much of what we saw then, and continued to see later was little more than posturing. In addition, there was a kind of groupthink or pack mentality that led one reporter to sound like any other. If this was what passed for investigative journalism, you could have it.

Anyway, who cared? I'd been in touch with the Senator during the trip and he was pleased with what we'd done in Europe. The reporters could write whatever they liked but we'd got what we came for, or some of it, evidence for the Senator to use as ammunition in future committee hearings. If I had been in doubt, I'd find out later how useful all this was to be to McCarthy, who continued to amaze me with his agility in questioning witnesses and coming up with new lines of inquiries on the spur of the moment.

Before leaving London, we took a quick trip to the Palace, but the Queen wasn't there, so we returned to the hotel and had dinner. It was time to go home.

Five

MADISON

Ed felt as if he was walking on rubber, sinking deeper with each step but unable to reverse course. At the office, he secluded himself and kept his gaze steady at the pebbled wall blank and white as he waited for what he assumed was inevitable. If he could magically wish himself out of this situation and save himself, he might have but it would be impossible to escape otherwise. Janey had been avoiding him at home ever since the article appeared in the paper and when he tried to explain himself further about the loyalty oath, she said there was nothing to talk about and turned away.

Only Little Ed seemed unchanged in his feelings, and the boy didn't really know what was going on. When Ed got home from the office, they'd walk down to the park together, throw their lines into the water and sit on the pier and watch the bobber for a while. They never caught anything, but Little Ed didn't care. The kid would just sit there on the dock and stare at the water, as if he expected a fish to jump up and bite him, but that was okay with Ed. He thought he should live like the boy: just focus on what was in front of him and let everything else slide, but he found this hard to do. The opacity of the gray-green water seemed in its lack of transparency to mirror his life. Now, he put his arm around Little Ed and pulled him close. The boy was small, with nut-brown skin and dark eyes. Not for the first time, Ed wondered if Little Ed was really his son. But this wasn't important. They loved each other and biology had never been Ed's strong point anyway.

When they were about to leave the lake, Little Ed, asked, "Can we come again tomorrow, Daddy?"

"We didn't catch anything," Ed said, and gave the boy a squeeze, struck as always by how warm he was, how trusting.

"That doesn't matter," Little Ed said. "I just like to sit there with you."

Ed was so moved by this, he felt his eyes water and had to look up at the agate sky in order to hide it from his son. For a moment, he thought about the possibility of losing this little boy and shivered. He valued his job, the house, his marriage, but in the end the only thing he felt he couldn't do without was his son. He shook his head to dismiss the thought. Then he hugged Little Ed to him again and they started walking home.

That night he tried again to talk to his wife, but Janey couldn't understand his reluctance to sign the oath. She thought he was just being stubborn or maybe even lazy which he found insulting. "You think I want them to lay me off," Ed said incredulously? "How could you think I'd want that?"

"Then sign the damned thing," Janey said. "What do you care really? Sign it and all of this will disappear."

"See, that's it," Ed said. "I do care whether you think it makes any sense or not. And do we know anything would disappear? Maybe this is just the beginning."

"Beginning of what?" Janey said. "Anyway, if your paycheck depends on it, then who cares what's right or if the guy asking you to sign is an asshole? You think I'm crazy about everyone I work with down at the Ben Franklin? You're not supposed to like the people at the office, Ed. That's why they call it work. If you loved going down there and seeing everyone else, you'd pay them instead of the other way around."

The way Janey talked, Ed felt like a student who'd disobeyed in class. "It's not a matter of me loving or hating everyone," he said patiently. "That's not even a part of it. It's the principle of the whole thing. Telling me I'm not patriotic if I won't sign something is bigger than that."

"What principle is that?" Janey said. "Maybe they're right and you're not patriotic enough," Janey said. "And if you are, what's wrong with saying so, with signing your name?"

"It's not that simple," Ed protested.

"It's exactly that simple," Janey said angrily. "Nothing's more important than keeping your job. Who do you think you are, some aristocrat with a trust fund? We need that money to pay the mortgage and the car loan. That's how simple the whole thing is."

"It's about my character," Ed said. "My reputation. That's not simple at all."

Janey snorted. "People like us can't afford character," she said. "That's for rich people or those up at the University."

Ed just shook his head at this. He didn't know when his wife had become anti-communist or even cared about the whole thing. "Anyone, can afford character," he said stubbornly. "You don't have to be rich or educated to have that." But Janey didn't answer.

That was the last time they'd talked, and Ed had been sleeping on the couch in his den since.

Ed hadn't heard directly from DiPietro since he'd been called into his office the week before. Because everyone else ignored him, Ed allowed himself to hope the whole thing had blown over. More important, since Jimmy's phone call there'd been nothing more about him in the paper and Little Ed was doing fine with the other kids at school.

Ed knew he'd reacted more angrily than he should have when DiPietro asked him to sign the oath, but the delay allowed him to think maybe they were actually giving him credit for sticking up for himself. Who could tell? In the midst of thinking this, however, DiPietro's secretary called and asked him to come down to his office. When Ed arrived, he saw DiPietro along with the head of the agency sitting behind a conference table. On it was a paper that looked like the one Ed had been asked to sign before. DiPietro indicated a chair and Ed sat.

"I've asked Mr. Morrey to join us," DiPietro said, "because I think we got off track the last time," DiPietro said. "That okay with you, Ed?"

Ed had only seen Morrey once before at an office barbecue, but he nodded his assent. Morrey was an older man with horn-rimmed glasses and what seemed like a kindly air. "Fine with me," he said.

"Okay," DiPietro said. "Well, last time I gave you a paper just like this one in front of you and asked you to think about it, talk it over with your wife, maybe your friends or pastor. Did you have a chance to do that?"

Ed nodded again but said nothing more.

"Well, since we heard nothing from you, I assume your attitude about this hasn't changed. Is that right, Ed?"

"I don't know that attitude is the right word," Ed said. "It's more a matter of principle, if you ask me."

"Okay, fine," DiPietro said, clearly annoyed. "Have your principles changed since the last time we talked? How about if I put it that way?"

Ed just looked at the guy. This seemed incredible to him, just as incredible as anyone really thinking he was a communist. But it must be so. All of a sudden, the big boss of the company who never gave him five minutes before was in here with DiPietro calling him on the carpet. "I don't change my principles like you'd put on a different shirt," he said. "Do you?"

"We're not talking about me here, Ed," DiPietro said. "We've tried to be fair in giving you time to cool down and think this over, but the point is are you going to sign this or not? That's what we need to know."

Ed looked over at Morrey. The older man hadn't said a word. Now he leaned across the table and said, "I know how you feel, son," he said in a soft voice. "No one here's going to say principles aren't important, at least while I'm in charge. I'm a veteran too. But if I were you, I'd just sign this paper and then we can all go back to work and forget about it."

On the face of it, this was completely reasonable, but Ed still reacted against the suggestion. If Morrey really knew how he felt, why was he getting this pressure? What difference could this possibly make to him or to the agency? He'd always thought Morrey seemed okay regardless of his feelings about DiPietro. Still there was an edge to the room. Ed knew about danger, had seen it, sensed it, and he thought he might be in danger now. At the same time, he felt something new, something approaching euphoria at standing up for himself against the other men.

"You might be right," Ed said finally. "I have no reason to think you're not, but I can't sign this because if I sign it's as if I'm saying I support the idea of these things, that there's a question about whether I'm patriotic or not and you have a right to ask."

Morrey nodded ponderously, seeming to think this over. Then he got up without another word and walked out, leaving DiPietro and Ed facing each other. "I'm disappointed in you, Ed," DiPietro said, "and I know Mr. Morrey is too. We've tried to make you see our point of view, but some people are just too stubborn to cooperate even when it's in their own interest to do so."

Ed was tired of talking to this guy. "Anything else?" he said. "I've got a lot of work sitting on my desk and I should get to it."

"Actually, there is," DiPietro said, and pulled another paper out of his folder. He slid it across the table to Ed. It was a letter telling him that the agency was putting him on furlough. Along with the letter there was a check for two weeks' pay. It struck Ed that they had to have prepared the letter and check before the meeting which meant they didn't expect him to sign in the first place.

"What's this?" Ed said.

"I think it's self-explanatory," DiPietro said. "We're putting you on a furlough with what I think is a very generous stipend considering the fact that you've been so difficult to deal with over this."

"You're firing me because I wouldn't sign a damned loyalty oath?" Ed said, amazed. "I've done great work. Ask my clients for Christ's sake."

"That's why we're only giving you a furlough," DiPietro said. "You may think better of this after a couple of weeks at home."

Ed stood and looked down at the other man. "No fucking way," he said, and brushed past DiPietro, leaving the check on the table.

Ed walked home again, skipping the University this time. What was the point? He'd never been much of a student and things weren't going to change now. It occurred to him that he'd been stupid not to take the check he'd been offered but to take it would be to play their game, accept their terms rather than to stick to his guns. To hell with DiPietro, to hell with Morrey, to hell with all of them.

Janey had a different response. When Ed walked into the kitchen, she looked up, fire in her eyes. "Your office called," she said.

"Oh, yeah," Ed said, noncommittal. Maybe they were asking him back after all. "What did they want?"

"They said you walked out and left a $200 check on the table."

"That's right," Ed said. "I got fired. They called it a furlough, but the fact is they fired me for not signing that loyalty oath."

Janey took a deep breath and crossed her arms across her breasts. "A furlough's different than being fired, Ed. It's temporary."

"Not really. Unless I sign the loyalty oath the furlough becomes permanent. They gave me a couple of weeks to think it over."

"And you're going to do that, right? I mean, okay, you made your point even if I don't understand what it is. When it comes right down to it, you're going to sign the damned thing, right?"

"No," Ed said. "I don't think I will. I thought it over already and I decided I don't want to be railroaded into anything."

Janey came over and put her hands on his shoulders. "Look, Eddie," she said. "I understand how you feel and maybe I wasn't fair to you before. But now you've just got to sign because you've got to hold onto that job. What I earn isn't going to be enough, not close to enough for us to make it without your check too."

"I'll find another job," Ed said.

"Without a reference from this one? I doubt it," Janey said. "If you're really that mad, grit your teeth and stay there while you look if that's what you want to do. It's always easier to find a job when you have one."

Janey said this in a monotone, as if she was talking to herself. Ed thought she looked shell-shocked staring straight ahead at the wall, so intense he looked just to make sure there wasn't anything hanging there he'd missed. He'd expected his wife to be angry, but more than that Ed could see she was stunned that he was going against her. She'd always called the shots in their marriage, made the important decisions, chosen the furniture, the doctors and he'd gone along because it was easier that way. Now Ed realized he was surprised himself. It was as if he'd discovered that he had principles while he was talking to DiPietro and Morrey, but that wasn't really true. He'd always known there were things he believed in. This seemed different, not that he was like Patrick Henry or any of those patriots he'd learned about in high school, but something unexpected had come along and it had pushed him in a new direction, making him take a step that might turn out to be irrevocable. So, surprised, yes but it wasn't any ordinary surprise but larger than that, maybe life-changing, who knew? And in that moment, despite his determination to follow his gut on this, he also felt regret for what it would do to Janey, and he suspected, to their life. He wasn't flippant about this; no survivor of the Depression was going to give up a job easily, but determined nevertheless.

"Sorry," Ed said, putting his hand on Janey's.

"I'm not signing anything, and I guess that means I'm not going back. We've still got some savings from my grandmother's old war bond, and we've got the house."

"That money was for little Ed's education," Janey said, her voice suddenly louder in the room. "And you want to sell our house just because of your pride? Are you serious, Ed? I mean, really, who gives a shit about the damned oath and what those guys think about whether you're patriotic? Let them think whatever they want, you've got a family to support and we're not using our savings to do it."

He had to admit it sounded crazy the way she said it, but that didn't change anything. "We'll figure something out," he said, meaning to reassure her.

But Janey didn't accept this. "You mean you will," she said. "I'm through." And she walked out of the kitchen.

"Through?" Ed said. "What do you mean? Through with what?" But Ed was talking to an empty room.

The office sent the check around that Ed had left on DiPietro's desk and Janey cashed it before taking Little Ed and going to stay with her sister. "I love you, Ed," she said, "but Little Ed and I can't sit around and see if you're going to be a responsible husband and father. When you get off your high horse and come to your senses maybe I'll be back."

And not knowing why he said it exactly, Ed replied, "And what if I don't, get off my high horse?"

"Well, you'll see what happens," Janey said. They hadn't spoken since.

Janey was decisive when she decided to leave but it wasn't easy for her to go if only because it meant giving up a way of life that she'd always wanted and planned for. She'd chosen Ed initially because she thought the big farm boy she met at the dance would be a good provider, responsible, steady, someone to count on. Romance had never been a part of it for her and hadn't characterized their marriage. They didn't go for long walks holding hands and sex was an occasional obligation to be fulfilled if not enjoyed. She'd been satisfied with Ed and with their marriage, until now. But she wasn't going to sit around and watch their life go down the drain because her husband was doing something stupid.

Without thinking consciously about it at the time, she'd blamed her mother for staying with her father when he stayed home listening to the radio and drinking rather than looking for a job after the mines closed down. Janey's mother didn't feel she could leave and maybe that was true for her. No one in their family had ever been divorced no matter how lousy their lives were; it was the Depression, and you accepted the cards you were dealt without complaining. But times were different now, Madison wasn't Mineral Point, and Janey wasn't going to make the same mistake her mother had. Living in two rooms at her sister's wasn't the same as having her own house, but the way Ed was acting they weren't going to have the house for long. Anyway, she was still young and might meet someone else who wanted to work for a living. Assuming Ed didn't change his mind, and Janey had a feeling in the end he wouldn't.

Ed wasn't used to being home during the day and at first he kept busy doing chores he'd put off. He got the lawn in shape for winter, trimmed the hedges, changed the storm windows and winterized the furnace. The realtor he called said it wasn't a great time to sell but when the agent came by,he commented on the improvements Ed had made on the house and guessed he'd make a few thousand over what they'd bought it for if they did sell.

Ed had never been big on cooking so he took most of his meals at Mickies a few blocks away. He'd sit at the counter with the roped off section of girlie magazines at his back and read the paper as he ate. McCarthy was making a name for himself in Washington chasing communists and Ed wondered if those people had been convicted on evidence as flimsy as what the agency had against him. It wasn't that he doubted there actually were people in government passing secrets. The war had gone a long way toward convincing him that not everyone in the world had good intentions. He knew about espionage in Washington and over in Europe but thought of it as being like a black cloud hanging in the sky some distance away and not likely to affect him or the people he cared about.

At the same time, having risked his life for the country, he now felt abandoned by it and, incidentally, by his employer, his wife and his friends, those he had left. Walking in the neighborhood after eating, Ed was aware of people looking out their windows and then hurriedly closing the drapes as if whatever he had was contagious. Since he had nowhere to go, he left his car out on the street for a couple of days and the guy across the street called the city to complain because there was an ordinance that forbade parking on the street for more than twenty-four hours. Why the guy didn't just call on the phone if it bothered him, Ed didn't know but the neighbors were no longer talking to him. When did people get so goddamned suspicious, he wondered? Madison used to be a friendly place, a typical college town with people greeting others on the street and selling parking spaces on their lawns on football Saturdays. No one suspected strangers of questionable behavior and neighbors waved cheerfully when they went by in their cars if Ed was out doing yardwork. At least that was the way it had always been. Not anymore.

The house seemed bigger with Janey and Little Ed gone and very quiet. So much so that when the phone rang one day Ed jumped out of his chair, not recognizing immediately what the noise was. When he picked up, he was surprised to hear a woman's voice.

"Mr. Malloy? This is Susan Rozelle. We talked at the University one day a few weeks ago?" She sounded doubtful, as if he had forgotten her.

"I remember," Ed said, not sure of what to say. Did he call her professor or dean or maybe assistant? He had no idea.

"Yes, well," Susan Rozelle said, "I was just calling to see if you'd had a chance to look at any of the information I shared with you when you came over here."

The brochures she'd given him were sitting in a pile in the corner of his den where he'd left them weeks ago. "Actually, I haven't," Ed said. "I'm sorry. I've been kind of busy." Right, Ed thought. Busy doing nothing but he didn't know what else to say.

"I understand," Susan said. "I hope you'll check it out, though. I think you might find our programs interesting."

Ed liked her voice, soft sand a little uncertain, as if she had been nervous about calling, though he had no idea why that would be so or why this woman would go out of her way to contact him, even if, as she had said the day they talked, it was her job. Did she do this with every vet who walked in the door? He didn't consider himself to be university material. No one in his family or even his friends from high school had gone on to college. It was a foreign universe, intriguing but more than a little intimidating as well. He had resented people like DiPietro who'd been to college, thought of them as snobs, looking down on people who hadn't had the same opportunities. Yet here he was, talking to a dean. Was this even possible?

"Well, okay," Ed said, hoping to extend the call, wanting to hear that soft voice for a few more minutes. "Maybe you're right. I'll definitely read it now." It was as if she'd given him an assignment that he hadn't fulfilled.

"Wonderful," Susan Roselle said. "And once you've done that, perhaps you could come back to South Hall, and we can discuss it. Sometime in the next few weeks or at least before the winter semester begins. Do you think you'd have time to do that?"

Time, all Ed had was time, but he didn't want to admit this. He felt inadequate enough as it was. "Well," he said. "I guess I can do that, sure I can."

"How about this Thursday?" Susan said, her voice bright and friendly over the phone. "Around eleven? Would that be convenient."

"Thursday would be good," Ed said. "I'll be there." And after hanging up, he found himself looking forward to something for the first time in weeks.

Six

WASHINGTON

Whatever else people said about McCarthy, no one who knew him ever suggested he was lazy. I thought of him as being like a billiard ball, bouncing off this idea and then that one, with everyone else serving as cushions on the table. Given his sometimes sleepy expression, I was surprised how energetic he was, always moving, pushing ideas and demands, never quiet. He laughed a lot and loudly, though he didn't tell jokes, and I wasn't always clear what was funny to him. In the time I worked for him, McCarthy almost never took a day off and was generally in his office late at night, often drinking bourbon with the reporters who hung around looking for material. People don't understand this about reporters. Most of them are liberals but that's not the important thing. They were all hungry for a story and McCarthy was always good for copy and a laugh when all the other politicians had gone home.

Even so, we were still gathering strength, developing material, sources, witnesses. It was the slow movement in our symphony, the preparation for more dramatic scenes to come. Even if I couldn't have identified it as such at the time, looking back, I see what was going on during those months.

Joe's appetite for work made us a good fit. He'd call me at any time of the day or night. "Roy," he'd say in the harsh whisper of a drinking man. "Did I wake you"" And before I could answer, he'd go on, his voice like a runaway train in the dark. "I got a problem here," he'd say.

Then he'd ask questions in a staccato tone. If I didn't know the answer, he'd order me to get it as if I had a library or newspaper morgue right there with me in my hotel room. Or he'd suggest we meet for a drink at three am to talk about some Committee business and assume that I had nothing else to do and, like him, never slept. While others with a family might have resented this, being alone as I was in a strange town, I welcomed it. To me, McCarthy's urgency spoke of his commitment, attested to the importance of the work we were doing, and said something both about what he demanded of himself and what he expected from me. Long days and extra hours were what I'd signed on for and I would have been disappointed if Joe had asked anything less from me and others on the staff.

Other than Joe's nocturnal calls, however, no one contacted me socially. Washington was famous as a party town, but Perle Mesta, the city's leading hostess of that time, must not have had my number as I was never invited, asked out for a drink after work, or even included in poker games. This was a contrast with my life in New York where I had a wide circle of friends and rarely spent a night alone. I wondered idly if I'd given off some kind of signal, an odd scent, like animals do when defending their turf.

With thousands of homosexuals supposedly working for the government, I knew there were bars and clubs where homos gathered to drink, dance, and I was eager to join in if I could do so without threatening my position. I had perfected the art of hearing without appearing to listen so I knew about Nob Hill and Casey's in Georgetown but given the rumors circulating about me, I couldn't take the chance of going to one of those places and revealing anything about my sexuality. What was I afraid of? It's hard to say, something vague and inchoate but present nevertheless. I might have said I didn't want to compromise the work of the Committee, which was true, but it went beyond that. In New York, I felt invulnerable, free to do what I liked, see whom I pleased. But in Washington I was isolated, out of my element and scared of being found out and humiliated. To me, the city was a large shooting range with me as the unwilling target.

Still, I wasn't used to being on the shelf sexually this long and finally overcame my discomfort to venture out one night to a place I'd heard about vaguely in one of the close-in Virginia bedroom communities that surrounded Washington.

It was a small bar called "Cozy Corner" on a country road surrounded by fields, as quiet and removed from the city as one could imagine. Inside, was a small room with a piano player in the corner, seating at the bar and a few tables that flanked the musician. Two couples moved slowly around the dance floor, but I was never adept at dancing so sat at the bar and ordered a beer from the bartender who was friendly but reserved.

After a few minutes, a man about my age with a poorly fitted rug sat at the next stool, signaled for a drink and then looked around the room before turning to me. "First time?" the man said.

It wasn't clear if he meant the first time at this bar or my first encounter of this kind, so I played it safe. "Just found out about this place," I said. "Someone at work mentioned it."

This wasn't true, but it didn't matter as the man just nodded. He drank his beer, and we sat silently listening to the music for a few minutes. I wasn't sure what came next, if he'd make a move or expected me to. I was about to excuse myself, when the guy said, "I've got a car."

I nodded as if I understood this was an invitation, but I was uncomfortable accepting a back-seat assignation with a stranger. On the other hand, I asked myself, why was I there? I turned and scanned the parking lot.

"It's the Cadillac on the end," the man said. "Dark blue." Then he put a dollar on the bar and walked outside.

Not sure what local customs were in such situations, I finished my drink and sat for another half-hour, thinking perhaps my prospects would improve, but nothing changed except the pianist moved from Cole Porter to something vaguely contemporary. In time, I put money on the bar and left but when I looked outside the Cadillac had vanished and I returned to Washington feeling lonely and a little foolish.

When Schine and I got back from our trip to Europe to investigate the overseas libraries, we filed a report detailing what we'd found but McCarthy didn't seem particularly interested. He was focused on following up on the VOA hearings. To be honest, before going to Europe, I hadn't understood what was so important about the VOA and had only a vague idea of what it actually did. As a young man growing up in

New York the agency was little more than a name. The idea of broadcasting to an audience in Bucharest or Tbilisi seemed exotic but nothing more. Now I knew better. When you consider the Voice was our main connection with most of the Communist world you could see why McCarthy was upset about the possibility of a subversive intrusion there.

One thing I was learning about Washington, however, was that it was hard to keep your eye on the ball and stay sharp. This was particularly true when working with McCarthy who had the attention span of a field mouse. Listening to him switching from one issue to another mid-sentence made me feel like my head was packed with cotton and I was going to have to fight to get air. So, while this might be considered the adagio or slow movement, to continue the symphony analogy, things were still moving pretty fast.

During this time there was also a lot of talk about what was being called the "Lavender Scare" that McCarthy and Hoover were ginning up even if it was another Senate Committee during the Truman administration that had gotten the whole thing going a few years before. Hoover had files on everyone, so we met and he passed on the names of government workers he suspected were faggots. This was ironic given that Hoover had never married and there were ongoing rumors about him just as there were about me and Schine. Still, given my concerns about being outed, it made sense to be inside the investigation if I could be.

Otherwise, I didn't really care because I knew that most of what people might say was bullshit. The real point was who was doing the talking and to whom? No one was going to ask me point blank if Dave and I were lovers because Hoover aside, innuendo was the order of the day.

What really mattered is that McCarthy didn't care or didn't seem to anyway. The thing about Joe was if he was with you, he was with you all the way and I admired that. I never met anyone as loyal to his friends and as vicious to his enemies. Since he had been on the offensive about homosexuals in the State Department, my being outed might trump his sense of loyalty. Just one more reason for me to be discreet.

You had to know there was a lot of pressure on up and down the administration when Eisenhower put out an Executive Order banning homosexuals from working in government. Dozens had been fired already with more likely to follow. I doubt Ike gave a shit, but he'd talked about it during the campaign and found people responded noisily when he did. Beyond the worry that homos were going to be vulnerable to blackmail, a surprising number of people thought there was a link between communism and sex, that who you fucked could indicate a lack of moral fiber. Considering the love lives of some of the Congressmen making speeches about homosexuality this was ridiculous, but hypocrisy was nothing new in Washington.

Even if it was Ike who signed the Executive Order, McCarthy had a gift for grabbing the narrative, regardless of the subject, when it served his purposes. "If you want to be against McCarthy, boys," he told reporters gathered around him at a hearing, "you've got to be either a communist or a cocksucker."

Talking tough worked for McCarthy even if there were still some rumors about Joe, including vague reports to the papers in Wisconsin who'd decided to bury the stories they heard about the Senator. No one was going to write about McCarthy's sex life unless you had pictures and an eyewitness, and no one did. McCarthy tried to short-circuit all this by announcing his engagement to his secretary, Jean Kerr, that spring. I think this surprised Jeanie as much as anyone else, but she was loyal to the Senator and happily went along with the whole thing.

Even before I got involved with the Lavender issue, however, I'd heard the stories. The talk was that homosexuals had first moved to Washington in droves in the Depression when FDR opened up government jobs as part of the New Deal. And after the War ended more supposedly decided to come to town. Some people estimated that there were 5,000 homosexuals working in Washington back when Clyde Hoey started yelling about all the sexual perverts in government and began his investigation. Hoey was from North Carolina, and I had no idea why this was so important to him but the Hoey Committee raised a lot of hell for a few years before Clyde passed away and the whole thing died with him. My personal experience with homosexuals in Washington was limited but even if I'd only been there a few months I knew one way to draw a crowd was to start screaming about communists or homosexuals. Homosexual communists sounded golden.

It had been an issue first with the Democrats and then later with Republicans when they came on in fifty-two. Still, beyond doing what McCarthy wanted me to in working with Hoover, I wasn't going to spend a lot of time looking in on other peoples' sex lives. Who was getting or giving blow jobs in Capital bathrooms didn't rise to a level of great importance as far as I was concerned. I got the part about security risks, but with the gossip about me and Schine, I figured it was best to keep my head down. I had slept with both men and women in roughly equal proportions in my life, but it was never a major concern for me. One way to put it was that I was young and hadn't made up my mind which way I was going sexually and didn't think I had to on anyone else's account. At the same time, if who I *shtupped* was going to hurt my effectiveness as McCarthy's counsel, it was in my interest to short-circuit any rumors which was part of the reason I'd avoided the Cadillac in the parking lot in Virginia.

An obvious way for me to combat all this was to date women publicly but I was new in town and didn't have a social circle. I made it a point to spend time with Barbara Walters, a pretty girl I knew because her dad ran a bar called the Latin Quarter in the city. Barbara was a student at Sarah Lawrence at the time though later she started working in television. I liked to take her out when I was in New York and even invited her to D.C. a few times to show her off at parties. There wasn't a lot going on for us between the sheets but no one else had to know that and Barbara and I always liked spending time together. Otherwise, I did what I was told and kept quiet about the rest. Staying on the edge of the Lavender investigation seemed like the best strategy and I had other things to work on at the time.

More hearings were about to start, and McCarthy and I spent a lot of time working on material Dave and I had developed interviewing possible witnesses in New York. Joe had been in touch with Dulles at State about this, but the Secretary was dodging and weaving artfully, claiming anything questionable that had been done had occurred under Acheson during the Truman years, that he'd just taken office and was still trying to find out where the men's room was. He claimed he knew nothing about anything we might be looking at.

"He says he's on our side," McCarthy said with a smile, "but the fact is he's on his own side. Like everyone else."

"I guess that's true," I said.

"Damned right it is," McCarthy said. "You remember that, boy, and you'll do all right in this town."

For reasons that weren't completely clear, my father started calling more during this period. We'd never been close when I was a kid, never had father/son talks or confessions. Because he was a boxing fan, we'd go to the fights at the Garden, but I never shared his fascination with the blood and gore of the so-called sweet science. He loved Jewish fighters like Battling Levinsky, Benny Leonard and Max Baer, never questioned their career choices or asked why they hadn't become lawyers or accountants. Did he envy them their toughness this man who would stand up to no one? There was no way of knowing. Not that I didn't like my father because I did. In fact, I looked up to him, and knew he was a respected judge and a mover in the New York political world, but I'd always been a Mama's boy and that wasn't going to change.

My mother was the one who made my father move us from the Bronx to Manhattan, even though his political base was in the other Borough. He couldn't have liked that, but my mother was hard to disagree with and basically immovable when she'd made up her mind about something. I knew this, my father knew, and everyone who had been around our family knew. It took me a while to understand the reason the old man was getting in touch now was that he was actually worried about me. I learned more when I went up to New York and had lunch with him at Lindy's. Dad liked the cheesecake there along with the fact that someone was always stopping by the table to shake hands.

"Everything okay down there?" he began today.

"Sure, Pop. Everything's fine," I said. "New set of hearings starting soon."

My father nodded ponderously. One reason we didn't talk much is you wouldn't have said he was much of a conversationalist. He worked words around in his mouth like pudding and it took forever for him to get to his point. Now he shifted in his seat, uncomfortable about something. "I hear you were in Europe with the Schine kid," he said.

This was common knowledge. Anyone who read the *Post* or any of the other New York papers knew our itinerary. Neither of my parents liked Dave or understood why I wanted to be around him. In fact, if I thought about it, almost no one really liked or respected him, but that didn't matter to me. I trusted my gut and this friendship worked for me.

"Very important trip," I said. "The Senator asked me to go and look into the overseas libraries and we learned a lot."

"The papers say there was something funny going on between you two," my father said, looking down at the table. This was as close as he'd ever come to talking about sex with me, but of course I knew what he meant.

I waved my hand between us, brushing this aside. "That's just the papers," I said. "They always have to say something. You know that." I believed this but of course no one had ever featured my father in a gossip column. Belatedly, I realized that I was embarrassing him. "I'm sorry about that," I said. "Really, there's nothing to do it."

My father nodded again. "Is this really what you want to do," he said, changing the subject. "Chase communists all your life with that *meshugah* McCarthy? First, you're after the Rosenbergs, which I have to say didn't do the Jews any good and now this."

There was no point in arguing with him about the Rosenbergs or whether prosecuting them had hurt the Jewish people. My father wasn't the only one going on about that, but to me, anyone who was passing information to the Russians should go down, whether they were Jewish or not. "I worked on that case because it was important and they were guilty," I said. "That's all there was to it."

My father dropped his silverware on the table with a clatter. "People died leaving *kleyne kinder* behind and that's all you can say? Where's your humanity, Roy?" He smacked his forehead. "They were guilty, or they weren't, I don't know, but you damned well ought to care if you're making orphans! You can't tell me there were no protestant communists, but you didn't see them executing the *goyim*."

There was no way to argue about this and he was right. I'd been so focused on the prosecution that what happened to the Rosenbergs or their children didn't concern me. Did that make me insensitive, inhumane, maybe it did, but the only thing that really bothered me was the pain and embarrassment I might cause my parents by what I did or was doing.

"I'm sorry, Pop," I said. "You're right. I'm going to think about what you said, I promise."

He nodded but I could see he wasn't really satisfied. "Anyway, who asked you to get involved in all this and then stay involved?"

"Well, no one really asked me, Pop, but it was my job then and this is my job now. The Senator offered me a position and it's not many men my age who're counsel on an important Senate Committee."

"So that's it? You were flattered to work for a Republican, a *shaygetz*?"

"McCarthy's okay. But him being a Republican, sure, that's part of it," I said. "So what? A job like this can lead to things later on."

He shrugged. "Leading to things," he said and laughed. "Fucking yourself is more like it. You have a good name in this town, Roy, but our people are Democrats and that's who we help get along. Republicans never had any use for the Jews, you know that."

"McCarthy does," I said. "And if you think about it, it could be good to have one of us working for a Republican senator. The Rosenbergs and their Communist friends didn't do our people any good. You'd have to admit that."

My father didn't like Republicans or me working with them, but that wasn't the only thing he disapproved of when it came to my life. He didn't like my wearing custom made suits when he bought his off the rack at Macy's and though he'd made some money, he didn't like that I was hanging around with rich people at 21 and the Stork Club. He didn't like Schine but that was only part of it. I knew even if I'd chosen to live like a Mormon there'd still be something my father would be unhappy about. I reached across the table and patted his hand.

My father wasn't responsive. "I can't talk politics with you," he said. "I've been doing this for decades. You're a *pischer* just out of short pants."

I had to laugh at this, but he was right. I never worked my way up from running errands at the Democratic Club in the Bronx or took a make work job an alderman had found for me. I never did favors for powerful older men or paid my dues in any other way. I was on a steep learning curve in Washington and my father wasn't the first one to make a point about my age. "I'm twenty-six," I said. "I have a law degree."

"*Mazel tov*," my father said. He blew out some air and ate another bite of cake. "Your mother wants you back home," he said, and I figured with this we got to the real reason for the meeting."

"What about you?" I said.

"Actually, I do too," he said. "So why don't you quit while you're ahead. Come back to New York while I can still help you get on with a good firm."

I didn't know if he was telling the truth or not but for the first time I wondered if it was possible that the work I was doing could hurt me rather than help. I doubted this but I knew my father was sincere and I appreciated his offer. I knew with his contacts, he could make things happen with a call. He might even be right about Washington, but I wasn't ready to leave. Because I admired my father and all he'd accomplished, I hated to disagree with him. I knew this conversation was making him self-conscious and he'd only called because he cared about what was good for me. But in this case, I felt I had no choice. "This is important, Pop, what I'm doing. I wouldn't stay if it wasn't important."

"I'm not saying it's maybe not important," he said. "But they're a bunch of snakes down there. They'd cut you up and have you for dinner. You don't watch out they're going to get you."

I was touched that my father seemed protective of me. Moreover, I took what he said seriously because he was connected politically and knew what was what. With hindsight, I can also see that he was right, even if it took the Washington hotshots some time to get at me. "Sok's the one who sent me down there," I said now as if this justified my work.

"And what did it cost him to do that?" my father asked. "Not a goddamned thing. More copy for his column, that's all he cares about."

"I thought you two were friends."

"We're friends as long as it makes sense for him," my father said. "That's all it is with any of those *goniffs*."

He was right, but in my youthful arrogance I thought I could stay ahead, at least for the present. "This won't last forever," I said. "A year, maybe two. And then I'll come back to the city like you want. There will be plenty of time later to write wills for old ladies at some firm."

My father grunted. "You got it all planned out, Mr. Smart Guy? And what if there is no work here after you've ruined your reputation down in Washington? What if whenever you're ready to stop chasing communists there aren't any old ladies who want you to write their wills for them?"

I should have been grateful and more concerned than I was, but I'd had enough and wanted to get out of there. "You worry too much, Pop," I said. "I'm not going to sabotage anything. Maybe I'll even help myself by being on television all the time."

But he wasn't convinced. "Okay, fine. You know everything, but I'm your father. It's my job to worry about these things even if you don't."

Seven

MADISON

Two weeks went by, and nothing happened except Janey got a lawyer. It happened accidentally like many things that later turn out to be life-altering. She had moved into her sister Patsy's apartment on Mound Street and was feeling out of sorts with her life having been changed dramatically. Living in two rooms with Little Ed was confining after the larger house they had on Madison a few blocks away but staying had been intolerable to her after Ed left his job. Patsy was understanding but made clear this had to be temporary and after a few days she started trying to influence Janey's life. She was the younger sister so was used to being ordered around and to please Patsy, Janey consented to join her church and found herself one Friday night at a fish fry listening to an attorney named Dennis tell her about himself.

Finally, Dennis asked Janey's last name and then his interest picked up dramatically. "You married to that communist?" he said, which struck Janey as rude and intrusive.

"He's not really a communist," she said, not sure why she was defending Ed.

"But he's the one who signed that petition, right?" Dennis insisted.

Janey acknowledged this and then said that they were currently separated, and she was living with her sister. Janey wondered later if this had been an arranged meeting but there was no way to tell for sure. Patsy gave nothing away and Dennis started calling her daily. Since Patsy was willing to babysit, Janey decided she could go to dinner and a movie with Dennis. She wasn't particularly attracted to him, but it was nice to be out with a man who seemed interested in her. She had thought that part of her life might be over. Who would want a woman who was nearly thirty with a small child, but Dennis claimed to love children.

One night he asked if she was moving on with a divorce and Janey said she'd been too busy to think about it. The truth was that she'd hoped that Ed might come to his senses, and they'd get back together.

"You should have an attorney," Dennis said. "Just in case."

"Are you volunteering?" Janey asked.

Dennis grinned. "Let's say, I'm willing," he replied. "And probably as good as anyone else you could hire."

The next week Janey signed a contract, not knowing exactly what she was doing or what would happen next.

Ed was rattling around in the house and figured he'd have to sell it if he got divorced, maybe move somewhere toward campus, get an apartment. He wasn't sure, but it made sense. He knew he couldn't afford the mortgage unless he got a job fast. He developed a routine of breakfast at Mickies where he'd read the papers after which he'd walk around the neighborhood or even down to the park to sit on a bench and watch the water. He went to the zoo for the first time in years, but he'd never been drawn particularly to caged animals, especially now that he felt like one. It occurred to him that most people in his situation would be lonely but strangely enough he wasn't aware of that. He remembered when his mother died, and he was left with the house and acreage since his father had gone two years before. He was only eighteen and had no brothers or sisters, so he wandered from room to room in the old farmhouse as if he was looking for something, as anchor, to hold him in place or if not, to release him. He had the same feeling now of being disconnected, floating from place to place, as if he was waiting for something without knowing what that might be.

In the meantime, he found things to do around the house, fixing cabinets, putting doors back on their hinges and mowing the grass. Often, he'd go to the library in the afternoon and read out-of-town papers to see what was going on in the world. What he learned was that it wasn't very different from reading the *Herald*. McCarthy was chasing communists and Ike seemed to be joining in. Ed had never cared before, but now he felt oddly sympathetic toward the people on McCarthy's list. He didn't know whether they were communists or not, but he knew he'd lost a job because people thought he was. Thinking was enough these days, a hell of a note, if you asked him.

As long as he was going down to talk to Susan Roselle, he checked on his veteran's benefits and learned that he could get $200 a month if he went to school, which wasn't that much less than he'd been earning at the insurance agency. Even with whatever he'd have to pay in child support for Little Ed, if Janey divorced him, Ed figured he could make it easily, especially if they sold the house.

He told Susan Roselle this when he appeared at her office the next week, but she didn't seem surprised. "Actually, I'd already done some research on that," she said and smiled.

"You're checking up on me?" Ed felt oddly flattered rather than invaded by this.

"I was curious," Susan said.

"I guess I could have saved myself the time then," Ed said. But why should he be surprised or pleased? It made sense that this woman would know what veterans got from the government if she was signing them up.

"Of course, it's not just a financial decision," Susan said. "It's a change in your lifestyle. Have you thought about what you'd be interested in studying?"

She had him there. Ed had never thought of himself as having a lifestyle before, but he liked the idea. "I wasn't much of a student in high school," he said slowly, "and that's more than ten years ago."

Susan nodded her head as if she understood which was more than Ed had gotten from Janey who'd never shown any curiosity about what Ed might have wanted. For people like them there was only necessity; choice seldom came into it. You got a job and worked at it and who cared what you wanted.

"Which subjects did you like then?" Susan asked, interrupting his thoughts.

It was a reasonable question, but Ed couldn't think of anything. It made him suddenly anxious as if this was some kind of test and he was failing already. He figured he should be interested in something or why even think about going to the University but his mind was a blank. "I guess I was pretty good at math," he said. "I always liked to read and then when I worked at the agency, I did some actuarial work."

"We have an excellent Commerce Department," Susan said. "Maybe you'd like to take some courses over there."

"To tell you the truth," Ed said, "I've had enough of business for a while."

They sat there quietly for a moment and Ed studied the woman across the table from him. She was older than he was, but not by much, maybe in her thirties. He didn't see a ring on her finger, and her strawberry-blonde hair was drawn back into a ponytail today, making her look like a co-ed. Then he checked himself; he shouldn't be thinking about this. They weren't dating and she was out of his league anyway.

"Like I said before, I'm a big reader," he said finally. "I go to the library in the afternoons to look at all the papers. I used to read about Korea and now the McCarthy stuff. That's how I got in trouble in the first place."

"Not from reading exactly," Susan said thoughtfully. Then she brightened up. "Maybe you'd like journalism?"

"Not really," Ed said and laughed, thinking of the story Jimmy had written about him in the *Herald* and the way papers twisted the facts for their own purposes no matter what they did to people like him.

"Politics then?" Susan persisted. You had to give the woman credit for hanging in, making more suggestions; Ed could see he wasn't making it easy for her but the idea of writing for the newspapers made him uneasy. He didn't want to be in the public eye any more than he was already.

"Sorry," Ed said. "I hope the other guys you talk to have a better idea of what they want to study than I do."

Susan smiled broadly at this. "Actually," she said, "you're pretty typical. Most of the men just want to get through college in a hurry and make money so they can buy a house. You haven't said a word about that."

It was true. Ed had never cared much about money, as long as there was enough. Now, he felt self-conscious with this quiet woman looking expectantly at him in her small book-lined office. Her name was on a placard on the door, Susan Page Roselle. Was Page her maiden name, he wondered, assuming she was married despite the lack of a ring. He couldn't remember the last time he'd actually sat and talked with a woman other than his wife and even then, they'd never talked that much, mostly fought. In high school, he'd had girlfriends and then in Italy he'd gone with prostitutes a few times. There had been women in the insurance office, but he'd never really talked to them and now here he was with a woman who wanted to know what he was interested in. Who had ever asked him anything like that before? It made him feel inadequate, foolish, but also in an odd way important, even interesting. But he had to forget all this and get to the point, tell Susan what she wanted to know. He tried to think.

"I already have a house," he said and felt as if he was bragging, putting himself up on the other vets. "Maybe politics," he said to get back on pace. "Are there courses in that?" This sounded stupid, but somehow it didn't seem to bother Susan Roselle.

She smiled sweetly and said, "Of course there are. Political Science is a very popular major, especially for students who hope to go to law school."

"I don't know about science," Ed said. He remembered flunking biology in high school when he couldn't see through a microscope. It still stung.

"It's not really science in that sense," Susan said. "It's more a way of looking at how other countries arrange themselves politically, studying the history of government and political figures, things like that."

Ed thought this might be good but was afraid of saying something dumb again. It was intimidating to be here; he felt the books on the shelves pressing down, suffocating him. "I have to tell you, I'm not sure I can do this," he said. "I don't think I'm smart enough to tell you the truth."

Susan smiled again. "Oh, that's silly. I don't know you very well, but I'm sure you're smart enough for whatever you want to do.:"

Ed didn't argue with her, not because he thought there was any chance she could be right but because he liked the idea of this educated woman thinking he was smart. As though she knew what he was thinking, Susan drew some papers out of her desk drawer and slid them across the desk. "Anyway, I need you to fill out these application forms for me."

Ed felt as if he was falling down a deep hole. His mouth was dry, and his eyes were burning but there was no turning back now. And if he didn't follow through on this what else would he do? "Now?" he asked.

"No time like the present," Susan said. "That way if there's something you're unsure about, I'll be here to help."

With no excuses to offer, Ed set to work filling out the forms.

Things began to move quickly once Janey's lawyer moved to end what he called a trial separation and file for divorce. Ed had hoped they might get together and talk, maybe work things out between themselves without representation. But when he suggested this Janey laughed derisively. "What's there to talk about? It looks like you don't want to work, and I don't want to be married to someone who doesn't have a job."

Neither of them mentioned love and Ed couldn't have said for sure if they had ever loved each other. They weren't expressive people; no one he knew was. He couldn't remember ever hearing his father tell his mother he loved her, and Ed had never really thought about it. He didn't know if the old man did or not. It wasn't the kind of thing that ever came up between working hard on the farm and trying to find a way to pay the bills. Now they were both gone and he wouldn't have known how to ask them anyway. He wondered about his marriage, if what was true of his parents was also true of him and Janey. It seemed a fair assumption that you loved whoever you were married to and, if not, why marry? Well, Little Ed, he guessed. Rather, he knew.

"I might go back to school," he said now, just to have something to say.

"Back?" Janey said and laughed again, her lips turning down in a sneer. "When were you ever in school to begin with."

"I graduated from high school," Ed said, insulted.

"Sure," Janey said. "So did I, but that was ages ago. A lot has happened since then. Aren't you a little old for college now, going to football games, pep rallies, all of that?"

Susan Roselle had said you were never too old that they even had something they called "Extension" for people who didn't live in Madison but were still able to take courses at the U when they were already working outstate. Despite Susan's reassurances, however, Janey's derision made Ed doubtful, and he knew that was her intention. Had she always been this cruel, this undermining of him, or had his decision to leave the agency really set everything in motion and caused her to change?

"They got something they call the G.I. Bill of Rights for vets," he said. "Maybe you heard of it? There's a special office down at the U for it and everything." He consciously didn't mention Susan Roselle. "The benefits are almost as good as having a job, $200 a month and it lasts for three years."

"I thought that was for younger guys," Janey said, an edge in her voice. "When you just got out of the service you went to Voch and took the insurance exam because you thought so too. I remember."

"Maybe I made the wrong choice," Ed said.

Janey nodded knowingly. "Maybe so. I know I did. See you, Ed."

And that was all there was to it. Inside a month, the papers were signed, and they sold the house on Madison Street that Ed had put so much into and been so proud to own. He moved into a one-bedroom apartment on Randall Street that wasn't far away and when Little Ed visited on the weekends, Ed moved into the living room and slept on the couch to give Little Ed the bedroom. Within months, Ed's whole life had turned, but it didn't seem that he'd actually had agency in all this or decided anything. It was more as if he was on a carousel watching his world spinning by. Starting with the business with DiPietro, things just seemed to happen and there was no way Ed could see to slow it all down.

Janey felt as if somehow she had come out of all this as the bad guy, the one hiring the lawyer going after her husband who to her now looked sad, almost pathetic, a shadow of the strong man she'd thought she married. It wasn't so much that others said this to her; most of her friends were sympathetic but rather than condemning Ed's behavior, they acted as if he was mentally ill or something. Maybe he was and when she thought about it, Janey felt bad about what had happened. She knew Ed thought she should have supported him no matter what he did, but she'd seen what happened when her mother did that and she wasn't about to get caught in the same web she had. That was why she'd left Mineral Point in the first place. If Ed were to have a change of heart and go back to work, that might have been fine, but Janey wasn't going to sit around and wait for him to come to his senses. She'd be thirty soon, and Ed had taken up a good part of the best part of her life. Maybe it was her error in judgement in choosing him, but what was done was done. It was obviously too late to get in touch with the other men she'd known during the war and say she'd made an awful mistake.

The sale of the house had given her some money to start with and staying with her sister for a few months allowed her to look around for a place of her own. The only course she'd really been good at in high school was typing, so she signed up for a course at a secretarial school and within a few months, even going part-time because of Little Ed, she'd got close to qualifying for a certificate as a legal secretary. Dennis even mentioned that his firm might hire her. It would be a way to get back some of the money she'd paid him for the divorce, but Janey was in no hurry to attach herself to another man. She'd bide her time and make sure whatever decision she made concerning men would be more successful than the first one had been.

Janey took Little Ed to visit her parents in Mineral Point over Thanksgiving and Ed was alone in his apartment, the white walls as blank as his mind. Ed hadn't had time to arrange anything and the furniture he'd taken from Madison Street lined the walls like forgotten soldiers. He couldn't think what should go where. The last time he'd had Thanksgiving out of a can was when he was eating C-rations in Italy and for the first time he felt real regret at what had happened, losing the marriage, not so much Janey but the daily interaction with Little Ed. He missed bedtime, when he'd sit next to the boy and read to him, or after school when they'd play ball in the yard or walk to the park to fish. He still had his son on alternate weekends and some weekdays when it was convenient for Janey, but an important part of life for Ed was lost and a gaping hole in his middle had taken its place. It was a hunger that couldn't be satisfied and now he thought he'd never feel whole again.

Time was slipping away from him, hours, then days, weeks, with no calendar he couldn't say. It was late November, cold and damp in his small enclosure but he didn't remember what the landlord had told him about heat. Dazed and mixed up, he sat on the floor, alternately in the present and back in Salerno in a bombed-out farmhouse devoid of furniture except for the paillasses, straw mattresses used by the medics that had used the place before they arrived. The bombing was incessant, and he couldn't get his bearings. Who would be bombing him in Madison? He was unable to get up and wondered what had happened to his legs.

Time went by and things slowed down. He was surprised how comfortable the paliasse was, the wood of the floor seeming to spread out to make room for his bulk. He couldn't remember when he had eaten or where he slept; he could smell himself so it must have been a long time. He knew he should find a way to right himself, but this seemed impossible.

Disoriented he heard a banging somewhere, the bombs again or pipes, the furnace, wherever it was. He should complain, he thought; this was unacceptable. He tried to focus to figure out where the noise was coming from and then he heard someone calling his name and he knew it couldn't be the pipes unless this was it, the big one, and he'd really gone crazy. The banging continued and finally, it came to him, dimly. It was the door, someone trying to get in. He balanced himself against the wall with difficulty and stood against it for a moment waiting for his legs to stop shaking. Then he walked slowly to the entrance and opened the door. A woman was standing there in jeans and a sweater. She looked familiar but he couldn't think where he'd met her; he didn't know any women.

"Mr. Malloy," she said now. "It's Susan Roselle, from the University. I tried several times to call, but you didn't answer."

As if he'd been accused, Ed turned around and saw the disconnected phone on the floor. He pointed at it as if speech was beyond him but if any of this bothered Susan Roselle, she didn't show it. She pushed him out of the way, walked into the room and looked around. Then she said, "You look terrible. Go take a shower. I'll wait here."

Ed stood under the shower for twenty minutes then dressed in fresh clothes and went into the living room. Susan had moved the furniture into a conversation group and raised the blinds. He smelled something good. "That's better," Susan said approvingly. "I made coffee. There isn't much food here, but you should eat."

Ed was immediately embarrassed that this nice woman had come over and was putting things in order. She was a dean, for Christ's sake. What was she doing here? Did this kind of a doctor make house calls? But he didn't say this. "I haven't really done much shopping," he said. "I get my meals down at Mickies most of the time."

"That explains a lot," Susan said, looking him over, but she smiled. "Come over and sit down with me and have a cup."

"You don't need to stay," Ed said. "Really, I'm fine. Your husband's probably wondering where you are."

"He would be, if I had one," Susan said.

Ed drank the coffee and looked at her. She seemed younger now, out of the office, and in jeans. "I didn't mean to pry," Ed said, feeling foolish. "I just thought you were married because of your name."

"Everyone in my family has three names," Susan said. "Page was my mother's maiden name,, but I was actually married a long time ago, when I was only seventeen. My husband died in the War, so I've been alone since then."

It was a surprisingly intimate conversation to be having with a woman he hardly knew, in his barely furnished apartment, but Ed immediately felt sympathy. "I'm sorry," he said. "A lot of guys didn't come back and left wives behind."

Susan nodded. "No kids, thank God. Anyway, a long time ago now. It's awful, but I can't even remember what he looked like unless I look at our wedding pictures." She ducked her head and took a deep breath. Then she said, "But you're married, aren't you?"

"Not anymore," Ed said. "Divorced." And then without being asked, he blurted out the whole story, told Susan how his life had changed because he signed a petition in Vilas Park on July Fourth. She listened attentively, not saying much, but nodding to encourage him to go on.

"I remember reading about it," she said when he'd finished, "but I didn't connect you to the story in the paper. It's kind of unusual to be asked to sign a petition at the fireworks but I remember thinking at the time I didn't understand why no one else would sign the Bill of Rights."

"Me neither, "Ed said. "The reporter said some of the people he asked thought it was some kind of communist thing, Russian or something."

Susan laughed. "Actually, it was written during a revolution, but I don't think that's what they meant."

"I doubt it," Ed said. "Anyway, that was just the beginning. Someone painted "Commie" in red paint on my sidewalk and my kid got beaten up at school. Then my boss called me in and said they wanted me to sign a loyalty oath if I wanted to keep my job."

"It's not that unusual," Susan said. "Even some universities have them, not ours, thank God. For some reason McCarthy's stayed away from the campus."

"Maybe so," Ed said, "My wife, my ex-wife, couldn't see why I wouldn't sign, and I couldn't really explain. I just didn't want to do it. I'm not political, never even belonged to a party, but I didn't want to be pushed and didn't see why I should have to prove anything to anybody."

Susan nodded. "I can understand that."

"My wife didn't, couldn't see why I wouldn't go along," Ed said. "She said if I signed the whole thing would disappear, and we could go on."

"You didn't agree?"

"I guess not," Ed said. "And look how well that's turned out for me. Pretty stupid, I guess." He laughed shortly and Susan smiled. Then he went on. "Considering that I'm living in this dump, you could say I was pretty stupid, and you might be right. But to me, the whole country seems different now and I don't know why or if it will ever go back to whatever it was. Not that it was so great when I was growing up. Even before the War, I remember as a kid in the Depression, people were taking food from each other, and then during the War stealing gas rations. Now everyone's reporting other people they don't like." He shrugged, embarrassed that he'd talked too much. "Anyway, since I'm not working, I read the papers more, about the Hollywood Ten, even going back to stories about Alger Hiss, the Rosenbergs."

"I hope you don't see yourself that way."

"Not really," Ed said. "I'm pretty sure I've never even met any communists. But I figure if something like this can turn my life upside down, who knows about all those other people McCarthy's after? Maybe they're as innocent as I am."

"There are actually some professors at the University who belonged to the party years ago," Susan said, "but for some reason no one's ever threatened them, at least as far as I know."

"Good," Ed said. "Good for them. Anyway, I'm not sure that's the only reason Janey left me, but it was the big one. Plus, when I talked to her, she said she couldn't really see me being a student."

"Is that right?" Susan said. "Interesting." But it wasn't really, and Ed could see she didn't approve.

As they sat there, drinking coffee and talking, it slowly dawned on Ed that unlike his previous assumptions, Susan was a single woman, and he was alone with her in his apartment. As if Susan had come to the same conclusion, they both laughed, the sound echoing in the near-empty room. And while this wasn't really a date, Ed noticed the shape of Susan's breasts in the soft wool and the fact that her brown hair curled nicely around her face. He didn't say anything and finally to break the silence, Susan said, "I'm glad you're all right. But that wasn't actually why I came."

"You didn't know I was sitting on the floor not sure what day it was?"

"No," she said and smiled again. "I wanted to remind you about registering for the winter semester and also to tell you about a job, if you're interested."

"I'm unemployed so I guess I'm interested," Ed said. "What is it?"

"The catch is you have to be a student," Susan said.

"I think I see what this is about," Ed said. "Is this the way you reel other vets in?"

Susan laughed. "It depends," she said. "As I told you, most of them are mainly concerned with getting through as soon as they can and don't really have time for other work."

"Well, I'm not worried about that since I have no idea where I'd be going," Ed said. "What's the job?"

"I was talking to the head of the student union the other day," Susan began, "and I happened to mention your situation, that you have prior managerial experience."

"If you could call it that."

"That's what I called it. Anyway, they need someone to run the boathouse, not just renting out the canoes and sailboats but keeping the books and running the office."

"An executive position then," Ed said.

Susan nodded. "Exactly, at minimum wage."

"I didn't know the University even had a boathouse." Ed said. "I do know about the lakes."

"And how long have you lived here?"

"All my life," Ed said. "In Dane County anyway, but I grew up on a farm, never spent much time around Madison until I moved over here." In saying this, he realized she knew more about him than he did about her. It would seem stupid at this point to ask her favorite color, what songs she liked. "Are you from Wisconsin?" he asked finally, just to say something.

Susan smiled. "I've been here for ten years but I grew up in a little town in Ohio and went to Ohio State for grad school. I could have gone home and taught school but when the job here was offered, I came to Madison and never really left."

"It's not a bad place to land," Ed said.

Susan nodded. Then she sat up straight and cleared her throat. Back to business. "Anyway, that's the job, but like I said you have to be a registered student." She looked at him expectantly.

For a moment Ed didn't know what she was talking about, his mind having dropped back to memories of the War, stacking the corpses of friends who'd died and were going home in rubber bags. This happened at odd times. He could be doing anything and suddenly he was back in Italy and nothing had changed. He shivered. "Sorry," he said. "What's a registered student?"

Susan smiled tolerantly. "Someone who's signed up for courses. I took the liberty of checking on the political science courses that are offered next semester," Susan continued without waiting for an answer. "There's actually an introductory course starting in a few weeks."

"Lucky me," Ed said even though he still didn't completely understand what political science was. He knew he'd just got a break; he knew that. "Where do I sign?"

Eight

WASHINGTON

Okay, this is how it works: the chairman of a senatorial committee can hold hearings on whatever he wants whenever he wants. I didn't come up with this, make it up, but that's the system. So even if McCarthy had gotten bored and cancelled the first VOA hearings in New York, by April he was ready to start in again focusing on the Overseas Library Program Schine and I had explored in Europe. It seemed obvious that the original purpose of the overseas libraries must have been to portray a positive influence of America and anything that got in the way of this was not in the best interests of the country. So that was our starting point. In addition, I'd given McCarthy a list of the commie books we'd selected out in the libraries and thought this would be a good way to begin.

Before we could get started, however, there was a deluge of new press attention to our trip and what we'd done there. American journalists got a kick out of our treatment by the European newspapers who seemed to want to make fun of us. We were called junketeers, adventurers, playboys, and a variety of other things. American columnists who hadn't been along, concluded that we'd done little to justify the cost of the trip to taxpayers. Which might have been true, but you can't tell me those "fact-finding" missions to exotic places senators are always going on are any different.

Still, while I didn't like it, I could see the point the papers were making. What qualifications did Dave, and I have to inspect American posts in Europe? Where was our authority to cross-examine career diplomats even if we were right about the subversive material they had in their libraries? Not that I would have admitted it then. Looking back now, I can see McCarthy sending us to Europe was probably a mistake. Things don't always work out as you plan.

Predictably, none of this bothered Dave much. When I called him, he was back staying in his family's apartment at the Waldorf, going out every night and then sleeping until noon. When I woke him, he said, "What are those guys upset about? We worked hard over there, and I thought it went pretty well."

Dave had his good qualities, but introspection wasn't one of them. Rich people are like that. They do what they do and let others figure it out. "Really?" I said. "Have you read what they're saying about us?"

"Some of it. They called us adventurers," he said and yawned. "I have to admit, I kind of liked that."

"Jesus, Dave. It wasn't junior year abroad. We're working for a senatorial committee for Christ's sake. The trip wasn't supposed to be a vacation."

"Sure," he said. "I know, but I liked it anyway. And you'd never been to Europe before, right? So doesn't that make it kind of an adventure?"

There was no arguing this with him and at least he hadn't been wounded by the press coverage. In the end, however, it didn't matter very much. Nothing anyone would write was going to discourage McCarthy, who scheduled the hearings and told me to put together a list of witnesses.

I wasn't exactly astonished that some commie authors had been included in the overseas collections. This was supposedly to suggest the range and variety of political ideas in America. But that didn't justify the number of anti-American titles we'd found. Though a House committee that looked over the list claimed only a handful of the books supported communism, we thought there were many more, perhaps thousands, by authors who were either communist sympathizers or had previously belonged to the Party. I'm not stupid enough to think Dashiell Hammett was actually encouraging revolution through his mystery novels but there was no question Hammett had been and still was a communist. He refused to talk about it to HUAC or name names of others who belonged to the Party. In my book that was a good enough reason to send him to jail.

Beyond individual authors, the question was whether the books in these libraries were merely supposed to represent all aspects of American life, as some claimed, or to promote America as the beacon of world democracy and freedom. McCarthy thought this should be the obvious goal but those that put these books on the shelves and the "blue-ribbon committee" of publishers who chose the books disagreed.

All this had become even more confusing when John Foster Dulles came in as Ike's Secretary of State and inherited the libraries as part of his portfolio. Dulles put out a new order saying no books by authors whose ideologies were questionable would be included in the libraries unless the books were "substantially better than other material available." This led to panic among overseas staff in charge of the libraries and even some book burning. The general assumption was that Dulles had given in to McCarthy, but actually no one gave in to anyone. Dulles had no stomach for a fight with Joe, but he had much the same attitude as McCarthy about communist authors being included so no arm-twisting was necessary.

Dulles said he wanted to avoid "past mistakes" regarding the libraries, but I'm guessing he knew nothing about the libraries before taking office. He wasn't really interested now, though he was happy to support what we were doing passively while letting Joe take the heat. But blaming the Truman administration for the libraries' collections wasn't really going to work with the reporters who were all over this, accusing us of censorship.

McCarthy was cool, as usual, and enjoying the uproar. "I never said anyone should burn any books," he said when asked about whether he was in favor of bowdlerizing.

"Do you disagree with Mr. Dulles then, Senator?"

"I haven't talked to him about it," McCarthy said. "Did he burn books? I didn't hear that. I know he's in favor of our investigation. I know that."

No matter who burned the books or if anyone did, Alfred Morton, the VOA director made things worse by stupidly saying he intended to use the works of communists in order to make them "eat their words." This worked so well that he got fired immediately.

It was in this general atmosphere that McCarthy convened the first hearings on the libraries in a windowless room in New York with the press and the audience practically on top of the Committee and witnesses. The Democrats on the Committee had some fun noting we had listed children's novels, hiking guides and nature books among the questionable volumes because their authors had either been communists or fellow travelers but after some fencing of this sort, we finally got down to business.

One of the first witnesses we called was James Wechsler, the editor of The New York *Post*, a *putz* I'd known for years and disliked. Wechsler had been president of the Young Communist League when he was a student at Columbia in the Thirties and we'd seen a couple of his books in the library in Austria. While he admitted writing propaganda for the Party then, Wechsler was backing away from that now, saying everything he did for the CP was a distant memory.

He was part of the intellectual left-wing in New York, which wasn't exactly my crowd, but while I say I disliked Wechsler, the truth is I didn't know him except for a few slighting comments he'd made about me in his column when I was working to convict the Rosenbergs. He claimed all his work for the communists was in the distant past, but McCarthy didn't buy it. Joe made little distinction between his work for the CP and writing for the *Post,* which he considered to be a secular version of *The Daily Worker*.

I started my questioning of Wechsler along this line. "Would you say you're encouraging communists and supporting communism with your column and with the books you write?" I asked.

"I'd have to know specifically what books or columns you're referring to," Wechsler said archly. "But everyone knows I'm anti-communist."

This wasn't going to stand with McCarthy who broke in immediately. "I don't know who everyone might be. What you mean is you're anti-communist now," McCarthy said. "That's your position, right?"

"Yes," Wechsler said.

I enjoyed watching McCarthy work even if it meant I could seldom finish a sentence. He'd sit quietly for a moment but then his leg would start jumping and you could practically feel the umbrage coming like heat from a fire. He made me think of those cartoons where characters had steam coming out of their ears. The two of them made an interesting tableau, Wechsler thin and scholarly in his chair and McCarthy large and practically sweating in his eagerness to skewer the editor.

"So, you don't deny that you were once very pro-communist, a card-carrying member of the Party?" he went on.

"Of course not," Wechsler said. "That's in the record."

"And you're proud of that, being a communist, writing propaganda and all the rest? That gives you a warm feeling on cold winter nights?"

"I'm not proud exactly of having been a member of the Party," Wechsler said. "But I'm not ashamed of it either. I was young and idealistic like a lot of people back in those days. There's nothing wrong with that I can see."

"You are proud of it then," McCarthy said, his chin hanging over the table as if he'd like to jump across and punch the witness.

"I just said I wasn't," Wechsler said raising his voice, but Joe had knocked him off his pace which was the whole idea. To see McCarthy work was a little like listening to classical music if only in the way he'd introduce a theme, circle back to it and repeat before continuing. And like the conductor in an orchestra, interpretation, pace, and timing were all up to the Senator. He was the only one who knew what was coming next while the rest of us sat there waiting.

"Okay," McCarthy went on now. "Just so we've got that straight. But tell me, is it true that the Communist Party no longer issues membership cards?" McCarthy was going off script again here. We hadn't talked about membership cards, hadn't done any research on it, and I didn't know if the Party still had them or not.

Wechsler seemed to be as surprised by the question as I was, but he covered up well. "I understand that this is the case," Wechsler said. "Since I'm not a communist anymore I can't say whether this is true or not."

"Let's say it is," McCarthy said.

Sure, I thought. Why not? Wechsler wasn't saying it wasn't true so maybe it was and maybe it wasn't. No one seemed to know. This strategy worked for McCarthy and was the kind of maneuver he loved. Head off into uncharted territory and then let the witness try to follow him. You might hate him if you were in the hotseat like Wechsler, but there was an art to what Joe was doing.

"If it is the case that members of the Party no longer carry cards,' Joe said now. "Then isn't it also true, that you can't tell whether someone is a communist by whether he carries a card. Isn't that so?"

"That's a very circuitous way to make your point, Senator. You can't use a negative to prove a negative," Wechsler said, but McCarthy was getting under his skin.

"Circuitous or not, the fact that you say you no longer have a membership card doesn't prove to this Committee that you're no longer a communist."

"No," Wechsler said, "but I never said it did prove it. What I said under oath is that I'm no longer a communist."

"And you think we should take your word for it,"

"You can do as you like, Senator. I'm not here as a friendly witness."

"Then why are you here?"

"I'm here, as you know, because I received a subpoena, and I believe that loyal Americans have a responsibility to show up and answer questions if they're called to testify before Senatorial Committees."

Wechsler sounded like a Sunday school teacher, his voice high and strained but this didn't faze McCarthy. "You say you're a loyal American," Joe said," but would you say you're critical of Joe Stalin in your paper, Mr. Wechsler?"

"That would be clear to anyone who reads the *Post*."

"Okay," McCarthy said, nodding his head like a scholar. "And you've also been pretty critical of the work this Committee is doing."

"Is that a question?"

It's a fact," McCarthy said. "But wouldn't you say it would be an effective strategy to set yourself up as anti-communist while also doing the bidding of the Communist party? To claim that you're out of the Party and an enemy of their leader while doing their work for them. Doesn't that make sense?"

"Not to me," Wechsler said, shifting uncomfortably in his chair, his mouth turned down in a sneer. He reminded me a little of a mark in a Three-Card Monte game outraged at being tricked. "That's ridiculous," he added.

McCarthy nodded and changed his tack, "Let's move on to another subject then," he said and looked at a paper on his desk. "Are you aware, Mr. Wechsler, that your books are in the libraries maintained by the State Department in overseas reading rooms?"

"I wasn't aware of that," Wechsler said. "That's interesting. Which titles are there? I've written several books."

"I see," McCarthy said. "And do you think these books you've written are in any way typical of the best of American life, that they should be held up to represent what's outstanding about our country?"

"That's not my decision to make," Wechsler said. "I can say I don't object to my books being in those or any other libraries."

"You're proud of both your books and your communist past?"

"I'm not going to be drawn into this line of questioning," Wechsler said.

"Okay," McCarthy said. "Then what we want you to do is give us a list of names of those people whom you know to be communists or may have been communists who are working at the *New York Post.*"

Wechsler should have known this was coming but the question of a list stopped him, at least temporarily. Unlike HUAC, we didn't maintain a list of communists per se "I don't know if anyone at the *Post* is a communist," he said. "We don't ask about peoples' political beliefs when we hire them."

"As long as they're left wing," McCarthy said.

"You can characterize us as you like, Senator," Wechsler said, moving papers back and forth in front of him.

"I don't read your sheet," McCarthy said. "As far as I'm concerned, it's an organ of the Communist Party. I don't allow it in my office. But I do want a list from you."

"A list of everyone I know who might have been a communist in the past or is one now?" Wechsler asked.

"Yes," McCarthy said. "Can you do that?"

Wechsler hesitated. People who wouldn't name names when they were in front of HUAC were later blacklisted but we weren't really interested in that. Our focus was on people working in government. If this wasn't clear to Wechsler, that was his problem. He knew no one went to jail after testifying in front of our Committee. "It might take me a while," he said, "and if I do make a list, I'd like for it to remain with the Committee and not made public."

This was ridiculous and Wechsler knew it. Anything the Committee had would likely be leaked one way or the other to the press, but McCarthy had him where he wanted him and went along with this request because he knew the Democrats on the committee would demand it. "That's okay," he said. "That's fine."

"And I'd like to review my testimony along with the list before it becomes part of the record," Wechsler said. "Would you agree to that?"

"It depends on when you get the list to us," McCarthy said. "We're on the nation's business here and we don't want to waste time."

"In my opinion this whole hearing's a waste of time," Wechsler said.

"Well, unlike the Russians you seem to like so much, in this country you're entitled to have your opinion of me and the Committee," McCarthy said. And that was it for Wechsler.

At least the weather had improved. The rain slacked off after February and now it was Cherry Blossom time with tourists clogging the hallways of the Capital and a parade messing up traffic in the middle of town. The festival's a big deal in Washington but neither McCarthy nor I gave a shit and probably wouldn't have noticed if it weren't for the pink blossoms littering lawns and sidewalks everywhere you walked. We were hard at work preparing for the next group of witnesses. The slow movement was winding down and what came next was bound to be more dramatic and consequential.

I met Joe in his office the week after Wechsler when the Committee was on recess to review the information we had. I say I met him, but the truth is you were never alone with McCarthy or to put it another way, there were always people around him. Staffers, reporters, constituents in town for a picture with the great man, it made no difference. He drew a crowd wherever he was. You wouldn't exactly say he had an entourage in those days but it hardly mattered. Now he leaned close and said in a half-whisper.

"It went pretty well with that newspaper asshole from New York."

"I think it did," I said, and it was true. At the end of the session Wechsler looked as if he'd been shrunk somehow, his wool suit hanging off him and his face slack and pale. Since then he'd been having us for lunch in his column but who cared? Let him say what he wanted. No one read him anyway.

"What we got to do now," McCarthy said is find someone else to bring in, but not anyone too tough or too easy."

"Too easy?" I asked.

McCarthy nodded. "It's got to look like we're pulling a rabbit out of the hat. Nothing amazing about showing what everyone already knows." He slapped his hands together at this and I half-expected to see a rabbit jumping around right there in the office. Then he said, "Surprise! That's the thing, Roy. Surprise." And he smiled with delight.

One night when I'd had enough of my own company I decided to drive out to Virginia and visit the bar I'd gone to a couple of weeks before. Nothing had surfaced about my first trip, and I assumed that it was far enough out of the way that no one who could hurt me would notice if I dropped in. I arrived a little after eight and the place looked exactly as it had appeared before as if it were a stage set that sat undisturbed during the intermission. The same sleepy couple, listlessly moving back and forth on the dance floor, the pianist playing songs Nat Cole had made familiar.

I sat at the bar but if the bartender recognized me, he didn't show it. It didn't seem to be the kind of place where you'd buy the barkeep a drink to listen to your troubles. I drank a beer and listened to the music and in time the same guy I'd seen the first time came and sat down next to me. "Are you here every night?" I asked.

The man smiled. "Just the nights you're here," he said. Then, "I know who you are, by the way."

"Is that right?" I said, starting to get a little bit warm. I had thought I would be safely anonymous in the suburbs and wondered if I should just leave, but curiosity held me there. Then the guy put his hand on my arm and squeezed my elbow.

"It's okay," he said. "I won't say anything. I work at State."

"That's interesting," I said. "I hear there are a lot of faggots over there."

The man laughed. "I probably wouldn't put it that way but you're not far wrong. Anyway. I'm not interested in taking chances either."

"And yet you're here."

"Like you," he said, and then we laughed together.

Later I followed him out to his car, and we spent the night at his apartment which was nearby. His name was Jerry, or at least that's what he told me. It didn't matter. As I drove home, I felt lighter, less embattled. For the first time since arriving in Washington, I felt as if I had a friend or something like a friend. At least, someone with as much at stake as I had, as much to lose.

It was vintage McCarthy to drag in something out of left field and then leave you to figure out what he was getting at. What I took out of the whole rabbit business was that I should find communist authors or fellow travelers, like Wechsler, whose books we'd found in the overseas libraries and bring them in to testify in front of the committee. But this was more difficult than it might seem. I looked around for a week but when I couldn't come up with anyone ideal by the time the hearings resumed, we decided to recall Morton.

When we reconvened, we were back in the cavernous hearing room, cold and dank, the large ornamental lights hanging out of the corniced ceiling like predatory birds searching for prey. As was the case with many rooms in the capital, this one reached for elegance but missed it and succeeded only in suggesting a kind of seedy ballroom in an out of the way hotel. We were only here because of the overflow audience at our previous hearing but this time the crowd was much less, suggesting that McCarthy might have lost some of his juice. Perhaps sensing this, Joe seemed pre-occupied this morning, involved in the papers in front of him, so he signaled that I should start.

"Mr. Morton," I began, "you admit, as we've shown before, that you have a number of books by communist authors in your overseas libraries. Can you tell me why?"

Morton cleared his throat. He seemed dispirited too, his pale green eyes watery, his tie pulled off his collar as if he was having trouble breathing. I didn't blame him but nevertheless had no sympathy. "I think the best strategy is to let them hang themselves," he said now.

"And how would buying their books and then including them in our overseas libraries accomplish that?" I asked.

Morton raised his shoulders and looked at the ceiling perhaps for divine guidance. "I would hope people would read them and see the error of their ways," he said primly.

"Are there any authors in particular you think would convince readers of the American way and our general superiority to the communists?"

"Or there are many of them, I think," Morton said.

"But none come to mind?"

"Not offhand," he said.

"Well, to help out," I said. "I have a list that Mr. Schine and I put together when we were visiting the libraries in Europe." I hesitated, then looked down at the paper in front of me. "Would you think, for example, the poetry of Langston Hughes would help put America in a favorable light??"

"I'm not familiar with the works of that particular gentleman," Morton said.

I hadn't expected Morton to be familiar with the Harlem Renaissance, but I was just getting started. "Well then," I said. "I'll give you an example of his work."

Though you may hear me holler,
And you may see me cry—
I'll be dogged, sweet baby,
If you gonna see me die.

I looked up at Morton. "Do you think that will convince many communists of the errors of their ways?" I asked.

"Perhaps not that exact passage," Morton said.

"All right," I said. "How about Richard Wright then? He had so little affection for our country that he moved to France to get away from America."

"I'm afraid I'm not familiar with him either," Morton said.

"The author of *Native Son* and *Black boy,* you've never heard of him?"

"A Negro author?"

"Yes, a Negro author," I said, "Like Langston Hughes and an avowed communist. He has a rather dim view of American democracy; says we're actually a slave state with white overlords. Would you agree?"

"Oh, no," Morton said. "I wouldn't agree with that of course."

"And yet you have three of Wright's books in your overseas libraries."

Morton made a note of this and said he'd check on it, but then McCarthy broke in, listless no more. "Thank you, Mr. Cohn," he said, "but I have a few more questions for the witness.

Morton looked relieved to be through with me, but he shouldn't have been. McCarthy cleared his throat and read from one of the papers he'd been looking at before. "Surely, you've heard of Paul Robeson?" he said.

"The Negro singer," Morton asked, looking pleased that McCarthy had mentioned someone he'd heard of.

"Yes," McCarthy said. "The Negro communist singer. Well, did you know you have a copy of a book his wife wrote in your libraries?"

Morton looked worried again. "I wasn't aware of that," he said.

We'd actually seen Mrs. Robeson a few days before when we were preparing for the hearings. Unlike most authors who hid behind the Fifth Amendment, she claimed instead "the fifteenth amendment as a Negro."

This had confused McCarthy since the hearings had nothing to do with her right to vote but he was unusually gentle with her. "You will receive no less attention because of your race," he had said. "Besides, I have no intention of arguing with a lady."

And yet here he had brought her through her work in front of the Committee. "Like Mr. Cohn, I'd like to read something to you, Mr. Morton," he said, smiling. "This is from a book called *African Journey,*" by Mrs. Paul Robeson. I assume you're not familiar with it since you seem to have no idea about any of the books by communists in your libraries. Is that right?"

"No," Morton said. "I mean, no, I haven't read that particular book. I'm not referring to books in general by communists."

"I see," McCarthy said. "But you don't deny that you have books by communists in the overseas libraries, are you? I mean, that's what we've just been talking about."

"I can't say for sure that we do or don't," Morton said. "I'll stand by my past statement on books by communists."

"I see," McCarthy said. "I think you mean that your intention is that the books will make the communists change their ways. Your exact statement was that you wanted to make them eat their words." He smiled and licked his lips.

"Yes," Morton said. "Something like that."

McCarthy nodded. "Something exactly like that, I think, Mr. Morton. Well, Mrs. Robeson says in her book, "...the one hopeful light on the horizon [are] the exciting and encouraging conditions in Soviet Russia where for the first time in history our race problem has been squarely faced and solved…" He looked up at Morton. "Would you think that would be very convincing to a reader who had questions about America."

Morton looked stricken. "No, Sir. I wouldn't say so."

"Mrs. Robeson doesn't seem inclined to eat her words, that's for sure. We had her in a private session and she didn't seem to want to say anything at all, like a lot of these communist authors. Do you have a reaction to that, Mr. Morton."

Morton shook his head no. "As I said, Senator, I haven't read that particular book, but I will now. It certainly sounds like something we need to review if it's in our library."

McCarthy nodded and shook his head. "You do that, Mr. Morton. And then you can come back and tell us what you've found. Does that make sense to you?"

Morton looked stunned and as if he wanted nothing more than to get out of the room. "Yes, Senator," Morton said. "I'll definitely do that. I will say that no one, certainly not me, had any intention of stocking our libraries with questionable books. I'll absolutely review the matter."

McCarthy nodded and excused Morton, who practically ran out of the room. What I noticed then and later was that people were always underrating McCarthy regarding his brains and preparation and it worked to his advantage. He was no intellectual, but he had a quick, native intelligence and was always well prepared. Although many tried over the next few months, no one was very skilled in diverting him or knocking him off his game. It was more often, the opposite. He might come into the room hung over and unkempt, his eyes bloodshot and his hair in disarray but then a miraculous transformation would take place, and he'd suddenly become focused and alert. He had presence and once he was in the hearing room, he never failed to surprise and impress me.

Nine

MADISON

Susan was born in New Paris, Ohio and grew up there where she went to public schools. Her father was an insurance salesman, and her mother was a homemaker so while Susan was a child of the Depression, her family never suffered the poverty of many. Neither of Susan's parents had gone to college and Susan was their only child, As such, she was beloved and highly valued by her parents who were pleased when after being valedictorian of the high school and a cheerleader, Susan married her boyfriend Gary who was shortly drafted and sent overseas during the War.

At eighteen, Susan expected to live the kind of quiet, well-ordered life her parents had, centered on home and family. She was a modest girl, so she knew her own strengths and had no great expectations for her life to come. Susan and Gary made love before he shipped out and Susan hoped this would lead to a child but as it happened, she did not become pregnant. Though her parents wanted her to stay home and wait for Gary, Susan decided she would rather go to college and thus be better prepared for the workforce when her husband returned.

Because of her excellent grades, Susan had been offered a scholarship to Miami University where she admired the Georgian architecture and enjoyed the intellectual challenge of her classes. Oxford was close to home and Susan came home most weekends, never dating or participating in campus activities. It seemed inappropriate since she was a married woman.

Susan finished her history degree in three years, graduating with honors. Just as she was about to graduate, however, she received news that Gary had been killed fighting in France and would not be coming home after all. This news, surprisingly, was oddly not as upsetting as Susan might have expected and the fact that it was not made her feel guilty. In part it was because of her habit of anticipating anything and everything that might happen. Gary was in a war and people got killed in wars so why shouldn't it be reasonable to think that this might happen to Gary, as in fact it had. But in retrospect, she wondered if she might feel relieved. Had she loved Gary or was it simply the expected thing for girls in her class to marry and start having children after graduation. She wouldn't have admitted this to her parents, but in the quiet nights that followed the news, she often wondered.

Susan had grown as a student at Miami and didn't really relish the idea of returning to New Paris, though her parents urged him to come home where they could take care of her in what they assumed was her sorrow. But New Paris really bore no resemblance to the city of light and there was really nothing there for her except a job teaching in high school, which wasn't appealing. Susan had been offered a fellowship at Ohio State because of her work at Miami so she went to live in Columbus, a much bigger city than any she had experienced before.

There were thousands of students at Ohio State and many graduate students whom Susan might have dated but perhaps because she was a widow whose husband had been killed in battle, the boys she met seemed young and inexperienced while she was a bit intimidating to them. So, while she was short, cute, smart and dressed well, except for a brief affair with her major professor Susan had no serious relationships in Columbus and was happy to leave when she was offered an administrative job in Madison. It wasn't exactly her field, but she enjoyed working with the returning veterans and had been told this might lead to something bigger. At twenty-six, Susan thought it was time for a fresh start.

Ed had been working part-time at the boathouse for a month. It had taken a week or so to get the office in order, but the truth was after that there wasn't much to do, and Ed almost felt guilty collecting his paycheck. When the weather was better, they rented rowboats, canoes, and sailboats but things were slow in the winter except for the few students who wanted to rent snowshoes. All Ed had to do for now was keep track of where everything was. Often when there was no business, he'd go out and sit in one of the wire chairs on the terrace and look at the water, iced-over and endless in front of him. Off in the distance was a peninsula they called Picnic Point where students and faculty could hike or camp though the campus itself was so beautiful that it was hard to imagine anyone thinking he'd have anything to get away from.

Once or twice a week Susan Roselle would come down to visit and they'd sit in the Rathskeller during his breaks from work drinking coffee and talking. While Ed assumed she was checking up on him, she was so relaxed and friendly that it didn't really seem official. Since her visits took place during the workday, Susan generally wore a dress but sometimes she'd be in slacks. She'd changed something about her hair and now Ed was even more aware that she was a very attractive woman, about his age, and apparently showing an interest in him. In the moment of thinking this, however, he'd correct himself. He wasn't in Susan's class, and he knew it. She was a dean with a Ph.D and he wasn't even really a freshman. Ed told himself she was only being friendly and reined back any expectations he might have allowed himself.

Susan was in charge of the program to bring vets back to school, but she made clear that she wasn't really Ed's boss. She left that up to a guy named Joe Turner who ran the whole Union building but even Joe didn't really seem that interested in cracking the whip. Somehow the place seemed to run pretty well anyway, and it occurred to Ed that however it may have seemed in his past life, you didn't have to be a pain in the ass to make things work efficiently. In his allotted time with his son, Ed would often bring Little Ed down to play in the boats and watching the boy working the long wooden paddles Ed was keenly aware of how different his own childhood had been, which was a good thing. Maybe Little Ed would end up in a better place.

Three mornings a week Ed went up the Hill to take his Political Science class, which was taught by a professor named Peter Sinclair, who was rumored to be an actual communist but if this was true, he was pretty low-key about it. Beyond a few glancing remarks about McCarthy that almost anyone might make, most of what Sinclair talked about was what he called "international power politics." Ed wasn't sure what this meant exactly but he figured if he stayed with it the whole thing would start making sense eventually.

At some point, after the first few weeks, Sinclair stopped Ed after class and said, "You're the guy in the paper, right?"

Ed didn't have to ask what he meant. "That's me," he said and smiled. "Joe Stalin's best friend in Madison."

Sinclair nodded. "Nice that you've got a sense of humor about it. Most people wouldn't in your situation. But from what I hear they put you through it anyway."

Ed assumed Susan had told Sinclair about his losing his job. "Nothing I can't handle," he said. Then he looked around the Hill bordered by elms and maples. "This isn't that bad a place to land anyway."

Sinclair nodded. He fingered the loophole on his tweed jacket. "You know, there's a group just getting organized you might be interested in."

Ed shook his head no. "I'm not much for groups," he said. "Actually, I'm not even political. I don't belong to a party or anything."

"I wasn't suggesting that exactly," Sinclair said. "This is a group to support people like you who've been victimized by McCarthy. The others have all been singled out too or know someone who has."

"I don't really feel much like a victim," Ed said. "I'm doing okay."

Sinclair nodded. "No problem then but keep it in mind. You might see a poster up on campus announcing a meeting of the group. It's called "Joe Must Go.""

"Go where? Isn't he from here?" Ed said and immediately felt stupid.

Sinclair laughed. "Maybe we should call it "Bring Joe Back Home." The idea is to get people to sign petitions to recall McCarthy. He's doing a lot of damage."

"Can you do that? Recall a Senator?"

"I'm not sure yet. But we'll cover that in class," Sinclair said. Then he tapped Ed on the shoulder and walked away.

Even if Janey was the one who'd left the marriage, Ed tried to keep things friendly between them, if only for Little Ed's sake. When he stopped that afternoon, however, Janey was in a prickly mood, her face set in a scowl. "What are you taking up at the Big U?" she said.

Ed didn't like her sarcasm, but it was the first time she'd shown any interest in what he was doing so he thought things might be improving between them. "Only a poli sci course," he said. "Nothing major, just enough to get the benefits. Interesting, though, I have to say."

"Poli sci, eh?" Got all that joe college slang already, don't you?"

Ed just looked at her. They had been married long enough for him to know when she actually wanted to fight, but he didn't feel like playing along today. "What's going on with you anyway? What's wrong with my taking a course?"

"Getting too smart for us, that's all," Janey said. "I'm surprised you even come around anymore, except to see Little Ed."

In fact, Little Ed was the real reason he'd come by; they were divorced after all. But Ed valued keeping things even between them. It was easier. He just didn't understand Janey's attitude. Somehow, she seemed to think he was putting on airs because he was taking a college course. He thought of telling her how lost he felt among all the college kids, how stupid, but knew it would do no good. Still, her anger made him sad. There hadn't ever been passionate love between them, but they had gotten along, at least in the beginning. And after they split, he hoped they'd remain friends. Now he wondered if this was realistic.

"Trust me, I'm not any smarter than I ever was," he said. "In fact, if you asked some people, it was pretty dumb of me not to sign the damned loyalty oath in order to keep my job, which is the only reason I'm even at the U."

"And I'd be one of them," Janey said, ending the conversation. "Just have Little Ed back on time and don't spoil his dinner."

Ed took Little Ed over to Klitsner's on Monroe Street, where he bought him new sneakers because the boy noticed a pair in the window the last time. Then they walked two blocks to Mickie's where Ed allowed Little Ed to order a sundae despite Janey's orders. Ed was only having coffee because he'd noticed a new layer growing around his belt. While they were eating, Little Ed said, "Dad, are you ever coming home again?"

Ed felt a sudden pain in his midsection, regret hitting like a blow. Not about Janey really, but losing the family, the closeness they'd had by default living with each other, putting Little Ed to bed at night, taking him over to school in the morning. He could spend time with the boy now, but it wasn't the same; he knew it even if it hadn't been enough to make him do what Janey wanted and sign the loyalty oath.

It wasn't like Little Ed to be this direct, but Ed figured it was best to be honest. "I don't know," he said. "Probably not. I'm not sure your mom wants me there." Then because he knew that was cowardly, he added, "Neither of us do."

Little Ed sat with this for a minute and then said, "But maybe you have a girlfriend, too."

Ed hadn't mentioned Susan so he wondered if Little Ed had been put up to this by Janey. "Where did you get that idea?" he asked.

Little Ed shrugged. "I just wondered," he said.

"I have some friends who are girls," he said. "Just like you do."

Little Ed shook his head. "Not the same," he said. "In the third grade, if a girl likes you, she chases you around the playground."

Ed laughed. He liked that Little Ed understood the differences in their situations. The kid was more perceptive than he would have expected. "That's interesting," he said. "And do any of them ever chase you?"

Little Ed shrugged. "Sometimes," he said. "But I don't even like any of the girls in my grade. They're all stupid."

"That can't be true," Ed said, having no idea why he was sticking up for little girls. "But you're right, it's not really the same."

"So," Little Ed persisted. "Do you have a girlfriend, Daddy?"

Ed thought it was best to come clean. He knew that none of this was easy for Little Ed. He'd lived in the Madison Street house all his life and now he was somewhere else and his whole world had been upset. In addition, Ed's notoriety had made things difficult for the boy at school with his friends. It seemed only fair that his father should be honest with him, but Ed still hesitated since he knew the whole conversation would be reported back to Janey. "I did meet someone I like," he said.

"And she likes you?" Little Ed said hopefully.

"I don't know about that," Ed said. "Maybe. We don't know each other very well yet. We'll see."

Little Ed nodded again satisfied with the intelligence he'd gained. "

"Maybe you'll meet her sometime," Ed said. "Would you like that?"

But Little Ed didn't take the bait. The boy was cool for his age and not ready to commit himself or choose sides. "Can I have a piece of pie?" Little Ed asked.

Ten

WASHINGTON

Being evil's a tough gig. Don't let anyone tell you otherwise. But now, the papers were calling me under-handed, a weasel, a scumbag, McCarthy's bag man, someone who was universally disliked and feared. To hear them tell it, Mephistopheles, the devil himself, had nothing on me. I got some of this from the liberals during the Rosenberg's prosecution, but I was only second chair then, not a primary actor. Now it was different, more personal and direct. One of the writers even ridiculed the scar I have on my nose from a childhood accident. Okay, I've never claimed to be a movie star, but I wouldn't call mocking someone's looks political commentary.

This began when I was on television during the VOA hearings and picked up steam later. Some columnist called me the most hated man in America which was not only overstatement but nonsense. Was someone doing a survey? Who was in the top ten? Most of America hadn't even heard of me before the hearings. I understand these guys have to come up with copy for their editors three times a week, but hated? I don't think so.

It might seem odd to some people given my reputation, but I never really understood hate. I was opposed to the Rosenbergs because I was an attorney prosecuting their case and it was my job to do it as thoroughly as I could. I'd even go so far as to say I thought they and other communists were the enemy but that was as far as it went. I didn't hate them. If anything, I respected them as being committed and tough adversaries, which made me work harder to put them where they belonged.

But hate is the American way, always has been. First with the Indians, killing them and moving them away from where they'd lived forever. Then we moved on to the Irish and the Italians, the blacks the Chinese and my people in the Twenties followed by the Mexicans and whoever might be coming next. Why hate and looking down on others is so essential to the American psyche is something I've never figured out, but it's been with us from the start, so why should I have been surprised that it had come down to me?

Let me be clear. I wouldn't say I was insensitive or wanted people to dislike me; it made doing my job more difficult and it was hard on my parents to see their son defamed this way. But it didn't keep me up at night. I took pride in my ability to absorb abuse, as all lawyers do. You could say it goes with the territory. And while like everyone else, I might have preferred popularity to disrepute given a choice, I accepted my role in all this. I always liked the Stoics, in part because they taught you to accept what you were given and not to expect more as most people do. I remember reading Epictetus at Columbia and him saying if you didn't spend your time flattering the Senator, expecting to be invited to his parties was foolish and stupid. The way I translated that to my world was that if I wasn't going to kiss asses, I shouldn't expect anything. It may sound harsh, but it worked for me.

Anyway, question my morals all you want, but no one could accuse me of going with McCarthy for the money or being insincere. I made $75 a week and lived in a room in the Statler where the bedspread was tattered and the pipes banged all night long. To put up with that, I had to think what I was doing was important, even essential. Joe made a good target and so did I. If anything, maybe I hate the columnists who use us for target practice, instead of the communists.

Later, *Time* put Schine and me on the cover with a puff piece calling us "McCarthy's Men." One of the papers made a mock-up of it replacing the Time cover line with "McCarthy's Tools," which I had to give them credit was kind of funny, unlike the innuendo about Dave and me sharing rooms when we traveled that found its way into the papers.

To combat this, I continued dating Barbara, which helped, and she was a great sport, coming with us to the Stork or 21. She was smart, funny and comfortable anywhere, having been raised around show girls when her dad owned The Latin Quarter. I wasn't sure how all this worked out with her professors at Sarah Lawrence who I figured were liberals like professors everywhere, but she'd make it work. Barbara could fit in anywhere and look she belonged. It was a gift.

Seeing me out and about with a beautiful woman made all the gossip columns and there were always pictures. Inevitably people asked if we were in love, and I always said we were. Why not? Who could it hurt? Still, the questions about my sex life wouldn't go away and some suggested Barbara was just my beard and that I was using her to cover up the truth about me and Dave. Why all of this should have been anyone else's business is beyond me, but eventually it reached my boss, and McCarthy called me into his office to talk it over. Immediately, I was worried about being discovered, thought maybe someone knew about my trips to Virginia, and this made me more defensive than I should have been.

"It's bullshit, the stuff about me and Schine," I told Joe when we met. "Noise and nothing else. Dave's not a homo, girls love him. As for Barbara, we've been friends for years. I knew her dad and used to go down to the Latin Quarter when he owned it. So now it's big news if we go out when I'm in New York."

"Relax," McCarthy said, smiling. "I'm not worried about you and don't care what you do when you're on your own. You're a young man and you can do what you want, but you've got to ignore that crap reporters are writing. They've been all over me for years, looking at my garbage, checking out hotels where I stay, every goddamned thing you could think of. Don't let it get to you. It's the old thing; any publicity is good publicity."

"Doesn't feel so good to me," I said, taking a deep breath. "Not with everything I'm hearing about this from my friends and parents who see it all too."

"What do they say."

"Actually, my father was pleasantly surprised. He thought we looked good on tv. My mother said my tie wasn't straight."

McCarthy laughed. "We'll have to work on that. Anyway, you've got to have thicker skin. Likely, this is just beginning for you."

He couldn't have been more right about that.

Spring was turning toward summer, hot and muggy every day, as if a large wet blanket had descended on my shoulders. Even wearing summer suits, my shirts stuck to my back and there was a permanent sheen of sweat on my forehead. McCarthy had already announced he was getting married to Jeanie Kerr and this was a good distraction given the rumors about his possibly being a homosexual, but I wasn't sure the marriage would actually happen. I liked Jeanie but she and Joe fought all the time, I mean fought viciously, usually when she found out he'd been with another girl, which to be honest was a lot of the time.

Joe had asked me to be an usher at the wedding, but I wasn't going in to get fitted for a dress suit. This would be in late June and that was a long way off. Jeanie was devoted to Joe when it came to politics; no one could be more committed on that level. But her faith didn't extend to McCarthy's personal life.

Along with this, what they were calling The Korean Conflict dragged on and we were losing, or at least not winning, which didn't make anyone happy. There are no ties in war. We'd won the Battle of Seoul but that was a year ago. The Chinese and North Koreans just kept on coming and there was no end in sight. I had gotten a commission with the reserves which got me out of things but now we were having more trouble with Schine. Dave had gotten a 4-F based on a report from a family doctor in California who said he had a slipped disc, but Drew Pearson did some digging and wrote in his column that Dave was a draft dodger which got a big reaction from the professional patriots. Why should a rich boy get out of the Army when poor kids were dying every day half-way around the world? There was no good response to this, but the pressure forced Schine to take another physical and this time he passed and was re-classified 1-A.

He called me up, hysterical. "That doctor in California said I was out, that I'd be okay, but now I'm I-A. I can't go to war, for chrissakes."

I didn't want to argue with him. "You should have done what I did and signed up for the Reserves," I said.

"Great, but I didn't," Dave said. "What do I do now?"

"Take it easy," I said. "I'll ask Joe to make some calls, maybe there's a way to get you a commission or something."

"A commission? Are you out of your mind? You can't make a private into an officer by snapping your fingers? Anyway, McCarthy hates me."

This wasn't far off, but I wanted to encourage Dave. When I was coming up, I was taught never to say something couldn't get done but rather to ask how do we do it. Problems were there to be solved so even if I was new to Washington, I assumed we could handle this somehow. "I don't know yet," I said to Dave. "But there's got to be a way. You're a valuable member of the committee's staff."

"What a joke," Dave said. "I haven't been to the office in weeks and when I'm there, I don't do anything. The papers are calling me a playboy."

The papers in this case weren't wrong and I didn't really like listening to his whining, but I wasn't going to say anything. He was upset enough already and for my own reasons I wanted to keep him around, even I wasn't sure how to do it. "Let me worry about this," I said.

I knew the custom was that every Senator and Congressman could ask for special consideration from the Army for friends and family. Not that either Dave or I were in that category, but I still thought we would have been given consideration easily if Pearson hadn't drawn attention to the case.

When I brought the matter to Joe, he said, "Look, Roy, I wouldn't care if they sent that guy to Madagascar, to tell the truth. I mean, during the War I didn't have to go since I was a judge, but I went ahead and signed up for the Marines. And the papers are right. Why should some poor kid from Mazomanie get his ass drafted and sent to Korea and Schine doesn't?"

McCarthy was proud of his war service and had his honorable discharge and medals framed on his office wall. "I know that, Senator," I said, "but maybe as a favor to me? He is on the committee staff."

McCarthy shrugged, unconcerned. "You can't make chicken salad out of chicken shit," he said, "and I know about chickens, used to raise them back in Wisconsin. But sure, if it's important to you, go ahead and make some calls."

If I had it to do over, I'd pass and let Dave take his chances, but life doesn't work that way. You don't get do-overs later for mistakes you made. I was young and full of myself, and my boss had just given me permission to intervene for Schine. I figured I could get this done and I was wrong about that.

Later, when the President's staff was trying to get rid of me, they claimed I made forty-four calls trying to get Dave a better deal. I'd be surprised if it was that few. It could well have been four hundred contacts in those months but who was keeping score? I tried to get him in the Army, Navy, Air Force, Merchant Marine. I would have put him in the Salvation Army if they were willing to take him, I didn't give a shit. But nothing worked out. In the end, Dave was assigned to Fort Dix out in Jersey.

Even then I didn't give up, demanding the commander give Dave leave so he could come into New York, almost nightly. It wasn't common for soldiers in basic training to have passes, especially to go into the city but I claimed important Committee business and it worked until they finally had enough and then Dave had to stay closer to the base.

Everyone from McCarthy to Barbara told me to lay off at this point; I'd tried and failed. Leave it alone. But for reasons I can't explain I couldn't help myself. I already said I wasn't in love with Dave physically. I didn't really think of him that way, didn't daydream about his well-muscled arms and torso or imagine us together in a hot tub. Was he good looking and sophisticated in a way I wasn't? Sure, but that wasn't what this was about. It was more that I was obsessed with getting these army assholes to do what I wanted and the more I failed, the more determined I became. I kept thinking there ought to be a way to accomplish this that I had not thought of, but if so, I never found it and Dave never got his commission. More important, as trivial as this might seem, with the fight over Schine, we started down a path that would ultimately result in the famous Army-McCarthy showdown a few months later. In the way naturalists track animals through the shit they leave behind on the trail, looking back, I can see the entrails of all this in my own stubbornness about Dave Schine's commission.

While all this was going on, we decided to convene hearings on communists who had been working at Fort Monmouth through the forties and into the fifties. You could say the slow movement was over and we were moving into the dance, a minuet. We'd move and the Army would counter, moving away, beckoning us on.

It always amazed me that the bleeding hearts in the liberal press acted as if we were pursuing the Fort Monmouth scientists for trivial reasons. The fact was we'd received hundreds of tips, including an FBI report about subversion at Monmouth where, among other things,

Julius Rosenberg had worked during the War. Now, they were working on the most sophisticated radar systems we had. This was obviously not information we wanted going directly to Moscow. Still, there was no question that until we started focusing on security problems and communists in the Army we'd been tolerated if not loved.

After reading the FBI report, I thought it was important enough to interrupt his vacation in Florida and bring him back to Washington. Joe never complained about this, Jeanie may have felt different.

During the hearings, we interviewed dozens of men who'd worked at Monmouth in the decades after the war, most of whom were lower-level scientists but had important information about what was going on out there. One that stood out was Tony Abruzzi, a G.I. who attended City College after the War and started working at Monmouth shortly after graduation. There wasn't much information about this guy beyond that. But he had known the Rosenbergs and Morton Sobell, the communist spy who was convicted along with them. That was enough to get him an invitation to testify.

Abruzzi was a solid man in his early thirties with a receding hairline and a five o'clock shadow and was obviously uncomfortable as we began. This might have been explained simply by the fact that we'd been assigned a close room that was made suffocating by the presence of reporters, cameras and curiosity-seekers. When I scanned the audience, I noticed a face I couldn't place immediately. Then it came to me. Jerry from Virginia was at my hearing. We made eye contact, and he nodded, in affirmation, and gave me the thumbs-up. He was obviously there to support me, but it had the opposite effect, making me feel exposed before the crowd. What had I been thinking when I drove out to Virginia to get laid rather than paying attention to business?

Something seemed to have gotten to Abruzzi too, as his head was on a swivel, jerking left and right as he looked nervously around the room. Now he took his chair, and we called the hearing to order.

I tried to put him at ease feeling that if he was too anxious, he wouldn't be useful to us. "Let's start with your military experience," I said. "You served in the War, am I right?"

"Yes, sir, Abruzzi said. "First in Africa and then in Italy."

"Thank you for your service," I said. "After your discharge you returned, went to college and started working at Fort Monmouth?"

"Correct," Abruzzi said.

"And while there you knew the Rosenbergs and their friend Morton Sobell, is that right?"

"I wouldn't say I knew them," Abruzzi said.

"You knew them well enough to go to meetings of a communist cell, didn't you?"

Abruzzi nodded. "I only went to a couple of meetings."

"Okay, but didn't you actually live with Sobell for a while?"

"I think he lived in an apartment I was living in with other people for a couple of weeks, that was all."

"Really" I said. "You mean you did not know the other people who lived in your own apartment? How big was this place anyway?"

"I wasn't really there that much," Abruzzi said, running his finger inside his shirt collar.

Okay," I said. "Fine. But going back, did you know other communists, either at Monmouth or earlier during the time you were in the service."

Abruzzi was sweating now, moving around in his chair as if it was on wheels. 'You have to remember it was different back then. The Russians were on our side in the War."

"That's true," I said, "so is that why you met with various other communists during the War, maybe in Italy?"

"You couldn't tell who was or wasn't a communist over there," Abruzzi said. "Nobody exactly advertised it. We were busy trying to stay alive, but yeah, we'd get together sometimes with the Russian soldiers when we had leave and talk, you know, bull sessions. Whether those guys were communists I don't know. None of us were sure we were coming back, so it wasn't the main thing we were worried about."

This was kind of a sentimental appeal to the audience using the dangers of war as an excuse for his actions, but it worked as was indicated by a sympathetic murmur in the press corps. I let this die down then continued my questions. "And would you say you're still a communist?"

"I never said I was one," Abruzzi said. "I just knew some people, who knew some people and went to a few meetings, first overseas, then here. That's it."

Abruzzi smiled at this and licked his lips, as if he was pleased with himself for this comeback, but it didn't derail me.

"A few communist meetings? I went on, "A few communists living in your spacious apartment but you're not sure you knew them. Sounds like they were all over the place, but you never noticed."

"Okay," Abruzzi snapped, defensive now. "Communist meetings, if that makes you happy. But like I said that wasn't really what we were thinking about back then, in Italy, I mean."

"Absolutely," I said. "There was a war to win, and I can see this is making you uncomfortable, but we're just interested in getting a picture of the whole scene. I'd like you to give me a few names of people who were at those meetings, even if they were informal. Can you do that?"

"You mean during the War?"

Abruzzi was stalling, hoping I'd forget where I was going but that wasn't going to happen. It was a dance, and I knew the steps. "Then and later," I said.

Abruzzi took a deep breath. "There were the people you already talked about at Monmouth. During the War there were some Italian organizers who I can't remember their names. And then there were some of the other guys in my squad."

"Names, please," I said.

"This is a long time ago. I don't even know where these guys are, what happened to them," Abruzzi pleaded.

"Let me worry about that," I said. "Just give me the names."

"Okay," Abruzzi said. "I ain't going to give you the names of guys who are dead but the ones I remember being there were Ernie Wagner, Jim O'Connor and Eddie Malloy."

"These were soldiers in your unit in Italy?"

"Yes, Sir."

"And they attended these communist meetings with the Italian organizer you mentioned earlier?"

"Yes, I think they did," Abruzzi said.

"You think so or they actually were there?"

"They were there," Abruzzi said, and I thought he was going to cry.

"And have you been in touch with any of these other men since you were discharged? Have they continued their communist activities?"

Abruzzi shook his head no. "Like I said, I don't know if they were communists then and I have no idea where any of them are now. We don't keep in touch. Tell the truth, I don't know if they're dead or alive, but they were all good men, I can say that."

"I'm sure they were," I said and printed the names he mentioned on a notepad. If they were still alive, we'd be able to find them.

Did I enjoy making a *shmendrick* like Abruzzi look bad, not really. I knew he wasn't central to our investigation, but I didn't care about his feelings. This was too important and unlike intervening in Schine's commission, communists working at Monmouth told us crucial things about the army's lousy security procedures. Looking back, I can't honestly say Abruzzi or the others we talked to that day helped us very much, but the top brass had started circling the wagons once we began questioning them, with good reason as it turned out.

Before any of that could happen, however, we got involved with Irving Peress. On the face of it, Peress was nobody you'd think twice about, a dentist from Elmhurst, Queens, who'd signed up for Korea the year before because the Army was looking for dentists. He had received an immediate commission as a captain, as any doctor would. What made Peress unusual from the start was that rather than signing off on the standard loyalty questions on the Army application, he took the Fifth, saying he couldn't answer questions about his past communist affiliation without jeopardizing himself.

This wasn't exactly unheard of but looking back it still surprises me that nobody flagged his paperwork at the time. Instead, Peress was assigned to basic training in Texas and then to Fort Lewis in Washington. This much was routine and wouldn't ordinarily have been worthy of McCarthy's notice. A pink dentist even in the Army wasn't going to make news. It was what came later that drew our attention.

While I was getting together the paperwork on Peress, McCarthy got a call from a high-ranking general who asked McCarthy to call him about what he called a serious matter. When McCarthy did, the general said he was calling about a breach in Army security that had to be investigated. He wouldn't say what this was exactly but that it was too sensitive to talk about on the phone. He was sending his adjutant down to New York and asked McCarthy to meet him there.

We were getting hundreds of tips a week, most of which went nowhere. I was in favor of ignoring this one, but McCarthy disagreed. "I can't go to New York," he said. "I'm up to my ass in these hearings.

But you don't ignore a general when he calls, so I guess you'll have to go and talk to his guy." He looked down at a note he'd made. "He's going to be in the bar at the Sherry Netherland."

"Jesus," I said. "The Sherry-Netherland? You think it's really worth taking the day to go up there?"

"Who knows?" McCarthy said. "It's like all the tips we get. Some are bullshit and some we need to look at seriously. You know that."

"By this time, you can't tell the difference?"

"No, Roy," I can't," he said, his voice rising in the small room. "Congratulations if you can, but it doesn't matter. We've already pissed off enough people in the Army and the way things are going, we'll piss off more a lot more before we're done with these hearings. So, if this general asks me to look into whatever he's got, we're goddamned going to do it, if that's all right with you."

I couldn't argue with this so while I didn't like it, I left the office and got on the train to New York.

Eleven

MADISON

As if the outside world had decided things were going too smoothly, Ed looked up one morning at the boathouse and saw Jimmy Simmons standing in front of him. He was wearing a string tie and a corduroy jacket. Ed didn't really dislike the kid, but just seeing the reporter made his throat suddenly close up. If experience meant anything Jimmy showing up was never going to mean anything good but whatever it meant or might mean, Ed had to find a way to relax and let things fall where they were going to fall.

"Slow news day, Jimmy?" Ed asked and took a deep breath.

The reporter's face was red and blotched as if he'd been in a fight on the way over. He ran his fingers through his crewcut. "Actually, it isn't, Mr. Malloy," he said. Then he looked around him as if someone else was listening. "I had to look all over for you. I didn't know you moved or that you were a student and had a job here."

"Kind of a student," Ed said. "Part time. One course so far. But I'm pretty sure you don't want to know about my studies. What's up?"

Jimmy took a notebook out of his pants pocket and looked at a page of notes. "You know a guy name of Tony Abruzzi by any chance."

Ed had to take a minute. In the benign light of morning, it was hard to think of anything other than the cerulean water stretching out in front of him toward the insane asylum across the lake where he might be going if this crap continued much longer. Abruzzi? The name was vaguely familiar. Then it came back full force. "Sure," he said. "I know Tony, or at least I used to know him. We were in the service together."

"In Italy?" Jimmy said.

"Yeah," Ed said. "In the War. Before you were born. So what? Why are you asking?" But Jimmy had already started writing in his notebook, a bad sign as Ed knew from experience. "Wait a minute," Ed said. "Stop writing for chrissakes. What's going on? And why're you asking about Tony Abruzzi? I don't need you putting any more stories about me in the paper, Jimmy. That last one was bad enough."

Jimmy smiled weakly. "Sorry, Mr. Malloy," he said. "Really, I am. It's not actually up to me, though. My editor told me to come down and not leave until I got to talk to you."

"Okay, we're talking. You're here, but you've got your notebook out and I know where that's going. I'm telling you, Jimmy, I don't need it. You already got me fired off one job and I don't want it happening again. I've got a nice little deal here."

Jimmy took a folded-up newspaper out of his jacket pocket. He smoothed it out and laid it flat on the desk, but Ed couldn't read it in the bright light without his glasses. He'd stopped reading the papers since coming over to the University and he noticed he'd been a lot more relaxed. "Okay," Ed said. "I give up. What am I looking at?"

Jimmy picked up the paper and read. "Tony Abruzzi, an admitted member of the communist Party, who is employed at the Fort Monmouth Military Base in New Jersey, was interviewed by the Senate Committee on Investigations Tuesday."

Ed's mouth fell open. "Tony's a communist?" he said. "Now you got me. That's got to be a mistake there, Jimmy."

"He admitted it. They quoted him directly," Jimmy said. "He testified that he knew the Rosenbergs and Morton Sobell. He says he went to meetings with them and even lived with Sobell for a while."

Ed knew who the Rosenbergs were, but Sobell was just a name to him, an engineer who turned out to be a spy. He couldn't see what it had to do with his old army buddy. "It still doesn't sound right to me," he said. "How would he know those people? I haven't seen Tony since the War, but he was a great guy, a good soldier."

"No doubt," Jimmy said, "but he was in New York yesterday testifying as part of the McCarthy investigation.

"McCarthy interviewed Tony?" This was beginning to sound like one of those fantasy novels to Ed. Maybe aliens had kidnapped Tony. Who the hell knew?

"The Committee did. Actually, McCarthy's counsel, a lawyer named Roy Cohn handled the testimony. A very tough guy on communists, they say."

"Sonofabitch," Ed said shaking his head. "Even so, why come all the way down here to tell me about it."

Jimmy nodded. "I'm sorry to be the one bringing the news, Mr.Malloy, but Cohn's always trying to get people to name others they knew who either were or still are communists. They let the witnesses off easier if they do."

Ed was beginning to get a glimmer of what was going on and his palms started to sweat. "Okay," he said. "So what?"

"Your old Army buddy Tony named you and a couple of other guys in his testimony in front of the Committee."

"Named me? What the hell you talking about? I haven't even seen Tony in ten years, almost ten years, like I said, since the War."

Jimmy shrugged. "Doesn't matter to Cohn. Anyway, this was during the War that Abruzzi was talking about, in Italy." He looked back down at the paper as if he'd forgotten something. "So, did you and this guy go to meetings with an Italian communist organizer over in Italy? Maybe when you were on leave? He says here you did."

"Come on," Ed said. "Where were we going? When we were on leave in the Army all we wanted to was get shit-faced and forget about the War."

"You sure you didn't go to any meetings?" Jimmy persisted. "Because your friend Tony says you were there, along with, let me see, Ernie Wagner."

"Ernie could give a shit about communists and neither did I," Ed said. Since the kid was standing there with his notebook, he tried to think back seriously to that time he had spent in Italy, but it was mostly a blur in his mind of mud, explosions and dead bodies. Now, he had the sense of a door closing on him, of being exposed and humiliated in print because his old Army buddy was shooting his mouth off in New York. And for what? To cover his own ass, Ed figured, no matter who it might bring along with him. The whole world was going nuts and there was nothing he could do to stop it. But he had to get a grip on himself.

He took a deep breath and looked out at the lake to gather himself. "Look," he said finally. "I guess I knew some Italians back then, everyone did. Mainly they helped us get girls and some of them took us to dinner. What we talked about then or who we talked with I have no idea. It's a long time ago, Jimmy."

Jimmy nodded but pressed on. "Okay, you can't say for sure that on one of those dinners or long nights in an Italian bar, that there couldn't have been Russians there and the subject of communism didn't come up?"

"I have no fucking idea if it did or not," Ed said, his voice growing louder. "I can't remember. And I'd tell you if I did. I'll say this, though, in the War the Russians were our allies, we fought next to each other and some of them died there, just like our guys. And, okay, I guess they were probably communists because their country is, but if we did ever talk to them about anything I have no idea what it was. The main thing on our minds then was keeping our heads down and staying alive. Same as it was for them. Soldiers aren't that different no matter where they come from. I've spent most of the last ten years trying to forget the War so thanks very much for wrecking a beautiful morning, Jimmy, just like you ruined the Fourth for me. Can you just tell me what the hell the *Herald* cares about my old friend Tony saying maybe he went to communist meetings with me ten years ago in Italy? I mean, what exactly about this ancient history matters right now?"

"It's news," Jimmy said weakly.

"News, my ass," Ed said. "It's just like last time. You're making it up as you go along, you ask me."

Jimmy was red-faced now. "Sorry, Mr. Malloy, I'm just doing my job."

"Some fucking job," Ed said.

"Anyway, we didn't make anything up," Jimmy said. "McCarthy's our Senator. What he does in his Committee is news and not just in Wisconsin, trust me on that. If a witness in his hearings testifies and names someone in Madison, then that makes it important here whether you remember anything about that meeting or not. I'm sorry if I'm wrecking your day, I really am. But if we don't publish this someone else will."

"Right," Ed said. "You're sorry but it's not your problem. I understand, Jimmy. Now get the hell out of here and leave me alone."

Jimmy's story came out the next day with a headline reading "Local Man Named" followed by a sidebar referring to the 4th of July article Jimmy had written about Ed in case any readers had failed to make the connection. Afterwards, Janey called him and said, "You never told me you went to communist meetings in Italy. I thought you were there to fight a war."

"I was," Ed said. "It's bullshit. They just want to sell their damned papers is all. I don't remember any meetings, swear to God."

"Well, your army buddy says you were there," Janey said.

"Who knows what they made him say," Ed replied. He wanted to stick up for Tony even if his testimony had put Ed in the shitter. "You get in front of a committee like that with all those lights, reporters everywhere, who knows what you'd say."

"Maybe the truth," Janey said. "Anyway, thanks to this Little Ed's having trouble with the kids at school again."

"Goddamnit," Ed said. "I'm sorry about that." The first story had been bad enough for the kid. He saw him now in his mind's eye, shrunken in fear, his little black eyes looking like currants in his narrow face. He knew he was setting a lousy example for the boy, that he was a lousy father, a failure in that sacred relationship. He could tolerate the rest, but not that. "I'll go back and talk to the principal again," Ed said helplessly.

"You do that," Janey said, "It sure helped a lot the first time. Anything else I need to know if people are going to talk about me in the store."

"Not that I can think of," Ed said.

"But you're not sure?" Janey said. "Like those meetings?" Then she hung up.

After that, Ed unplugged the phone. If anyone really needed to reach him, they could write a letter. He was sorry to be causing Little Ed more trouble and there was no way to explain the situation to a kid. He didn't understand it himself. If they were lucky, it would all blow over in a day or so unless Tony kept on talking or got himself indicted. Even so, it was hard to see what more they could do to him. He'd lost his job, his house, his marriage. Thinking of it that way, he almost felt optimistic. There was that about hitting bottom, he thought. The only way his life could go was up.

Ed spent the weekend alone in his apartment staring at the four walls. When it got to be too much, he went out to see a movie. Other times he'd go for a walk but then the signs in people's windows sent him back to the apartment. "I'm with Joe," one said under a picture of McCarthy in his Marine uniform. "The Tailgunner's my man," said another with a steely-eyed McCarthy in a flight suit surveying the horizon. It was everywhere, inescapable, and the streets themselves in the neighborhood seemed to be narrowing, the dark trees pressing in upon him, the dead leaves like black snakes preparing to strike.

When Ed got to work on Monday, there was a note asking him to come and see Joe Turner when he could.

Ed had only been upstairs at the Union a few times, spending most of his time either in the Rathskeller or at the boathouse. He'd been in one of the meeting rooms when he was taking orientation, but generally he was on the main floor. Now he walked up two flights instead of taking the elevator to give his annoyance time to wear off. Joe's note hadn't said what he wanted but Ed figured it had to do with Jimmy's article, and it turned out he was right. Joe walked him back to his inner office and offered him coffee. Then he said, "You know, Ed, it doesn't matter to me."

"Funny how everyone says that" Ed said. "My friends in the neighborhood, my kid's principal, my boss at the insurance agency said that and what you do know I'm on the street a few weeks later."

Joe smiled. "That's different," he said. "The University's all about free speech, various ideas and ideologies. We welcome that."

"That's fine," Ed said. "But this has nothing to do with me. I just had this buddy in the army who's turned out to be a communist, I guess. Who the hell knew over there?"

"You don't need to tell me; I was in the War, too." Joe smiled and reached across the desk to pat Ed on the arm. "No big deal, I'd just like you to come over and talk to our Board when they meet. They might have some questions."

Ed felt the familiar chill coming over him, the feeling of dread. "Questions? What do you mean? What kind of questions?"

Joe shrugged. "I don't know, but it's always best to get this out in the open before people start making assumptions. It's mostly a student board so they'll probably think you're a hero."

"Sure, they will," Ed said. "But their parents would have a different idea. Most people I run into think McCarthy walks on water, his picture on matchbooks. Tailgunner Joe and all that bullshit."

"Maybe," Joe said, "like I said it doesn't matter to me, to any of us here at the Union who know you. Just do me a favor, talk to the Board, okay?

Before Ed had a chance to meet with anyone, his political science professor stopped by the boathouse. Sinclair did seem to think he was a hero, which in its own way was more irritating than Janey's attitude.

"Look," Ed said. "The whole thing's ridiculous. Nothing happened, really. Tony's just covering his ass if he's talking about me and Ernie Wagner being reds. I don't remember being at any meetings if there were any. Anyway, it's nothing to get excited about."

"The reporter who wrote the story that was in the paper seems to think something's happened," Sinclair said.

"They're looking for headlines," Ed said. "It's what they do. Tony was just trying to get off the spot and, you know what, I don't blame the poor bastard. Who wants to be in that situation?"

Sinclair nodded. "Sure, but what happened to your buddy is exactly what's happening to people all over the country. McCarthy throws their name out there and it costs him nothing, gets some headlines. But the next thing you know, they're out of a job, losing their homes, losing friends. You know what I'm talking about first-hand, Ed, and it's not just McCarthy. This hysteria about communists is everywhere. The president's doing the same thing behind the scenes. Hundreds of people in government have lost their jobs because someone somewhere said they were communist or homosexual or might be one. You're part of all that. That's all I'm saying."

"And that's supposed to make me feel better?" Ed said. "To tell the truth, I don't feel like I'm part of anything," Ed said. "Not a goddamned thing. I wake up in the middle of the night in a cold sweat and see searchlights outside my windows like in the war. Walking down the street I turn around every three steps because I'm sure I'm being followed. It's crazy what's going on inside my head."

Sinclair nodded. "Well, I can't help with that but maybe you should meet some people who are in the same position and get out of your head for a while. It isn't just you, but misery loves company."

For the first time, the idea of getting together with other people seemed appealing to Ed. For all he knew, Tony would keep on talking and Jimmy Simmons would keep on writing stories. But he was aware of what seemed like a chasm between him and everyone else, a kind of invisible barrier, like the isolation booths they used on the fake tv shows to convince everyone the questions were on the up and up. Walking down State Street he noticed people looking over at him as he passed and wondered how many knew who he was and what they thought he'd done. "Maybe," he said now. "Maybe I would do that, meet some people."

"Good," Sinclair said and got up from his chair. "Got to go, but I'll see you later." He patted Ed on the back and started back up the Hill.

Tired of talking, Ed took his break and walked down the path along the lake just watching the icy water, the birds hovering over it looking for flies. The crew team went by, rowing their asses off while the guy in the bow yelled at them to go faster. If the lake wasn't frozen solid, they'd be out there at six am. It seemed insane to Ed but what wasn't anymore? He sat on a rock and looked down at the water, intent on nothing when he heard someone behind him.

"They told me you'd walked up this way," Susan Roselle said. "Can I sit?"

"It's a public rock, I think," Ed said and immediately regretted it, being harsh. He was waiting for her to mention the article in the paper but when Susan spoke it was in a dreamy voice without urgency. "Isn't a little cold to be out walking?" he said, to soften what he'd said before.

"You're here," Susan said, and pulled her coat around her. "I love this path," she said. "When I first came to Madison I'd walk back and forth to class on it rather than going up on the Hill. It reminded me of the country back home even though it's so close to the city."

She was right. The lake path could well be in the country, Ed supposed, though it was completely different from the rocky soil in Dane, where you couldn't walk anywhere without turning your ankle or stubbing a toe. Susan was wearing a skirt today but unlike Janey, she didn't seem to worry about getting it dirty or starting runs in her stockings, if she was wearing stockings. She seemed comfortable with herself, unself-conscious. It was one of the things he liked best about her.

"You just came out here all by yourself without knowing anyone?"

Susan smiled. "That was one of the most attractive things about it, not knowing anyone, starting over. Back home, I was just that girl whose husband didn't come back from the War. Everyone felt sorry for me and that wasn't what I wanted."

Ed nodded. "I can see that," he said. "I'm still surprised no one you met wanted to marry you, though."

"How about that?" Susan said. "I think I was too serious for most of the other students and now everyone I meet is older and married already. I guess that train passed by when I wasn't looking."

Except for me, Ed thought, but he knew better than to say anything. They were quiet for a moment and Ed wondered if he'd gone too far by talking about her being single, but she'd brought it up in a way by mentioning her dead husband. He'd never been at ease with polite conversation, ether at neighborhood parties or even meetings at the school, not to mention with a woman about his age. It was new to him and hard to know what was acceptable and what might be rude or inappropriate. "I guess you saw what they said about me in the paper," Ed said, figuring it was best that he change the subject.

"Saw it, haven't read it yet," Susan said.

"Don't bother," Ed said. "It's all crap anyway."

Susan didn't respond to this. "That's not why I came down here," she said. "I was looking for you because I thought you might like to come over for dinner. Nothing fancy, just a cookout on my covered patio."

Patio? Ed thought. He wasn't sure he'd ever been on one. "To your house?" Ed said, stalling for time.

Susan laughed and Ed noticed for the first time that she had dimples and that her whole face opened up when she smiled. "Well, we could go out to a restaurant instead, I guess."

Ed was still amazed at Susan's continued interest in him and now she'd invited him to dinner. But he decided not to question it, at least for now. For reasons of her own this pretty little woman seemed to be drawn to him and if he had trouble believing it, he wasn't going to deny having some good luck for a change. For the first time today, Tony Abruzzi and the *Herald* were the farthest things from his mind.

Ed's confusion was obvious to Susan, who thought there was nothing unusual about her pursuing him. She couldn't afford to wait around forever, and the options were limited. Anyway, why wouldn't she be interested in this tall, handsome man who had somehow wandered into her life? It was true that they had significant differences, that some might see a disparity in their relative positions in the world, but what of it? Anyway, despite being employed by the University, Susan had never been especially attracted by the tweed legions that walked up and down the Hill every day, much less the men in her office who made passes at her while expecting her to ignore the fact that they were married. Ed was a breath of fresh air compared to them. She hadn't yet given up the idea of being married again or having children, even if she was older than most of the young mothers she met. Things were changing in the world and not always for the worse. She would follow up with Ed and see where the relationship went if it went anywhere. Moreover, having him off balance wasn't entirely against her self-interest. She enjoyed the feeling of being a step ahead. Too often, life had seemed to have unpleasant surprises in store for her. This was a chance to reverse the equation.

The Union Board met in a conference room and when Ed was ushered in he felt as if he was on trial, no matter what his boss said about his job being safe. Joe had been right about the Board, though, all of whom seemed to be college kids. Ed supposed he was technically a student too, but these kids were different, residential students living in dorms and fraternity houses, sent here by their parents with tins of cookies and cake, and strapped laundry boxes to send home to mom when things got out of hand. To Ed, they exuded privilege, though there was nothing overt about this except their presence in the room. They were different was all, different from him and Janey and the kids he'd known growing up, none of whom had been sent to the big U after graduation. It wasn't that Ed had never seen students like this before since they passed him every day on the street and in the Union, but he'd never been in a room like this when the space between them seemed impassable.

When the board members identified themselves, it turned out they were heads of various committees that ran Union programs for the students. It seemed amazing to Ed that a place this size could have a bunch of kids running it, but there were also a few older staff members there who he guessed supervised or handled budgets.

Joe started by saying, "Ed, the reason we're here is that you've gotten a lot of publicity lately either because of things you've said or that friends of yours have said, but this is only an informational meeting. No one's accusing you of anything.

Ed shifted in his chair. Joe was a decent guy and a good boss, but he sure felt as if he was being accused of something and had to defend himself. No one had said so, but he knew if these kids decided he was a radical he'd lose his job. If that wasn't the case, what was he doing there?

To gather his thoughts, he looked out the window where he could see iceboats on the lake, people walking on the path, doing normal things, living their lives. He tried to imagine he was somewhere else, anywhere else.

"Okay," he said finally. "But just to be clear with all of you, I didn't actually say anything to that reporter."

A boy who'd introduce himself as Harrison Bradford and was the president of the fraternity council spoke up. "Maybe not this time, but you signed a petition last summer. That's right, isn't it? And that's what the first article was about?"

Joe had indicated that the students would be sympathetic, but this kid seemed aggressive to Ed. He'd never trusted the sort of person who had a last name for a first name, as if his family came over on the Mayflower or something. But this kind of thinking would get him nowhere. For all he knew, the fraternity members were like their parents, fans of McCarthy, members of Young Republicans exposing commies on campus. Who could say for sure? "Some petition," Ed said now. "It was a copy of the Bill of Rights. You all read that in high school. Is that something you'd refuse to sign?"

"I don't know, but a lot of other people refused," Bradford insisted. "Why do you think they did that?"

Ed felt himself getting hot and willed himself to hold back and not attack this boy. "Because they were scared, I guess."

"Of what?"

"Actually, I don't know," Ed replied. "I've been trying to find out. What I know is that McCarthy has people looking over their shoulders, suspicious of everyone else."

"I might have refused to sign it under the circumstances," Bradford said. "My dad says Senator McCarthy is a great American."

Ed had been right about the boy. A young patriot defending the republic for sure. But there didn't seem to be any good response to this. Ed didn't want to get into a political argument or insult the kids by saying anything about their parents. He was relieved when a girl down at the end of the table rescued him by asking, "What about your friend, who testified to the Committee in New York?" She looked down at a note. "Mr. Abruzzi."

"I think Tony Abruzzi's a great guy," Ed said. "We fought together in the Italian campaign in the War. He was seriously wounded, and we thought he might die, but he recovered, left the hospital and came back to fight some more."

"Maybe so, but he's still a communist, isn't he?" the girl persisted.

"I don't know what Tony is or isn't," Ed said. "But he was a good friend to me when I needed friends. He saved my ass more than once, pardon my French."

The girl smiled. "It's okay," she said. "So, you don't know if he's a communist or if you went to meetings with him?"

"I don't know, and I don't care," Ed said. "It's a long time ago."

"Were you ever a member of the Party?" It was the fraternity kid again.

"I'm not a joiner," Ed said. "I didn't even belong to 4-H in high school. I'll bet some of you kids know what that is, right? Every high school kid belongs to 4-H where I grew up out in Dane, but I didn't."

Bradford didn't react to this, and Ed guessed 4-H didn't exist wherever he came from. "Is that a no?" he said.

"That's a no," Ed said.

He looked around the table at the others, but it turned out no one else had much more to say. Ed looked at Joe and raised his eyebrows, wondering if there was anything else, but Joe just shrugged. "Unless someone else has questions for Mr. Malloy, I think we'll let him get back to work," he said. Thanks for coming in, Ed."

"No problem," Ed said. Then he got up and walked out of the room but before returning to his post, he went down to the rathskeller and had a beer, unusual for him this early in the day but a way to let all this roll past. It was unclear whether he'd be asked back by the Board for more questions, but now he smiled to himself as he rolled the beer around in his mouth. He thought he'd handled himself well with those kids and if he had to, he'd do it again.

Susan lived in a bungalow in University Heights, an area adjacent to the campus that Ed had always thought of as being remote as a foreign country. The winding streets of the neighborhood contained large mansions honeycombed with smaller houses braided around rolling hills. While Ed was pleased by the invitation, he was still unsure of his standing with Susan. Was this a date or had she just taken pity on him after seeing his empty apartment?

He couldn't remember ever having gone to dinner with anyone other than Janey and it wasn't the kind of thing they did as a couple. Maybe meet someone for a beer at the bowling alley or the tavern near the park after work but that was all. People at the University were different. He guessed they got together for cocktail parties, dinner, who knew? It was all exotic to him. Yet here he was, getting ready to go Susan's house. He had spent time thinking about how to dress and whether to bring flowers or a bottle of wine like he'd seen men do in the movies. Susan was wearing jeans and a sweatshirt when she visited him, but Ed didn't even own a pair of jeans and didn't want to be disrespectful.

In the end, he settled on khakis that were reasonably new and a crew-neck sweater. He remembered his mother saying it was never a mistake to be over-dressed but in the end he decided against a jacket and tie and walked over from the apartment on Randall, enjoying the warm night and the hum of traffic on University Avenue. He could look across the street and see the University barns in the distance which made him feel more comfortable. There was a slight smell of manure in the air, and he could almost imagine being back home in Dane. He had decided against bringing wine, but Susan obviously didn't care. She had the gift of making you feel welcome regardless of where you came from or what you were wearing. She put her arms around Ed at the door and ushered him into a small living room, lined with books and pictures. Ed thought the art might be Chinese or Japanese, something Asian anyway. He hadn't fought in the Pacific, but he knew guys that had, and their stories hadn't made him that fond of the Japs. Still, you couldn't blame an artist for what happened during the War. It struck him that there were no drapes and rather than a carpet just a throw rug over an oak floor.

Ed had never been inside a professor's house before, even if Susan wasn't exactly a professor. He didn't know what he would have expected but definitely not this. He didn't see a television set. "Nice," he said, just to say something. "Have you read all those books?" he asked and again felt stupid.

Susan laughed. "Of course not," she said. "I guess they're all books I either think I should read or want to read someday. It's kind of a wish list maybe."

"It's still a lot of books," Ed said. "Even if you've only read some of them."

"You're right about that," Susan said. "Let's move into the other room."

They sat next to a fire pit in an enclosed patio and ate hamburgers, coleslaw and baked beans. As the evening went on, Ed became more comfortable, but he still didn't really know why he was there and wasn't sure how to ask. Fortunately, Susan anticipated the question.

"I'll bet you're wondering why I invited you over tonight?" she said. "It's the first time we've met away from the University."

"No, not really," Ed lied. "But thanks. It's a nice house."

"Even so," Susan said. "I think you're feeling a little awkward so let me tell you." She hesitated and smiled at him. "It's nothing to do with school, your job at the boathouse or that article in the paper. I have no idea why they print that stuff.

"That's a relief," Ed said. "I think it's those hearings in New York. If my old friend Tony hadn't mentioned me...well, I don't know what's going on, to tell the truth. But I guess it's news, at least according to the reporter I talked to down to the paper."

Susan nodded. "Those hearings are getting a lot of national attention. And like I said before, even some universities are requiring everyone to sign loyalty oaths and anyone who refuses to sign can lose his job. Lots of people already have."

"My wife couldn't see why I didn't just sign the damned thing," Ed said. "Who cares, you know? And then if you sign it all goes away, or at least that's what Janey thought."

"And you disagree?"

Ed shrugged. "I don't know who's right but say I had signed it and kept my job and then this thing with Tony comes up. I'd probably have gotten fired then anyway. Once it's out there the thing just keeps gaining power so who knows what's going to happen next?

"Makes you feel vulnerable," Susan said.

It wasn't a word Ed often used but now he thought she was right. "It's like I have this target on my back," he said.

"Anyone would feel that way," Susan said and hugged him to her.

They were quiet for a moment, then Ed said, "Before you were talking about why you asked me over here."

Susan laughed. "I was, wasn't I. Well, the truth is, like you said, I work at a large university with thousands of people around all the time, but I don't know many people my age who aren't married. And my friends who are married don't include me very often. I think they're afraid I'll steal their husbands." She smiled to show she wasn't serious, but it made a lot of sense to Ed. When they were married, Janey would never have invited a single woman into their home.

"Still, I'd figure you had a lot of friends from work," Ed said.

"Not really. Most of them are men and, like I said, married. Not that I'm lonely," Susan said quickly. "I just thought we could get to know each other a little. And maybe you could forget that I'm a dean."

"That could take a while," Ed said.

"It's okay," Susan said. "We're young, we've got time."

"I don't always feel that young," Ed said, and it was true. By the time he was thirty he'd been through war and seen enough death and destruction to last the rest of his life. Divorce hadn't been pleasant either and he still felt guilty for what he had done to his son. He shook his head to drive the thought away. Tonight, he was in this nice house with a pretty lady who seemed to like him. He wasn't sure if they were dating and he hadn't been on a date anyway in ten years or more, but this was close enough.

Susan cleared the table and then led Ed back inside where they sat on the couch and drank coffee. Ed wasn't sure what was supposed to come next, but he decided he'd made enough progress for the evening and left early. Susan walked him out and then kissed him on the cheek. "See you soon," she said.

"I hope so," Ed replied.

"Count on it," she said.

It was mid-winter but milder than usual which allowed people to hope for an early spring. The boathouse was open though not busy as students came and went, some renting equipment for ice fishing or skating on the lake. The hearing with the Union Board had apparently gone well enough. Ed received no further requests for meetings the following week and he allowed himself to think that the uproar over Tony Abruzzi's testimony had died down. He and Susan had seen each other two more times since the dinner at her house. Ed wasn't sure what holding hands in a movie represented these days, but he was enjoying the idea of having someone he looked forward to seeing. He was debating having Susan meet Little Ed, but thought it was probably still not the right time for that.

Then one morning he got a note from Professor Sinclair asking if he could stop by his office that afternoon, that he wanted Ed to meet someone. This was unusual since he and Sinclair didn't really know each other, but Ed walked up the Hill after lunch to see what was on the professor's mind.

When Ed got there, Sinclair was sitting next to a stocky man of medium height who had his hair parted in the middle of a low forehead. "I want you to meet Leroy Gore," Sinclair said with no other explanation.

Gore stood now and shook Ed's hand. "I read about you in the paper," he said. "Damned shame, but not surprising considering what else is going on in the country."

Ed nodded his head. He wasn't sure what he was doing there, a common feeling for him these days. "Leroy's editor of the Sauk Prairie *Star*," Sinclair said, as if this should mean something but Ed had never read the paper or even knew the town had one.

"We used to go down to Sauk City when I was growing up in Dane," he said.

"So, you're one of those kids," Gore said, then smiled to show he was joking.

"The reason I asked you here is that Leroy is the head of the 'Joe Must Go' Club," Sinclair said. "I mentioned it to you before when we talked."

Ed remembered but didn't know what more to say. To his relief, Gore started talking. "I'm no radical," he began. "Actually, I'm a registered Republican and supported McCarthy in '52. But in addition to these goddamned hearings that are wrecking the lives of good people like you, he's been attacking General Zwicker, a great Wisconsin guy from way back. The worst thing is he's screwing the farmers and that's where I come in."

"The farmers?" Ed said. "I didn't hear about that."

"If you come from Dane, you know that most of the folks here are dairy farmers because the ground's too rocky to grow anything. Well, right now there's a shitload of butter and cheese we can't sell so we've been asking the government for help. We wrote McCarthy since he's our Senator, but he can't be bothered to even answer a letter. Too busy chasing communists and kissing up to millionaires. He's forgotten where he comes from, who he's supposed to be representing out there. That's why I started the club."

"Sounds like a good idea," Ed said. No one in his family was a dairy farmer but he'd known plenty growing up..

"We hope so," Gore said. "Thing is we've got to get 400,000 people to sign petitions to force a recall election. That's a lot of signatures and we've only got sixty days to get them."

Ed was about to say he didn't join clubs when Gore stopped him. "I'm not asking you to sign anything."

"The last thing I signed got me in a lot of trouble," Ed said. "And the funny thing is it wasn't even really a petition."

At this, Sinclair jumped in. "Wouldn't you like other people like you to avoid the trouble McCarthy got you in, Ed?"

"Sure, I would, if I could. But most people I know think McCarthy's the right hand of God. My kid put a nickel in a gum machine and the prize he got was a ring with McCarthy's picture on it in an army uniform. What I'm saying is this guy is really popular with most people, like a movie star or something."

"Maybe here in the city," Gore said, but go out in the country and talk to some of the farmers and you might hear different. Anyway, we've got some college kids going around trying to get signatures, but they get discouraged and give up when people call them names."

Ed was getting the man's drift. He'd been so absorbed in what was happening to him that he hadn't really considered what McCarthy's crusade was doing to other people in Wisconsin, like the dairy farmers. "And you figure that wouldn't bother me because I've been taking shit so long that I'm used to it?"

Gore smiled. "I don't know if anyone ever gets used to it, but maybe something like that. You're a veteran, been in a war, and you're not afraid to step up to defend yourself, am I right?"

Ed nodded. "I'm maybe a little too good at that. I stood up for myself so well that I got my ass fired and lost my wife and kid."

Instead of responding to this, Gore just nodded and put what looked like a membership card on the desk in front of Ed. It showed McCarthy in a Cadillac driving through a forest of oil wells, apparently a reference to his friendship with the Texas millionaires who were funding his campaigns and fixing him up with teenaged prostitutes. "We're not asking for money, Ed," Gore said. "If you'd just go around, maybe with some of the kids and try to get people to sign the petition and maybe buy bumper stickers. It would be a big help." Then, as if it was an afterthought, he said, "Do you have children?"

"A son," Ed said. "Eight years old."

"Great," Gore said. "People can never believe communists have kids." He held up his hand. "Joking, I know, you're not a communist."

"Maybe you could tell my neighbors," Ed said. "People I've known for years defaced my home and terrified my kid. They won't talk to me on the phone and pull their curtains closed if I walk by their houses."

"Nice folks," Gore said. "Just like you said about people who love the Senator. Well, how about it. Will you help us?"

Janey wouldn't be thrilled if he took Little Ed around on this kind of thing, but why should he care what she thought anymore? She hadn't really liked anything he did since he came home from Italy, found her in the family way and married her without asking questions. Anyway, no matter what she thought, it would be time together with the boy and Little Ed was the kind of kid who might like going door to door with him. Ed smiled at the thought of Little Ed ringing doorbells with a purpose.

Ed picked up the membership card and Gore gave him a yellow button to go along with it. "Sure," Ed said. "What the hell, if there's really a way to bring that sonofabitch down, I want in."

"Good man," Gore said. "But I should tell you none of the bigwigs in the state are supporting the Club. Neither the Democrats who hate McCarthy nor the Republicans who are afraid of him. We can't even get Bill Evjue at the CapTimes or the Milwaukee Journal editorial board to write us up. They say it's unconstitutional to recall a Senator, but I've got a lawyer who thinks it would be a hell of a court case to try. Anyway, we've got to do something even it's mainly shitkickers like me who are pissed off enough to make the effort. I have to say there are a lot of us in Wisconsin."

"Ed thought of DiPietro and of the kids giving Little Ed trouble at the school and the memory made him hot inside his shirt. You can't choose your enemies and sometimes not even your friends, he thought and offered Gore his hand. "Well, I guess I'm one of them," he said. "Okay, when do I start?"

Before talking to Janey, Ed discussed the canvassing with Susan the next night. "Maybe I'll go with you," she said.

Ed was surprised. "Can you do that? I figured that since you work for the University, they wouldn't let you."

"One of our professors is the person who brought you into it," Susan said. "If it's okay for Sinclair to be involved, why not me?"

He was impressed, but Ed hadn't really meant to invite Susan and in a way, he wished she hadn't inserted herself into things. Not that he thought she was pushy; he knew she was trying to be supportive. But it made it all more complicated. Still, it might be a good thing. He'd been considering whether to introduce her to Little Ed anyway. "I thought I'd bring my son along," he said slowly.

Susan smiled. "And you're not sure if you want him to meet me yet? That's okay. I don't have to come if it's going to make things difficult."

He knew she was trying to let him off the hook, but disappointment was clear on her face. "Maybe I need things to be more difficult," Ed said. "Maybe that's the right thing. I want him to meet you. I just thought I'd wait a while longer."

Susan laughed. "That's usually the woman's line, isn't it? See where this is going before taking the guy home?"

"You're right,'" Ed said, "but to hell with it. That's great if you can."

"I'll take that as a vote of confidence," Susan said.

"Now all I have to do is tell my ex-wife I want to take Little Ed around with me to spread commie propaganda around town."

"I think I'll let you handle that on your own," Susan said. "You can let me know how it turns out."

Twelve

NEW YORK

The Sherry-Netherland was nearly deserted when I got there at ten o'clock the next morning. Not that this was one of my regular stops. The Sherry was the sort of hotel that appealed to upscale goys but not to people like me. It wasn't exactly stuffy but strait-laced, the kind of hotel where old ladies would have High Tea in the afternoon, not that I really knew what High Tea was. I preferred places that were noisier, lively, like Lou Walters' joint or the Astor in Times Square. The Waldorf was high-class but livelier than the Sherry-Netherland, but this was where the general had decided that I should meet his adjutant to find out what his phone call was about.

I looked around the empty lobby and finally found my contact at the bar, a man about my age with small narrow eyes and a widow's peak, nursing a cup of coffee. I could tell he was military because he looked ill at ease in civilian clothes, and someone had forgotten to take the stick out of his ass. I figured he was maybe a lieutenant or even a captain, whatever rank being a gofer for the general got you. I sat down next to him and though we shook hands, neither of us bothered to identify ourselves. We knew who we were and what we were doing there.

"The general called Senator McCarthy," I began. "The Senator's busy so he asked me to come up and meet you."

The other man nodded. "I'm supposed to tell you that Dr. Peress was a card-carrying communist before he signed up," he said.

This was the big news that made me take the night train up from Washington and sleep on my parents' couch. "Irving Peress? We know that already," I said.

"Right," the man said. "But you probably don't know that he was transferred from Texas to Washington State and then back here and got promoted to major along the way without any of his superior officers knowing what was going on or doing anything to stop it."

He was right. This was new and worth knowing. "Okay," I said. "I'll bite. What is going on and why aren't they doing anything about it?"

"That's the question," the man said. "The general thinks someone should have held things up. There were red flags everywhere with this asshole. It's more than just the usual fuckup that goes on all the time."

A general accusing other officers of what amounted to a conspiracy to abet a communist was new, but I couldn't see what would be in it for them. "Why would they do that?" I asked. "Maybe they're just inefficient, not paying attention, I don't know."

The adjutant nodded. "Okay, sure, that's true. But there was also a First Army report that recommended Peress be discharged that no one paid attention to. Instead, the army and General Zwicker just passed him along from one place to another without the paperwork on him ever catching up."

"So why did that happen? Are they all communists too, are you saying there's some kind of conspiracy in the general staff."

"No, not saying that," the adjutant said quickly. "But it's more than just inefficiency and sloppy staff work. The general thinks it shouldn't be that easy for an admitted communist to get promoted from captain to major without someone asking questions about it."

"You're right about that," I said. "But fill me in. Has Peress admitted to still being a communist?"

"Not exactly, but he refused to answer questions on the commissioning exam, took the Fifth instead."

In McCarthy's mind pleading the Fifth was tantamount to admitting you were a communist. Constitutional rights never got in Joe's way. "So that's why the general called the Senator and why we're talking here today?" I asked.

"That's it," the man said. "We think that's enough, more than enough. The man had been disapproved by the First Army after they investigated his background, but instead he got a promotion."

"Sounds bad," I said, looking around the empty room. "And the general couldn't have just told the Senator this when they talked on the phone?"

"Too sensitive for the phone," the man said. "This involves the general's friends, men he was with at the Point, and in the War. We're careful talking about that. You never know who might be listening to a phone call."

"You've got a point there," I said.

"Damned right," the man said. Then without waiting for anything more from me, he picked up his hat and left me sitting in the bar. I stayed for a while alone and drank a coffee. The whole thing had a nice clandestine feeling to it, kind of cloak and dagger, a meeting with an unknown and unidentified man at a bar in New York. It should probably have been in some dive in Hell's Kitchen to complete the illusion. We should have been wearing trench coats and talking out of the sides of our mouths, but this would serve the purpose. It did seem as if there should be an envelope with classified information taped under one of the bar stools, maybe a microdot that would yield evidence under further examination, but in the end the adjutant was gone and there was nothing more for me at the Sherry, so I retraced my steps to Penn Station, thinking this was mostly a wasted trip and wondering what I'd tell McCarthy about it.What I didn't know when I met the adjutant was that the Peress case was significantly different than that involving the researchers we'd interviewed before. Ft. Monmouth was the center for the Signal Corps, employed some of the best scientists in the country, and had projects involving guided missile controls and radar systems. At first glance, Peress was nothing more than a pink dentist who had managed to get promoted by staying ahead of his paperwork. Through moving around the country, he'd managed to keep everyone in the dark about his politics. Big deal, or so it seemed.

But I was wrong. It turned out the general was right to blow the whistle on the Army's handling of the case. McCarthy was sure they were stonewalling when we asked for details on Peress and figured questioning the dentist might allow us to learn more about the holes in Army security. Looking at Peress was important for another reason. The hearings when we questioned him propelled us into our first big conflict with the Army's top brass who it turned out weren't happy being accused of accommodating a communist through the ranks. If I had been as smart as I thought I was, I might have suspected that this could backfire or at least have prepared for the possibility that everything would blow up rather than breezing through the hearings as if we had free rein and there were no consequences for what we did.

Peress was the son of Russian immigrants and like a lot of Jewish kids attended City College in New York. He got out of the War in Europe because he had hernia but by 1952, he'd made a miraculous recovery, got drafted again and passed the physical this time. He got a commission as a dentist and the only thing that looked funny was that he refused to answer routine questions on his application. Instead, Peress claimed "federal constitutional privilege" to any questions about subversive organizations. Mysteriously, no one in the Army seemed to give a shit about this.

Meanwhile, as my friend in the bar said, the First Army back in New York ran a check and found enough evidence of subversive activities to recommend that Peress be thrown out. But nothing happened. The report got lost, who knows? It took nearly four months for the First Army paperwork to catch up with Peress who by then had asked to be sent back to New York and applied for promotion to major. How could this have happened? There are only two reasonable conclusions: either Peress was one slick operator, or the Army was even more incompetent than we had previously thought.

Most of what we knew came through tips and calls, like the one McCarthy received from the general. But when I reported back about my meeting in New York, it was enough to get McCarthy interested in bringing Peress in front of the Committee. At first, Peress refused to appear, but finally General Zwicker ordered him to show up.

Though I would never have admitted it, the pace and pressure of the hearings was beginning to get to me, along with McCarthy's demands and the fear that I'd fall on my face on national television. I was a Jewish prince, raised by a doting mother to believe I could do no wrong, but this was a different world, one that was hostile and actively wanted me to fail. I slept fitfully and during the day the onset of more preparation, interviews, and private meetings was like the hot breath of a blast furnace on my neck. Was it exciting? You could say that I guess. But the idea of my making a mistake in judgement, showing finally my youth, inexperience and McCarthy's mistake in hiring me wore on me as the weeks went by. As much to escape as anything else, I re-traced my steps and found myself back at the Cozy Corner in Virginia a day before I was to go up to New York.

Jerry and I hadn't exchanged phone numbers or even last names, though of course he knew who I was. If he didn't show up at the bar, I'd just return to the city but at nine he sat down next to me and ordered a drink. "I thought you might be here," he said.

"Oh, why?"

"You looked a little frayed at the edges at the hearing," he said

Frayed was an odd word to use and it made me wonder fleetingly about his background, if he was a blue blood gone bad, disgracing the family name. I doubted he'd tell me. I just said, "Damned right. What were you doing there anyway? Your boss send you over to take notes?"

Jerry feigned outrage falling backwards on his stool and then regaining his balance with difficulty. "My boss has his own problems. He didn't even know the hearings were going on. Anyway, I was there to support you. Didn't you feel supported?"

"Not exactly," I said, but I was touched. "It wasn't what I'd call a friendly room."

"Are you always so suspicious?" Jerry asked. "So afraid?"

"I wouldn't say I'm afraid," I said. "But I've got a lot to lose and now it's all on television. Beyond that, I have to spend time handling the rumors about me in the papers."

He nodded sympathetically. "It's tough for all of us now," he said. "But you don't have to worry about me."

He was right. I was too suspicious, on my guard to such an extent that I couldn't even recognize when someone was trying to help. We sat there for another half hour and would have made an odd couple if someone was noticing. Jerry was a large shambling man in a worn tweed jacket in contrast to my suit and careful haircut. Around ten, we went back to his apartment which now seemed a bit safer than it had before. I've never thought of sex as a solution to your problems but it's something on a dark night when you're alone.

The day the hearings were to resume McCarthy was late and when he showed, up he looked even worse than he generally did. His brilliantined hair was askew and his tie was at half-mast. He had the usual cuts from shaving, a knob on his forehead and his eyes were bloodshot. I assumed he'd either been on a hell of a bender or gotten in a bar fight. Of course, both could have been true.

"What happened to you?" I asked, assuming he'd been out all night and forgot about the hearing.

"We had an accident in a cab last night," he said. "I slept in a chair at the hospital next to Jeanie's bed. She's still there. Let's take care of this asshole so I can get back."

Given McCarthy's condition, I almost felt sorry for the witnesses coming before the Committee today. Anyone, claiming the Fifth or clamming up was likely to get McCarthy in all-gangster mode, going down his throat, pounding the table and demanding answers.

Peress showed up mid-morning with his wife and lawyer, wearing civilian clothes rather than his uniform and was obviously uncomfortable, like everyone else who came before our committee. I always figured if you weren't nervous when you faced Joe, you didn't really understand the situation you were in.

Peress was a man of medium height with jowls, a receding hairline and a habit of wiping his rabbit mouth frequently with a pocket square. There was a rumble of anticipation in the press row with some scribes moving around for a better view. When everyone was seated, McCarthy signaled that I should start the questioning.

"Major Peress," I began, "You should know you're allowed to consult with counsel whenever you feel the need. He can talk to you or nudge you and you can do likewise."

Peress nodded and smiled weakly but before I could continue, McCarthy pushed me aside. "Actually, I'll start on this, Roy," he said. Then to the witness, "Did anyone in the Army ever ask you if you were a communist or a communist organizer?"

"I refuse to answer under the protection of the fifth amendment because it might tend to incriminate me," Peress said.

"Okay," McCarthy said. "That's your right, even if I don't like it or respect it. I see you came with your wife today. Is she also a communist?"

"I refuse to answer," Peress said, "for the same reason."

"Well, then," McCarthy said, "have you attempted to recruit soldiers you may have met into the communist party during your term of service?"

"I refuse to answer," Peress said.

McCarthy nodded, as if Peress' refusal to say anything was answer enough. Then in a conversational tone, he turned to me and said, "I find it interesting that known communists find it so easy to circumvent the Army, to fool the most senior officers into giving them promotions rather than busting them down to private or court-martialing them. Don't you find that peculiar, Mr. Cohn?"

I shrugged but didn't say anything because it wasn't really a question, and we were in front of a packed room rather than having a private conversation. But once McCarthy got going there was little point in trying to head him off. The fact was it didn't matter what Peress said, he was fucked anyway you looked at it. Peress could take the Fifth all day for his own reasons and it wouldn't matter to McCarthy. It wasn't that I felt sorry for him but looking back, I can see that the poor *schlemiel* was screwed the moment he walked into the room. He had as much chance in front of Joe as a juicy steak would have with a hungry wolf.

McCarthy's foot was bouncing up and down beneath the table and he started beating his pen on the desk in front of him. In rapid fire, Joe asked Peress about the communist leaning of his brother, sister, parents, and other relatives before wrapping up with this.

"Were you in the Boy Scouts, Dr. Peress?"

Peress nodded.

"All right, then, was your scoutmaster also a communist?"

Peress looked stunned. "I don't know," he said.

"Great," McCarthy said. "Finally, we get a goddamned answer."

The room erupted in laughter and Peress leaned over to talk to his lawyer though it was hard to imagine what they had to talk about. He'd already pleaded the Fifth ten times. What more was there to say? But McCarthy wasn't through.

"So even though you were a member of the Communist Youth League and an organizer in the Party and even though you made no pretense about this, didn't hide it, probably were even proud of it and refused to answer basic questions about your background on your

Army commission papers, not one of your commanding officers ever got in your way. Is that right, Mr. Peress?"

"I prefer Dr. Peress," the witness said.

McCarthy smiled at this, and I could see what was coming next. "Oh, is that so? And at which university did you get your medical degree?"

"I'm a dentist," Peress said. "Not a medical doctor."

McCarthy had the poor *schmuck* now. No dentist's chair in the world could be as uncomfortable as the place Peress was in. Joe hesitated for a moment then moved in for the kill. "And you think jawbreakers are doctors? I disagree."

"I think dentists are doctors," Peress said stubbornly, proud of his position and refusing to accept McCarthy's characterization of him, but Joe just smirked.

It was kind of pathetic that Peress had to insist on his title to hold on to what dignity he had left in the face of McCarthy's barrage but it wasn't going to help. He was like a dog caught in a trap and he didn't even seem to know it. But this line of questioning didn't make sense to me and didn't come up in our pre-hearing planning. Who cared about Peress' scoutmaster or what he liked to call himself?

But the Senator was a freelancer and never consulted a script so there was no telling what would happen when he was off on a tangent. I knew he was trying to get under Peress' skin, and he was succeeding even if some of the questions had nothing to do with communism. The witness was sweating noticeably, and his face was a deep red. He ran his fingers underneath his shirt collar as if it had shrunk during the hearing and took deep breaths trying to regain his composure. "Dentists are absolutely doctors," he repeated stubbornly now. "I think everybody would agree with that." He looked over at McCarthy. "Most everybody anyway," he added.

McCarthy smiled, pleased that he had gotten to the witness. "Okay, then answer the question, Doctor," McCarthy said.

"I refuse to answer for the same reason I stated before," Peress replied in a strained voice. "Isn't this obvious by now?"

McCarthy never exactly denied a witness his constitutional rights, but he treated those who claimed them with disdain, and I didn't really disagree. If you were or had been a communist, and this was common knowledge, as it was in Peress' case, why not admit it? All this talk about thousands of people having their lives ruined by our Committee and HUAC might be true, but that wasn't the point. Had those people done nothing to make that happen? You make choices in life and then live with them, God knows I have. Wechsler at least had the balls to admit his communist past and name names of others, even if this got him into trouble with the liberals. I hate to grant that bastard credit for anything but give him that. He answered the questions.

In this case, however, McCarthy didn't just ask questions, he called Peress a communist and challenged him to deny it. Then Joe followed up by saying, "I'm kind of curious as to how communists can get their status changed so easily in the army. The average guy would be sent to Timbuktu just for asking, but you somehow got rewarded, transferred and promoted as well. How does that happen? You said your wife and daughter were ill and that's why you needed a transfer. If it doesn't violate your constitutional rights, tell me what was wrong with them?"

"That's personal," Peress said.

"I don't really care what it is," McCarthy said. "I'm not just asking, I'm going to order you to answer that, mister."

Peress leaned over to talk to his lawyer for a moment. Then he said, "They were undergoing psychiatric treatment."

"In other words, there was no physical ailment," McCarthy said. It was a snide thing to say but in a perverse way it made me admire McCarthy. There was simply no place he considered off-bounds, no place he wouldn't go.

Peress, understandably, didn't share this feeling. "I don't think you can distinguish between mental and physical illness," he said stiffly.

"Even though you admit you're not a medical doctor, you think you can make that judgement," McCarthy said.

"Yes, sir," Peress said, his voice strained.

"Okay," McCarthy said. "Now I understand you're resigning from the Army. Is that correct? Are you receiving an honorable discharge?"

"I don't know exactly," Peress said.

"You don't know if the fact that you're a communist and organizing others in support of communism on Army bases might affect your chances of receiving an honorable discharge. Is that correct? Do I have that right?"

"There was no discussion of that," Peress said.

McCarthy looked at Peress with scorn. "No discussion? Sonofabitch! What do you think of that?" Then he turned to me. "I'm through with this guy, Roy."

I didn't make much more progress with Peress than Joe had but it was important to get some things on the record, so I asked, "You are a graduate of the leadership training course of the Inwood Victory Club of the Communist Party, are you not?"

"I decline to answer under the fifth amendment," Peress said.

"Okay," I said. "Then can you tell us if you attended courses in leadership at the Inwood Communist Club?"

Calling it a club made it sound social, as if they had an annual picnic with games, one-legged races, a raffle maybe, but it didn't matter because Peress refused again to answer.

I pressed on. "Were you involved in recruitment for the Communist Party and specifically, when you went down to Ft. Kilmer, did you attempt to recruit any of the Army personnel there into the Communist Party?"

After a hurried conversation with his lawyer, Peress refused to answer, as he did our other questions. He refused to answer questions about the cell we'd heard he organized on the base. He refused to answer how much of his Army salary he might have donated to the Party. The more he refused to answer, the guiltier he sounded. We didn't have proof of any of these things but Peress' refusal to answer any question we set to him gave the impression of guilt. Over the course of the hearing, the witness grew increasingly uncomfortable as he went again and again to the pocket square to wipe his forehead and his mouth. Just before noon, I decided there was no point in keeping Peress further. I'd covered everything I could think of, and Joe was already on his way back to the hospital.

We'd poked the bear and there was an immediate response. Peress' testimony was an obvious embarrassment for the Army. Two days later he met with General Zwicker, his commander at Ft. Kilmer, and requested an immediate resignation along with an honorable discharge. This was granted before a letter from McCarthy demanding Peress be given a courts-martial and dishonorable discharge could reach Zwicker.

When he heard this McCarthy pounded his desk and yelled, "We proved he's a communist and now they're giving him an honorable discharge anyway. The sonofabitch should be in prison."

McCarthy was predictably infuriated by this and before we could talk, he wrote Robert Stevens, the Secretary of the Army, not naming Zwicker but calling for an investigation to reveal which Army officer had allowed a communist to be promoted through the system. The letter got kicked up the chain of command until finally it landed on Eisenhower's desk.

It was no secret that Ike didn't like Joe, even disdained him, but he never came right out and said anything. The story was that he wouldn't "get down into the sewer" and fight with McCarthy but we thought he was afraid to do so. The new Gallup Poll had McCarthy's popularity climbing with more than 50% approving of the work we were doing. When the same poll asked what the President could do better, a majority said, "Fight communism."

No surprise here. The fact is the polls win out in America. Has it ever been different? Of course not. Politicians aren't going to support anyone who's down in the polls, whether he's a good guy or not. And if you're riding high in the polls you can be the most unscrupulous bastard in the world and money and support will find you quickly.

Eisenhower knew this. Like him or not, McCarthy was wildly popular around the country, almost a folk hero in some places. He had a committee chairmanship and a large budget. No one ever said Ike was brilliant, but you didn't have to be a genius to see that getting into it with Joe right then would be a losing battle. Instead, Eisenhower sent some staff members and finally Dick Nixon to meet with McCarthy and ask him to back off on his investigation of the Army. McCarthy refused and said if the Army wasn't harboring traitors, they would have nothing to worry about.

After his meeting with Nixon, I met with Joe in his office. "They're sweating, Roy," he said, a crafty smile on his face. "The polls and our mail have them nervous."

Of course, I was still being criticized in the press for making calls about Dave Schine. Remember Dave? The Democrats did. Not that my efforts had done much good. Dave was out in New Jersey and staffers for the Democrats were threatening to put together a chronographic list of all the calls and other contacts I'd had with the Army going back to the previous summer. McCarthy wasn't happy about this but there was no way I could call back what I'd done, even if I'd already started to regret it. And so, the hearings reconvened with General Zwicker scheduled to be in the hot seat.

Joe and the general swapped stories about Madison and football at lunch before the hearing, which seemed to lull the general into false comfort. Once we were seated in the hearing room, however, things got serious quickly. Zwicker seemed hostile and defensive, refusing to respond to the simplest questions we put to him. Predictably, this pushed Joe to the boiling point.

"Tell me this, General," McCarthy said, "How did Peress get his honorable discharge so quickly after refusing to give testimony before our committee."

This put Zwicker off his game for some reason even if Peress' appearance was part of the public record. He cleared his throat and shifted in his chair before saying he was unaware Peress refused to answer questions when he was before the Committee.

"Really?" McCarthy said. "That's strange because I know you've seen all the press reports about this."

This was true and we all knew it. Zwicker just didn't want to accept responsibility for what he'd done. At this point the general adjusted course quickly. "Change that," he said. "Actually, I was aware that Peress had pleaded the Fifth. But I didn't know it was in reference to any communist activities."

Improbably, at this point McCarthy shook his head and started laughing. When he had recovered, he said, "That's hilarious, General. What else in the world would we have been asking him about? Can you tell me that?"

Zwicker wasn't used to being mocked. When he replied, he was tight-lipped. "Yes, yes, okay, I see that," Zwicker said. He stopped in mid-sentence to whisper to his lawyer sitting next to him. Then he said, "All right, I can say I did know which questions Peress refused to answer."

Zwicker obviously knew everything Peress told the Committee, and we knew he knew so why bother stonewalling? Joe was right to laugh at the absurdity of the whole thing. At this point, in desperation

Zwicker pulled out the so-called Truman Doctrine saying personal questions of federal employees should be kept in total confidence.

This was ridiculous since we weren't talking about civil servants and McCarthy was becoming more irritated all the time, trying and ultimately failing to hold his temper. "General," he said at last. "Why don't we at least try to be truthful and forthcoming.

Zwicker was clearly trying to maintain his dignity in the face of McCarthy's assault but it wasn't easy. "I don't like to have anyone impugn my honesty," Zwicker said now. "Which you just about did just now."

But McCarthy had had it. "Either your honesty or your intelligence," he said. "I can't help impugning one or the other when you sit here and tell us that after a major under your command was known to have come before a Senate committee, the transcripts of that testimony I know you've read, to have you come here and tell us that you didn't know Major Peress had refused to answer questions about his communist activities when it was all on the record. And then back up and say well, maybe you did, after you talk to your lawyer, but still you don't seem sure. So, when you say you weren't aware of this or that I'm forced to question your honesty or your intelligence. I want to be frank with you about that."

Zwicker was white with anger but bit his lip and said, "I have no control over your assumptions, Senator. No one does. That's well known."

They sat looking at each other silently for a few moments while everyone else in the room waited for McCarthy to explode, but Joe kept his composure for once. Finally, he asked whether the commanding officer of a communist who'd received an honorable discharge should be held responsible, obviously referring to Zwicker.

"Well, that's pretty hypothetical," Zwicker said.

"No, General," McCarthy said. "That's very real."

Zwicker danced around the question, had the court reporter repeat the question several times and at last refused to answer. Then McCarthy said, "Okay, here's a simple one. How do you feel about getting rid of communists in the Army."

"I'm all for it," Zwicker said.

"Okay," McCarthy said. Then he asked again that Zwicker answer the hypothetical question about where responsibility lay and said,

"We're going to be here all day until you answer that question, General."

"Do you mean, how do I feel about communism?"

"I mean the question I posed before," McCarthy said. "Even a five-year-old child could figure that out."

At this point McCarthy had questioned Zwicker's intelligence and honesty, so comparing him to a five-year-old had the effect of making him withdraw further into what remained of his dignity. "I really can't answer that," he said. "I don't actually know what you're asking."

"Is that right," McCarthy said. "We've already had the court reporter read the question five times but still you don't understand. General, I think you're a disgrace to the uniform. Anyone who says I'll protect a communist who gets promoted to major and is given an honorable discharge is not fit to wear the uniform or to rise to the exalted rank of general as you have. This is an embarrassment to the service and an awful thing to give to the public, but I will because they deserve to know who's serving in the highest rank of the armed services. You will be back here, General."

My stomach dropped and I sank my head on the desk hoping when I re-emerged the whole scene would have disappeared. He may have been provoked but it was the stupidest thing McCarthy could have done and there was no way to call it back, to unsay what had been said. There's no question McCarthy shouldn't have said this and maybe I should have tried to control him, but I'd been working with him long enough to know that was virtually impossible. He was like a two-ton truck running downhill that had lost its brakes. What's more, while the way he said this was neither elegant nor appropriate, I thought he was right to be frustrated by Zwicker's refusal to respond to questions.

Even if McCarthy was right, he caused us irreparable harm that day by publicly insulting a general from his home state in a public hearing. I knew then with the certainty of death that this would be a turning point, one we'd be held accountable for in the future. No matter what we thought, our investigation would suffer for what Joe had done, as in fact it did.

Being right wasn't much comfort but the principle McCarthy was insisting on was important. Wasn't this the same kind of laxity allowed David Greenglass, Ethel Rosenberg's brother, to be sent to Los Alamos where he could learn atom bomb secrets and then pass them on to Julius Rosenberg. It was the same looseness of discipline that allowed Julius Sobell and even Tony Abruzzi to be working at our leading center for radar research without anyone raising a red flag.

Did either McCarthy or I think Peress' case was as important as Greenglass and Rosenberg? Of course not, but it was the Army security procedures in both cases that we were trying to focus on. It's a fact that sometimes personal style and behavior get in the way of making your point. God knows it's been true for me. But even as I felt misgivings about how all this had developed, I understood what McCarthy was doing, and I was proud to be by his side. McCarthy was history and history is never neat and tidy.

Thirteen

MADISON

To Ed's surprise, Janey made no objection to his taking Little Ed around with him to canvas for McCarthy's recall. Though it was clear she had no enthusiasm for his new affiliation, she didn't want to deny Ed time with his son and Little Ed needed his father. Ed thanked her as they were leaving and Janey just said, "Be careful. No one likes the communists."

Ed started to say once again that he wasn't a communist but caught himself and just nodded his assent. Since he'd never done anything like this before, Ed figured the smart thing would be to start with an area that was familiar, so he and Susan and Little Ed started walking together around his old neighborhood. The streets were lined with tall dark trees covering the sidewalks in shade and had been named after Presidents: Adams, Madison, Jefferson, Monroe, Grant, Lincoln. Ed wasn't big on patriotism, but he wondered how the Founding Fathers would feel about McCarthy's crusade. He had decided to wear his service cap to show he was a veteran while Susan was in jeans and a Wisconsin tee shirt. Little Ed had a big yellow Joe Must Go button pinned to his baseball cap.

No one was home at the first house and at the second when Ed tried to hand the guy a brochure the man yelled, "Commie bastards, you don't deserve to wear that cap."

"Sure, I do," Ed said quickly. "Where did you serve, brother?" This stopped the guy.

"The Pacific, like McCarthy. I was in Guadalcanal, and I damned near didn't make it back," the man said.

"Thanks for your service then," Ed said. "I was in France and then Italy. I know what you went through. But I'll tell you this. McCarthy never got near combat, and he doesn't care about you, about me."

"He's against the communists," the man said. "Like I am. You should know better if you were in the War." Then he slammed the door in their faces.

"Why was that man so mad, Daddy?" Little Ed asked. "We're nice people."

Ed put his arm around his son's small shoulders. "Of course we are," he said. "He didn't really mean it."

But Little Ed wasn't convinced and seemed to shrink back as they made their way to the next group of houses.

"Not as bad as it could have been," Susan said to comfort Little Ed. And then to Ed, "That was quick thinking on your part. Maybe you're more skilled at this than you imagined."

"I thought I had him," Ed said, shaking his head. "I didn't think another vet would fall for that 'Tailgunner Joe' bullshit."

"Bad word, Daddy," Little Ed said. He had started holding Susan's hand when they crossed the street and hadn't let it go.

"You're right," Ed said. "Sorry."

They walked up Adams to Grant and then down to the park and actually got five signatures on the petition along the way. One woman invited them in for hot chocolate and cookies. There was a picture of McCarthy in uniform on the wall, along with a panoply of family pictures and one of Jesus with a bleeding heart in a gold frame. The woman had been hesitant at first, but Little Ed's magic worked with her.

"Honestly," the woman said, "you seem like awfully nice folks, but I can't sign this. My husband would kill me."

"Don't tell him," Susan said. "We won't."

"Really?" the woman said and nodded her head, thinking about it. "Well, then, okay. I will." She signed in a slanting scrawl and gave them the names of a few friends in the neighborhood.

"People will disappoint you," Ed said afterwards. "But sometimes they surprise you too. I never would have expected you to tell that woman to go around her husband."

"Desperate times bring desperate measures, "Susan said, laughing. "It needed to be done. And it worked."

"Maybe that's a good reason then," Ed said. "Reason enough for me, anyway."

They were out for two more hours and ended up with ten signatures. "Pretty good," Susan said, "especially for the first time out."

"Right," Ed said. "Too bad we need 400,000."

After dropping Little Ed off, they stopped for coffee at a café on Monroe Street. "He's a sweet boy," Susan began.

"I saw you two holding hands," Ed said. "That's not something he'd do with just anyone."

"I got the feeling he was being polite," Susan said. "That you or his mother told him to do that when you're crossing the street. Still, he didn't let go when we got to the corner. I guess that's a positive sign."

"I never thought of him being especially polite," Ed said. "He never holds my hand I'll tell you that. I think you're a success."

"Let's wait and see," Susan said.

Wait and see for what, Ed thought, and not for the first time, he wondered what Susan saw in him. He didn't know how to broach this question so instead, he said, "Have you ever thought about having kids?"

Susan sighed. "I guess everyone does, or at least everyone does where I come from. If my husband had lived, sure, but now it's probably too late for me. How about you? Did you want more than one when you got married?"

"It wasn't really a decision," Ed said. "I was overseas, and Janey wrote to say she was pregnant and it was mine. I never questioned her about it since we didn't have much time together before I left, but we got married anyway. Having another was something we were talking about when all this came up, mainly Janey's idea. She came from a big family, but I was an only child."

"Isn't that unusual on a farm?" Susan asked.

Ed nodded. "More hands to help, but it didn't work out for my parents, I guess."

"But even if it wasn't planned, you're happy now, aren't you? I mean, you love Little Ed, and he loves you, it's obvious."

There was that business about love again. It wasn't something Ed had thought much about before, but it seemed important to Susan.

"Sure," he said with more certainty than he felt. "I mean, you love your kid. But it's different. Parents and kids. Not that I ever meant for it to happen, but you can divorce your wife, or she can divorce you. It's hard but you're adults so you make the best of it and go on. You never divorce your kids, and you wouldn't want to."

Susan reached over and stroked his hand. "You make it all sound pretty grim," she said. "I'm not trying to cause trouble, but did you ever feel Janey forced you to marry her?"

Ed shook his head. "I wasn't about to question her about it, whether she'd been with other guys besides me. I guess it's possible but it's a long time ago now."

"You're such a good guy," Susan said.

"Not really," Ed said. "Getting married was something I was fine doing and I always liked Janey. It doesn't look like such a smart idea now. I wouldn't mind having more kids, though," Ed said, then regretted what it might suggest or what Susan might think it suggested about them.

But she just nodded, leaving the subject lying between them on the table. "Well, he's a nice boy," she said. "I'm glad I got a chance to meet him. That you were ready to introduce him to me."

"It didn't do him any harm," Ed said. "Of course, now he's going to tell his mother."

"And tell her what, that you've got a girlfriend," Susan said, smiling.

"Something along those lines. And that's okay with me," he added quickly.

"That's good to hear," Susan said. They sat silently for a few more minutes, then she got up from the table. "I've got to be getting back to work," she said.

It seemed abrupt as if he'd said something wrong and Ed wondered if he should apologize but maybe it was true and not an excuse. He hadn't really said he'd like to have more kids with her or even with some other person. It was more an abstract wish but unlike others, like getting taller or smarter, something that was attainable. And for all he knew it could happen with Susan in time. He didn't really think she was too old and for reasons he didn't fully understand, he doubted she thought so either.

The Unitarian Church stood on a hill on the West Side just past the University and the Forest Products lab. It had a dramatic green copper roof and slanting angles that made it look like a giant prehistoric bird had landed on the bluff overlooking University Avenue. The church was designed by Frank Lloyd Wright and had already become a tourist attraction. Ed knew this because he had read about it in the paper and seen the postcards, but he'd never been to the church before or known any Unitarians. He had the vague idea that Unitarians were like Jews, though he had no idea why he thought so.

He'd seen Wright once in Cross Plains when he was home visiting. He remembered because the old man was wearing a gray Astrakhan coat, black-brimmed hat and a long cape. The great man arrived in some huge European car and stopped in front of a restaurant in town. Ed hadn't known why Wright was there or who the architect was, but it was clear he was *someone*. Later a friend told him Wright's studio and school were nearby which explained him being in town that afternoon, but whatever the reason it made an impression on Ed.

Ed parked in the lot and noticed that parts of the church seemed unfinished, and groups of men and boys were carrying pieces of stone from one place to another. He thought of offering to help but that wasn't why he was there, so he walked up the stairs and went inside. A sign on an easel in the front read "Joe Must Go" and then "Today."

Leroy Gore was just inside the door and when he saw Ed, he came forward enthusiastically. "Glad you could make it," he said. "There are some people here I want you to meet."

Ed followed Gore into the church where there were perhaps thirty people standing in a small enclosure drinking coffee. Ed noticed the women were mostly wearing pants and either had their hair down or bunched in ponytails. Except for a dab of lipstick, none of them wore makeup and didn't resemble Janey or her friends. They looked, he thought, like college girls but older, grayer. On the walls were engraved quotations from Thoreau and Emerson, writers Ed remembered vaguely from school.

One read: "Sermons in stone, books in the running brooks, and good in everything." Ed thought it was a nice sentiment, though it was unlike anything he'd seen in churches he'd attended as a child. Where was the looming statuary, the bleeding hearts of Jesus, candles, incense? It was a different kind of church, that was sure.

Gore took Ed by the arm and introduced him to a man named Charlie Sprague. "Charlie is a vet, like you," Gore said, then walked away as if this was reason enough for the two men to want to know each other.

Sprague was a few inches shorter than Ed but had a high gleaming forehead and a disarming smile that made him feel welcome immediately. "Read about you in the paper," Sprague said.

"Like everyone else, I guess," Ed said. "Bullshit, I have to say." When Sprague didn't reply, he added, "Where did you serve?"

"Army Air Force," Sprague said. "In the Pacific, mostly, and over the hump flying transport into China."

"A pilot, like McCarthy?"

Sprague laughed. "Not exactly. We were hard up but not that hard up."

Ed was about to respond when Gore tapped the table with his pen, and everyone turned expectantly toward him. "I want to thank you all for coming out today," he said. "Especially the Republicans." There was polite laughter at this, and Ed guessed it was because there weren't any Republicans in the room.

"Like you all know," Gore went on, "we're trying to get people to sign our petition to recall McCarthy." Here there was scattered applause and Ed joined in. Then Gore continued. "We've done well so far, especially out in the country where I live but we need more people like Ed back there, to go out and canvas in their neighborhoods."

Several people looked to see who Gore was referring to and Ed waved his hand, though he wished Gore hadn't singled him out. He felt self-conscious enough already in this crowd. The men had a kind of rich-guy casualness in their corduroys and jeans and the women were unlike any women he knew, except Susan. Everyone seemed friendly enough in a curious way, as if he was some rare species to be examined and perhaps admired from a distance. He wished he had ornamental feathers or maybe a headdress, something to indicate he was worth consideration but there was nothing. He waved again and a few women wiggled their fingers in a response.

"What we need," Gore continued, "is for those of you who have the time to sign the petition and give a few bucks if you can. We've got less than two months to get this done so any help at all is a lot of help."

A man in the back raised his hand and when Gore recognized him asked, "How many signatures do you need, exactly?"

"A little more than 400,000," Gore replied and smiled.

"That sounds like a lot," the man said.

Gore nodded. "It is a lot, but it's the law. A successful recall petition is based on the number of votes in Wisconsin during the last Presidential election. There were 1,600,000 in 1952 so we need 25% of that."

Someone let out a slow whistle and others shook their heads, but Gore charged on undiscouraged. "Just because it's a lot of signatures doesn't mean we shouldn't do the best we can. What we're trying to do is important. And you know what, it ought to be hard to recall a U.S. Senator. It's no surprise that it is. Are you with me?"

There was more vigorous applause at this and some movement toward the table with sign-up sheets but not as much enthusiasm as Ed might have expected in a place where McCarthy supporters wouldn't exactly be welcome. He didn't know what it would take to succeed or if it was even possible. Maybe Gore was right that there was more support among the farmers who were directly affected by the butter surplus but in a place as liberal as Madison it seemed surprising.

Ed had been out twice more with Little Ed and Susan, and they'd managed to get a couple of hundred signatures, but he could see it was going to be an uphill battle, at best. The last time, when he'd dropped Little Ed at his mother's, Janey said, "I hear you've got a girlfriend."

"I wouldn't say that exactly," Ed replied.

"That's what Little Ed told me," Janey said. "He said she was nice."

"He's right about that," Ed said.

"Then I'm glad," Janey said. "Glad for you."

This surprised Ed. He had expected her to be angry, to make some sarcastic remark. "It's not really anything much," Ed said. "Not yet. But thanks."

"Well, whatever it is," Janey said. "I'm still glad."

Oddly enough, Janey's generous reaction made Ed feel guilty. He didn't know why he should feel this way but when Susan offered to come with him to the church he'd demurred and again thought he might have hurt her feelings.

Now, Gore came over and stood to his side. "A decent turnout but maybe not the most enthusiastic crowd you could get," Gore said. "Still, they're Unitarians. Good people but I think it's against their religion to get too excited about anything."

Ed nodded. He knew nothing about Unitarians and what they might or might not do. This wasn't like any church he'd ever seen, more like a YMCA maybe or a community center but who was he to question it, and he wanted to seem hopeful. "Maybe they'll come around in time," he said.

"That's the trouble," Gore said. "We don't have much time. But you've done great work, Ed. I appreciate it. What we need is another fifty people like you who are willing to walk around their neighborhoods and bother their friends and neighbors."

"I don't mind," Ed replied. "I don't have that many friends and like you said, I've been through war so someone calling me names isn't going to make much difference. We met some nice people out there and my son got a kick out of it. He thinks it's funny when people shake their fists and yell at us."

Gore laughed at this. "I guess the apple don't fall far from the tree then."

"I guess not," Ed said.

"Well, keep up the good work," Gore said. "One thing I wanted to mention is all this is starting to get to McCarthy. One of the columnists in Washington wrote us up in the paper out there and I hear McCarthy had a fit. There's talk he might even send his assistant out here to meet with voters and try to calm things down. Jewish fellow named Cohn, his top assistant, works with him on his special committee. Supposed to be a tough guy but I'll bet he's never run into anything like these dairy farmers."

"Probably not," Ed said, but he recognized the name. According to the *Herald,* Cohn was the lawyer who'd questioned Tony Abruzzi when Tony called out Ed and his other army buddies. "When's this fellow supposed to be coming out?

Gore shrugged. "There's no way to know if he will or he won't. They don't clear their travel schedules with me, that's for sure. But one thing I know is that if Cohn does come, we'll be ready for him. It could backfire and be exactly what we need to get folks excited enough to fight back. Wisconsin people don't like smart New York lawyers telling them what to do, how to think."

That sounded right to Ed, but he hoped he'd get a chance to talk to Cohn. He'd met a couple of Jewish guys in the Army, and they seemed okay but kept to themselves. They wore these little hats on their holidays and weren't allowed to do anything then. Since he wasn't religious himself, Ed always felt awkward among the devout, intimidated maybe, and envied them a little. But those guys weren't Cohn or what he knew about Cohn. He didn't know what he'd do if he met the man, or if he'd do anything. He just wanted the chance to see the guy who'd gotten to Tony and through that fucked up his life some more. "I appreciate your letting me know," he said.

"No problem," Gore said. "And thanks again for all you're doing."

Fourteen

NEW YORK

Like a million other people, I felt I knew Edward R. Murrow. I'd listened with rapt interest to Murrow's broadcasts night after night, sprawled in front of the big Victrola in my parents' living room following the progress of the War in Europe. I was too young to fight, but throughout my teens Murrow brought the War home to us, making the explosions of the Blitz seem a living thing in our homes safely across the ocean from England. Morrow's terse announcement, "This is London" became a catch phrase that would resonate for many of us throughout our lives, along with his sign-off, "Good Night and Good Luck," which became vague and almost meaningless once the War was over but nevertheless had the same chilling effect on me whenever I heard it many years later.

Murrow was a living presence, as real as my mother and father, aunts and uncles, down to his tattered mackinaw and slouch hat, his rasping cigarette voice, a constant in my ear as I grew up and later when I'd finished law school and started making my way around New York. I wouldn't say he was a hero to me, but I admired him. Murrow had returned from London by this time and gone to work at CBS, even if he never dominated television as she had radio. Occasionally I'd see him at 21 in his bespoke suits and English shoes, cigarette held jauntily in his lips, talking and gesturing with his hands as he drank martinis.

Beyond what was generally known about Murrow, the thing that made him more real and identifiable to me was that I knew despite his patina of class, he was no Ivy Leaguer but rather an ordinary guy who'd grown up in West Virginia and went to a cow college in Washington. He may have been Churchill's intimate friend, but he was no Oxbridge gentleman. Regardless of his appearance, he wasn't one of them, which meant he was really one of us. I chose to believe this was privileged information which bound us together, if only in my mind.

I bring all this up to explain the almost personal sense of betrayal I felt when after making the transition from radio to television, Murrow decided that spring to launch an attack on my boss. And this on CBS, which was often referred to as the "Tiffany network" because it vowed to stay above the fray of partisan politics. Previously, they had taken pains not to take sides in what was shaping up as the Army-McCarthy battle. Now Murrow had decided to change all that and, at least from my perspective, there was no need to do this. We had plenty of enemies in the press already. Drew Pearson was after us and Wechsler and his attack dogs at the *Post* never lost a chance to take aim at Joe. Herbert Block, the star cartoonist of the Washington *Post* had been publishing his black and white shots at Joe for years by this time.

What I'm saying is Murrow was late for the game, his broadcasts what in football parlance would be called piling on. And even if he was the most famous person to go after McCarthy so far, it wasn't his fight until he decided to make it so. This irritated the liberals who'd been in there slinging mud from the beginning. Where had Murrow been, some columnists asked, and though we were on opposite sides, I had to agree with them.

Ironically, we might have provoked Murrow. One of our staff leaked that Murrow had once been on a Soviet payroll. This was technically true, but it was a stupid mistake and was too much for Murrow. The evidence, such as it was referred only to a study session Murrow had been part of twenty years before prior to his becoming a broadcaster. It was the kind of red herring that thrilled people trying to poke holes in a legend, but it was a cheap shot. No one had asked me about this, but now it was out there and made Murrow angry enough to move on to McCarthy where he had been quiet before.

The broadcast itself was nothing special, consisting entirely of old clips of McCarthy, some of which were only damning because Joe lost his temper or seemed to belittle the president. Nothing new to be excited about. What's more, it was bush league for Murrow to include shots of Joe spitting, giggling and pounding the table during one of the sessions. It could have been worse and the fact that Murrow ran with this made me disappointed in him. You could build this kind of case on anyone in public life if you wanted to. To me, the program was embarrassing but little else.

There were some people, of course, who would say Murrow brought McCarthy down, but this was ridiculous. The only one who could do that was Joe and he was doing a pretty good job of it when he decided to attack the army's top generals publicly. Murrow's smear was an afterthought, if anything, but it served as a kind of canary in a coal mine, signaling to everyone on the left that it was safe to join in now that CBS and Murrow were on the job. What's more with the CBS broadcast, criticisms that were familiar to everyone in Washington now made their way into the public and this hurt us.

Murrow's program appealed to the American ideal of black and white thought, presenting a world without nuance. You're right or wrong, in or out, with me or against me, for or against everything that is right and good in the world. Given those choices, who would you pick? McCarthy seemed created especially for the role of bad guy with his blue jowls, spreading gut and greasy hair.

To simple-mindedly brand McCarthy as a red-baiting ignoramus with bad teeth as they had Whitaker Chambers a few years before when he testified against Alger Hiss was an easy call and Murrow had to know it when he came out against McCarthy. To no one's surprise the mail to CBS after the broadcast was overwhelmingly in Murrow's favor.

Murrow did make the gesture of offering McCarthy equal time to answer in a second telecast. Big deal, a chance for Joe to embarrass himself with nothing to gain from it. I counseled him to pass it up, as did a few others like Bill Buckley and Fulton Lewis. "What do you have to gain?" I argued. "The people who are against you aren't going to be persuaded by anything you say and the people who are backing you won't agree any more than they already do."

"I can't let that bastard get away with it," McCarthy said stubbornly. "That smug sonofabitch can't just go ahead and say that shit about me."

"He already did, Joe," I said. "You're not going to make him unsay it."

"But I might make it worse you're saying?"

"Yes," I said. "You could do that."

Naturally, McCarthy did the rebuttal show anyway, lashing out at Murrow and waving his arms around in a way that made him look more crazy than effective. Television was a cool medium and out of the hearing room, Joe's voice was shrill and papery without its menacing quality. All of that being, so, I thought he did all right but despite this and all arguments to the contrary Murrow somehow won this round too, or at least most of the people who commented on it seemed to think so.

The viewer mail favored Murrow again and some reporter made the astute observation that the letters supporting Murrow were typed and well written while those in McCarthy's favor were scrawls on note paper heavy on vulgarities, which served to reinforce the stereotypical view of McCarthy's supporters as being sub-human. There were a few voices in our favor that made the point that Murrow had cherry-picked examples to make Joe look especially bad, but in the end, there was no question who won and lost. McCarthy looked like he'd eaten some bad fish when he came into the office the next, day his face ashen, even if he was mostly just pissed off at himself.

"You were right," he said. "I should have kept my mouth shut, but I've never been worth a damn at that."

"Not many people are when they're being attacked," I said. "But what's done is done. The important thing is what's next?"

"For us, you mean?"

"Who else? Us and the Committee."

My question might seem odd since I was Committee counsel and would logically know our agenda but while others may have thought McCarthy sly and conniving, the fact is he flew by the seat of his pants, if he flew at all. There was no real plan of action and little strategic planning. I seldom had any sense of where we were going, and I doubt Joe did either. You could say he was intuitive, but the truth was the whole process was a kind of involved dance as I said before, and McCarthy was the only one who knew the steps.

McCarthy smiled now, his eyes dark slits in his puffy face. "I'll tell you what's next. We nail the Army's ass to the wall. That's what's next."

It turned out, however, that some Committee members had other things on their minds. This didn't come completely out of the blue. Symington, the leading Democrat, had already warned me privately that I should watch out. He pulled me aside after one of our meetings and said, "I don't know why I'm telling you this since you can take care of yourself but watch your ass. There's some shit coming down. It would be too bad if you got caught in the crossfire."

I didn't really know Symington or why he'd concern himself with me. He was the kind of tall, elegant aristocrat that I wouldn't have normally gravitated toward, so I was surprised when he reached out. I had run into him once or twice at parties but that was all. Before I could figure out what crossfire I should avoid, however, the other members of the Committee called for a meeting with Joe in which they demanded he fire me, or they would release a report detailing our efforts to pressure the Army on Schine's behalf.

"What did you say?" I asked the Senator when he came back to the office and told me about the meeting.

"What do you think I said," Joe replied. "I told them to go straight to hell, that it was blackmail. If I let you go it means the communists win."

I appreciated the support, but I wasn't surprised. Beyond Joe's loyalty to me, he wasn't about to let himself be pushed into something even if in this case it might have done him some good politically. We never really talked about what you might call our relationship, because we didn't have one. I think we liked each other and in my own way, I admired him. Beyond that, I was useful to Joe in his work. Maybe his attitude had to do with his Wisconsin values, that you didn't cave to pressure and turn your back on your team. Since I've never visited Dairyland, I have no idea. But as passionately as some senators and others wanted me off the Committee, McCarthy wanted me to stay on, so I stayed.

Looking back, I'm not sure Joe was right in saying the Army's report on me was blackmail. No doubt they were trying to sensationalize my relationship with Dave and turn us out to be homos making out on the government's dime. This was bullshit, but it's true that I wrote, called, and contacted many officers over a six-month period after Schine was drafted. It's also true that I tried to get him a commission in the Army, the Navy, the Air Force, Marines and even the Merchant Marine. I would have tried to get him a commission in the Salvation Army if I'd thought it would do any good.

I assumed incorrectly that if a Senator tried to get a subordinate commissioned, it would automatically be done. But the Army's case against me was nothing more than this. Whatever they might say or imply no one had evidence of anything improper. There were no incriminating pictures of Dave and me at Provincetown or Fire Island; no one had caught us *in flagrante* or had any other damning information. Despite the whispering campaign, no one really had anything on us except the charge that I'd inappropriately pressured the Army on Dave's behalf. That was it and that was all. Looking back, it doesn't seem like much but in the end, it was enough to cause a hell of a lot of trouble.

Before going any further with this, I want to clear up the confusion people have between our Committee and HUAC. I'm not sure why, but the press kept writing about McCarthy and me as if we had anything to do with the House committee, which was hard at work in 1947, long before Joe was even in the Senate. More important than that is that we had no interest in actors, directors or screen writers. I'm not even sure McCarthy had a tv set but if so, I'm certain he never watched "I Love Lucy," or knew who John Garfield was. To me, none of what was going on in Hollywood mattered very much compared to trying to find communists working in the government. Those actors might have gone to meetings or even started committees to do who knows what, but in the end, who cares? What I'm saying is, if you're going to hate me or McCarthy, do it for the right reasons. We didn't even know the people involved with HUAC and the so-called "Hollywood Ten" had nothing to do with us even if Murrow thought it did.

The Senate Democrats were bad enough, but it turned out neither Murrow nor the liberal press were done with us after Joe fell on his face rebutting Murrow on "See it Now." The next person we interviewed was Annie Lee Moss who worked as a clerk in the Pentagon but had been identified as a communist by Mary Markward, a woman whom the FBI had placed as a source within the Communist Party. Mrs. Markward had become membership director of the Party in Washington and knew all the members, which seemed like reliable information to us. The Army had been notified several times about Annie's past but did nothing about it. This was consistent with what we'd observed about Army security previously.

Mrs. Moss was a small Negro woman who showed up wearing a long black overcoat and dingy white gloves. She had horn-rimmed glasses, wore a kerchief over her head and looked more like someone's cleaning lady than a spy. I have to say that if they had decided to outfit her in such a way that she'd look nothing like a security risk, they'd have done a good job. She was right out of central casting, even though the Army had suspended her a few days before.

Joe ushered her into the room that was packed with a standing-room-only audience with Murrow's cameras looming behind us. I felt rather than saw the pressure of the crowd, imagining them pulling on my coat and breathing down my neck. As if this were real, I sat up several times and checked behind me to see who was leaning over my shoulder. There was no one there but I felt the pressure just the same.

Before we could begin, however, an uproar broke out in the packed gallery. "Monsters," someone yelled. "Criminals, Red-baiters" called another and suddenly there was a small riot in the room as capital police attempted to get at the protesters while others rose up to defend them. McCarthy turned around and shook his fist at the people in the back, but this predictably made it worse. Before we knew it, we were being pelted by bottles, cans, eggs, anything the hecklers could get their hands on. This went on long enough that it became obvious the only thing was to close the hearing down while the police restored order.

When we were able to re-convene, Mrs. Moss took her seat, looking, I thought, a bit surer of herself than she had earlier. As was his habit, McCarthy got right to the point, asking "Are you a communist?"

"No, sir, I am not," Mrs. Moss, her voice barely audible in the crowd.

"Could you speak up?" Joe said. "I can hardly hear you. This is a big room."

"Sorry, sir," she said. "No, I am not a communist."

"Have you ever been a communist?" Joe asked.

"I never even heard of communists until a few years back," Mrs. Moss said. "When they first asked me about it, I had to ask what was that?"

"Never heard of it," Joe said. "I'll just bet you hadn't."

Then he surprised me by announcing he had an important meeting to get to and left the room. I wanted to grab him and ask what was going on but by that time he was out the door. He left us in a bad situation, and I didn't know why, but I didn't want to draw any more attention to ourselves, so I just sat down as if this was all planned. The worst thing was that McCarthy's leaving turned the chair over to Senator McClellan and the others on the Committee who wanted to get rid of me. I had no idea what meeting Joe could be going to that could be more important than what we were doing, or if there even was a meeting, but I had no choice than to carry on the questioning.

"Mrs. Moss," I began. "Your testimony is that you were never a communist despite the fact that the membership director of the Washington Communist Party has told this Committee that Annie Lee Moss was on her list during the forties and was an active member then. Is this correct?"

"Maybe there's another Annie Lee Moss," the woman said. "Ever think of that? It must be a case of mistaken identity." This was absurd but I had to admire her quick thinking under the circumstances. She might look like a bag lady, but she wasn't stupid, that was clear.

"There's only one Annie Lee Moss FBI file," I said, turning to address the senators on the panel. "And only one Annie Lee Moss Justice Department file. We also have corroborating evidence supporting Mrs. Markward's testimony."

Then I turned back to the witness. "Isn't it a fact," I said, "that you've received *"The Daily Worker"* on a regular basis through Rob Hall?" Hall was one of the leading communists in Washington, but the question seemed to bewilder Annie Moss.

"Well, let me see," she started. "There was a colored man from my union who used to drop off some newspapers from time to time, but I never read them."

"And was *The Daily Worker* one of those papers?" I asked.

"I don't know, sir," she replied. "Like I said I don't read no newspapers in general."

At this point, McClellan jumped in. "Mr. Cohn, I think the only fact revealed here is that you've done a shoddy job preparing this case. You've wasted the Committee's time and dragged this poor, innocent woman down here and attacked her for no reason."

"As I said, Senator, we have good reason," I replied, but McClellan shook his head angrily, unconvinced.

Then Bobby Kennedy, who had been hired as the minority counsel for the hearings, broke in and said, "I'm informed that Mr. Hall is white. We were all under the impression that the union organizer Mrs. Hall referred to was a colored gentleman."

"I don't know if he was an organizer," I said quickly. "We only said he was a communist and that he was in touch with Mrs. Moss."

"So that means there's both a white Rob Hall and a colored one," one of the other senators said facetiously as the reporters in the room started laughing.

"I don't know if there is or not," I said, feeling hot but determined to keep control. "Our information is that it's the same Rob Hall."

"Well, if one is black and the other's white, they can't be the same," Senator McClellan said reasonably.

"I think that's something we need to look into," I said because there was no other way to get out of this conversation. Even if Kennedy and I hated each other, I had to give them credit for turning things around on us, but McCarthy was equally to blame for leaving the goddamned room.

Regardless, the Democrats were in control now. Symington broke in to say he'd looked in the Washington phone book and there were three A.L. Mosses listed. "We need to make sure we have the right person before allowing this woman to suffer more abuse and innuendo," he shouted. Then he turned to Mrs. Moss and asked her to read out loud her suspension notice. Why he did this is a mystery, but if we'd been wondering it proved that Mrs. Moss didn't read well.

When she finished, Symington asked, "Is that the best you can do?"

"Yes, sir," Mrs. Moss said. "I was never much good at reading."

"And yet you were supposedly getting and passing on complicated messages to our enemies in Soviet Russia."

"No, sir, I never did none of that," she said.

"I may be going out on a limb here," Symington said, "but since you've been suspended by the Army are you now looking for work?"

"Oh, yes, sir," she said. "I got to feed my family and if I can't find nothing I'm going down to the welfare."

Symington nodded. "Of course, you would," he said. "But I'll tell you what, if it turns out you don't find anything pretty quick you come on down to my office and I'll hire you. Will you do that?"

For the first time, Mrs. Moss seemed to brighten up at this. "Oh, yes, sir. I'll do that for sure. And thank you."

It was a grandstand move by Symington. Even if he had graduated from Amherst he could lay on that Southern accent when he wanted to charm the crowd. I didn't know if he was serious or really had a job for Mrs. Moss, but it didn't matter. The fallout from the meeting continued for days and weeks. Murrow went ahead and made her a heroine on one of his programs, stating that our investigation showed the way a poor Negro woman can be falsely accused as a communist spy with little or no justification. And the liberal columnists, not stopping at me or McCarthy, castigated Mrs. Markward as an informer, an irony since the FBI had hired her to be just that.

The *coup de grace* was that the harpies were still after me. Word came out that week that a "confidential report" had been prepared concerning the efforts I'd made to secure a commission for Schine. This was another publicity play. The report was so confidential that in the following days it was hard to find anyone in a position of influence in Washington who hadn't seen it.

At this point, I thought of handing in my resignation. After Zwicker, the Murrow business, and now the Annie Lee Moss hearing, it had been a bad few weeks and it looked as if it was about to get worse. Even McCarthy looked grim when we met in his office to talk about strategy for the continuing Army hearings. It seemed like a good time to leave and in fact, it would have been, but there was something that made me want to stand and fight, not to let the other Senators and Bobby Kennedy shake me from an investigation that I still believed had right on its side. I might have been wrong there, but it was the way I felt. Looking back, I'd do nothing different if faced with the same decision today.

Fifteen

MADISON, NEW YORK, WASHINGTON

Janey didn't think of herself as a jealous person. If Ed wanted to have a girlfriend, why should she care? After all, she and Dennis had been spending more time together and he'd even invited her to come up to Eagle River with him for a weekend where they could spend more time alone. She hadn't decided to accept this invitation, but she hadn't said no either. Even if she wasn't jealous, she had become increasingly uneasy about her ex-husband's activities, their effect on Little Ed and the fact that when she saw Ed during handoffs of the boy, he seemed happier than she could ever remember seeing him. She wasn't an expert, but she thought if he was going to be a communist, Ed should be unhappier about things, not just the divorce but the way things were going, the state of the world and he was the opposite of this.

She supposed she should be glad for him. She knew it would be generous of her to feel this way, but she just didn't, and she couldn't help that. Dennis said that with all the new stories in the *Herald* about Ed's communist friends testifying in Washington, he could be having even a worse influence on Little Ed than before. Dennis said he might even be taking the boy along to meetings of communist cells he belonged to, maybe down at the University in one of the coffee houses or in the Union. Janey supposed she could tell him not to take Little Ed along on his canvassing trips, but she enjoyed having some time to herself when she could go shopping or even see an afternoon show at the Orpheum.

Dennis kept after her, saying she should change the custody arrangement they had, maybe require Ed to have supervised visits with Little Ed if he was going to continue being a communist. That's how they work, Dennis said, little by little they work their way into your lives and next thing you know you've lost everything. Janey wasn't an alarmist, but this was Ed as she'd never seen him, self-confident and moving ahead with things she hadn't heard of before with him. It scared Janey to think Dennis might be right. She didn't know exactly how he knew all about communists, but he said he had sources she wouldn't know about and seemed very certain about how communists worked. Lawyers were smart people, Janey knew that, and they knew a lot she couldn't know.

Gore started dropping by the boathouse during his frequent trips to Madison. Ed would take his break with the editor on the terrace where they'd sit drinking coffee and watching the waterfront. "If you've never seen the Mediterranean this is pretty good," Gore said one day.

"When I saw the Mediterranean, it was full of gun boats, submarines and dead bodies," Ed said. "I'll take this."

"Good choice," Gore said. Then, "I told you before McCarthy's started to notice what we're doing. I think he's nervous now."

"I saw he was back in the state last week," Ed said.

"Every weekend since we got organized," Gore said. "It's like he's running for re-election, which he will be if we get all the signatures."

"Well, we're working hard," Ed said. He'd been out with Little Ed and Susan three times in the past week, venturing far from the West Side, going downtown first and then all the way out to Maple Bluff, a Republican stronghold on the far East Side where he'd been amazed how much anti-McCarthy sentiment he'd seen. One lady told him, "I just wish he wasn't so rude when he's interviewing those people on television. I mean, I know they're communists and all, but still, he doesn't have to be that way."

Gore patted Ed on the arm. "I'd like you to take a trip with me."

"Up north?" Ed said.

Gore laughed. "No, I mean a real trip. To the East Coast. New York, Boston, Philadelphia, maybe Washington D.C."

"Why would we go there," Ed said. "Assuming there was any way I could afford it, which I can't."

"We need more money," Gore said, ignoring Ed's objections. "We've done well with fund-raising here, but let's face it, the big money is in the East. And don't worry about expenses. I'll cover yours, not first class, but I'll get you there, put you up in a hotel and make sure you get three squares a day."

The idea appealed to Ed. He'd never been able to do any traveling except when he was in the service, which wasn't really traveling at all. Just moving from place to place. New York and the other cities Gore mentioned were no more than names to him. The idea excited him, particularly because he'd never thought of himself as being very worldly, travelling around the country, maybe influencing people. On the other hand, he'd have to lose time with Little Ed and he had begun to wonder about the effect Janey's new boyfriend was having on him. The last time they'd been together Little Ed had asked, "What's a fellow traveler?"

"Where did you hear about that?" Ed said.

"Dennis told me," the boy said. In the moment, Ed had made a joke about people liking to travel but it made him wonder what they were saying about him to Little Ed.

"I'd have to ask my boss for the time off," he said.

"Sure," Gore said. "I already talked to Professor Sinclair. He says you can miss class, that you can write a paper on it when we get back." The editor stood up now and stretched. "So, go ahead talk to your boss, make whatever arrangements you have to make because we're leaving in two days."

Boston, Hartford and Philadelphia passed in a blur of suburban living rooms, men in suits and women in flowing dresses. Gore introduced Ed as a veteran who'd been slandered by McCarthy which inevitably brought applause and pats on the back along with the expected donations. Ed felt uncomfortable in these groups and dishonest at still being called a veteran years after the war had ended, but Gore was at ease with these people, laughing with the men and hugging the women who'd brush his ear or neck with lipsticked kisses as they moved on past. How a small-town editor could know his way around Boston or

New Haven was a mystery to Ed, but plainly there was much about Gore he didn't know.

On the train to New York, Ed asked, "How did we do there? Looked like a lot of checks to me."

Gore shrugged. "Good but not good enough. We need to do better."

Ed had never either done fund-raising or given money to worthy causes himself. Everything he made at his job had always gone to the simple requirements of living and he had assumed everyone else was in the same situation. It seemed incredible that complete strangers would casually show up and give what seemed to him to be a lot of money to support something that had nothing to do with them. "Better than what?" Ed said.

"Better than what we've got so far," Gore said. "Don't worry about it, we'll get there." Then he tipped his chair back and went to sleep.

They reached New York in the morning and checked into a hotel. Gore got on the telephone immediately, but Ed wanted to walk around and see the city. They were staying in Midtown, so he walked over to Times Square, a neon masterpiece unlike anything he had ever seen or even imagined clogged with throngs of people moving back and forth with complete disregard for travel signals or intersections. Ed was looking at the signs and window-shopping when a black woman in a shiny orange dress sidled up to him. "Want a date, soldier?" the woman asked.

Ed had known a few prostitutes in Italy but as far as he knew there weren't any in Madison. Still, he understood when he was being propositioned. "How did you know I was a soldier?" he asked.

The girl smirked and looked Ed up and down. "I've known a few soldiers," she said. "How did you know I was a hooker?"

"The same way, I guess." Ed smiled. The woman was maybe twenty-one. Her hair was frosted-blonde, and she was practically spilling out of her dress. She wore bright crimson lipstick and had a quizzical expression. "10:30 in the morning's a little early for your line of work, isn't it?" he said.

"Girl's got to make a living," the woman said and patted him on the shoulder. "Welcome to New York, soldier."

Ed walked uptown as far as Central Park and then back to the hotel where he put his feet up and took a nap. Gore had told him that they had a couple of cocktail parties to go to and he had to be rested. When he woke up, Ed took down the ironing board he found in the back of the closet and ironed his pants and jacket. He'd brought along three shirts but even with alternating them daily he was down to his last one. Gore came in around four and threw two new ones in wrappers on the bed. "I got a friend works at Macy's," he said in explanation. "He said they fell off a truck. Didn't cost me anything."

"You've got friends in New York?"

"I wasn't always a small-town editor," Gore said, smiling. "I've been around."

Ed wanted to ask where exactly Gore had been, how he'd known those elegant women at the Hartford country club, but he didn't want to pry where it was none of his business. "Well, you didn't have to do this," was all he said.

"We need you to look sharp," Gore said. "Ready to go?"

The first party that night was in an apartment on the Upper East Side filled with people who were unlike any Ed had known in Wisconsin. He might have said they were rich or sophisticated or cultured though none of this meant much to him and it was more than that. They just seemed very different, slurring their words in a kind of drawl, moving their polished foreheads around to see over the head of whoever they might be talking to at the moment. Ed found them hard to talk to but tried gainfully and smiled like the yokel they must assume him to be until Gore made his pitch for money. He introduced Ed as his primary exhibit at which point some of the people who'd been looking over him turned to regard him with new interest.

When they were going down in the elevator after the party, Ed said, "We did well there at least, right? Lots of checks anyway."

"Pocket change to those people." Gore said, dissatisfied as usual. "You ever been to a wedding where a couple of families get together to give you a towel set instead of each of them getting you a gift themselves? It's like that."

Ed remembered his marriage to Janey at City Hall with only her sister and a friend in attendance. Neither the sister or Janey's friend had brought presents to the ceremony and to make things worse, Ed had to take them all out to lunch afterwards at the Hoffman House. He always thought he should have gotten credit for stepping up and never questioning if the baby was his even though Janey hadn't been his girlfriend. He nodded at Gore's remark, as if he knew all about weddings.

When he was overseas, he didn't think much about Janey until he got her letter saying she was expecting and would he do the right thing. If there were other candidates neither of them had mentioned it and it didn't matter to Ed. They had never been the couple you'd see romantically holding hands in public, deep in conversation at a restaurant or sending each other little notes at work. There hadn't even been valentines or birthday cards. They didn't have that kind of relationship. A towel set would have been the best gift they got at their wedding, but he supposed most people made more of a fuss over getting married than they had. In fact, he hoped they did.

The next stop was in an area of New York called Greenwich Village, though it didn't look like any village Ed had ever seen, being a bunch of run-down brick buildings crushed together on top of each other block after block in lower Manhattan. The men at this party were mostly dressed in corduroys and the women sat on the floor on large pillows, had hair down to their shoulders and wore sweaters that reached below their waists. Ed had never been around people like this either, but he found them more approachable than the group at the first party and some seemed to listen with real interest when Ed described his experiences with the McCarthy fallout. Afterwards, Gore was pleased with the results of the evening.

"These folks had less and gave more than the high rollers Uptown," he said. "Figure that one out."

They stayed in New York overnight then took the train to Washington, the last stop on their tour. Again, they got in before noon, left their bags at a hotel and headed for Capitol Hill.

"I've got some people to see," Gore said. "Walk around, see the sights. Everything's nearby, the Supreme Court, Washington Memorial, Jefferson too."

Ed nodded but he had a different idea, something he'd told himself he'd do if he ever made it to Washington. Especially after the skein of towns they'd run through on the trip so far, he was determined to do something he'd remember here. Ed asked a cop where the Senate offices were and then climbed the stairs up to McCarthy's suite. There he found a secretary sitting inside the front door in front of a huge Wisconsin flag and a poster touting the state as America's Dairyland next to bronze busts of McCarthy and Abraham Lincoln. The secretary told Ed the Senator was always eager to greet constituents, but unfortunately wasn't available and might be held up all afternoon. Ed could wait, however, in case he found time to stop in.

"Anyone else I could talk to?" Ed said.

"There's Mr. Cohn," the secretary said and shrugged. She indicated another door just beyond her desk.

Ed knocked and entered to find a small man with slick-backed brown hair sitting behind a large desk talking on the phone. When Ed came in, Cohn held up his hand like a traffic cop and pointed Ed to a chair next to the desk. Even though Ed was waiting, the other man seemed in no hurry to end his call, saying over and over, "Okay, I get that, I do. I get it. But listen, do this for me, okay? Will you just for Christ's sake this one thing?"

Finally, he hung up and looked across the desk at Ed, a crooked smile on his face. "How can I help you, Butch?"

This seemed a little disrespectful but also casual, like this was just the way they talked out here, so Ed let it go. Cohn was wearing a dark gray suit and a deep blue tie. He was clean-shaven but had what looked like a bruise bisecting his nose that made Ed dislike him. His hair glistened in the overhead light. This was the man who'd interviewed Tony, the one who'd been described by Gore as a tough guy.

"My name isn't butch," Ed said. "I'm a constituent of your boss," Ed said. "From Wisconsin."

"Sorry," Cohn said, but he didn't seem sorry. Ed thought he'd never met anyone who seemed less likely to apologize. "And I don't think Joe's got constituents anywhere but Wisconsin. Someday maybe but not now. Anyway, welcome, the Senator always likes to hear from Wisconsin people. What's your name again?"

Ed hadn't given his name to the secretary but now he said, "Malloy, Edgeworth Malloy. I go by Ed, though."

Something moved behind Cohn's eyes at this, something like recognition. He nodded and smiled. "That's familiar and I never forget a face or a name," he said. "Don't I know you from somewhere?"

Ed smiled at the unlikeliness of this. "Not really," he said. "This is my first time in Washington. But maybe you remember Tony Abruzzi, an old army buddy of mine. You might say you met him. How about that?"

Cohn smiled slowly and nodded again. "Yeah, that's it," he said. "Abruzzi, the guy who worked out at Monmouth, the pink vet. He named you to our Committee when we were grilling him, am I right?"

"Tony wasn't really a communist," Ed said. He felt hot under his coat and tie but was determined not to lose his temper. "But that's right. He named me at that hearing and you were the one questioning him, put him on the spot."

"What I do," Cohn said simply, neither apologetic nor proud of this. "My job."

Ed looked at the little guy, smug behind his big desk and thought of jumping over and wrapping his hands around his stringy neck. "I guess you're proud of that, bringing people down here to a hearing and then embarrassing them, maybe ruining their lives?"

Cohn shrugged. "Not really," Cohn said, examining his hands. "Just not my concern. I didn't tell this guy to go to commie meetings over in Italy, did I? I didn't tell him to live in a rooming house filled with communists when he got home. I would never have heard of him if he hadn't hung out with those other guys out at Monmouth." He shifted in his chair. "Think about it this way. Maybe your buddy should have been more careful in choosing his friends. Maybe you should too."

Ed considered what he had said to be confrontational, but he'd had almost no effect on Cohn, and he was impressed with the other man's recall of Tony's case. "I never chose anything," he said now. "The Army took care of that for me. I never went to any meetings over there either and I lost my job anyway. What's more, my kid got beat up at school and they put red paint all over my sidewalk."

"Too bad," Cohn said but he didn't really sound concerned. "But tell me, if you never went to meetings why did your old pal Tony name you, can you tell me that?"

"I don't know," Ed said. "But I don't blame Tony. Probably you scared the shit out of him, and he thought he had to say something. I'm guessing he's not used to being questioned by sharp New York lawyers."

"Oh, I get it," Cohn said, and flapped his wrist next to his face. "You mean like me?" He seemed pleased with Ed's description of him.

"Hey, if the shirt fits, wear it," Ed said.

"That must be one of those Wisconsin sayings I've heard about," Cohn said and smiled. "Got a nice ring to it. I like it; okay if I use it?"

It was an odd moment for Ed. Standing outside himself for the moment, it was almost as if he was a stranger watching the whole scene, impressed that he was sharing wise remarks with a smooth customer like Cohn. He was different than the people at the New York fundraisers, though he seemed to be a New Yorker too. Smart and sharp in a way the others hadn't been, at ease with the give and take, not polished but sort of rough in the way he moved his mouth around words. Without willing it, Ed found himself perversely admiring the other man for his aplomb. He'd just barged in the office with no warning, but Cohn didn't seem unnerved or even surprised, and Ed wondered if anything made this man uncomfortable, if he was always in control of the situation. Even if Ed had prepared for the moment mentally when he would confront his accusers, the reality was completely different from what he would have expected. He was angry but he found himself respecting Cohn's arrogance and self-assurance. Cohn made no apologies for anything he and McCarthy had done, no matter how destructive it might have been or whom it had hurt. Not his concern was all he said. Back home, Ed was surrounded by people who apologized constantly for things large and small that in truth should have required no apology. He could probably learn a lot by being with this guy longer, but Cohn was looking around the room as if he was expecting to see something new on the walls. Now he patted his desk pad in a kind of dismissive gesture.

"Anyway, what are you doing here, Ed?" Cohn said, finally getting to the point. "Seeing the sights? Anyone I can introduce you to?"

"I'm part of a group you might have heard of," Ed said. "The Joe Must Go Club. I'm out here to raise money for that and try to get rid of your boss."

Cohn slapped his forehead and said, "Sonofabitch! Of course, I read about you and your buddies in the paper. Where's your button, though? I like those yellow buttons." Cohn fixed his fingers in a circle that might have been a parody of the buttons they handed out.

"I doubt you'll be laughing in a few weeks," Ed said. "But how about I make sure you get one when I'm back in Madison?" He stood up quickly, but his feet had fallen asleep and for a moment he lost his balance.

"Take it easy there," Cohn said. Then he offered his hand and grinned. "Hey, I enjoyed this, Ed," he said. "Honestly. But I'll tell you, you haven't got a snowball's chance recalling McCarthy. He's going to be here for a long time."

"That right?" Ed said. "Then tell me why he's flying home every weekend, going to coffees and boy scout dinners if he's not worried?"

Cohn shrugged. "I don't make up his schedule. Maybe he just likes those cheese curds, what do I know? But thanks for coming by. You lit up what was looking like a pretty boring day. And you'll make sure I get one of those buttons, right?"

And then Ed was back out in the hall with people walking back and forth and no one paying the smallest attention to him. Later, when he saw Gore at the hotel and told him about his meeting with Cohn, the older man seemed amused. "You thought you'd shake him up by going in there to his office?"

"Maybe a little," Ed said. "Didn't work. I was surprised, though. He's a young guy, younger than me."

"But a pretty slick operator, right?"

"You can say that again," Ed said, shaking his head.

"He's supposed to be the most hated man in the country," Gore said. "Even more than his boss. Does that make sense to you?"

"Not really," Ed said. He hadn't thought about how he felt about meeting Cohn, if you called their interaction a meeting, It wasn't something he'd planned or even considered ahead of time. He had hoped to see McCarthy but should have known the Senator wasn't going to be sitting around waiting for people to drop in on him. "I've never met anyone like that before," Ed said slowly. "But, no, I didn't hate him, not at all. It wasn't like that really."

"Even with what he's done to you."

"Did he do it?" Ed said. "Cohn? All by himself? I don't think so. It took a lot of people and reporters to write about those hearings and get everyone excited about communists everywhere. And before that, did Cohn make my neighbors write "Commie" on my sidewalk? Did he give my boss the idea of having me swear out a loyalty oath? Whatever Cohn or even McCarthy's doing here, I think it doesn't really have much to do with me, even if I've caught hell for it. If the whole country is so scared of communists that they're willing to look at someone like me, you have to think everything was ready to explode at any moment and all it took was someone like Cohn or McCarthy to throw on the match."

"Well, you're a more forgiving man than I would be in your situation, that's all I'd say about that," Gore said.

"I haven't forgiven anyone," Ed said. "I'm good and pissed off or I wouldn't be here. I just think it's bigger than Cohn or even McCarthy maybe."

"Well, you're right about," Gore said.

When Ed got back to Madison, a letter from a law firm he'd never heard of was waiting for him announcing that "Janemarie" Malloy was suing for a change in custody arrangements. The reason stated was Ed's "poisonous" influence on their son. In addition, the letter stated Ed had neglected his financial responsibilities and asked that his lawyer contact them as soon as possible.

Ed knew Janey meant business when she used her full name, but the letter caught him by surprise and felt like a kick in the gut. He was willing to admit he lacked something as a father, but a poisonous influence on Little Ed? What kind of poison, he wondered, and how had he administered it? He knew he had missed a few support payments, but he'd been busy and hoped Janey would understand that. She had to know he loved his son; how could she not know that? Even with the exaggerated language, Ed knew the letter was serious. If Janey got the change in custody she was asking for, it could limit his contact with Little Ed or even cut it in his home. It was the one thing he couldn't imagine losing, the only thing he couldn't be without.

Ed didn't have a lawyer, though he had met a few through his work with Gore. Not knowing what else to do, he called his ex-wife. "I'm not supposed to talk to you," Janey said when she picked up. "What do you want?"

"Not talk to me? Jesus, Janey we've been married for ten years. We have a son. Just tell me what you're so upset about," Ed said. "I thought we were doing okay."

"You did, did you?" Janey said, her voice brittle as glass.

"Yes, I did. What's wrong," Ed said. "I just got back from a trip to find this letter from your lawyer. Did something happen while I was gone."

"That's it," Janey said. "You're a big man now with your name in all the papers, a fancy girlfriend and no time for Little Ed."

"I wouldn't call her fancy," Ed said, feeling a little guilty for not sticking up for Susan. Maybe to Janey or Little Ed she did seem fancy. Who could say for sure?

"Little Ed said you're living with her, going up to the big U now for classes and then taking him along on those communist things you're working on. You've changed, Ed. You used to be a hard-working guy that came home every night. Getting to be too big now for ordinary people, like me and Little Ed."

Beneath her anger and sarcasm, Ed heard the hurt in her voice and there seemed to be some nostalgia there too, which struck Ed as odd since Janey had been the one who left. He couldn't deny that he'd changed but none of it had been by choice. He hoped he was stronger now, but he wasn't sure he was any better. Where did all this come from?

"I'm not a big man" he said. "I'm the same as I ever was and I'm no communist either. That's the whole point of Joe Must Go. Lots of innocent people like me are having their lives wrecked and we're getting together to protect ourselves. Anyway, you said it was all right to take Little Ed along when I canvassed."

"I changed my mind," Janey said. "I think it's the wrong influence for a young boy. They're picking on Little Ed at school again."

"Goddamnit," Ed said. "I'll go back and talk to Dr. Silbert. He told me he'd take care of the whole thing when I went the first time."

"Don't bother," Janey said. "I think you've done enough. More than enough. And don't call me anymore." With that, she hung up the phone, pleased with her firmness in the face of Ed's protests. It was true, Janey thought, not just that Ed was different but that the ways he had changed frightened her. She didn't know if he was really a communist and she didn't care. Her responsibility was to protect Little Ed, and she took this more seriously than anything else in her life.

There was a part of her that regretted this. She knew at base Ed was still a good man, but he seemed to have forgotten himself or been transformed by other people whom she didn't know and didn't trust.

Everything in her background taught her to feel that these educated, upper-class people not only looked down on her but would be perfectly willing to steamroll her in order to get what they wanted. Was that communism? She wasn't sure but she knew she didn't like it and needed to protect her son from it.

Ed tried to make sense of it all, but the conversation had upset him more than he would have expected. Sitting in his kitchen with a cup of coffee in front of him, he thought he saw small insects crawling around inside the tiles on the floor, as if it was a moving thing and he moved his feet to avoid whatever was down there. Even after the tiles calmed down and stopped moving, he noticed his hands trembling. What the hell was he going to do?

That night, he described the exchange to Susan. Despite what Janey had said, they weren't really living together, and he doubted Little Ed had told her they were. How would an eight-year-old boy even think about that? On the other hand, if that was what Susan wanted, he saw no reason not to at this point. Still, it wasn't like Janey to be jealous after all this time.

"It's not that I expected a brass band welcoming me when I got back from Washington," he said. "But a letter like that from my ex-wife's lawyer was a shock, I'll tell you. I didn't even know she was thinking about changing custody."

Susan nodded sympathetically. "She must really be furious to go to those lengths, hiring a lawyer."

Ed nodded. "That's what confuses me. It doesn't seem like her. Now I wonder if I really knew her at all."

"People change," Susan said. "Not that I've been through a divorce, but you said she mentioned me when you talked."

"Oh, yeah," Ed laughed. "She says you're a fancy woman and a bad influence on Little Ed. She kind of suggested we're both communists."

"Fancy, really?" Susan seemed pleased. "I've never been called anything like that before. And communists! God knows, from some of the reactions we've gotten when we were out canvassing, she wouldn't be alone. A lot of people seem to think so."

"Nice of you to see her point of view," Ed said.

"Sorry," Susan said and put her arms around him. "She just sounds jealous to me."

"Jealous?" Ed said, incredulous. He'd never thought of Janey that way. "What could she be jealous about? She's the one who left."

Susan smiled. "It's the most natural thing in the world. Any woman would feel that way if she thought her ex-husband was going to be happy with someone else, especially if she doesn't have anyone herself."

"Sonofabitch," Ed said. "Jealous."

"We could stop seeing each other if you think that's a good idea," Susan said.

"I think that's a terrible idea," Ed said. "You're the best thing that's happened to me in what's been a pretty shitty year. I keep thinking you're going to come to your senses and stop answering when I call. I mean you're a dean and I'm not even a college graduate. How does that look?"

"I don't care how it looks," Susan said.

"Other people might not agree," Ed said.

But Susan wasn't worried. "I hear there could be possibilities for advancement at the Union," she said. "Joe told me you have a way with the students."

Just talking to her made Ed feel better. And it was true. Things were looking up, despite Janey's action. "Sky's the limit down there," he said.

"That's what I hear. So what are you going to do now?" Susan asked.

"I guess I'm going to find a lawyer," Ed said.

Sixteen

WASHINGTON

Just when I think nothing can surprise me anymore, something comes along to convince me I'm an idiot. It happens like this. McCarthy's out somewhere and I'm in my office, talking on the phone, trying to get ready for the Army hearings that are bearing down on me like an avalanche and suddenly there's this galoot standing in my doorway. A big guy with shoulders on him, hands all red knuckles, packaged in a suit he got at Sears that won't ever fit. The words raw-boned come to mind but I don't know what that means any more than I'm sure what a galoot is really. Just seemed right for this guy. He was more broad than tall but tall too and you could tell he wasn't used to wearing a jacket and tie. He made me a little nervous standing there, so I stayed on the phone longer than I had to, even after the other party had hung up and all I heard was buzzing in my ear. I needed to get my bearings to deal with this guy who was there God knows why but didn't look like a long lost friend.

He wasn't any agency staffer, I knew that, and I thought I'd recognize assistants to the other senators. I figured it was maybe one of the secretaries sticking it to me because I didn't see anyone as a rule or take appointments. But still there he was in front of me and the guy wasn't moving. Finally, I asked how I could help him and for no reason called him Butch. Butch the galoot. What the hell was I saying? This guy knocked me off my game is the truth.

Turned out he was from Wisconsin and not only that but one of the leaders of that fucking club they have out there trying to impeach McCarthy. To make things worse, it turned out this guy, Malloy, knew me or thought he did because he'd been named during the Monmouth Hearing by some commie friend of his. What was funny was Malloy didn't really seem pissed about this, just kind of curious, interested in seeing the villain who had outed him, like poking a bear in the zoo to see if he could make it growl.

This was a little off my usual beat, but I tried to play along. I told him I don't do constituent relations, don't answer letters or make nice when people from Wisconsin call on the senator. We had staff for that, but in a pinch, I was supposed to fill in. McCarthy got a ton of mail and a lot of it had to be answered. In addition, we followed the local newspapers: if someone did something important, like celebrate a fiftieth wedding anniversary, turn 100, or had a kid who made Eagle Scout, we were supposed to write and congratulate him. But this wasn't why Malloy was there. He had a bitch and wanted to be heard so, okay, I was on the spot. Still, like I said, he didn't really seem as much mad as curious, so was this some kind of weird courtesy call, a warning, we're coming to get you? What? Who knows but when I mentioned the meeting to McCarthy later, he wasn't amused.

"Those bastards are causing me all kinds of trouble," he said. "Their fucking petition. From what I'm hearing it might even work."

"Who says so?" I asked. "They haven't got a prayer."

McCarthy shrugged. "People I know back home in Appleton say they've got support. I heard a hundred thousand have already signed the goddamned thing."

This surprised me. I didn't know there were a hundred thousand people in the whole state and wouldn't have imagined a guy like Malloy could get that done. Maybe I'd underestimated him. "Well, what do you think?" I asked. As far as I could tell McCarthy was phenomenally popular and not just in Wisconsin. Senators from other states were afraid to go against him because he had followers where they lived too.

"Beats the shit out of me," he said. "But that's why I've been going back there every weekend for the last six weeks."

"Yeah, this guy mentioned that, Malloy. Seemed to think maybe they had you on the run or something."

McCarthy smiled that ragged smile at this. "That's what he thinks? That's funny. I ain't running anywhere. So, what did you tell him?"

"I told him to send me one of those buttons they've got," I said. "The yellow ones that say, 'Joe Must Go.' And you know what, I'll bet he will. He just seemed like that kind of guy."

But whatever was going on in Wisconsin with the petition, we had bigger things to worry about. The Army/McCarthy hearings really got serious after Joe stuck his foot in it by insulting General Zwicker. This was where his bluster had got us and my stomach was in an uproar as I tried to figure how to get us out of this. It didn't help that now we had major television coverage, and the general was raising hell about it all over town. I knew McCarthy wouldn't back down or apologize but for some people the business with Zwicker was the last straw and the leadership was going to make us pay. The dance was coming to an end, and we were on the cusp of the fourth movement, the Allegro when things move faster and faster.

The way it started was the Democrats drafted Estes Kefauver, a senator who wasn't really involved in this fight, but, unlike Joe, was a member of the club and disapproved of McCarthy's style. Kefauver submitted a formal request to the Armed Services Committee to start an inquiry into our actions. When its chairman passed on this, Joe demanded that his own Committee handle the investigation. Getting named to investigate himself was a stroke of genius but what was more surprising is that the Democrats went along with this.

A special seven-member subcommittee was set up and since he was a focus of the investigation, Joe had to step down as chairman in favor of Karl Mundt. Outside counsel and staff would be hired, all hearings would be public and witnesses would be sworn. No one imagined at that time that this inquiry would become a circus that went on for six weeks, be televised nationally and become a sensation. The idea was to bring in some generals, reveal the truth quickly and that would finish us. But these guys had no idea what they were up against.

Joe and Jeannie McCarthy lived in an old frame house on Third Street in the Northeastern part of Washington that Jeannie's mother had bought for them, a good thing since Joe had no money. The old lady lived in half of the house and Joe and Jeanie had the rest. They had knocked down a few walls and created a large open living room and office that was perfect for our staff meetings. Joe, Frank Carr, Jim Juliana and I met there most nights and early mornings during the Army hearings, which were really a witch hunt whose only purpose was to embarrass Joe and get rid of me. It was great theater I suppose but an incredible waste of money, not to mention the television networks who lost untold millions in advertising in order to show the whole thing.

But before we could really get started, there was a final attempt at a compromise: the leadership proposed that the Army would get Adams to pull his chronicle and resign and Joe would fire me. Tit for tat. This made sense and I wouldn't have blamed McCarthy for accepting the deal but that would have been uncharacteristic of Joe. "Those sonsabitches may have started this fight," he said, "but I'm damned sure going to finish it. I'm taking names and I'll get every one of those bastards even if I have to wait for the next election. I'm more popular in their districts than they are and I won't let them forget it."

I'm not really a stickler for fairness when you're in a fight like this, but I'd have to say it wasn't clear who started what. We were looking for communists in the government and the Army was protecting their asses. But I doubt the proposed agreement would have worked anyway. The word we got from the White House was that the President wanted an investigation that would settle things once and for all. "One thing I've learned," Ike was supposed to have said, "is that you can't compromise with Joe McCarthy."

He was right about that. There were six weeks between the time the Army produced that Adams memorandum listing all the times I'd been in touch regarding Schine and our response with memoranda of our own detailing the fact that the Army had essentially been holding Dave hostage as a way of getting back at me. While this war of words was going on, Joe went on the road to gather support from his fans, traveling to St. Louis, Omaha, Houston, Chicago and Milwaukee. He finished the tour in New York where I joined him along with a wild crowd of 6,000 members of the Police Department's Holy Name Society.

When Joe got up to speak, he shouted, "I can't see what kind of sense it makes to support an Army bureaucracy that gives promotions and honorable discharges to communists while Americans rot in Chinese jails."

I don't know where he got the comment about Americans in Chinese jails and I don't even know if it was true, but the crowd didn't care. They went crazy, chanting, "Joe, Joe, Joe," until finally Cardinal Spellman walked out on stage to shake hands with Joe which quieted things down

McCarthy said later it was the greatest night of his life, and I couldn't disagree even if I knew some of these people were lunatics and would clap at anything McCarthy said. It didn't take much to get them excited and if I'd thought about it, I might have been bothered by the fact that they were our base. What's more, I knew my visitor from Wisconsin was ramping up Joe Must Go excitement and getting more signatures on their petition. Word was they now had more than a quarter of a million signed up. I'd seen pictures showing signs attacking McCarthy all over rural Wisconsin and though it was hard to believe, it seemed they were just getting stronger all the time.

With all this going on, Malloy still found time to remember our talk. A few weeks after his visit, I got a padded envelope at the office. Inside were a bunch of yellow buttons and a baseball cap with "Joe Must Go' above the brim. "Pass a few out to your friends, if you have any," he had written.

I was amused by this and liked Malloy's moxie, but of course we had our supporters too, thousands of them. The letters and calls poured in, so many we had to hire extra staff to handle the crush even if most of the messages were unusable because of profanity and anti-semitic raving. I could never figure out how Joe appealed to the proto-nazis since he had a Jew for his chief counsel, but hate has never made sense. It exists in its own universe and multiplies constantly without logical sequence.

The world collapsed for me during those weeks and days when we were meeting to decide on a strategy for the hearings, usually at night and mostly on a diet of beer and hamburgers, courtesy of Mrs. McCarthy. I was on a virtual trolley between McCarthy's, the Statler where I got a few hours of sleep some nights, and the office. Time became an unruly continuum rather than being sharply delineated into hours and minutes, days and night, light and dark. The other side had hired Joseph Welch, a tall, elegant lawyer from a distinguished Boston firm. The contrast between me and Joe couldn't have been greater and I figured it must have been intentional. Welch gave the appearance of being a Boston brahmin, but appearances were deceiving since he was from Iowa and had graduated from Grinnell, a little college out there, whose other distinguished graduate was Harry Hopkins, FDR's trusted advisor.

Welch was tall and balding with a bow tie that gave him the look of an elegant clerk. Also, he frequently adopted a puzzled look though I doubt there was much than confused him. The hearings would make Welch a television star, however, and, ironically, we later became if not friends, at least friendly acquaintances. At one point after hearing I frequented the place, he asked me about the Stork Club. "I've never been there," he said smiling. "It must be an expensive place. I'll bet I couldn't get in, could I?"

"Oh, I don't know," I said. "They cater to television celebrities, so I think they'd probably find a place for you. Maybe not a good table, but you could get in."

For all his good humor and likable qualities, Joe Welch was an effective counsel for the majority, perhaps the most effective weapon they had. In addition to Welch, the Committee hired Ray H. Jenkins, a lawyer Everett Dirksen had met on a visit to Tennessee. Jenkins was a huge man with a shock of red hair who bragged that he represented "only the most evil of criminals" in his law practice. The rumor was that he had never lost a case. He reminded me a little of Malloy in the sense of being big and rough looking. As it turned out, however, they were nothing alike. Jenkins was a superb lawyer and more a friend to us than an adversary in the end, despite our relative roles.

Given this lineup of legal talent on the other side, the question arose as to who should be hired to represent the Committee. We went through lists of lawyers we knew were sympathetic or had worked with Joe in the past but in the end, against the advice of some good friends, I raised the question of whether we really needed to hire an outside representative.

"I'm a lawyer," I said during one of the evening meetings at the house. "I can prepare the case probably better than anyone else. There's nothing devious here, nothing too difficult to research, no complexities in our story. Why can't I just defend us?"

"But you're one of the primary people being investigated," Jim Juliana said reasonably. "What's that saying, any lawyer who defends himself has a fool for a client."

He was right, of course. But I thought I was the most brilliant lawyer in town and besides God was on our side. We'd done nothing wrong, or at least nothing others hadn't tried to do on behalf of their friends or relatives, so why shouldn't I just handle the defense? McCarthy had no objection, so that's what we decided to do. It was a fateful decision, and I've lived to regret it.

While Joe liked to play down Gore's recall movement in Wisconsin, there was no question the Joe Must Go group had gotten his attention and caused him to travel back home frequently. This and the repeated trips he'd made to gather support had had its effect on his health. He gained ten pounds then promptly lost it back. He was drinking more, sleeping less and was admitted to Bethesda Naval Hospital on several occasions for what we described to the press as kidney problems, but were really successive attempts to dry him out and get him back on his feet for the hearings.

When I visited Joe in the hospital during one of his stays, I told him, "You're not going to accomplish anything by killing yourself before we can even get at the Army."

"I'm not going to kill myself," Joe said, his eyes racing, "but I'll tell you this, I'll sure as hell kill some of them if I get the chance."

Despite the passion in his voice, I didn't take this threat very seriously but on one trip I ran into his old Wisconsin friend Van Susteren who told me he was worried too. "Joe was telling me the other day he's gotten death threats," Van Susteren said.

"Nothing new about that," I said. "He's always gotten them; so have I. They never come to anything. Writers aren't killers."

"Maybe not," Van Susteren said, "but I can tell you Joe's taking them to heart. He even went out and bought himself a gun."

"Jesus," I said. "Can he shoot? I mean, he was in the service, right."

Van Susteren laughed. "Sure, the Marines, but he never took a shot at anything that might shoot back. He couldn't hit the side of a barn. But it shows all this is getting to him. I'm worried. You should be too."

I was no fan of Van Susteren, who'd criticized me before Joe even took me on, but in this case, I wondered if he was right so I talked it over with Jeannie and it turned out she was as concerned as Van. "Maybe you two could take a trip," I said. "We've got a few weeks. Maybe go down to Florida fishing or something. You always liked that."

"The last time I suggested that Joe said he couldn't get away. Then he went to Pittsburgh to give a speech," Jeannie said. She shook her head. "I honestly have no idea what to do, Roy," she said. "I really don't."

I couldn't help her, but Joe regained some strength after a week in the hospital and was again in a fighting mood when he got back to Washington. He started posting signs in the office like "Quitters Never Win, Winners Never Quit," "The Only Good Red is a Dead Red," and "Tough times Never Last; Tough people do!" He told me that he intended to win this battle or die trying and got comfort from a poster that read:

> *Oh, God don't let me weaken*
> *Help me to continue on*
> *When I go down,*
> *Let me go down like an oak tree*
> *Felled by a woodman's axe.*

I didn't really get this or see why it comforted Joe. The office looked like a high school locker room before the big game.

If Joe didn't need a break, I did, so I went up to New York, collected Barbara from Sarah Lawrence and we drove out to Connecticut for the weekend. We hadn't gone away before, but I didn't want to go alone. I felt comfortable with Barbara and if she wasn't my girlfriend, she was as close as I could come. I liked spending time with her and to be honest I liked sleeping with her. Who wouldn't? A friend had loaned me his house in Stonington and after getting unpacked we went out for a shore dinner at a nearby restaurant.

Barbara was a very beautiful woman and not what you'd think of ordinarily as a college girl perhaps because of the time she'd spent hanging around showgirls at her dad's club. She had a knowing sophisticated look despite her age and when we walked in, the whole room stopped what they were doing to look.

"You're drawing attention," I teased her.

"Maybe they're looking at you," Barbara said. "After all, you're the one who's on television all the time."

I laughed but knew I was right. Barbara had long brown hair and large, sensuous eyes that drew you in forever. Looking at her, I thought maybe I really loved her. She was that gorgeous, smart and easy to be with. Anyway, no matter who the other customers were looking at, it didn't do me any harm to be seen in a romantic restaurant with a beautiful woman. I'm guessing some people thought Barbara was nothing more than my beard, a way to distract from the truth about my sex life but this was ridiculous, unfair to Barbara, unfair to me. Okay, I slept with men, many men, I'd be stupid to deny that, but no one with any brains would consider Barbara second best to anyone or anything.

While I had been a regular at the bathhouse in the Village for some time, I'd always gone with women too. Some people want to make sex simpler than it is. You're this or you're that. You're heterosexual or homosexual or maybe bi-sexual if you want to go that far. But to me, classification is a waste of time. The fact is that there's little in life that's more complicated than sex, less programmatic, or at least that's how it always seemed to me. Nothing's really comparable or superior to anything else as far as that goes. How to compare the weekend with Barbara to a furtive blow job in a rest room with someone I'd never see again. I may not have been everything Barbara would have wanted in a man, after all, she married someone else a few years later. But we always had a good time together, in and out of bed. If she wasn't satisfied, I certainly never heard anything about it.

In part to rid myself of these thoughts, I said, "My mother thinks I look lousy on tv. She says my ties are bad."

"Your mother's right," Barbara said. "I can help you with that. I've got a contact at Saks. Let's go over there when we get back to the city. By the way, I've got a friend who works at CBS, and she says you really got under Murrow's skin, or your boss did."

"You've got friends all over," I said smiling. "Saks, the Murrow show, and who knows what else?"

"I get around," Barbara said modestly but I knew that she did, moving effortlessly between worlds in New York and Washington. Sometimes, I wondered how she had time for her schoolwork, but no doubt she handled that without much effort, like everything else she did.

"Anyway," I said, "most people think Murrow won that one. He was way ahead on the mail, that's for sure."

Barbara shrugged. "I don't know, that's what I heard. But listen, Roy, what's so important about the hearings, television and all that? I can see it for McCarthy and the other senators, but is it really that vital to you? For all the crap you take in the press, I don't really see it. You could quit and come back to New York and do really well."

I wondered if maybe my parents had been talking to her. "Actually," I said, "it might seem funny, but right now there's nothing more important than these hearings and not just to me."

This seemed to make her sit back in her chair and I realized I'd raised my voice. "Sorry," I said, and I was, realizing it was stupid to be away for the weekend with her talking about politics.

"Don't apologize," Barbara said, smiling. "I like your passion. It's one of the things I like best about you."

Was she flirting with me after all the time we'd spent together? Doubtful and there was no need, but it was fine with me. "Well, anyway," I said, "We should order. What looks good to you?"

We stayed in Stonington until Monday sleeping late then walking on the beach and going through the shops in the village buying unnecessary things. We didn't talk about politics again and I found myself thinking Barbara might be right in saying I should give it up and come back to New York where I was more at home anyway. Who needed the headaches and toadies of Washington, the one-up-man-ship and outright childishness of half the senators on the Committee? It was a game, maybe even an important game, but did it have to be mine?

The last day we were in Connecticut, I was on the verge of proposing to her but stopped just short though I would follow through and ask her to marry me a few years later. I now think I missed my chance. I've lived long enough to know that timing is everything in life. It doesn't really matter now. The moment passed, I didn't propose, and then it was time to leave.

We drove back to New York, and I caught the train to Washington. When I said goodbye to Barbara, I found myself wondering why we hadn't done this more often. We were both busy but not that busy. "I'll see you soon," I said to her.

"Promise?" Barbara said, smiling.

"Sure," I said. "Absolutely."

What the Army grandly called the Adams Chronology was nothing more than a list Adams had put together of all the times I'd made calls pressuring various offices on Schine's behalf. To me, it was bullshit even though I had trouble letting it go. Was it accurate? Probably about as accurate as the list of commies McCarthy had at the Wheeling speech in West Virginia. I didn't check. I never denied calling Adams and anyone else I could think of trying first to get Dave a commission but so what? Adams and I were lawyers fencing with each other. *Quid pro quo* was the grammar of our lives, the way to tell if we were still breathing. No mystery there. Adams called me as often as I contacted him, asking for favors of one kind or another. Seats for a Broadway play, a good table at 21, box seats for a Yankees game, or his real objective, a cushy job at a white-shoes New York law firm. When we talked, he bitched endlessly about the lousy salary the Army paid him and whined that he was worth more.

I listened because it was in my interest to do so. In my world this was the way things worked: You scratch my back, I'll scratch yours. Except Adams welched on the deal. When I couldn't get him a job in New York, he figured he'd get even by putting together his big list give it to the Democrats and get my ass fired. It didn't turn out to be that simple, but we didn't know that at the time.

Bullshit or not, though, Welch used Adams' Chronology when he filed his Bill of Particulars on April 11. "The Department of the Army alleges that Senator Joseph R. McCarthy and chief counsel Roy M. Cohn, as well as other staff members, sought by improper means to obtain preferential treatment for one Pvt G. David Schine, United States Army."

Along with this was the *sub rosa* whispering campaign about Schine and me being homosexual. This wasn't the kind of thing you could deny on the radio, but it was out there, not just around the Capitol but also in Washington society or as much as I knew of it. I had done my best to shield the Committee from this, but there were only so many times I could bring Barbara down and show her off to rebut the rumors and I disliked doing that to her anyway.

McCarthy wasn't going to take this lying down. After Welch filed his bill, Joe hit them with one of his own, accusing the Army of lax security and blackmail. He said that *Res ipsa loqiuitur* the Adams Chronology had given aid and comfort to the Communist Party arguing that by making this accusation they were giving the party camouflage and protecting them from our attacks.

He also said Secretary Stevens and Adams were civilians and had no right to speak for the Army. He called the hearings "nothing more than a Cohn, Schine television show" and finally, he took a shot at Adams personally, saying that far from objecting to doing anything for Schine, he'd wanted to trade preferential treatment for Dave in exchange for a place in a better job in New York. He said the Chronology was nothing more than a bargaining chip and shouldn't be taken seriously.

What he said was true, but I thought he should have kept quiet about the Army sheltering communists. Joe wasn't much of a strategist, and it was a measure of loyalty to his staff that he spoke out about this. The Army wanted to get me and so did the Democrats on the Committee, but I wasn't important in the larger picture. Their ultimate target was obviously McCarthy and while I appreciated his support, Joe should have been more concerned about protecting himself. I think he knew this but in the end it hardly mattered. The Army had their Bill of Particulars, and we had ours. The sides were clear and the time for compromise had passed. The battle was drawn, and we were ready to fight.

Seventeen

MADISON

One of the leaders of Joe Must Go was a Madison lawyer named Ivan Nestigen, whom Ed hadn't known until Gore made the introduction. Nestigen was sympathetic when Ed called asking for advice, but he was serving on the Common Council and said he didn't do family law anyway. He suggested a colleague named Charlie Myers whom Ed went to see the following week in his office on the Square.

Myers was a man of medium height wearing a rumpled tweed suit, crepe-soled shoes and a slightly frazzled look when Ed was ushered into a room cluttered with books and papers falling off the desk under the windows.

"Sorry, sorry," Myers said, reading the look of alarm on Ed's face. "It's not you, I just lost my damned car keys. Again. Third time this month." Myers shook his large head and rubbed his face with rubber hands in disbelief at this relatively simple failing. "Okay," he said when he'd recovered himself. "I'm fine now. How can I help?"

Ed described his life for the past year ending with his return from Washington the week before to find the demand letter from Janey's lawyer about changing their custody arrangements. Like everyone else in Madison, Myers had seen the stories about Ed in the paper but didn't seem overly concerned. "Even in this environment, the fact that you're a communist isn't reason enough to change a custody arrangement," he said.

"I'm not a communist," Ed said.

"I know," Myers said. "What I mean is, even if you were, it doesn't matter. The Court doesn't really care what party you belong to, or if you belong to a party and the law doesn't either. Now if being a communist made you neglect your obligations or stop paying child support according to the Separation Agreement you and your ex-wife have, that would be different, but you've done all that, right?"

Ed nodded. "Mostly, I missed a payment because I was out of town, but that's all. She's mad because I took my son along on Joe Must Go canvassing trips around town."

"What about these indecent living arrangements," Myers said reading from the lawyer's letter. "Anything to that?" He was smiling as if he was hoping it was true, so Ed wasn't worried.

"It's ridiculous. My girlfriend's a dean at the University."

"Good for you," Myers said, as if Ed had won a prize in a gumball machine. "Nothing illegal about having an accomplished girlfriend if you're divorced. Now if it was a boyfriend, we might have a fight on our hands. Not that it matters to me," he said quickly.

"Will it matter in court?" Ed asked.

"If you're co-habiting?" Myers said. "It shouldn't but let's be realistic. It could." He looked again at the letter. "How did your wife find Thorndike? Her lawyer."

Ed shrugged. "I don't know. The Yellow Pages or friend of a friend maybe. Why, do you know him?"

"I wouldn't say I know him," Myers said. "I kicked his ass in court a few times last year but that didn't bring us closer together, if you know what I mean."

Ed immediately felt guilty, as if he was taking advantage of Janey by having a better attorney than she did. He thought he should call her up and tell her what Myers had said, offer to help her find someone better. With all that had happened he still felt oddly protective toward her. "Maybe my ex-wife should get someone else," Ed said.

"No," Myers said quickly. "We want to keep Mr. Thorndike in the case."

"So you can kick his ass again?" Ed said.

Myers laughed. "I don't really care about that so much," he said. "But if I remember it you can bet, he does, too."

"The language in that letter kind of bothered me," Ed said. "Saying I was a bad influence on my boy and that stuff about Susan being indecent."

Myers waved this off with his hands. "You're too sensitive. That's just lawyer talk, Thorndike justifying his fee. Don't take it seriously.'"

Ed suspected the lawyer was right, but it wasn't only that he might be thin-skinned where Janey, and his son were concerned. It got to him that Janey might really believe this crap. What did she imagine he'd do, kidnap the kid, take him to a communist indoctrination camp? How did a person he'd lived for years come to that? Sensitive, sure, but the truth was it pissed him off. "It's not easy," Ed said. "But I won't if you don't."

"I've forgotten it already," Myers said. "Look, I'll call Thorndike and get back to you. Maybe we'll have a meeting to talk it over, but probably not. With luck we can get this cleared up in a week or so on the phone with no more trouble for you. Anyway, if you get any more letters from him, don't respond. Just call and let me know. And don't talk about this with your ex-wife."

"I shouldn't tell Janey?"

Myers put his big hand on Ed's shoulder. "Tell her what? That you're going to countersue?" Then seeing the look of confusion on Ed's face, he said, "Just joking. My job is to make this disappear, as quickly as possible. But there's no guarantee I can do that, so we've got to work up a defense if you want to keep the rights you have with the boy. I know, it's a shit deal. But whatever you'd like to think, your ex-wife isn't on your side; she's not your friend anymore and you can't confide in her. Getting together for coffee, whatever you might say in an unguarded moment is just going to hurt you, so don't do that. Trust me, if she really wanted to talk about this with you, she wouldn't have had her lawyer write a letter in the first place. Does that make sense?"

"It does," Ed said. "It's just kind of sad, not that things were so great between us before, but not like this."

"Welcome to my world," Myers said. "It's why a lot of lawyers don't want to do divorces. Marriage is a very optimistic institution, till death do you part, and all that, so when it doesn't work out, it makes people crazy sometimes. Which means I always see people at their worst, nothing personal. Anyway, go have a beer with your girlfriend down at the Union and let me worry about this."

Ed left Myers' office and started walking down State Street, heading to the University. Myers hadn't mentioned a fee, but he had a feeling they'd give him a break because of the Nestigen connection. And while he was relieved by Myers' optimism about the case, he felt depressed about Janey's suspicions. They hadn't had the best marriage, but he'd always imagined they cared about each other and had never considered the possibility that things would sink to this level. No one in his family had ever been divorced, in fact no one he knew had ever gone this far and it made him feel he'd failed in a significant way. Without seriously planning anything, he supposed he had thought they'd work it out eventually and get back together. He wondered if Janey's sister or maybe this lawyer had pushed her to take this step.

It shook him that she could really consider him dangerous. And the thought of having less time with his son gave Ed chest pain so severe that he had to stop and lean against a building for a moment. Even if Janey were eventually to apologize, he knew it was one of those comments that couldn't be forgotten or taken back later. Regardless of what happened with the lawyers, this changed things between them forever.

The weather in Madison was variable and likely to change at any moment. When Ed started walking at the Square, it had been warm with a slight wind blowing, but by the time he got down to Johnson Street dark clouds had started gathering in a mauve pyramid overhead and the wind had turned cold and threatening. Small bits of moisture bit Ed's cheeks and he increased his pace, hoping to get down to the Union before the storm hit the shore. He barely made it, and thunder was crashing overhead when he crossed Langdon Street.

Ed walked over to the boathouse, shook off his coat and toweled down his hair. When he looked up, he saw Jimmy Simmons sitting in his chair playing Solitaire. "Jesus Christ," Ed said. "Where did you come from. You tailing me?"

Jimmy got up quickly from his seat. "Sorry," he said. "I didn't mean to scare you. I've just been waiting here."

"Everything scares me these days, kid," Ed said. Then seeing Jimmy's face, he said, "Didn't rent out any boats to your friends, I hope," Ed said.

"No, Sir," Jimmy said. "Not in this weather. I'm not sure I'd even know how anyway. Anyway, no, I was just sitting here. Honest."

Jimmy seemed to have grown since the first time Ed saw him, let his butch haircut grow out and he was filling out his clothes better than before. Ed didn't think he'd ever feel comfortable around the reporter, however, and he wondered what bad news the kid was bringing him now.

"You know, Jimmy," he began, "I'm sure you're a nice young guy but somehow whenever you're around something happens that's going to be bad for me."

"I know, Mr. Malloy, and I'm really sorry about that," Jimmy said. "But it's not my fault. My job is to report the news, and you might not like it, but you're news."

"I'm not news, goddamnit," Ed said irritably. "I'm just some asshole who got caught in the middle of something thanks to McCarthy. Anyway, what's happened now to bring you down here."

"Actually," Jimmy said, "it might be good for you in a way. McCarthy's Committee's going to have their hearings into the Army on national television."

"I heard something about that," Ed said. "What's that got to do with me."

"My editor thought maybe either you could write something for our Op-Ed page or I could just interview you again and write it up. You know, a reaction to what's going on in Washington from a local angle."

"I don't have any reaction," Ed said.

"But you're active in Joe Must Go," Jimmy said. "Out there going block to block getting signatures on the recall petition, right?"

"So what?"

"That's a reaction to McCarthy and what he's doing, wouldn't you say so." Jimmy looked so pleased with this insight that Ed almost felt sorry for him.

"The only reaction I have is that I hope we can recall the sonofabitch," he said. "Can you put that in your paper?"

"We don't print profanity," Jimmy said sadly, "but I can probably cut that one word and use the rest."

Ed laughed. "Well, then, knock yourself out, Jimmy. That's all I have to say."

When Ed saw Susan that night however, she said, "Maybe you should have written the article or at least let Jimmy interview you. What's the harm in that?"

"I thought signing his damned petition in the park was harmless and look where that ended up," Ed said. "You think you know how these things are going to work out, but it turns out you never do, or almost never."

"I wonder," Susan said. "I think the *Herald* could use some of that outrage I hear in your voice. It might make for more interesting reading than they usually have in the paper."

"If it's okay with you, I'd rather not be any more interesting than I already am," Ed said. "Last week, when they published a story about my working for Joe Must Go it caused more trouble for Little Ed. I can't have that happen again especially with Janey suing me."

"Did you tell Jimmy that you met Roy Cohn in Washington?"

"God, no," Ed said. "He'd run all the way to Milwaukee with that."

The visit with McCarthy's lawyer still resonated for Ed, the way Cohn sat at his desk with his foot on the chair, not even getting up to shake hands, his cocky manner and the fact that he'd called him Butch and mocked "Joe Must Go" by asking for a button. Ed had thought of a thousand things he should have said, ways he could have told Cohn off, set him straight about what was going on, and the threat they represented to him and his boss, but he hadn't and now he'd likely never have the chance to see Cohn again. He couldn't really see the little lawyer coming out to Wisconsin and when would Ed ever get back to Washington.

"Oh, well," Susan said now. "A lost opportunity." But Ed could see she was bantering with him and not really serious. "You could stay overnight," Susan said. "Try to live up to what Janey's lawyer is saying about us."

Ed was tempted. Things had developed naturally, easily between them, and now they were meeting several times a week for dinner. After one of these dates, Susan had invited him back to her bedroom and they'd made love. Anticipating this, Ed had been nervous. Sex with Janey had been an occasional thing, anniversaries and birthdays maybe, but always programmatic. Susan was completely different. She came at him quickly in bed, aroused in a way he hadn't expected, so much so that it was all over much faster for Ed than he would have liked. He apologized but Susan just smiled and straddled him, her hands on his shoulders as she moved rhythmically.

"I don't think I can do it again so soon," Ed said, embarrassed.

"You under-rate yourself," Susan said before moving lower and taking him in her mouth, bringing him alive again. This time it was better, slower, more in sync as they moved with each other.

"You're amazing," Ed said afterward. Given her demure appearance, he was surprised by her inventiveness and enthusiasm.

"I've been on the shelf for quite a while," Susan said laughing. "I've got some time to make up for, years, in fact."

"From the way you look, I expected something different," he said. Susan smiled at this. "Good," she said. "How do I look?"

Ed was sorry he brought it up. "I don't know," he said. "Modest, maybe. The way you dress, I mean."

"It's the way I was brought up," Susan said. "Small town. Conservative parents. My dad thought drawing attention to himself could hurt business. My mother used to say he was so modest he'd go into the next room to change his mind."

Ed laughed. "Well, you've got that under control." Then, he said, "I'd really like to stay but maybe tonight's not the best time. Little Ed might call or something."

"Does he call often at eleven o'clock at night?" Susan asked and laughed. "But don't worry about it. I'm fine with you going home to sleep if that's what you want."

"Thanks," Ed said and made his escape. He understood that living together would be the logical next step. They'd talked about this in a glancing way with Ed trying to make a joke out of it. "I'm pretty sure you'll get tired of me in time and start looking for someone more appropriate, which means anyone really. I wouldn't blame you."

This made Susan flush with irritation. "You're not getting rid of me that easily. I'm not looking for anyone else and I won't be. I'm satisfied and I wish you were too."

"It's not that," Ed said, and he didn't think it was. "But you're a dean with a Ph. D and I'm a special student taking one course. I had to go to the library to look up veldt when you mentioned it the other day. I had no idea what you were talking about."

"Who cares," Susan said. "If I wanted to marry someone with an interest in African History, I would have looked for one." Then she smiled. "Not that there was much to choose from in that lot. But still, I just don't think it matters."

"It may not matter now," Ed said. "What about later?" The thought that ten years down the road, she'd look up one day and be dissatisfied seemed inevitable.

"That's not the kind of thing that will ever matter to me," Susan said. "Like I told you, I got the degree when my husband was killed, and I needed to make a living. I thought I'd be a spinster."

"Really? I surprised you?" Ed liked the idea of being a revelation to someone like Susan.

"Yes," she said quietly. "You're actually a very surprising guy."

This was as far as the conversation got but they'd walked back over this several times since with Ed sure that in time myriad reasons they were mismatched would present themselves to Susan and she'd end the relationship. Whether this was true or not, however, Ed knew he wasn't being completely honest and that his indecision had little to do with education or Susan's seeing his flaws. In the past, he'd been reasonably confident in his ability to take the next step, whatever it might be, but things were different now. He found himself holding back, hesitant, now the lawyer had said that co-habitation could matter in court.

Ed had no idea what had changed in him or why but there it was. Janey was the only person who'd known him long enough to ask and he figured she'd have no interest in discussing his personality changes. It was one of the things you lost in divorce, that sense of where you fit in the world and a common history you shared with another person.

Despite his misgivings, he thought he should take the leap of faith and move in with Susan before she changed her mind. It made no more sense to continue to live alone in his run-down apartment. Given what Janey had said about Ed's deficiencies as a parent, it made sense to wait until the custody question was decided but he loved Susan and didn't want to wait. He hadn't really ever loved Janey. Their marriage was different than that, a necessity presented to him with no possibility of refusal. If Little Ed had ever asked him, he would have moved the question aside, said that he and Janey didn't really have that kind of relationship, that they were more of a team, maybe a partnership, though that sounded overly practical, at least to Ed's ears.

He knew he was grateful to Susan for rescuing him, and missed her when he wasn't with her, liked being together in and out of bed. She'd been clear about how she felt, and it seemed somehow ungracious not to reciprocate so what was holding him back? It was a mystery having to do in part with what he considered a new freedom to choose what sort of life he wanted to have. He'd been in lockstep from high school to the army and then back home to marriage and family and the job at the insurance company. Now through a string of circumstances all those obligations had been left behind but what would take their place?

Outside Susan's house, the street was empty though Ed thought he saw shadows move farther down the block. He squinted into the darkness but could see nothing clearly. He shivered in the cool night air and pulled his collar close around his neck. It wasn't the first time he'd sensed people being after him, behind him, unseen but following, keeping tabs on his movements. Once he noticed the headlights of a strange car in his rearview mirror following him all the way home at two in the morning. And now this, whatever it was if it was even anything. Was he paranoid, imagining enemies in the night down the empty block? What could make him important enough to shadow, keep tabs on to be written down in secret notebooks kept by whomever was on the prowl? He didn't know, but it was a strange, fearful time, and it made him jumpy,

Just that afternoon he'd bitten Jimmy Simmons' head off when he surprised him in the boathouse and the kid was only doing his job. Ed told himself he was going to have to get a grip. Whether it was the McCarthy stuff or Janey's new lawyer and his demand letters, Ed knew he'd been more irritable than usual. Susan had even noticed it, though she explained it away by saying anyone would feel the same way given everything that had happened to him lately. But Ed didn't buy it.

A magazine had done a big feature a few years before saying Madison was the ideal American city, a mixture of culture, beautiful parks, and friendly, well-educated people. They'd featured the University of course but also mentioned the LaFollettes, long gone now, of course, but along with milk and cheese about all most people outside the state could say about Wisconsin. Ed remembered reading the feature with pride, even taking the trouble to frame the magazine's cover with the Capitol lit up at night.

The magazine ended up calling Madison the Paradise of America and the Chamber of Commerce ran with this, printing bumper stickers saying "Welcome to Paradise" that soon dotted cars all over town. Maybe the city was actually that way or had been in the past. Ed couldn't say for sure. A couple of years ago he would have agreed with the reporter who wrote that story. But lately Madison had been nothing but trouble for him, the ease and friendliness gone, replaced by suspicion and fear of what or whoever was different. And Ed sensed there was nothing temporary about this. He remembered Cohn saying McCarthy was going on to bigger things and the hearings and newspapers articles wouldn't be ending anytime soon.

A car backfired down the street and Ed wondered if this would presage things to come. Gun battles on the quiet streets seemed beyond possibility, but who could say for sure? Reporting friends and neighbors as enemies of the state might only be the beginning.

Eighteen

The mail keeps coming. Stacks of it in large burlap bags the post office delivers twice a day. There are letters in business enclosures, others in smaller envelopes, boxes large and small and post cards. Some letters are typed, but the large majority are not, often written on note paper, pages from a Big Chief notebook or scrawled on the back of a card or letter the correspondent had previously received from McCarthy. They are supportive, sometimes profane, always direct, as if they imagine they're speaking to Joe himself: Get the commie bastards, Joe; string them up; nail their asses to the wall and worse. "Fire those Jew faggots working for you" was a frequent theme.

He is their friend, their pal, their champion, to hear them tell it the only one in Washington that's listening, the only one who cares about the fate of the country. There's a Christian tone to the notes, frequently quoting scripture, accurately or not. The writers have a direct line to God and He's a supporter of McCarthy too. And they're not wrong about Joe's passionate commitment to the cause which, if anything has gotten stronger, more intense over the preceding months. Regardless of the attacks that run in the liberal press, the almost daily Herblock cartoons showing him with black beard and hangman's noose, McCarthy's no opportunist grabbing onto the first available issue. He cares, sometimes too much, sometimes to his detriment and the stress is showing in sleepless nights and ever more disreputable dress.

Often there are direct accusations in the letters. Eisenhower's a commie sympathizer. Sherman Adams is pink just like Truman and Marshall. More mail about me and Schine. "Get rid of the kike bastards," one said. "It's the sheenies that started all this," said another. "The Commie Rosenbergs were Jews, just like Cohn and Schine." The fact that I'd had something to do with sending the Rosenbergs on their way to the hereafter didn't seem to matter to these writers. In a sense they weren't interested in policy but had discovered the true faith in McCarthy's crusade. They believed in Joe and weren't concerned with the fine print. The antisemitic attacks continue unabated even if we were helping their hero. They question our draft records, our parentage, our "Jewishness," our arrogance and our presumption.

And then there are the tips, meant to be helpful but seldom leading anywhere. Look into this, Joe, they demand, as if he works for them. Investigate that, so and so is hiding something, Symington's a red, so is McClellan. Someone else has evidence showing how and where commies might be hiding out. They heard it on the Winchell show on the radio, got it from a friend, their brother, their niece or nephew who knows someone on the inside who knows something. Fucking commies are everywhere, screwing up America. Look into it, Joe. Please.

McCarthy doesn't read any of this: the truth is Joe doesn't read much of anything. Newspapers, books Who has the time, he's fighting a battle that takes every minute of every day. He leaves the mail to his staff and if there's ever anything worth looking into, any book that's important, they'll tell him about it, summarize, give him talking points, if necessary. But what the mail tells me is that the fear of communism in this country is deep and wide and growing exponentially. It's not transient and won't go away, even if McCarthy and I do.

What I see is a deep undercurrent of fear and hate in America, all directed at the other, those who are different, often the newest arrivals, whether Irish, Italian, Greek or, as in my case, Jews. The attacks on homosexuals and Negroes are a variation on this theme. All of this has little to do with my job, of course; I don't experience the crazy mail as being supportive or critical. But it does convince me if I hadn't been convinced before that more than liking or approving of Joe, these people need McCarthy and what he represents in some deep and hidden way. His anger and passion are narcotic to them and far from being unique or what some might call a bad apple, he's more representative of America than most would like to think.

There will be more McCarthys just as there have been his like in the past, the Father Coughlins, J. Edgar Hoovers, and all the rest. There will be others. Count on this.

To clear my head, I walk outside between bouts with the letters and planning sessions for the hearings. Living in a hotel, as I do, I have little sense of Washington being an actual town with neighborhoods where people are born, live their lives and die. The buildings near the Capital are monuments, functional during the day, deserted at night making the city a ghost town of white marble and granite. They're completely different from the streets in Manhattan, always alive with foot traffic, hustlers, and movement, noise, smoke, sweat, most of all life, vibrant life never-ending. Here, there's none of that. The air is heavy and moist, making your face greasy no matter how many times you wash. People go to work and then home to their families, though some are more adventurous and frequent the bars and restaurants near the Hill. Even the parties, at least those I've been to seem like work with people trading cards and making appointments for the next day or the next week.

Otherwise, the city is a moribund animal during off hours or even the late afternoon. Occasionally I go down to Georgetown to Charlie's or OJays where homosexuals gather in clumps to drink and dance. It's reckless of me given my situation, but I'm desperate to find life in this mortuary. Generally, I sit by myself at the bar where the tattooed bartender recognizes me but has the good grace not to say anything, silently filling my glass until I signal that I'm done and ready to leave.

It seems like months since the weekend in Stonington with Barbara, though it's only two weeks, and the isolation is getting to me, so I decide to drive out to the country to the Cozy Corner in Virginia. I don't call Jerry because we haven't exchanged numbers, but he always seems to be at the bar when I visit, and this time is no different. He looks different to my eyes, though, haggard, a little rough around the edges. His shirt collar is frayed, and his tie is halfway-down his shirt. He nods when I walk in, and I take the stool next to his

"You don't look so good," I say, not beating around the bush.

Jerry smiles ruefully. "No shit. Maybe because I got fired this week." When I raise my eyebrows, he says, "Someone outed me to those lavender assholes. Not that it was a big secret, but my boss said he had no choice. I guess he figured if he didn't fire me, he'd be next."

'It wasn't me," I said. "I'm sorry."

"I know," Jerry said and shrugged. "But watch your ass."

"I always do," I said. "That's why I'm out here instead of in Georgetown."

Jerry nodded. "Smart but smart guys get caught too. I did. I thought I had it covered, knew what to do and what not to do, but I guess I was wrong about that."

I took this as a cautionary word, a friendly warning, and put my arm around Jerry. "What now?" I asked.

"There's nothing for me here anymore," Jerry said. "I'm going back to Albany. I've still got my law degree and some contacts."

It put a damper on the evening and when we left, he stopped at his car, and he said, "I'm just going to call it a night if that's okay with you. I'm leaving early in the morning."

"It's fine," I said. "Then I held him in my arms and kissed him in the dim light of the parking lot, saying goodbye to my only friend in Washington.

The next round of hearings was held in the Senate Caucus chamber, a grand room with sculpted ceilings and hanging cut-glass chandeliers that cast a sickly yellow haze over everything. Despite the size of the room, however, there was a standing room audience daily starting with VIPs like Perle Mesta, Washington's leading hostess and Alice Longworth Roosevelt. Then you had the press filling in on either side of gawkers and finally Committee members and counsel all jammed together at tables in the front. It reminded me of some championship prize fights I'd been to in Madison Square Garden. All it lacked was the fat guy in the tux standing in the middle of the ring and some babe in a swimming suit parading around the ring at the end of each round with a placard.

You want to know how I felt being in front of millions of people and under those goddamned tv lights day after day? The truth is I was like a rat in a maze fighting to find a good way out. Barbara and my parents came down for the first few days to offer support but then I told them to stay away since the mounting attacks on me in the papers upset them and I worried about their being targets. I had more than enough to deal with without that.

From our perspective the goal, the real point of the investigation was to spotlight and make undeniable the security lapses that allowed communists to serve in the military and even be promoted as Peress had been. The Army was doing their best to obscure this through their smear campaign on me. We knew their constant focus on what I'd done for Dave was just a smokescreen, but it was effective, blinding some people and causing others to wonder. The fact that McCarthy might have a couple of godless Jew homos working for him was red meat, there was no denying that. Still, we tried to maintain focus on the investigation starting with our first witness, Robert Stevens, the Secretary of the Army, who took the stand and started to read through a lengthy prepared statement.

"It is my responsibility," he said, "to speak for the Army, for the million and a half men and women..." Stevens intoned, but immediately McCarthy was on his feet interrupting.

"Mr. Chairman," Joe said. "Point of order." They'd already disallowed Joe's points of order on other occasions but he was impossible to shut down once he'd decided to speak. "Mr. Stevens is not speaking for the Army," Joe said. "He is speaking for Mr. Stevens. I resent this attempt to connect our great servicemen and women with the attempt to sabotage this committee's investigation into communism."

This set off a mild uproar in the room but both Jenkins and Chairman Mundt agreed with Joe on this point, not that it stopped Stevens from making the same claim again once he was allowed to continue. But then he got down to business. "From mid-July of last year until March 1 of this year possibly promoting Private David Schine was the subject in no fewer than sixty-five phone calls and nineteen meetings between Army staff and Senator McCarthy's committee counsel, Mr. Cohn."

This was bullshit. Stevens didn't know how many contacts we'd had with the Army and neither did I. It could be 650 as easily as sixty-five. What it all came down to was Stevens' claim that I was applying pressure to get Dave first a commission, then various leaves and passes once he'd enlisted. This was true and I was happy to admit it, but the picture Stevens painted was of me being a kind of Quixote on a lunatic mission driven by homosexual frenzy with McCarthy simply the passive partner, going along, afraid of displeasing me if he objected. Which was a joke because Joe was anything but passive and had never been afraid to displease anyone. The real question was why the Army didn't just tell me to go to hell with my requests for favors in the first place or refuse to take calls about Schine. That never happened and the reason was that they were perfectly happy to talk about a deal as long as it got us to let up on the investigation into Monmouth.

The real surprise of the hearing was Jenkins, the committee's counsel, even if he was less celebrated than Welch. Leaning his huge body into Stevens as he questioned him, all you could see from our side of the room was his red hair bobbing up and down as he pounded away on the Secretary. I don't usually agree with the *Times*, but in this case, their description of Jenkins fit. They called him "...The kind of lawyer who completely dominates a case and the court...in his thirty-four years of practice, Ray Jenkins had defended 600 murder victims without losing one to the electric chair. The secret he said was to get the jury so damned mad that they want to dig up the body and kill the SOB all over again."

I was glad we had him on our side even if Stevens got in some shots at me and Schine along the way. At one point, Stevens described a conversation with Dave saying, "It was along the lines that I was doing a good job of ferreting out communists. I took this as a compliment coming from young Schine who seemed to consider himself an expert on the matter."

This got a good laugh out of the spectators. Then Stevens added, "David was nice enough to say he thought I could go a long way in this field and that he would like to have helped me by becoming my assistant rather than being drafted into the Army."

When the laughter died down, Stevens added that he'd never had trouble with me except around the issue of Dave's induction, managing to avoid entirely the question of Monmouth, which was why Joe held the hearings in the first place.

Finally, they let Stevens go for the day and we went back to Joe's office for drinks and a strategy session. When we were sitting down, I asked Dave if he ever really made that suggestion to Stevens.

"I don't know," Dave said. "It's possible."

"He had his notes right there in front of him, for Christ's sake," Joe said. "He had the date and time."

"I guess I said a lot of things," Dave admitted. "Maybe some things I shouldn't have when I look at it now."

"Yeah," McCarthy snorted. "Maybe, my ass. You shouldn't have said any of that shit. You should have kept your goddamned mouth shut. Simple."

The hearings went on and Stevens stayed on the stand with Jenkins cross-examining him. The lawyer talked rapidly, his words rat-tat-tatting across the crowded room like rounds on a firing range. Occasionally, he'd emphasize points by exclaiming "Yes" and clapping his hands together. He was something to watch. Jenkins asked Stevens if the Army had been examining Monmouth before we started our investigation. Stevens admitted they had and that six people who worked there had been suspended previously for questionable activities, including organizing for the communists.

Jenkins nodded his huge head and leaned into the secretary again. Stevens pulled back as if he expected the lawyer to grab him by the neck, but Jenkins just turned to the audience and smiled before resuming. "And can you tell me how many were suspended after the McCarthy investigation began," Jenkins asked.

"Twenty-nine," Stevens said quietly.

"So," Jenkins said, clapping his hands for emphasis, "wouldn't you say then that the investigation had an important effect, and that it enhanced national security in a way that hadn't occurred before?"

"Not really," Stevens said. "We were on top of all that already."

"I'm sure you were," Jenkins said, his voice booming. "But all this was in this context, meaning that communists had been working at our vital post in Monmouth? Is that right, Secretary Stevens? Am I understanding you here?"

"Yes," Stevens said. "If you want to put it that way."

"Okay, then," Jenkins said, "Where did David Schine fit into all this? He had nothing to do with Monmouth except that he was working as a consultant to the Committee during the investigation which as we just established resulted in twenty-nine communists being fired. Isn't it a fact that you were being especially warm and tender to this boy?"

"Absolutely not," Steven said, and there was more laughter in the room.

"I see," Jenkins said, his face wreathed in a cagy smile, like a wolf who had just come into an open cage of chickens. "So, what you're saying is that the treatment you gave Schine was just what any other private would receive?"

"I would absolutely treat them all the same," Steven said, chin up, jaw tight.

Having established that, Jenkins got down to the meat of his cross. He asked if the Secretary hadn't been to dinner at the Schine's Waldorf Towers apartment. And if later he hadn't been driven around New York in a Schine limousine? And that subsequently he'd called Allen Dulles about a job for Schine. Stevens seemed to pull back in the face of this, to shrink then nearly disappear in the presence of the huge lawyer. Then Jenkins closed in for the kill.

He gestured at the pile of paper as if it somehow represented all the calls I'd made and Stevens' responses. "When you get right down to it, sir," he asked, "wasn't all this done in an attempt simply to get McCarthy and Cohn to back off their investigation because they were getting too close to the truth about Monmouth being a stronghold for communists?"

"It was absolutely not done for that reason," Stevens said stubbornly, though I doubted anyone in the room believed this.

Jenkins drew back theatrically and said, "I see. Then why was it done?"

"It was just a matter of convenience, actually," Steven said. "That's all it was."

"I see," Jenkins said, and turned to the room. "That's all it was."

As dramatic as this was, however, it was only the prelude for one of the big moments of the hearings for then Jenkins asked if Stevens ever had his picture taken with Schine since he claimed he treated him exactly as he would any other private in the Army. Stevens looked surprised by this. He said he couldn't remember anything like that, but he supposed it was possible that he took pictures with many people for various reasons.

Jenkins paused and then leaned forward, towering over Stevens again. "Possible, you say, Mr. Secretary?"

Stevens nodded. Then Jenkins held up an over-sized reproduction of a photograph of Schine and Stevens standing shoulder to shoulder in front of a military plane. And all hell broke loose in the room.

Stevens was red in the face, embarrassed by Jenkins' surprise and sat rigid as a scarecrow in his witness chair staring straight ahead. When things quieted down, he said in a soft voice, "It does look like me. I can't say I recognize the soldier for sure."

If Stevens didn't recognize Dave in the picture, he was the only one in America that wouldn't have since Schine's picture had been plastered across newspapers and magazines for weeks. I remembered the photo. It had been a cold afternoon, the rain blowing sideways into our faces like tiny pellets. We were on our way to Boston when Stevens offered the use of his private plane for the trip, likely just being friendly again.

Stevens cleared his throat then and corrected himself, his voice small in the big room. "Actually, I do recognize Schine now along with a rather grim-looking Secretary of the Army."

People in the audience laughed at this since Stevens didn't look grim at all in the photo, but rather like a proud uncle sending his nephew off to college. Given the undercurrent of suspicion regarding homosexuality since the Lavender Scare other questions might have been raised about their friendship, though no one had ever suspected Stevens of being queer. But the larger point, not really a question but an assertion, was why Stevens would be in the picture at all if he wasn't trying to curry favor with Schine's parents. To me this was typical not just of Stevens and Adams but all the top Army brass. They thought of themselves as entitled grandees, feasting off the nation's wealth, helping themselves to whatever they could get with little or no concern either for the good of the country or the soldiers they were supposedly serving.

The emergence of the photo was bad for Stevens and for the Army. I tried to avoid smiling but I had a feeling that we'd knocked them back in a significant way. When the noise in the room subsided, Welch, the aristocratic defense counsel, stepped up to try to stop the bleeding. He asked Stevens if he could remember anyone else being in the picture beside him and Schine.

It was an odd development in the chaos of the chamber, the shuffling of papers, books briefcases, the whispering that represented a steady undercurrent of noise and the reporters all scribbling their notes in the corner. I had no idea what Welch might be getting at and Stevens looked perplexed by the question, but then Welch said, "What I'm asking is if you were you photographed only with Private Schine or if there were others present that day?"

Because Stevens looked baffled and unable to answer, Welch provided his own. "I submit this is a shamefully doctored photograph," he said, "made to appear as if Secretary Stevens and Schine were alone when actually they were part of a group. I offer here the original, un-doctored photograph." And he held high over his head a photo with Stevens, Schine and a third man, Colonel Bradley.

I felt sick, my stomach moving somewhere in the direction of Potomac but there was nothing to do about Welch's move and it's an example of how quickly things can shift in a situation like this. We had them and then we didn't; in fact they had us. Though we could slow things down, I had the sudden knowledge that no matter what we would do from here on, we were fucked, and there was no way to avoid our fate.

McCarthy had seemed to be asleep but now he came awake and sat up quickly. He covered his microphone and said, "What the hell, Roy? What's this all about." I shrugged my shoulders, having no idea. Then he shouted "Point of order. Point of order, Joe's default in these situations whether it was actually a point of order or not. This did get people's attention, which was the idea.

"Mr. Welch says the picture is doctored, that this is actually a group picture, which is completely false," Joe shouted, waving his arms.

Except that it wasn't false and now Welch looked triumphant, having made his point. Now the Democrats on the committee seemed to come back from a seance, raising their hands and demanding loudly to know the facts of the matter. To this end, Stevens was excused from the stand and Welch called the man who supposedly had the facts, Roy Cohn, to answer for the artful distortion of the picture.

Jenkins for the first time seemed speechless. I'd given him the picture without mentioning Bradley being missing and now he was upset about it. I didn't really blame him, but unlike Stevens, I knew my way around the witness stand and wasn't going to be bullied as he'd been.

Jenkins brushed his mane back and recovering from his surprise took over from Welch. "Did you or did you not tell me," he asked, "that you had documentary evidence of the relationship between Private Schine and Secretary Stevens in the form of a photograph."

I had. He knew it, and I knew he knew it, but I finessed him. "How about if I do this my way?" I asked, trying to regain control. "Would that be all right?"

This didn't really answer Jenkins' question, but he shrugged, indicating that would be acceptable. I knew I had to regain control of the hearing and was doing what I always did and would later counsel others to do: deny knowledge of whatever I was accused of and then blame others for it.

I said I had indeed told him about the photo but the reason I didn't tell him it had been doctored is that I didn't know it myself.

"Mr. Cohn," Welch said, interrupting. "Would you admit that you're well connected here in Washington?"

"I don't know about that," I said.

"Really," Welch said. "I'd say no one here is as well connected as you and not just here, but maybe anywhere."

This got a big laugh from the room. When everyone quieted down, I said. "Okay, but I don't really see what you're getting at."

"My point," Welch said, "is that since you're so well connected, know so many people, you must also know people who enlarge and edit photographs. So how could you possibly not know this picture had been doctored?"

"That's easy," I said. "Because I didn't actually have the picture or arrange to have it enlarged myself. An associate did and then cropped the picture on his own because all we were interested in was showing the Secretary and Schine knew each other. After that he gave the picture to me, and I gave it to Mr. Jenkins. But it doesn't matter. The point is that Schine and Mr. Stevens knew each other better than Mr. Stevens was letting on. They were obviously well acquainted, and the picture offers undeniable proof of that."

Except it wasn't that simple. Without realizing it, I'd fallen into a trap that Welch had cleverly set, and I was kicking myself because I should have known better. Welch resumed the questioning. "Although we sit at the same table, you'd agree that I'm not your counsel, wouldn't you, Mr. Cohn."

"That's true, but I don't need a counsel," I said, arrogant as usual. "Roy Cohn represents Roy Cohn."

Even thinking of this now makes me cringe, but I couldn't help myself. Why could I go on at this length and given a choice, why would I? A good question and the answer I suppose is I couldn't help it. Climactic points in life are like that. What art critics call chiaroscuro, the play of black and white on canvas. It's hypnotic. You go over and over memories of these times like a bad painting, thinking if only you could improve this corner, increase the shading on the upper right, everything would be all right. But it wasn't to be in this case and now Welch headed in for the kill.

He smiled and said, "Okay, good. And I'm satisfied from my end, that it shouldn't appear that I'm representing you."

The audience laughed again at this. We'd lost the momentum due to my stupidity. But Welch wasn't through. He held up the photo and said, "Wouldn't you agree that it appears that Mr. Stevens is looking to his right?" I hesitated and he said, "Come, you can answer that easily. Yes or no?"

I didn't know where he was going and was angry with myself for getting out-maneuvered by this slick. "Yes, I'd say Mr. Stevens is looking to his right. So what?"

"And there are two figures to his right, isn't that so?"

"I guess that's true," I said.

"Well, then," Welch said, "couldn't Mr. Stevens be looking at either Mr. Schine, Colonel Bradley or both of them and smiling."

"Maybe he's smiling in anticipation of the steak dinner he's going to have later on compliments of the Schines," I said, always the wise guy.

"If so," Welch said, "Considering the expression on his face, Private Schine must be looking forward to a haunch of beef, maybe the whole cow."

The crowd laughed and clapped and stopped everything for five minutes. What had begun as a positive development for us turned out to be a fiasco, as in addition to me other McCarthy staffers were called to the stand until finally Jim Juliana took responsibility for cropping the picture.

"Ah, so at last we have the person responsible," Welch said to Juliana. "And why did you do that?"

"I was asked by Mr. Cohn to provide a picture of Mr. Schine and Mr. Stevens," Jim said. "So, I provided one."

"And are you quite sure that no one ever suggested to you that it might be a good idea to crop the photo so as to take Colonel Bradley out of the picture and make it appear to be a photograph of Mr. Schine and Mr. Stevens alone?"

"No," Jim said. "No one ever said anything like that. Absolutely not."

"Then who cropped and reproduced the photo if Mr. Cohn didn't and you also had nothing to do with it, a pixie perhaps?"

Before Juliana could respond McCarthy interrupted. "I'd just like to ask learned counsel," he said, "to give us a definition of pixie."

A muted reaction in the crowd followed this but then Welch said. "I think a pixie is a close relative of a fairy."

There was a general intake of breath at what seemed to be a reference to the rumors of Schine and I being lovers. Welch didn't seem like the kind of guy to be making homosexual jokes in a Senate hearing, but he'd gotten the crowd behind him, you had to give him that.

It didn't bother Joe who came right back at him. "I think you may be an authority on fairies, counselor," he said, and we had the crowd back, if only briefly.

Still Welch had turned the momentum around on something that should have been a big score in our favor. Stevens' claim that he had treated Schine no differently than any other private made no sense given the photograph, doctored or not. If Stevens didn't know Schine, hadn't pulled strings or tried to ingratiate himself with us, why had he accepted the hospitality of Schine's parents, driven us out to the airport and then offered his personal plane to fly to Boston? All of this made our case that he was clearly not as upright as he'd claimed. But thanks to Welch's brilliance, all that had disappeared in the talk of fairies.

More important, Welch had gotten under McCarthy's skin and caused Joe to explode publicly, which made McCarthy appear to be as wild and uncontrolled as our enemies wanted people to believe he was. We all valued the fact that Joe stood behind his "boys" as he called us, but in this case, he might have done more good by letting us stand on our own. That, however, wasn't and would never have been Joe McCarthy. It was his strength, and I was learning, his great flaw.

Nineteen

MADISON

Despite Ed's suspicions, Janey didn't really mean to attack him or even to deny him parental rights. When you were married, everything was a we. We're buying a house, we're buying a car, we're having a baby, we're going to the park or the beach, even if in her marriage, the we had mostly consisted of Janey making plans and telling Ed what they were. Now it was different. There was no we, only Janey alone trying her best to decide what to do. So no matter how Ed might see her wanting to change the custody situation, from her point of view, it was nothing more than protecting Little Ed from unhealthy influences, especially since Ed seemed more and more out of touch, traveling to places that were only names to Janey and spending most of his time with his high and mighty friends up to the University. Janey supposed that since there was no more we and they were each on their own, what he did with his free time was his own business, but she still felt increasingly helpless before meeting Dennis Thorndike at a social at the new church her sister had convinced her to join.

Not that Janey was really looking to meet anyone, but Patsy said she was closing in on thirty and still taking the course to be a legal secretary. To be honest Dennis would not have been Janey's dream date if she had been looking. He was short, beginning to go bald and had one eye that seemed to have a life of its own. It was always staring over your shoulder when he talked to you. But that wasn't really important. He was a lawyer, presentable and, as Patsy said, who was she to be picky at this point? They'd had lunch and then spent a few evenings together during which Janey filled Dennis in on her divorce and the current situation with Ed. Dennis listened politely and then asked why she hadn't had her own lawyer during the divorce, why she'd just agreed to handle everything off a form Ed got at the stationery store on Monroe Street? Janey didn't know the answer to that since no one she knew had ever gotten divorced before.

It came as no surprise that Dennis knew Ed's name from the articles in the *Herald* and he was outraged that Little Ed would have been recruited for canvassing trips for Joe Must Go. He said it was typical of communists to prey on helpless children and that they were even infiltrating schools and trying to put homosexual communists in a position to pervert America's youth. Janey had never been political before and she had always liked Little Ed's teachers, but she couldn't say Dennis was wrong nor could she stop worrying about the reach of communism in the life of her family. Could all those lawyers and Senators be completely wrong?

So when Dennis advised Janey to try to make a change in their custody arrangement and said he'd help with the paperwork, it felt to Janey that someone was finally looking out for her. To Janey this made sense and if her ex-husband didn't like it, well, that was just too bad.

Ed got a call at eight in the morning asking him to drop by Myers' office. They were drinking coffee, still in their bathrobes.

"What do you think they want at this hour?" Susan said.

Ed shrugged. "He said it should be fast. Maybe something's going right for a change and all I have to do is sign some papers."

Susan nodded. "That would be nice, but bad news travels fast and it's odd to me that they'd call so early. There's nothing urgent about signing papers."

"What kind of bad news are you talking about?"

Susan sat back in her chair and looked at him in amazement. "Ed, how can you be so naïve about other people, especially considering everything that's happened to you? There's evil in the world. You have to be on the lookout for it."

"Evil? You mean like my ex-wife?" It was a new thought to him and though it seemed absurd, he wanted to defend Janey.

"I don't mean anything specifically," Susan said carefully. "I just want you to be careful and protect yourself, that's all."

No matter what had gone on before, Ed didn't like the suggestion that Janey was evil and out to get him, but it wouldn't do any good to strike back at Susan, especially since she turned out to be prescient. When Ed got to Myers' office, the lawyer looked nervous and even more unkempt than usual. He took Ed into a conference room and said, "Okay, not a crisis, but we didn't exactly get the judge I wanted."

Ed didn't know what the difference would be. He had somehow thought you could pick and choose judges if you got one you that seemed wrong, but he didn't want to admit this to Myers. "What's the matter with him?"

Myers hunched his shoulders. "It's the luck of the draw. The way it works and too bad for us. We got Cooper and he's a big supporter of McCarthy."

"Great," Ed said. He had a sinking feeling in his stomach. "What does that mean exactly?"

Myers ran his fingers through his hair and sighed. "Well, it doesn't mean Thorndike's a genius because like I said it's luck of the draw. But it's probably given them some confidence. Now you're going to have to go through discovery."

"Discovery?" The term meant nothing to Ed. He thought of Columbus, Vasco de Gama, but he had the feeling it wasn't that kind of discovery.

Myers nodded. "Not a big deal, or it shouldn't be. They get to ask you questions and you respond, that's all."

Ed felt a chill on the back of his neck. Nothing seemed to be a big deal to Myers and now he wondered if his lawyer was sugar-coating the reality and things were actually much worse than he had feared. He wondered when this would end, he being under suspicion. "What kinds of questions?"

"Anything they can think of some of it completely irrelevant. No matter what they ask, though, it's important not to lose your cool because that's exactly what they'll want you to do. Also, some of the questions could be pretty personal."

"Maybe this guy's a better lawyer than you thought," Ed said.

Myers smiled. "Maybe, but I doubt it. Thorndike doesn't have a great reputation around town. I'm not the only lawyer who's kicked his ass."

"Well that's something," Ed said. "Have you been in touch?" It bothered him to be on the outside with all this just as his life had started to make some sense. He hadn't expected to have trouble with Janey after the divorce. At the beginning, she'd seemed very detached about the whole thing, but her lawyer's demand letter had rocked him. Now, according to the letter, he was a danger to their son and when he'd tried to talk it over with her, she refused to discuss it without her lawyer in the room.

"I talked to him once to set this up," Myers said. "He sounded kind of cagey, as if he had something I didn't know about. Which could be true. But the way this works is they have to share everything they have with us, so we'll know sooner or later what they have or think they have."

"I suppose the judge read the articles about me in the paper and "Joe Must Go," Ed said. "It seems like everybody has."

"Probably," Myers said, "but as I told you in our first meeting none of that should make any difference in a divorce hearing. Unless there's something you haven't told me."

Ed searched his mind, trying to think of what might be important that he hadn't already mentioned to the lawyer, but came up blank. "I told you everything I can think of," he said. "The truth is there's not much to tell."

"Okay," Myers said, "then go home and try to relax. Maybe go to a movie. I'll meet you at Thorndike's office tomorrow."

"Okay, I'll try, but, look, you don't need to take it easy on me. Am I in trouble here? I want to know what my situation really is."

He tried to follow Myers' advice, but relaxation proved difficult. Ed walked out the lake path to Picnic Point and then re-traced his steps, trying to think what had brought all this on. Could Janey really be angry about Susan and even if she was, would she go to these extremes only out of jealousy? He stopped and looked at the green algae washing up on the shore dying the rocks a sickly gray. He remembered when the lake had been clear as glass, but it didn't seem to matter to the ducks who bobbed in and out of the dirty water, looking for flies, breadcrumbs, whatever ducks ate. Students walked by arm in arm and Ed envied them the apparent simplicity of their lives even as he knew life however one lived it was never simple.

That night, Susan suggested they try to anticipate the meeting at the lawyer's office. "We could work on it together to help you prepare. Just think of what they could possibly ask you." she said.

"That's it, I have no idea," Ed said. "Myers said it could be anything."

"That leaves a pretty large window," Susan said.

"He did say it could be personal," Ed offered.

Susan raised her eyebrows at that. "About us?"

"I guess," Ed said. "He also told me the judge we got is a big backer of McCarthy."

"What difference should that make?" Susan asked. "I thought they were supposed to be impartial."

"Myers said it doesn't usually figure in during a custody hearing but from what I've seen McCarthy always makes a difference. Look what they did to my pal Tony when he got in front of that Committee."

"That's the guy who passed the buck to you, right?"

"Sure, but what could he do, what could anyone do under that kind of pressure? He'd probably name his own mother if he thought it would get him off the spot."

"Sounds like a great guy," Susan said.

"Actually, he was, probably still is," Ed said. "You know, he grew up in Jersey City, family was broke during the Depression like everyone else. Then he gets his ass drafted, serves for five years and somehow manages not to get killed over in Europe. He comes home and before he knows it, he's in front of some damned Senate Committee asking him if he's a communist." Ed shook his head. "I'll bet it scared the shit out of the guy just like it would anyone, so he gave them the names of other guys he knew over in Italy, including me. I'm not happy about it, it's been a huge pain in the ass. But I don't blame Tony."

"Maybe you should start blaming people, Ed," Susan said. "Starting with the papers, your former boss and then your ex-wife. A little anger might do you some good, as long as you're not angry with me."

"I've never been good at that," Ed said, thinking about it. "I don't know why but I just don't get mad, even like you say when I should. Sometimes I wish I did but if I feel it boiling up inside me, at the same time, there's always this voice that says, 'Come on, it's not that big a deal.'"

Susan pulled him close and kissed him. "You're such a good guy," she said. "They all depend on that."

Thorndike's office was just off the Square like all the other lawyers who wanted to be close to the courthouse. Ed thought it wasn't as busy as Myers', and he hoped that meant something. The deposition was in a shabby conference room with a couple of chipped tables pushed together to make one. Thorndike, Janey and a stenographer were on the side near the windows while Ed and Myers sat near the door. The lawyer had told Ed not to bring Susan along for fear of inflaming Janey.

They started with Thorndike naming everyone in the room for the benefit of the stenographer. The lawyer was a little guy, wall-eyed in a gray suit and a white shirt that was a little gray itself. Janey's face was stitched tight, and she didn't look at him when Ed greeted her. Thorndike started with a couple of puffball questions.

"Mr. Malloy, you are the former husband of Janemarie Malloy with whom you formerly resided at 1705 Madison Street in Madison, is that right?"

"Sure," Ed said. Everyone knew this so why ask the question?

"And you're now renting an apartment at 535 Randall St."

Ed nodded. Thorndike dived right in. "Are you a communist, sir?"

"No," Ed said. He sighed and looked at the ceiling.

"Have you ever been a member of the Communist Party?"

This was starting to sound like one of those McCarthy Committee meetings. "That's ridiculous," Ed said. He turned to Janey. "You know this, Janey. What's going on?"

"Please answer the question," Thorndike said, sounding like a schoolmarm. Ed wondered if he had a thimble to rap him on the knuckles if he misbehaved. "And in the future direct any questions to me."

Ed looked at Myers, who shrugged. "No," he said. "I've never been a member of the Communist Party. Jesus."

"Nevertheless, you're aware you've been named as a communist by Anthony Abruzzi at a hearing of the Senate Sub-Committee on Investigations in Washington chaired by Senator McCarthy."

"I'm know about the hearings, but I don't think Tony ever said I was a member of the party."

Thorndike backed off for a moment but then continued. "Maybe not, but Abruzzi did say you were involved with communists when you were supposedly serving our country, isn't that the case?"

"No," Ed said. "That's bullshit. Tony was just covering his ass. I never went to any communist meetings with him in Italy and I was serving my country."

Thorndike smiled tightly, pleased to have gotten under Ed's skin. "You're sure you never accompanied Mr. Abruzzi when he went to such meetings in Italy, even though he swore under oath in Washington that you did?"

This prissy little bastard was beginning to get to Ed. He had told Susan he didn't usually get mad, didn't fly off the handle, but now he took a deep breath and exhaled. Take it easy, he told himself. "Yes. I'm sure," Ed said. "I'm not a communist and never have been."

Thorndike looked at his notes. Then out of the blue, he asked, "Are you prejudiced against Italians, Mr. Malloy?"

"Prejudiced? Sure I am. That's why me and a bunch of other G.I.s fought to save their asses during the War," Ed said.

"Which might have made you dislike Italians even more, resent them for the trouble they'd caused you and your friends, some of whom unfortunately died over there?"

"Maybe for some people," Ed said. "But Italians are okay with me, like everybody else."

Thorndike nodded and looked again at his legal pad. "Do you know a man named Edward DiPietro?"

"Sure," Ed said. "He used to be my boss before he fired me."

"Do you think Mr. DiPietro is of Italian extraction?"

"How do I know?" Ed said. "But, yeah, I guess it's an Italian name so he's probably Italian or his parents were. So what?"

Thorndike patted a briefcase by his side and said, "Mr. DiPietro has given me a sworn affidavit saying you made anti-Italian remarks directed at him when you were employed in his office."

Ed's mouth dropped open. Where was this coming from, he wondered and what did it have to do with custody? But Myers had said they could ask him anything they wanted and that their intention was to piss him off, knock him off balance. A good reason to try to hold in his irritation. "I never said anything about DiPietro being Italian," Ed said.

"And were these anti-Italian remarks perhaps the reason for your dismissal?" Thorndike persisted, ignoring his answer. "A secretary of Mr. DiPietro, Miss Betty Simmons, quotes you as calling him 'A lousy wop,' when you left his office."

"I never said that, never called DiPietro anything. I don't care what Betty says," Ed said. He knew this was true, but at the same moment, he began to doubt himself. He couldn't remember saying anything about DiPietro but was it impossible? Who knows for sure what he'd said about a boss who was letting him go? Ed had nothing against Italians, and it wasn't the kind of thing he'd say, he knew that, but did he anyway? Was it possible? "The point is that had nothing to do with my leaving. I got fired because they wanted me to sign a loyalty oath, and I refused to do it."

Thorndike nodded. "Like other communists who've been discharged from the government and other employment for refusing to sign loyalty oaths."

Ed couldn't believe where this was going. He looked over, but this wasn't court. As Myers had told him, they weren't limited to questions related to custody and his lawyer couldn't object. "I don't know about any of that," Ed said. "I'm a loyal American," Ed said. "I've got a Purple Heart and an honorable discharge. I don't need to sign anything to prove that, so I didn't."

"Yes," Thorndike said," but despite this, you still dispute Mr. DiPietro's statement that you're anti-Italian?"

"I'm not anti-anything and Janey damned well knows it." Ed was starting to heat up again and he knew he had to control himself.

"Please confine your answers to yes or no and direct any comments to me," Thorndike said looking at his pad again.

"Okay, fine," Ed said. "Sorry."

"Moving on," Thorndike said, "are you an officer of an organization called Joe Must Go, whose stated goal is to recall Senator Joseph McCarthy?"

"We don't have officers," Ed said. "But, sure, I'm a member."

Thorndike didn't respond to this.

"And have you taken your young son Edgeworth along with you and other communists when you tried to get residents to sign petitions in support of this organization."

"We're not communists, okay?" Ed said. "Some of the members are Republicans, just like McCarthy, but, yes, I did take my son along canvassing, with his mother's permission." He looked over at Janey. "You know this," he said.

"And you don't think there's anything inappropriate about exposing your young son to this kind of controversial activity?" Thorndike said. "I understand that some of the residents you approached were angry and insulted you when you came to their door. There might have been violence directed at you and the boy. Weren't you concerned?"

"There are some pretty crazy people out there," Ed said. "But nothing like that happened and Little Ed seemed fine with it. He's a pretty tough kid."

Thorndike nodded. "So apparently you believe children should be, as you put it, tough enough to be exposed to such things? Insults, violence."

"I didn't say that, goddamnit."

"Mr. Malloy, please," Thorndike said but he smiled again, as if he was enjoying this and Ed supposed that he was.

At this point, Myers indicated he wanted to talk so Thorndike told the stenographer to take a rest, and they went out in the hall. "You've got to control yourself," Myers said. "Getting angry at Thorndike's questions is going to hurt not help us."

"It's hard," Ed said. "These are all bullshit questions."

"Do it anyway," Myers said. "That's the game. Thorndike's trying to get under your skin so you'll say something incriminating that he can use against you in court."

"If he's trying to piss me off, he's succeeding," Ed said. "They're trying to use Little Ed against me."

"It's a custody trial," Myers said. "If they can show you're any kind of improper influence it's going to look bad. Dial it down, all right?"

"Okay," Ed said. "I'll try." And they went back inside.

"Just a few more questions," Thorndike said. "Do you know a woman named Susan Rozelle, an assistant dean at the University?"

"Yes," Ed said. "You know I do."

"And have you and Miss Rozelle been keeping company, sometimes in her residence on Van Hise Street?"

Keeping company? Jesus. Were they in the nineteenth century? "I've visited her a few times," Ed said. "That's not against the law."

Thorndike consulted his pad again. "Perhaps not, but according to our operative, you've been observed there sixteen times in the last four weeks. Do you deny this?"

"Operative?" Ed said, his voice rising. He was sweating through the cardigan sweater Susan had made him wear. "You mean you've got private eyes spying on me. Jesus, Janey!"

"Yes or no, Mr. Malloy."

'I didn't get the question."

"Were you at Miss Rozelle's residence sixteen times in the last few weeks often leaving after midnight?"

"If you say so," Ed said. "I wasn't counting."

Thorndike took a piece of paper out of his briefcase now and held it up. "I have here a signed affidavit from the University Heights Association for Moral Life, protesting the existence of this relationship in their neighborhood."

"Let me see that," Myers interrupted and gripped Ed's shoulder hard. Myers read the paper over and then said. "I'm instructing my client not to respond to this."

Thorndike nodded. "One more question then. Were there ever any occasions in which you involved your son, Edgeworth jr. in these immoral meetings?"

"Immoral?' Ed said. He took a deep breath and looked at the ceiling. "No. He met Susan once or twice. They liked each other. That's all."

"Nothing more than that?" Thorndike said. "Are you sure Edgeworth Jr. wasn't present at any of these late-night assignations?"

Ed looked hard at the lawyer. He wanted to choke the sonofabitch and, in another minute or so he would have, but Myers interrupted. "Okay, that's enough. We're out of here."

Then they were on the street walking fast back toward Myers' office. "That was the worst hour of my life," Ed said. "I can't believe Janey said that shit about me. We've known each other since we were kids for Christ's sake. That was worse than getting bombed at Anzio. I'm not kidding."

"Pretty bad," Myers said and for the first time Ed thought the lawyer might be worried. "But it could get worse. Be prepared for that."

"What about this University Heights morality thing?"

"It's bullshit," Myers said. "I'm willing to bet there's no real association at all. He just made it up to get to you, which he did. But we'll be okay. You were fine, though I was afraid you were going to punch him at one point."

"Believe me," Ed said. "I wanted to."

"Hell," Myers said and laughed. "I wanted to. Now go home and take it easy. Have a drink, call your girlfriend, go for a walk, do something completely unrelated to all this."

Like what, Ed wondered. Since the fireworks at Vilas Park everything that happened seemed to have some relation to that night.

Ed showed the petition to Susan at home that night and to his surprise, she smiled. "What's funny?" he said.

"It's not really," Susan said. "Ironic, though, that there could be an association for morality in this neighborhood. "Considering all the divorcees and homosexual couples living up and down the block."

"So where did it come from then?" Ed asked. "My lawyer thought it might be phony. Maybe someone at the University who doesn't like the idea that we're dating."

"I doubt it," Susan said. "It's a pretty liberal place. They might question your taste in seeing me but it's hard to imagine that they'd have moral objections. People who live in glass houses and all that."

Ed nodded. It was comforting to think it could be all smoke and mirrors, though God knew what had gotten into his ex-wife to even start the custody lawsuit. All this could have driven her crazy, his being called a communist, the Joe must Go business and whatever Little Ed had told her about Susan. She wouldn't be the first one. Ed thought of the neighbors looking anxiously out their windows when he walked by and then drawing their curtains. And the people they'd seen when they were out canvassing who looked nuts with their wild eyes slamming the door in their faces.

"I did have a thought about a possible way to end all this," Ed said smiling. "And it might work."

"Oh, yes," Susan said. "And what would that be?"

"They're supposedly objecting to my immorality, being with you, maybe our moving in together, right?"

"Sure, but like I said, I don't really believe it," Susan said. "Morality's been having a pretty rough time of it around here lately, not to mention at the University."

"Okay," Ed said, "say that's true. "But how could anyone object to any of this anyway if you were my wife?"

Susan sat back in her chair as if she had been pushed and started turning red. She hugged her arms around her waist and Ed wondered if he'd made her angry with his proposal. But then she smiled widely. "Are you asking me to marry you?" Susan said. "To be honest, I'd prefer the traditional kind with you on your knees and maybe some flowers."

Ed got on his knees in front of her in the little living room. "I haven't got much to offer," he said. "But what I have is yours. Will you marry me?"

At this Susan fell into him and they both ended up on the floor. "Oh, god, yes," Susan said. "Yes, yes, yes."

Twenty

WASHINGTON

I had never been especially conscious of the weather before unless it was the weather inside my brain, which was variable. Back then, we didn't have cute weather girls in front of pastel charts to look at. Tornados, hurricanes, typhoons were all remote occurrences but irrelevant to me. Weather was just something that happened, uncontrollable, to be accepted and borne, but that spring, it was on my mind if only because it was usually lousy. Most days, we woke up to an overbearing gray sky and it rained frequently, though not every day. When the sun occasionally broke through the clouds, it felt like a benediction but one that seldom lasted more than a half-day at best.

Inside the hearing room, of course, the weather never changed. It was always close, claustrophobic, with the smell of mold everywhere in the room, and the omnipresent humidity settling on our shoulders like a heavy robe. Sitting at our table for hours, I was acutely conscious of the sweat dripping down my chest and my shirt sticking to my back under my jacket. My eyes ached under the lights and the television cameras raised the heat, actually and metaphorically. And while I was a principal in the proceedings, I had the unsettling feeling that we were going round and round without making progress or proving anything. The repetitious questioning and circuitous structure of the whole thing was Sheherazade without the exoticism and virgins. I often wondered what anyone else could see of interest in all this sparring between the opposing sides, yet every day the silent cameras were there, and thousands tuned in to watch.

Stevens had been on the stand for two weeks now and was starting to fade under our questioning. He sat lower in his seat, head dropping to his chest only to be raised with heroic effort. Everything he said amounted to "I don't know" or "I can't recall." I thought we had beaten him but now McCarthy made another crucial mistake. Pulling a document from his briefcase, he leaned over and whispered, "Should I hit him with this?"

"God, no," Ralph Carr said. And when I saw what he was referring to, I agreed. It wasn't necessary. But McCarthy never listened to us and introduced the document anyway. "Mr. Secretary," Joe said. "I want to show you a letter, one incidentally that was written before you took your position but has been in the file since you have been in office. It's from the F.B.I. pointing at the urgency of our investigation in connection with certain cases at Fort Monmouth."

Thus, began what we called the case of the purloined letter. What Joe had given the Secretary was a carbon copy of a letter from J. Edgar Hoover to the Army in 1951 stamped "Personal and confidential." The letter detailed thirty-four security risks at Fort Monmouth and went to prove once and for all that the Army's security had been so lax that communists were allowed to move and act freely within the fort for several years with no interference from anyone.

Once the letter's contents became obvious, the effect was explosive. There was a rumbling behind us in the room as reporters moved around to get a better look at what was going on. Jenkins was excited too, just as he had been about the altered photograph, jumping to his feet and holding the letter in front of him as if it were a flag. True to form however, Welch immediately questioned the letter's authenticity.

"I'd like a statement from Mr. Hoover attesting to the fact that he wrote this letter. I noticed it isn't signed by him," Welch said. "I have no idea where the Senator got this, but it's not in the Army files, I'm sure of that."

"That statement is untrue," McCarthy shouted. "You should be sworn in as a witness if you want to testify to that idea."

"I didn't say there isn't a letter in the files, Sir," Welch responded. "I don't know about that. But this purported copy isn't there. I repeat, I'd like to know where you got this."

McCarthy demurred on this point because he had no idea, not having seen the letter before that day. Despite his bluster to Welch, I could tell he was worried. He leaned over to me, his breath a mixture of garlic and alcohol, and whispered, "Where did we get the damned thing, Roy?"

But I didn't know either. Moreover, our arguing about the authenticity of the letter had the effect of obscuring its basic point, which was the lax security at Monmouth. This was Welch's intention of course, but it didn't matter as a recess was called and messengers from Welch's staff were immediately sent to the F.B.I. offices to ask Hoover if indeed he'd written the letter.

The next day Robert Collier, an assistant counsel to Welch, was called to the stand and testified that Hoover had no recollection of writing the letter. Not good news, but there was a fifteen-page memorandum sent on the same day in 1951 that touched on the relevant points. So even if Hoover didn't remember writing it, he admitted it was possible he had. It might be semantics, but in my experience slicing and dicing language is a full-time job among bureaucrats.

"Mr. Hoover advised me," Collier said, "that the FBI memorandum and the two and a quarter page letter contained the same information. And the exact or identical language appears in both documents."

This should have sealed it, but of course it didn't. Welch was like a bulldog. "Let's get this straight," he said, facing Collier. "You're saying this carbon is in fact a copy of absolutely nothing, is that right?"

"So far as I know," Collier said, "Yes, but that's a conclusion."

"Fine, a conclusion. But you're saying that despite an exhaustive search neither you nor Director Hoover could find a trace of an original in the FBI's files."

'I wouldn't say exhaustive," Collier said.

"Is that no?" Welch persisted.

"That's correct," Collier replied.

There was an under-stated rumble in the room as reporters and onlookers digested this. Just as with the doctored photo, Welch had managed to turn a bad moment for the Army into a revelation of misdeeds on our part. Welch's strategy was brilliant, and he was killing us. Having known nothing about the letter before it was introduced, I felt alone, as if McCarthy had put me on an island and taken away the only way to shore. Now they called McCarthy to the stand. Given the crowding at the table, we had to play musical chairs to make room.

"All right, Senator," Welch said, obviously enjoying his new-found advantage. "Can you please tell us where you got this letter?"

McCarthy turned to the audience and held his arms wide as if to suggest he had nothing to hide. "Well, Mr. Welch, I can tell you that I got it from a young patriot in the services who was deeply disturbed by the Swiss cheese of the Army's security measures." He stood for a moment letting the metaphor sink in, then continued. "This young man was dismayed by the failure of the Army to respond to the FBIs warning about communist subversion at Fort Monmouth and so he turned to me." Joe paused dramatically at this point and dropped his head as if in sorrow that matters had come to this. This was all fiction of course since McCarthy had been unaware of the letter until the day before and as far as I knew there was no patriot who had been in touch. But as was often the case, the facts mattered less than style. And Joe was the picture of confidence and determination in his testimony, holding up his right fist now as if to challenge anyone who chose to dispute his version of things.

"That's very interesting," Welch said. "And who was this young patriot? Will you name him as you asked previous witnesses to name communists? Will he come forward?"

McCarthy sat back in his seat, stricken at the suggestion that he compromise confidence. He held his hands to his chest and said, "There is no way on earth that any committee, any force can get me to violate the confidence of the young man who brought forth this damning evidence from within the government."

Welch then cited the U.S. code which makes it unlawful to provide classified information to those not authorized to receive it. To Welch's eyes, McCarthy's informant was a criminal who had placed his personal convictions and judgments above the law. And McCarthy was equally guilty for having encouraged this person.

This argument would have had more effect on a rock than it did on McCarthy who now saw this as a matter of violating his principles. The halo act had to be wearing thin at this point, but I had to admire Joe's creativity in coming back against Welch and invoking patriotism regarding the phantom soldier. Senator Mundt, the Committee chair, backed him up and said no one could make him name a source.

Still, Welch kept egging him on. "Senator McCarthy," he said, "like all witnesses, you took an oath, which included a promise that you would tell the truth, comma, the whole truth, comma, and nothing but the truth. Isn't that correct, sir?"

"We're not debating grammar here, Mr. Welch. I've never claimed to be an English teacher. But I can tell you you're not the first person to try to get me to betray a confidence and you'll be no more successful than the others."

Welch was right in suggesting that Joe's refusal to answer was similar to the way Joe treated so-called "Fifth Amendment Communists" who refused to answer questions. McCarthy didn't answer, just shook his head.

"All right," Welch said, "So even if you refuse to identify your source, will you at least tell us where you were when you got this letter?"

"No," McCarthy said.

"All right. How soon after you received the letter did you show it to anyone."

"I don't remember."

"To whom did you first show it?"

"I don't recall."

This would have gone on all afternoon if Senator Dirksen hadn't mercifully intervened. Then Jenkins stood and said in his opinion it was one of the elementary principles of law that a witness could not be compelled to reveal sources. Otherwise, Jenkins said, "Law enforcing officers would be so hamstrung and hampered that they would never be able to ferret out crime."

In all the back and forth between Welch and McCarthy, the substance of the letter had long been forgotten but that was never the point. Despite all the bullshit thrown out by other senators, these hearings were never more than an elaborately produced show playing to the large audience viewing us on television. These weren't closed hearings in a remote room where some truth might be told, but melodrama displayed in dramatic fashion day after day during April, May and June of that year. With the passage of time, I can admit now that Welch played that game better than I did. Because of my arrogance, I failed to respect his intelligence and ability to shift in midcourse and cross us up. I should have listened when my father and friends told me to get a lawyer rather than defend myself. But I hadn't and now we were paying the price.

Later, when we all got together for a drink in Joe's office, the consensus was that despite his truculence, Joe had been successful at least in refusing to reveal the sources of the document, whoever they were. "By the way," McCarthy said, "I'll ask again, where the hell did we get that letter?" Everybody in the room laughed. There was no answer to Joe's question and obviously none was expected.

For all the talk about him, Dave Schine seemed to have disappeared from Washington without a word. He'd checked out of his room at the Statler and disappeared. The last time I'd talked to him was during the cross about the purloined letter. In the middle of the debate, he asked me to get him a pass and I refused. He looked over and said, "I've had enough of this" and left the room. It struck me as ironic since the reigning assumption of the Army was that we were inseparable lovers.

Even if Dave was gone, however, he was anything but forgotten. Both Welch and Jenkins dragged out our relationship repeatedly as did a Senator named Flanders who in a speech on the Senate floor likened McCarthy to Hitler and made lewd innuendos about my "mysterious personal relationship" with Schine. Flanders was a crank and didn't matter but his speech gave rise to more letters attacking McCarthy for keeping us on his staff. Flanders backed off eventually but neither the reporters nor our anonymous correspondents did, and this carried on into June.

The homosexual attacks might have been personally embarrassing had these things not been like an echo chamber in my head for the last year. Besides, it was impossible to respond in any sensible way. When I was called to return to the witness stand, Jenkins asked if Schine and I were close friends, wink, wink; if I might even love Dave while admitting that he too had friends he loved. I didn't respond directly beyond saying I had many friends, and Dave was one of them. The irony in all this was that Dave was quite the ladies man, even Barbara was charmed by him. Because I lacked his social ease and envied it, I had found him attractive too but lovers? Not even close. When pushed by Jenkins, I said he was an expert on communism and economics, which was a joke, but it was necessary to say something. I was determined to be more composed on the stand this time than I had been before, to respond directly but not to be reactive or defensive.

Even with my determination to relax, I was exhausted as the month wore on. The hearings were like a sponge that soaked up all my time and attention. It would be hard to overstate the impact they were having not just on us but nationally. I could say it was a game, but it was deadly serious and played out before a cumulative audience larger than that of "I Love Lucy." That kind of attention is narcotic to politicians and like a drug has its poisonous side effects. McCarthy looked awful. He'd often come in with liquor on his breath, eyes bloodshot, and looking as if he'd slept in his clothes. More and more, he was standing and shouting "Point of order" at almost anything, desperate to reclaim the momentum Welch had interrupted.

Joe's poll numbers reflected this as he'd dropped from around 50 per cent approval to thirty in a little less than four months. You could say forget it, the public was fickle, but McCarthy had always gained energy from the polls. He could say to hell with his colleagues in the Senate as long as positive mail was pouring in and speaking requests were coming from all over the country. He could talk for an hour revving up a crowd in Omaha or Des Moines and seem to literally become taller and stronger the longer the speech went on. It's the most remarkable thing I've ever seen. But things were changing now. Joe was in trouble, we all were, and we knew it. The worst was yet to come.

Eisenhower chose this moment to issue an order making everyone in the executive branch unavailable to our committee. This had the effect of waving a red flag in front of a bull and McCarthy immediately called a press conference to announce the President was trying to stifle free speech and that he'd personally guarantee protection for any of the people affected by this. This was a pyrrhic gesture since the executive order had little effect and Joe succeeded only in further irritating Eisenhower. He would have done well to keep quiet about it, especially since more questions about our so-called eleven memoranda were coming daily and I'd been called to testify about them.

The memoranda which were dated between October 1953 and March of 1954 was our response to the Adams Chronology of my contacts with the Army in support of Schine. They detailed efforts by Stevens and the Army to blackmail us to stop our investigation into Fort Monmouth. We'd released them right after the Adams paper had been put out by the Army and they inspired widespread incredulity given the timing and the fact that no one except me, McCarthy and other staff members had previously known they existed. Senator Potter called the documents "mysterious and unbelievable" and he wasn't alone. Now, in the summer heat of June, the memoranda were read into the record.

We were tired and virtually insensate by this time. The lawyers were like exhausted fighters, carrying on even though the fight was no longer in doubt largely because of the politicians' love for the television audience. McCarthy, Frank Carr and I stuck to our story about the memoranda because circling the wagons was about all we could do in the way of a defense. And now I was back on the stand, having been advised by my father and others to back off and try to be less presumptuous. I'd been called an arrogant little bastard before, and I suppose this wasn't too far off. The truth was I enjoyed matching wits with others older and more experienced. Obviously, this hadn't served me well in the past, so I was determined to be more subdued now, a new Cohn, if that was possible at this late date.

Jenkins started off the questioning and asked where I had dictated the memos. "In Senator McCarthy's office," I said.

"To whom?"

"Mary Driscoll."

"She is the Senator's secretary?"

I indicated that she was and then Jenkins asked, "Would you consider it out of order if I asked you to step aside for Mrs. Driscoll?"

"That's up to you," I said.

Mary was the sister of David Brinkley, the television newsman. She was about fifty and looked like someone's wife or mother, dressed always in modest dresses or suits, her brown hair drawn back from her forehead, Mary had been Joe's loyal secretary for six years. She was a wonderful office manager and had been personally helpful to me during the time I'd worked for McCarthy. I thought it was unfair of

Jenkins to bring her into it, but Mary was more than willing. She came before the Committee on a very hot day and calmly testified that all the memoranda were legitimate and that she had typed them personally.

"Do you recall Mr. Cohn dictating any of these documents to you?" Jenkins asked.

"I have no independent recollection of that," Mary said, "but I'm sure he dictated some of them to me otherwise I would not have put his name on them."

Mary seemed neither perturbed nor nervous to be in the hearing and answered in a quiet, determined voice. She was going to be tough for them to shake but that didn't mean Jenkins didn't try.

"Do you remember the content of these memoranda?" he asked.

"I take too much dictation to remember what any of them are about," Mary said.

"Do you have your shorthand notebooks to refer to then?" Jenkins asked.

"I never keep my shorthand notebooks," Mary said, as if this was a stupid question.

"Well, then did you separate these memoranda from other documents in a single file and if so, what did you call it."

Again, Mary looked as if the question was too obvious to be taken seriously. Her aplomb was admirable, and I was impressed. "I called it Investigations Committee," she said.

Jenkins pressed on. "And how did you know where to look for the file when you were called upon to produce it."

"I can't tell you that," Mary said.

Jenkins looked as if he'd at last come on something. "I see," he said. "And can you tell us why that was?"

"I can't tell you because that is my way of filing," Mary said, and got a big laugh out of the audience.

Welch took over after this and started by saying he found it awkward to examine a lady, but he managed to get over this and turned to Mary who continued to seem completely at ease on the stand.

"I think you have told us you have three typewriters in your office," Welch said.

Mary indicated that this was true but the only reason the question was important is that it had been determined that the memoranda had been written on three different typewriters. "The one at your desk is an IBM," Welch said.

"There's an IBM on my desk now," Mary said.

"Was it there in October?" Welch asked.

"I don't recall," Mary said. "To me, a typewriter is a typewriter. I don't pay attention to the type of typewriter it is."

Welch nodded as if this made sense then asked about each memorandum in turn until he came to the last one dated March 11 which Frank Carr had dictated saying he was looking for another concerning Schine. This didn't make sense because Mary had already said she'd put all the memoranda in a file so where was the one Carr was referring to?

"It's simple, Mrs. Driscoll," Welch said. "You had them all together, did you not?"

"Maybe I overlooked one," Mary said. "I don't really remember."

This was ridiculous because Mary never overlooked anything. Welch was trying to do what lawyers do, knock her off her game and make her lose composure. This wasn't likely as Mary stood there, calm and stocky, her skin translucent in the room's lights, her lips set in a frown. "May I ask you this then," Welch said, "Did you ever find a memorandum that Frank Carr dictated after putting this file together?"

"Mr. Welch, you're confusing me," Mary said. And that was all Joe needed to jump up and object to the whole line of questioning. "This very very clever little lawyer has been harassing this good woman, and I want him sworn in as a witness, Mr. Chairman, and I want him to take a lie detector test. I'll take one too, we can all take one."

But this wasn't going to happen because the Committee was tired of delays and Joe wasn't serious anyway. He just wanted to get Mary Driscoll off the stand, and it was a good thing. Neither she nor anyone else could have answered Welch's questions about the memoranda because the whole lot was phony, dreamed up by Frank, Joe and me in response to the Adams Chronology on the spur of the moment in our office late one night. This doesn't mean the bases of the memoranda weren't true; we did think the Army had tried to bribe and blackmail me. But the memoranda were false, and we didn't want to have to take our final stand on them.

It was hot and close in my hotel, and I was too aware of my own stertorous breathing to sleep. I had suffered from childhood asthma and now without warning it recurred as a result of the stress of the hearings. My breathing was like an echo chamber in my head, a knocking of pipes and drums that made me wonder if guests in other rooms heard me hacking away. I got up and took a walk around the block remarking as always on the emptiness of the city, the absence of life on the streets after dark. Since Jerry left town, I had no one to seek out for companionship so I sat in the hotel bar for an hour, but no one approached me, not even a sad hooker wearing too much makeup at the other side of the room.

Finally, I went back upstairs, lay down, and spent the next few hours going over the coming day's testimony in my head. Despite my attempts to tone down my answers and keep any anger I felt on low ebb; it seemed to me that we'd lost our edge over the last few days and were going to have trouble recapturing it. Welch was gaining strength with the passing weeks and the cyclops of television in the corner recording everything was unyielding. At around three my phone rang and when I picked it up, I was surprised to hear Jeannie McCarthy's voice as we weren't really close friends.

"I'm sorry to wake you, Roy," she began.

"It's okay," I said. "I was up anyway."

She let that settle between us for a moment. Then she said, "I'm worried about Joe, and I didn't know who else to call."

How about Van Susteren or one of his other old Wisconsin buddies, I thought, but I didn't say this. "How can I help?"

Jeannie didn't respond directly. "He's like a madman," she said. "He won't stop drinking except when we take him over to the Bethesda Naval Hospital for a day or so. Then when they release him, he just starts up again. He doesn't sleep and he wanders around the house all night, talking loudly even though there's no one else here. He's exhausted and he's wearing me out. But he's got those stomach aches and headaches again and I'm worried."

I knew Joe was hanging on by a fingernail because of the stress brought on by the hearings, but I hadn't heard from Jeanie before, and this signaled a new level of distress. It was essential to find a way to help Joe hold things together for another week or so but I had no idea how to accomplish this. I called a cab and went over to their house where I found Joe sitting in his armchair in an old bathrobe, hair moved over in a mat on his forehead and a scowl on his face. The ruins of a chicken dinner sat on the side table and the room was in its usual disarray.

"Bastards," McCarthy said as a way of greeting me. "Fucking bastards. They hate us. You know they hate us, Roy, and you know why."

"Okay," I said sitting down. "Why?"

"Because we're fighting communism and we're the only ones that are, that's why. The Army doesn't give a shit, not really. Neither do Eisenhower or Dulles. They just want to get rid of me. Same with the Democrats." He was silent for a moment, took a sip of bourbon from the glass at his elbow. "And those goddamned Joe Must Go assholes," he added, waving his arm as if they were in the room. "Like I haven't got enough to worry about."

"They'll never get anywhere," I said. "People in Wisconsin love you."

"Used to be," he said. "Not anymore. That fucking Welch," he said suddenly. "Fucking stuck-up, Ivy League bastard. I hate that sonofabitch."

"He's from Iowa," I said irrelevantly.

"You'd never know it," Joe said, and he was right about that.

There was nothing to say to this, so I got up and went into the kitchen where Jeannie was drinking coffee. She reached over and squeezed my arm. "I'm sorry to get you out here in the middle of the night," she said.

"Don't worry about it. Like I said, I was up."

She smiled and patted my hand. She had aged in the past year, crows' feet climbing the sides of her pretty face. "I called you because you're the only one of those guys who never flirted with me behind Joe's back."

This seemed like as good a reason as any, even if there was the suggestion that she like everyone else assumed I was homosexual. What difference did it make there, in the middle of the night? I sat with Jeannie at the kitchen table as the sun turned the kitchen windows crimson then gold. Neither of us said anything more and when I got up to leave, I saw McCarthy had finally fallen asleep in his chair.

It was June and Washington was heating up, just as things in the Committee room were reaching their climax. With all the dramatic rises and falls, the changes of momentum, what you might call the brilliance of the lawyers, if you ask me, the crux of it all had to do with a young associate of Welch's named Frederic Fischer who has been mostly forgotten now.

Fischer was a member of Welch's Boston firm and was originally supposed to be part of his team at the hearings. When asked by Welch if there was anything questionable in his background, however, Fischer answered that in the forties he'd belonged to the National Lawyers Guild, a group that had been described as subversive by HUAC. Fischer said he'd never been a communist himself but had friends who were and this was enough for Welch to decide to send him home.

I was on the witness stand when all this became relevant, Jenkins having finished his examination and now Welch brought up my draft status. "I've seen questions raised about your status," he said. "I'm sure you're aware of them."

I replied, "I assume by now articles have been printed about almost anything about me, but, yes, sir. I'm aware of those."

Welch backed off with the suggestion that I research my draft status, which was unnecessary, as he well knew. During World War II, I'd dodged the service when my father arranged for a family friend to nominate me for U.S. Military Academy. I failed the physical because of my inability to do push-ups but fortunately the War ended in time that I wasn't drafted again. Anxious to avoid this situation in the future, I enlisted in the National Guard knowing that Guard members were exempt from the draft. I had avoided serving in both World War II and the Korean War but there was nothing illegal about this despite Welch's acting as if this was a big reveal. If I were now labeled a draft dodger, however, it could affect our case whether it was relevant or not. That was all I cared about, and Welch knew it, which was why it came out in cross-examination.

Welch was never short on surprises, however, and since he was unable to do anymore with my service record, he suggested we meet and discuss both Fischer's association with communists and my dealings with the draft. We found a conference room just down the hall after the hearings ended that day and made a deal: We'd forego questioning about Fischer, and they'd similarly neglect to mention my draft status any further. Neither subject seemed worth more committee time, so I thought it benefitted both sides. I mentioned this casually to McCarthy that night and he nodded his approval but predictably he'd forgotten all about it the next day.

This came out when Welch was questioning me again about Monmouth. "Isn't it true," he said, "that if you knew about a bad situation at Monmouth, you'd want to cure it by sundown, isn't that the case?"

"By sundown, I don't know, sir. We'd try to cure it as fast as we could."

"Then, why on September 7 when you first questioned Secretary Stevens about Monmouth, didn't you say there was something that wouldn't let you sleep at night?"

Who remembered a conversation held six months before? Not me, but I allowed as that might have been the case. I had no idea where he was going with this, but Welch stepped back dramatically now and said, "Every time you learn of a communist or a spy anywhere, isn't it your policy to expunge them immediately?"

"We want to get at them as soon as possible," I said.

At which point McCarthy broke in. "Mr. Chairman, on that question..."

Mundt asked him if he had a point of order, and the audience laughed since by now Joe's point of order complaints had become automatic.

"Not directly," McCarthy said, "but in view of Mr. Welch's question I should mention that he had a young man in his firm named Fischer whom he had recommended for work on this hearing who had a history of work with an organization that was helpful to the Communist Party. You have a gift for theatrics, Mr. Welch, a genius for playing for the easy laugh, but I don't think you have any real conception of the danger of the Communist Party."

No one else on the committee understood what was happening but Welch looked stricken. "This is no laughing matter," he said, "but while I may have certain gifts, unlike you sir, I don't stoop to the use of scare tactics with regard to innocent people."

"Mr. Welch, I have no need for scare tactics; I am scared of the danger being done to our great country and this is why I raise the issue.

You're making a burlesque of the facts we're trying to bring out here and I am conscience-bound to raise the issue."

The chairman interrupted at this point to say he had no recollection of Mr. Welch having tried to bring Fischer onto the Committee's staff, but this had little effect on either Welch or Joe. Welch said, "Mr. Chairman, I must have something approaching a personal privilege."

Mundt granted this and Welch went on, apparently deeply disturbed though I suspected he'd prepared his remarks ahead of time, because he thought Joe would be unable to control himself and disregard the deal. Sadly, he was on target with this. "Senator, may I have your attention, sir?"

"I'm listening," McCarthy said. "I can listen with one ear," though in fact, he wasn't listening but rather examining papers on his desk.

"This time, I want you to listen with both," Welch said, raising laughter in the room. The reporters who'd been somnolent were now sitting up, notepads ready and of course the television eye never faltered.

McCarthy meanwhile kept shuffling papers. *Soto voce,* he asked Jim Juliana to find an article that had been published about Fischer's previous affiliation. At the same time, I whispered to him to back off, knowing he'd abrogated the deal I'd made with Welch which he'd approved. But it was too late.

"Senator," Welch continued, raising his right hand to the ceiling for emphasis. "When I learned of this young man's previous membership in a communist organization, I asked him to go back to Boston and said that we wouldn't use him, but I didn't dream that you could be so reckless and so cruel as to smear this lad's reputation in this way. He will stay with our firm, but he will always bear this scar in the years to come. If it were in my power to forgive you, I would, but forgiveness in this matter will have to come from someone other than me."

Welch was embroidering a bit here as the "lad" he was talking about was a partner in a prestigious Boston law firm and was getting to be a little long in the tooth. Fisher was going to be just fine and wouldn't be tortured by anything Joe said now or later. Still, it was a nice flourish and might have stopped some people in their tracks. It only succeeded, however, in making Joe furious with the man who, in his view, had been criticizing one of his boys. Turning dramatically to the room,

McCarthy shouted, "Mr. Welch talks about being reckless when he's been baiting Mr. Cohn for days now. What hypocrisy! I mentioned only the man's record of communist activity..."

Welch interrupted at this point, obviously anxious to regain momentum, and then bring this to a close. For once I agreed with him, though Fischer was a red herring and Joe was right in saying he'd been badgering me for days, trying to make me lose my temper. It hadn't worked; I'd done well on the stand, and I knew it but what was coming now would be disastrous.

You want to know how I felt sitting there? I felt like a caged animal or perhaps like a butterfly pinned to someone's bulletin board. I was hot and tired and the sickly-sweet smell of McCarthy's Wildroot hair tonic assaulted my senses. We'd been on national television for months and though I knew we were right that there were communists at Monmouth and shuffled throughout the Army, I also knew that right or not we'd lost this battle. The sight of Joe's five o'clock shadow and otherwise disheveled appearance along with his constant interruptions had doomed us in the public eye. The people who supported us, who believed in McCarthy, would still believe, but the Gallup Poll didn't lie. We'd had our day in the sun, and it was over.

I lowered my head to the table and closed my eyes, hoping still to somehow keep to my agreement with Welch even if I knew it meant nothing to Joe.

Welch paused theatrically. "May we bring this to a close?" he asked. "We know Mr. Fisher belonged to the Lawyer's Guild and I see Mr. Cohn agrees with me on this. I did you no personal injury, did I, Mr. Cohn. If I did, I beg your pardon."

I indicated that I wasn't insulted by what he'd said and then Welch went for the kill, turning to McCarthy, and saying his voice raised with a flourish that would have been appropriate to an operatic aria, "Let us assassinate this lad no further, Senator. You have done enough. Have you no sense of decency, sir, at long last. Have you no sense of decency?"

It was a seminal moment, Welch with his head tilted slightly, his right hand raised and his eyes glistening with the emotion of the moment, was to me nothing more than a martinet but whatever my opinion, he dominated the room. For a moment, there was complete silence, then the whole room was standing, clapping, cheering, everyone veteran reporters, celebrity guests, hangers-on, even the cameraman. It went on for what seemed like hours but must have been only a few minutes. It was enough.

The phrase "sense of decency" was all most people would remember of the hearings years later while having no idea what Welch was talking about that day, and it would remain tattooed on my brain for years to come. Theatrical as it was, it expressed what many felt about Joe. It was the idea of McCarthy's indecency being asserted to the nation that would dominate headlines in every paper in the country the next day. As for Joe, he'd barely heard the other man and now looked up, questioning what had just happened and why the room was suddenly so quiet.

Mundt called for a recess and after a stunned silence the audience erupted in applause with even the reporters joining in. Welch lingered dramatically, enjoying the moment and then walked out holding a handkerchief to his eyes. This was ridiculous, of course. He'd won and everyone knew it, except perhaps McCarthy who hadn't moved from his seat where he sat bewildered, hair and clothes in disarray, as the room emptied and reporters rushed to the phones,

I was exhausted and felt as If I'd just been through a fifteen round prize fight. I'd had enough of the Army, of Welch, of McCarthy, Washington, the whole damned thing. I'd put everything I had into the hearings and though nothing final had happened that day, I felt in my bones that this was the end for us.

McCarthy was still sitting immobile in his chair. Now he turned slowly to me and said, "What the hell just happened, Roy?"

I wanted to say he'd fucked us by losing his temper, going back on the agreement I'd made with Welch, and yelling about Fischer, but I didn't. I wanted to give him hell, ask him why he'd played into Welch's hands, why he was what he was, but what good would it have done? "You saw it," I said. "Everyone did. Ask one of your reporter friends, Joe, they'll tell you."

McCarthy didn't respond to this. I got up to go and then in a low voice, as if it was a prayer, he murmured, "But what did I do? What did I do?"

Twenty-One

MADISON

Leroy Gore had agreed to stand up for Ed and Ivan Nestigen was going to be an usher along with Sinclair and Ed's boss from the Union. It was odd but Ed thought he had more friends now than he'd accumulated in Madison since coming back from the war. Previously, his life had revolved around work and his family, and he'd been content with this, if not completely happy. But getting fired and having Janey leave forced him to move beyond boundaries he hadn't known he'd created. Of course, Susan had been a lifeline, which is why he was here today.

He pulled into the parking lot of the Unitarian Church but before he could get out of the car, he saw Jimmy Simmons coming toward him notebook in hand. That kid was like a rash, he thought. Just when you think you're clear, it pops up again.

"Jesus, Jimmy," he said. "What are you doing here? You're covering marriages now? I don't remember you being on the guest list."

"I know, Mr. Malloy, and I'm sorry to intrude," Jimmy said. The reporter thrust out a bony hand but instead of shaking he offered only cold asparagus fingers. "Congratulations by the way," the kid said, then went on in a rush, the words rolling out his mouth like marbles on the playground. "Like I said, I'm really sorry but I just wanted to get a quick quote from you, if I could."

Ed knew what Jimmy was talking about. He'd seen the banner headline in the Herald before he left home. " Have You No Decency?"

Screamed the large type above a frontpage story on McCarthy's public humiliation in Washington.

"I've got nothing for you, Jimmy," Ed said. "I'm getting married. That's all I'm thinking about today."

"But you must have a reaction to McCarthy being taken down with all you've been through," the reporter persisted.

Ed took a deep breath. "Okay," he said, "off the record. See, I know how you guys work now. Unless I go back on, you can't quote anything I say."

Jimmy laughed. "Fair enough. Okay, something's better than nothing. Off the record, then. What do you think?"

"I think the sonofabitch is getting all that he deserves and more," Ed said. "He ruined a lot of lives, came close to ruining mine. Almost makes you sympathize with the communists in the government, if there really are any." Ed hesitated and thought if there was more he wanted to say. There wasn't. "I've got to go," he said." Then he took Susan by the arm, and they walked into the church.

The sanctuary was probably half-full of Ed's friends, Susan's family and her colleagues from the University. Little Ed was the ring bearer, and a tiny niece of Susan's went up and down the aisle with a basket full of lilies, dropping them here and there. The Church had brought in a new minister recently, a short, red-haired man who had come from Harvard and was rumored to be too High-Church for the liberal congregation in Madison. Ed didn't know about this. He and Janey hadn't had a church wedding since Little Ed was two by the time he got home so this was all new to him. Susan was beautiful in a simple white sheath, and he'd rented a tuxedo downtown at Nedrebo's.

Susan's father walked her down the aisle, the minister read some poetry and said a few things about love and commitment, but Ed wasn't really listening. The sun came through the large, slanted windows, someone had gathered wildflowers from the University marsh fields nearby and placed them around the church and the turquoise cushions on the seats seemed welcoming. He had the feeling that something good was going to happen, had already happened. It was a new sensation for him.

The minister had offered to provide vows for them, which was okay with Ed, but Susan wanted them to write their own. She read an Irish poem and then said, "How but in ceremony are innocence and beauty born? Let us discover our own innocence and beauty together."

Ed felt tongue-tied but finally managed to say, "Susan, you saved my life when it needed saving. I'm going to do my best to improve on that for you."

Everyone clapped which surprised Ed, but he guessed Unitarians did things like that. Then after the minister pronounced them married, he kissed the bride, which was a little embarrassing in front of everyone but okay in the end.

Afterwards, there was a reception at the University alumni center where they ate canapes and drank wine. Susan's mother approached him and gave him a kiss on the cheek, her lips dry and papery against his skin. "I had about given up," she said. "I really didn't think Susie was going to find anyone to marry, even a communist."

It was an odd thing to say, so rude and inappropriate that it was funny. Ed started to object that he wasn't a communist but why argue? Mrs. Rozelle had a sweet smile on her face as if being a communist were similar to belonging to the Kiwanis or the Lions Club. At base, he figured he just wasn't their kind of people which was fine with him.

"Well, you're wrong about that," Ed said now. "Susan wouldn't have had to look very far if she was interested in finding a husband. I'm a very lucky guy."

Susan's mother just nodded at this and moved on leaving Ed standing alone with his wine glass in his hand. Little Ed was moving around the room, charming people and Ed was grateful and a little surprised that Janey had allowed him to come to the wedding. He hadn't received any more letters from Thorndike and Myers had given him the idea that the worst might be past. Now Gore walked over. "I guess you heard about the hearings in Washington, what happened yesterday?"

Ed was going to tell him he was getting married and wasn't thinking about anything else, but he couldn't blame Gore for having McCarthy on his mind. "Saw the paper," he said. "In fact, there was a reporter out there in the parking lot waiting for me when I got here. Those guys don't sleep much."

"I think he might be finished, McCarthy," Gore said now. "And good riddance, you ask me. But we're not."

"No?" They'd gotten almost two hundred thousand signatures on their petitions, but Ed knew they needed more to get a recall election.

"I'm going back East," Gore said. "There's talk that when these hearings are over, they're going to kick McCarthy out."

"Of the Senate? I didn't know they could do that."

"You didn't think he could be recalled either," Gore said. "But look how well that's gone. We've got him on the run."

"Why go back then?"

"Because we're not quite there and I'd just like to see the bastard squirm. Want to come along? Not now. I mean, in a month or so when these Army hearings are over."

Ed had enjoyed their last trip together, but it seemed impossible for him to travel with all that was happening in Madison. "We're going to the Dells for a honeymoon," he said. "And my custody hearing is continuing. Not a great time for me to leave town."

Gore nodded. "Sure, I get it," he said. "But I'm not talking about now. In a month or so it might be different right?"

"Sure," Ed agreed. "Maybe."

Ed and Susan spent a long weekend in Wisconsin Dells, rode the Ducks and watched the kids playing in the water. Ed wished he could have brought Little Ed with them, but that wasn't going to fly with Janey, and it was probably just as well. They stayed in a little motel on the edge of town, ate dinner at local restaurants and Ed couldn't remember feeling quite as relaxed in his life. In bed, Susan huddled against him and said, "I'm glad I married you."

"I'm glad too," Ed said but the truth was he was still surprised it had worked out, especially since at least part of his motivation in proposing had been practical. He wasn't entirely kidding when he said he thought marriage would improve his prospects regarding the custody fight, but Susan didn't seem to care. It turned out that what he wanted was what she wanted.

When they got back to Madison, Ed went to his lawyer's office and found Myers disorganized as always. "I had a letter here from the other side," Myers said, leafing through the piles of paper on his desk. "If only I can find it."

For a moment Ed wondered if he had the right representation but then he reminded himself that he hadn't had much choice and Myers came well recommended. At last, the lawyer found the letter and held it up to the light from the window to read it. Then he turned to Ed. "Getting married was a good move," he said. "That whole business about the moralist society seems to have gone away. Can't really object to your living in sin if you're married."

"What else does the letter say?" Ed asked.

Myers sighed. "I was hoping we could just have a meeting and settle everything, but your ex-wife seems pretty determined."

"About what?"

"She wants to limit your contact with the boy. Says she still considers you to be a bad influence." He shook his head in bewilderment. "As long as I've done this, I don't understand people. Was she like this when you were married?"

Ed shrugged. "I thought we got along all right," he said. "She was upset when I got fired and didn't beg for my job back. That seemed to be her main problem."

Myers nodded. "Well, it looks like she's discovered a few other things since then. And now we've got a court date so unless her lawyer comes forward and tries to make an agreement, we'll have to settle it in front of the judge."

"Why would her lawyer want to propose an agreement now?"

"If he thought he'd lose," Myers said. "Like I told you, Thorndike and I have history. Still, I'm not happy about this judge we caught. If we could find a way around facing him, I'd listen."

"What's the worst that could happen?"

"They're not going to deny a father his right to see his son," Myers said. "But if Judge Cooper buys the idea that you're a bad influence, they could require you to have supervision when you're together, no overnights, things like that."

It gave Ed a chill to think of it. No more walks in the park with Little Ed, no ice fishing or skating in the winter, no trips to the zoo. "I thought they only did that with criminals," he said.

"You're right," Myers said. "It would be outrageous but that doesn't mean it can't happen in this climate. The communist bullshit in this state is as poisonous as gas."

Poisonous was a good way to describe what Ed had been seeing when he was canvassing. Hate, suspicion, above all fear of him and what people imagined he represented. It didn't make any sense and the atmospheric change in town was amazing. He remembered coming home after the War, to parades and strangers stopping him on the street to thank him for his service. Then in what seemed like no time at all that went away, replaced by neighbors reporting on one another along with the general belief that there was a huge conspiracy of communists threatening to take over and change the United States into a suburb of Moscow. How or why this happened, Ed didn't know, but it was with them now.

'Isn't there anything I can do?" he asked, referring to the courts.

Myers got up and walked to the window. "Normally, we wouldn't even be having this conversation. You're a good man, no criminal background, a veteran and now you're married and a student at the University."

"But it doesn't matter is what you're telling me."

Myers hunched his shoulders and sat back down. "We could make them a pre-emptive offer and see if they'd go for it."

"Offer what?"

"Part of what they want, but not everything. It's called negotiation. Your ex-wife already has residential custody, so we could say we're willing to cut down on your visiting days but not agree to supervision. That wouldn't be great, but half a loaf is better than none."

What Myers was suggesting sounded awful, but Ed had gotten used to awful over the past year. "From what you say they think they can win," Ed said slowly. He still found it hard to believe he was in this situation, that Janey thought he was some kind of monster, a danger to their son. The whole idea of his relationship with Little Ed being something he had to win was a lot to absorb. "But, sure, see what you can do. What the hell."

"I'll get back to you," Myers said.

It turned out, however, that Janey had no interest in compromise. So, Ed and Susan along with Janey and her lawyer were in front of Judge Cooper two weeks later to decide the whole thing. The court was a smaller room in the County Courthouse and what Ed might have called less formal than the larger courtrooms, though there was still a dais, and they all had to stand up when the judge came into the room. Cooper himself was a small man with steel-rimmed glasses and white hair parted in the middle allowing a pink scalp to peek out. He looked like a high school principal or maybe a Lutheran pastor from the Missouri synod. There was nothing about him that suggested leniency and Ed felt himself losing hope.

Thorndike was dressed in a pin-striped suit and his hair was slicked back to show to best advantage an advancing widow's peak. The court was called to order and then Thorndike rose. "I call Janemarie Malloy to the stand," he said.

Ed had seen Janey since their divorce but now he felt as if she'd changed into someone else when he wasn't looking, someone he didn't know, one of those country club women he'd see downtown in Manchester's tearoom or walking on the Square. She was wearing a purple sweater set and had her hair tied back severely into a knot. Her face seemed hard and narrow, and she looked straight ahead, avoiding Ed's eyes as she walked to the front of the room. When had all this happened, Ed wondered. He and Janey had never been one of those couples you saw walking on the Lake Path holding hands, but he thought they were reasonably happy or at least she'd never said otherwise. Where had all her anger come from and why? She knew he wasn't really a communist no matter what she said for the benefit of the court. And could she really be jealous as Susan suspected? If so, why, when she'd been the one who pushed for divorce in the first place? This made Ed sad, which in turn seemed weak and annoyed him. After all, Janey and her lawyer were coming for him. They wanted to take Little Ed away if they could. She didn't need or deserve his sympathy.

When Janey was settled, Thorndike leaned against the witness stand in what seemed almost an intimate way and now Ed wondered if they were seeing each other, if that was how Thorndike had come to represent her, why she was being so aggressive? In other circumstances, he might have been happy for her but not now.

"Mrs. Malloy," Thorndike began in a syrupy voice, "I know how unhappy you've been, how worried you are about your young son. Why do you think your ex-husband should be limited in being able to see Edward?"

"I think he's dangerous, a bad influence on Little Ed," Janey said in what seemed like a rehearsed speech.

"I see," Thorndike said. "That's awful. But you were married to Mr. Malloy for a number of years and knew him before you were married. Certainly, you didn't always feel this way?"

"He's not the same as he was. He's changed," Janey said, biting off her words. "Ever since he became a communist."

Immediately Myers was on his feet. "Objection, prejudicial," he said.

The judge allowed this, but the damage had been done, they'd been able to get the accusation into the transcript. "I understand your outrage," Thorndike said, patting Janey's hand. "But when do you think this change took place exactly?"

"Around the time he got fired," Janey said. "He started just staying in his room, didn't go out to look for a job, didn't do anything."

"And since then?"

"Well, it's just gotten worse and worse," Janey said. "Something's got to be done about it." She dabbed at her eyes with a handkerchief, but Ed knew she wasn't really crying. She hadn't even cried when her mother died. What got to him now was the anger, even hatred, in the way Janey spoke about him. Where did that come from, or rather where had it been all those years they lived together, shared a bed, a life. Could he have missed it somehow, this anger, even hatred, mistaken it for love. It seemed impossible and yet there it was in front of him.

Thorndike thanked Janey for her testimony and Myers approached the stand. "Mrs. Malloy," he began. "Was Mr. Malloy a good husband."

"Depends on what you mean by that," Janey said.

"Did he drink, gamble, abuse you or your son? Did he ever stay out all night without notice or go with other women, for example?"

"He didn't do any of that," Janey said. "Doesn't make him good."

"Perhaps not," Myers said. "But he went to work, brought home his paycheck, paid the bills, and supported you and your son while you were married, isn't that right?"

"The minimum," Janey said. "That's what Ed did. No more, no less."

Her mouth was set in an unforgiving line, and she seemed to spit out her words. If she had never been passionate in their marriage, Ed thought she was today. Had he really caused all that? How was it possible?

"And when you separated," Myers continued, "Did your ex-husband leave suddenly?"

"I kicked him out," Janey said. "Glad I did, too."

Myers nodded, letting her talk. "So despite the fact that as you say your husband did all the things most people would expect of a husband, went to work, supported the family, and gave you no particular reason for dissatisfaction that you can name today, you still think he's of bad character and that it would be a good thing for your child to be deprived of contact with his father?"

Janey sat up straight and looked right at the lawyer. "I think that would be one of the real advantages of all this," she said.

Ed felt a sudden pain in his breastbone as if someone had driven an ice pick into his chest and he was glad he was sitting down. The idea that Janey thought it would be good for Little Ed to keep him away hurt in a new way, a way he'd never expected, never imagined. It might be possible for them to be polite when talking in the future, but he'd never again think of Janey as anything other than cruel. It was the kind of remark you couldn't apologize for, even if you wanted to.

Myers pressed on. "You think it would be good for your son to lose contact with his father?" he said, nailing it down.

"Yes," Janey said. "Absolutely."

Ed felt sick and wanted to leave the courtroom, let her have what she wanted just as long as he never had to see her again. But he knew they couldn't allow this to stand, give up now. Susan took his hand and feeling her warmth against him helped a little.

Thorndike, who had seemed to smirk when Ed and Susan walked in earlier now called Ed to the witness stand. The lawyer paced back and forth several times, looked at the yellow pad he carried and then started in. "Are you presently a member of the Communist Party?" he asked.

"I already answered that," Ed said.

Myers objected. "Relevance, Judge, this is a custody case, not political."

"Goes to character," Thorndike said, "which is what this is all about."

"Witness will answer the question," the judge intoned.

"I'm not a communist and never have been," Ed said.

"So you say," Thorndike intoned. "Others seem to disagree. Well, then, do you subscribe to the *Daily Worker*?"

"This is ridiculous," Ed said.

"What the witness reads is neither here nor there," Myers said.

"Witness will answer," the judge repeated.

"No, I don't read the *Daily Worker*," Ed said. "I've never read it, never seen a copy. I don't think you can even buy it in Madison."

Then they went through the business of Ed's friend Tony being a communist and testifying in front of McCarthy's committee. "And despite all this," Thorndike said, "despite the obvious fact that you associated with known communists in the past, called them your friends, you still claim you're not one yourself. This seems incredible."

"It's true," Ed said simply. And having got the issue out in front of the judge, Thorndike said he had no more questions.

This gave Myers a chance to cross-examine. He went through Ed's service record, his medals for valor and the Purple Heart. Then Myers said, "You're a member of the Joe Must Go organization, isn't that true?"

"Yes," Ed said.

"And could you tell us why?"

"Because McCarthy almost ruined my life," Ed said quietly. "Me and lots of other people. I don't think he deserves to be a Senator."

"But you're not a communist."

"Of course not. It has nothing to do with that. Most of the people in Joe Must Go are Republicans," Ed said.

Having got that out in rebuttal, Myers let Ed return to his seat.

Next Thorndike called DiPietro to the witness stand. Ed hadn't seen his former boss since leaving his office the day he was fired and thought DiPietro looked distinctly uncomfortable now, re-arranging his clothes, and taking several deep breaths after sitting down. To begin with, Thorndike asked DiPietro where he worked and whether Ed had formerly been his employee. Then he got down to it.

"Would you say that Mr. Malloy was a good worker?" he asked.

"He was fine, I guess" DiPietro said. "No real complaints. Always met his marks, clients liked him."

"Nevertheless, you decided to change his employment status last fall and then you discharged him. Isn't that true?" Thorndike asked.

DiPietro nodded. "We took him out of direct contact with clients after a while," DiPietro said. "Put him on a desk because he was good with numbers."

"Was that the only reason?" Thorndike asked.

DiPietro shook his head. "After he got quoted in that newspaper story some clients and people in the office didn't want to work with him," he said. "Didn't feel comfortable around him."

"And then you terminated Mr. Malloy's employment. Can you tell us why?"

"He refused to sign a paper saying he was a loyal, patriotic American," DiPietro said. "We really tried to get him to sign but he just wouldn't do it."

"An oath asserting that he was a patriotic American?"

DiPietro nodded. "That's right."

Thorndike looked at his legal pad again as if there was some abstruse information there that needed to be interpreted. "Would you say Mr. Malloy was popular with other employees?"

"He was okay," DiPietro said. "No complaints up until then."

"Did he ever make prejudicial comments about other workers?"

Myers immediately objected. "Question has nothing to do with custody," he said, and this time the judge upheld him.

Thorndike had nothing more and Myers now rose to cross-examine. "Mr. DiPietro," he began, "Isn't it a fact that beyond being a good employee, Mr. Malloy actually had the best sales record in your office the year before he was terminated?"

"That's true," DiPietro said. "I had just come on that year, but he was the best the year before that."

"So, isn't it true that rather than just being fine, as you said, actually, Mr. Malloy was an excellent employee?"

DiPietro looked quickly at the other lawyer and shifted, uncomfortable in his seat. He was sweating and now he took a handkerchief out of his pocket to mop his forehead. Ed felt a brief wave of sympathy for what the other man was going through but checked himself. Had DiPietro cared when he cut him loose, took away his livelihood, caused him to lose his house, his marriage? To hell with DiPietro's discomfort. Let the sonofabitch squirm.

"Mr. DiPietro," Myers said. "Please answer the question. Wouldn't you say Mr. Malloy was an excellent employee?"

"You could say that, I guess," DiPietro said.

"I know I could," Myers said. "But what I might say isn't important.

The question is would you say that, as his former supervisor?"

"Yes, I suppose I would," DiPietro admitted.

"Now regarding this loyalty oath," Myers went on, "How many people work in your office, would you say?"

"I suppose there are twenty-five or thirty of us," DiPietro said. "I don't know exactly off-hand."

"And were all of these people in your office asked to sign a loyalty oath?" Myers asked.

DiPietro now looked as if he had just run a marathon. His chin dropped, he breathed deeply and shook his head. "No, we didn't ask everyone," he said.

"Just Mr. Malloy?"

"That's right."

"Despite his outstanding war record and the fact that he was the highest earner in your office the previous year, you picked him out among everyone in your office and demanded that he sign a loyalty oath? Why was that sir?"

"I wouldn't say we demanded it," DiPietro said weakly. He ran his fingers inside his shirt collar as if it had suddenly become too tight.

"Is that right?" Myers said. "My client had a choice as to whether or not he signed this loyalty oath you put in front of him? He could just as well have refused, as he did, and gone on working at his job?"

"No," DiPietro said weakly. "When you put it that way, I guess he didn't have a choice."

"All right," Myers said. "Then could you tell me why you and your supervisors decided that you should require this excellent employee to demonstrate his patriotism in this way?"

"I guess it was after he was in the paper for signing that petition some people had questions about him."

Myers nodded and now he held up a copy of the *Herald.* "The so-called petition you're referring to was actually a copy of The Bill of Rights, isn't that, right? Says so right here, in the paper."

DiPietro looked as if he wanted to run out of the courtroom, but Myers had blocked his way, so he just moved to the far side of the witness stand. "Just to be clear," Myers said, "it was either sign that loyalty oath or he'd get fired, right?"

DiPietro nodded.

"I'd call that a demand, not a choice at all," Myers said and dismissed DiPietro.

Thorndike decided not to call the people who'd signed the petition saying Ed and Susan were immoral and rested. Myers in turn called Gore, Professor Sinclair and Bill Boyer from the Union, each of whom attested to Ed's honesty and good character. Both sides had agreed not to bring Little Ed into the courtroom, so the case was given over to the judge who adjourned, saying he'd give his verdict that afternoon.

Janey left the room quickly but before Ed and Susan could leave with Myers, Thorndike walked over and asked if he could talk to them. "I just want to know if your offer is still on the table?" he asked Myers.

Myers looked over at Ed who shook his head. "I think we like our case," Myers said. "So, no. You had your chance."

As they sat at lunch, Susan said, "Do you think that was wise?"

"He wouldn't have asked if he thought they were winning," Myers responded.

"But you said before that Cooper is a McCarthy supporter," Susan persisted. "That hasn't changed, has it?"

Myers shook his head. "No, but that doesn't mean he can't be fair. I think Ed showed up well in court and DiPietro looked like he wished he'd never said a thing. What made it better is that they couldn't get that anti-Italian bullshit in there."

"Thanks to you," Ed said.

"Thanks to the judge," Myers corrected him. "That's one reason why I think we might have a chance."

After the recess when they were all seated and the judge had taken his place, Cooper looked at each side in turn and then began to speak in a low voice. "Divorce is always sad," he began. "It's the end of something that started out in a wonderful way and while sometimes inevitable always leaves wreckage behind. That wreckage tragically often involves children. While two people can decide they can no longer live together, they must still remain true to their responsibilities as parents." Now he paused and drank from a glass of water.

"In the present case, one side insists that the other is an unfit parent, a person of low character who cannot be allowed to remain actively involved with their son and should be allowed only supervised visits with the boy. This is a very serious charge and should be sustained only in the most dire situations." Cooper paused again. "Unfortunately, I am persuaded that this is one of those cases.

Mr. Malloy is a distinguished veteran and despite being let go from his previous job, he is in the process of trying to improve his life through education, as attested to by his professor at the University. All of this is admirable. But while Mr. Malloy denies that he is a communist, there has been testimony before a Senate committee chaired by our senator from Wisconsin that he has associated with communists in the past and as if in revenge for this, he is now involved in what I believe is an unconstitutional fight to remove Senator McCarthy from office. Moreover, he has taken his young son along on petition drives without apparent concern for the danger he might have been placing the boy in. All of this is disturbing and tends to undermine his claims of good character and patriotism. This may change in time but none of us can predict the future. Accordingly, I am ruling for the plaintiff and direct the Department of Social Services to determine a schedule of supervised visits during which Mr. Malloy can visit with his son. Court is adjourned."

Twenty-Two

WASHINGTON

McCarthy's house was like a morgue that night. We'd all gone by because we didn't know what else to do but there was a mournful quality about the gathering. While previously the living room had been a hive of activity with phones ringing and staffers running around carrying memos and notes, now Jim and I moved like sleepwalkers, careful not to interfere with one another's dreams. Jeanie McCarthy tip-toed daintily in and out of the room so as not to disturb anyone. Meanwhile, her husband sat in his bathrobe staring fixedly into the fire but saying little to anyone.

I had come by to tell Joe I was leaving, that the other side won, and my usefulness would be limited in the future. But he didn't want to hear it. I told him everyone else on the Committee wanted me to go and would eventually find a way to force me out anyway, that I would just make things hard for him by staying.

"I don't give a shit what those assholes want," Joe said. "I need you. No one else knows where the files are, hell, no one else knows how I think, what I want to do. I need you for contacts, ideas, scheduling, everything."

"You'll be fine," I said gently, though I didn't really believe it.

"Don't be so sure," Joe said. Then he repeated, "I need you."

We left it at that, but it didn't change anything. The newspapers were reprinting Washington gossip that I'd soon be forced out as Committee counsel for McCarthy. In Washington no one's ever actually fired so the Democrats' plan was to make a ruling that all Committee staff would have to be re-submitted to the Committee before being hired to do the jobs we were already doing. Those who didn't receive Committee approval would be dropped, which ran against the traditional method of letting chairmen choose their own staff members.

"Why don't you be direct about it and just kick me out?" I asked Senator Potter, but he patted me on the shoulder and denied that the resolution was aimed specifically at me. This was ridiculous but there was no point in arguing with an old man.

My friends in New York all thought I should quit. When I talked to my father, he sounded resigned. "I told you before you should come back home," he said. "I don't know why you took that *furshlugginer* job in the first place, who needs to be on television all the time? But you did good work and now everyone in the country knows who you are. You think they're going to fire you, why not just walk away? Do yourself a favor. This is the time to come back to New York and take a real job."

McCarthy, typically pugnacious, said if they fired me, he'd just create a new position for me as his executive assistant. "Maybe they can control the Committee, but they can't tell me who to put on my own staff."

I like to think of myself as being decisive but in this case, I was confused by conflicting emotions. I had never liked Washington and felt like an outsider there, but I still wanted to stay on with McCarthy and I'm not sure why. True, there was unfinished work to do but the writing was on the wall. The only real question was how to handle my resignation. So why the confusion? Even now, I'm not completely sure.

Had I known then what my future path would be it would be understandable. Had I known I'd eventually be advising presidents and future presidents, that I'd be representing everyone from world leaders to mafioso, that I would re-invent the profession of lobbying, and that things would never work out with Barbara, it might have made sense for me to want to stay on in Washington. But I knew none of these things. My father had said I should just walk away quietly, but he didn't understand that it was hard for me to do anything quietly. Did the rumors Flanders and others had thrown out on the Senate Floor play a part in all this? Of course, they did, even if no one had caught me with a boy in Lafayette Park or having drinks at Mickey's with questionable characters. The talk was out there about me and Schine. They'd even tarred McCarthy with the same brush though he was married. It all had an effect. Leaving quietly wasn't really an option.

Since the choice was either to resign or let them vote me out. I figured it was better to leave voluntarily. I can't say it was a bad decision at the time, but I ended up thinking it was a mistake. In retrospect, I felt I'd been a coward and should have faced down the members that wanted me gone, made them take their goddamned vote. I don't usually dwell on my mistakes, but I was wrong this time.

I wrote a rather vainglorious resignation letter saying, in part, "It has been a bitter lesson to come to Washington and see a reputation gained at some effort torn to shreds merely because I was associated with Senator McCarthy, who has become the symbol of hatred for all who fear the spread of communism."

McCarthy and Dirksen issued statements praising my work; the others were silent. With that, I was gone as Committee counsel.

No one who knew me would believe I'd slink out of town with my tail between my legs the way my friend Jerry had and indeed I didn't. Eight days after my resignation two thousand people paid for tickets to a banquet in my honor at the Astor Hotel in Times Square. E.F. Hutton, Westbrook Pegler, Fulton Lewis, Jr, Bill Buckley, and Bishop Sheen were there as well as Barbara and my parents. The tributes went on throughout the evening with one speaker describing me as the "American Dreyfus." The event was covered by all the papers as well as *Newsweek, Catholic World* and *Commonweal*. There were in fact so many Catholics present that someone called it an "Irish-Catholic gathering."

This wasn't quite true, but for me, the most important speech was by none other than Joe McCarthy who had made the trip up from Washington with Jeannie for the event and held court in a corner surrounded by admirers. When Joe got up to speak, he said, "Roy thinks he has resigned, but the truth is Roy Cohn can never resign from the fight against international communism. I need him too much for that; the country needs him too much. The Roy Cohn who worked as my counsel may have left, but there's going to be a new Roy Cohn tomorrow to carry on the fight now and forever."

And to cap off the evening, Rabbi Benjamin Schultz of the American-Jewish Joint Committee Against Communism said, "America is for Cohn; the people are for Cohn; he stands for McCarthyism and God bless it."

It was a great evening, and it should have left me on top of the world, but the truth is I felt the way anyone would who'd been fired from a job he valued. Empty inside hollowed out and left a husk by Bobby Kennedy and the Democrats. I truly believed we had left work undone and that my resignation would further enable the communists in government we might have identified and eliminated to gain a toehold.

I'm not stupid about this and I wasn't going to sit around licking my wounds. In my own way I'd given as good as I got, and the New York banquet was the *coup de grace*. That was the best that could be said about the whole thing. It was better to leave than to hang on in some subordinate position Joe would have created for me. So, I was gone but perhaps not quite forgotten. Unfortunately, the story, or my part in it, doesn't end on that high note.

The Senate hearings on the McCarthy censure took another two months to organize and it was billed as being the equivalent of a trial. The truth is it was a charade, a public lynching with the new committee that had been formed to run things acting as both judge and jury. In saying that, I don't mean to make McCarthy sound like a victim since Joe was less helpless than anyone I ever met. He had his chances to wriggle out of the situation he was in, but it would have been totally out of character for him to take advantage of them. Rather than apologizing to his colleagues for his bad manners, bad taste or both, he chose to go right at them, yelling insults and point of order to the end. That was Joe and there was no changing him. And even if the charges were no more serious than being accused of farting during mass, the Senate took their rules, official and unofficial, seriously.

The whole history of censure in the Senate was a joke. It had only happened a handful of times in the past and then when a member pulled a gun on a colleague or when two others had a fistfight on the Senate floor. Senators had seduced page boys and fallen asleep drunk in their chairs, when they showed up, which wasn't often. The worst Joe had done was make fun of some of his colleagues. First, they wanted to strip him of his chairmanship, but this wasn't going to happen because the old timers in the Senate knew if it happened to him it could happen to them. They didn't like McCarthy, but they were experts in self-preservation. And there were still no formal charges. No one was eager to go public condemning the one Senator a good segment of the American people thought was trying to fight communism.

What was to be done? In typical Senate fashion, they decided to name a committee to study the whole mess. Nixon had been deputized by Eisenhower for this duty and the names submitted were all members of the Senate's inner club. Unlike Joe, they played by the rules and some others they'd made up. And while the original hearing had been in the Senate Chamber with a packed gallery looking on, Chairman Watkins directed that the censure debate would be held in the Hearing Room and the press and cameras would not be allowed. Finally, to make sure these hearings didn't turn into a version of the Army/McCarthy debacle they limited cross examination so even though Joe had hired Eddie Williams to represent him, it didn't have much positive effect. Some court of law.

Even if the final verdict was thus pre-determined, as you might expect Joe didn't make things easy for them by constantly interrupting during the debate and finally being closed down by the chairman. You ask me, it was a clown show carried about by a bunch of losers who couldn't shine McCarthy's shoes but no one in the Senate was interested in what I thought of their process.

What it all came down to in the end was that rather than being penitent, Joe fought all the way. Whatever they said, he was really punished for saying of Flanders "I think they should get a man with a net and take him to a good quiet place." Of course, Flanders had compared McCarthy to Hitler but that was somehow forgotten. Then, if that wasn't enough, Joe said of Senator Hendrickson that he was "A living miracle in that he is without question the only man in the world who has lived so long with neither brains nor guts."

Behind all this, the White House publicists were pushing a notion that the era of McCarthyism was past. This version of the truth had it that if there were any communists or homosexuals in government they'd already been found out and punished during the Lavender Scare and it was time to move on. The only trouble with this story was Joe maintained his popularity with an important part of the public. The polls reflected this with McCarthy continuing to have significant popularity even after Welch's denunciation of him. Eisenhower's men could say what they wanted but their handling of the censure issue hadn't gained them any new friends and probably lost some supporters.

The Watkins committee submitted its report at the beginning of September. Shortly after this, Joe entered the Bethesda Naval Hospital complaining that the headaches he'd been suffering were getting worse. When I visited him there, he was grimly realistic. "I know I'm getting censured," he said. "And you know it too. That's not the important thing."

"No?" I said. "What is then?"

"I'm not going down without a fight," McCarthy said. "Once I get well, I'm going back up there and I'm not apologizing for a goddamned thing."

"You might think about that," I said. "Dirksen thinks this would all go away if you just wrote a note to Watkins."

"Fuck him," Joe said. "I'm not apologizing because I'm not sorry. I did nothing wrong and neither did you."

I agreed with him then and agree with him still. But looking back I'm still not sure why Joe wouldn't take the easy way out and apologize. What would it have cost him really? He had millions of supporters around the country and there was no need to go down the way he did. But McCarthy wasn't much on reflection or self-examination. He did what he did impulsively and let others worry about his motivations. His colleagues had backed down before when they challenged him, so why not expect them to do so now? In addition, there had been talk of his organizing a Third-Party candidacy to challenge Eisenhower in '56. That would have been a longshot, to put it mildly, but Joe's whole career had been about taking long odds. The truth was that if McCarthy had given up and apologized, he could have kept his chairmanship and gone on hunting commies as long as he wanted. So why not take the reasonable step? If I knew, I'd tell you but it's still a mystery to me.

I thought the time in the hospital might make him more cooperative, but when Joe emerged in November, he was no less pugilistic. "I will be censured," he told the reporters who were waiting for him, "because I am the last remaining symbol of American resistance to communism, which has now extended itself into the U.S. Senate. I can go fifteen rounds with these guys, believe me in that. I'll be there at the end."

Ever since Marquette, McCarthy had been a bruiser, what in boxing circles was called a bleeder, a fighter who didn't care what happened to him and just kept on coming and coming until the other guy got tired of punching. He reminded me of Carmen Basilio, a fighter my father and I had seen at the Garden whose face looked like a scarlet cauliflower after his fights but who somehow managed to win championships in two divisions anyway. That was McCarthy, the Basilio of Politics.

The debate began on November 8 and Watkins started off with a recitation of the findings of the committee with respect to McCarthy's errors of judgement and behavior. Joe responded in writing by saying he had been targeted by the reds as "a symbol of resistance to communist subversion."

After that, Watkins talked for an hour, exhausting himself and everyone else in the chamber. At the end, he asked his colleagues, "What are you going to do about this?" and left to a standing ovation from those present.

I didn't really take an old fool like Watkins seriously and I doubt anyone else did either. Instead of moving immediately on the censure, Dirksen came up with a compromise: The Senate would draft a new Code of Senate Behavior, and all future cases would be punished. Future cases. Which meant Joe would be off the hook if he apologized to the members he'd insulted, Hendricksen and Watkins.

Why anyone thought Joe would go for this is beyond me, but before they could ask, he dropped out of sight again. Word eventually reached the Senate that he was back in the Bethesda Naval Hospital, this time with bursitis in his elbow. Bursitis my ass, I thought, and no one else believed the story either, but there wasn't much they could do.

Joe was stalling, of course, because he had no interest in compromise. "The word I'm hearing is that I'm getting more support all the time," he told me when I visited. "We got invitations to give speeches in Houston and Boston. People are writing letters, holding rallies. Why should I give in now? Tell me that."

Rabbi Benjamin Schultz held a rally at Washington's Constitution Hall and three thousand people showed up, including a trainload of

New Yorkers. I sat with Sok in the audience and there were others with signs reading "Moscow Hates McCarthy, too."

An even larger group gathered in New York with a simple message: there was a "hidden force" deep inside the government that was trying to oust McCarthy because he had resisted their attempts to "Sovietize" America. I don't know who came up with the hidden force idea, but I could see it might be a winner. Everyone loves a good conspiracy theory and the idea that there was an underground group in the government working against McCarthy was classic. I was out of things officially by this time but having been attacked by the same people who were now trying to censure Joe, I was in some demand by groups protesting his censure. I didn't accept many invitations to speak, but it was hard to feel sorry for the hypocrites in the Senate.

Meanwhile at Bethesda, Joe's recovery was going well. I went down to see him again and while I was there Barry Goldwater and Eddie Williams came by too. Eddie had put together a couple of letters of apology for Joe to sign. Both were mild and neither admitted malice nor any serious wrong-doing. "If you sign these," Eddie said, "especially the one to Hendrickson, I think they'll vote against censure."

"You know me better than that," Joe said. "I don't crawl. I don't give up. I learned to fight in an alley and that's all I know."

The Senate finally voted on December second following three days of debate and angry speeches on the Senate floor. The resolution read in part that in characterizing the Select Committee and its members as the "unwitting handmaiden" of the communist conspiracy Joe acted "contrary to senatorial ethics and tended to bring the Senate into dishonor and disrepute...and to impair its dignity."

As far as I could tell neither Joe nor I could have done more than the Senators themselves to dishonor the body and if anyone figures out what Senate ethics are, I'd appreciate their telling me. In the end, though, it didn't matter. Joe had misbehaved and refused to apologize for it. The final vote was 67-22 with a few abstentions, including Jack Kennedy who was in the hospital and Joe's Wisconsin colleague, Alexander Wiley who had arranged to be in South America.

In one sense, you could say it didn't matter much. McCarthy was still in the Senate but having been censured he couldn't chair a committee. Over time they found ways to kick him aside, ignore his speeches and distance him in other ways. Joe was through as a national figure.

I watched the debate from the gallery. While I was sympathetic, I didn't really see Joe as a tragic figure. The way I saw it he'd fought the good fight even if in the end he lost. It had been the most stimulating and exhausting year and a half of my life, and I wondered if anything would ever equal it in the years that followed. I'm not dead yet, but I can say that so far nothing has. That may sound melodramatic but it's the truth as I see it.

After the Senate debate, I walked down to the floor and found a crowd of press and hangers-on waiting outside the Senate chamber. I didn't want to comment and wasn't in a mood for socializing so started working my way through to the exit when I saw someone familiar standing in front of me wearing a "Joe Must Go" button. It was the galoot from Wisconsin who'd come to my office the year before. What the hell was he doing here, I wondered, but when I stopped in front of Malloy he offered his hand. What was it to me to refuse so I shook hands with him.

"Nice to see you again, Butch," I said. "And thanks for the buttons you sent. I have to say I really liked the baseball cap."

Malloy smiled at this and took the "Joe Must Go" button off his coat. "Here," he said. "Here's another one. A souvenir. We didn't quite get there with the petitions but it's okay. He's out anyway."

"Not out, exactly," I said.

Malloy shrugged. "Maybe not out of the Senate, but down anyway. That's enough for me. He's done enough damage."

I looked back at the Senators now emerging from the Chamber and talking to reporters. "Good enough for them, too," I said.

I expected Malloy to move on, but he stood there on one foot, showing no signs of moving. "Let me ask you something," he said. "You were the Committee Counsel, real tight with McCarthy, right?"

"We weren't friends," I said. "I worked for him. But yeah, we spent a lot of time together. In that sense, we were close. So what?"

"What I want to know," Malloy said, "and you can be honest with me. Was it worth it? Was it worth wrecking lives like you did, getting people fired, ruining their reputations? I lost my job, my house, my marriage and my kid because of this shit. Does that bother you at all?"

It was an odd question in that it was direct, man to man. Beyond all the posturing of the senators in public most of us were polite if we were to run into each other outside the hearings. Unlike McCarthy, I hadn't gone out of my way to insult anyone, certainly not the man standing in front of me wanting an answer.

But here we were in the Senate anteroom, with people all around us talking at each other and this guy I didn't really know and wouldn't ever know wanted a mea *culpa*. I'm guessing he'd come all the way out from Wisconsin expecting to get it. I imagined him sitting on the bus for hours running versions of this conversation over in his mind, thinking confronting me would be payback for whatever had happened to him. It would all be worth it to him if he could just see Joe publicly humiliated. I was frosting on the cake. But whatever it was that Malloy wanted or thought he wanted; it wasn't going to come from me.

"I'd do it all again," I said. "The work was important."

"So that wasn't just a line of bullshit you put out?" Malloy said. "You actually believe ordinary guys like me are part of some big communist conspiracy to overthrow the government?"

This almost made me smile. I'd always heard people in Wisconsin were so nice, but this was a pretty damned aggressive thing to say. The odd thing, though, is that Malloy didn't seem as much mad as curious, maybe even incredulous. I wondered if he thought I was evil too, but he didn't really seem like that kind of person.

"Yeah," I said. "Actually, I do. I wouldn't have worked so hard if I didn't."

Malloy nodded as if he was taking that in but didn't say anything in response, so finally I patted his shoulder and said, "Got to go, Butch." And with that I pushed past him and out into the street. I didn't want to be late for the train to New York.

Epilogue

Following his censure, McCarthy was successfully marginalized. Though he remained in the Senate until his death, he never again took a central role in its business. His speeches were largely ignored, even by the reporters who had previously gathered around him eager for a quote. He was no longer news. While he remained popular around the country and continued to draw large crowds for speeches warning of the continued presence of communism in the government, McCarthy increasingly declined into depression and alcoholism. One bright spot in his life was a baby daughter he and his wife Jean adopted in 1957.

As it turned out, Edward R. Murrow's best days were behind him too. A celebrity in radio reporting from London during World War II, Murrow was ill-suited for television, and he never fully believed in it as a medium for serious broadcasting. Several of the "boys" from his staff in Europe, including Charles Collingwood, Eric Sevareid, and Howard K. Smith stayed on, however, and became fixtures in television news in the years to come.

Annie Lee Moss, the Army clerk whom McCarthy had been accused of bullying by other Senators and Murrow, who devoted one of his programs to her, was later found to have been a communist, just as McCarthy and Cohn had claimed. At least one of the senators involved in the investigation later sheepishly apologized for his role in the matter.

Roy Cohn returned to New York and enjoyed a successful career as a lawyer defending a wide variety of people, including mobsters, George Steinbrenner and the Roman Catholic Archdiocese of New

York. He was an advisor to Ronald Reagan and later defended a young real estate magnate named Donald Trump who had been sued by the government for discriminating against blacks in his rental units. Cohn counter-sued on Trump's behalf, asserting the government's position was baseless and the case was settled out of court.

Despite his stated intentions, Cohn never proposed marriage to Barbara Walters who married Robert Katz in 1955 and after her divorce was rumored to be involved with a variety of high government officials, including Henry Kissinger and Senator Edward Brooke. In time, she became the first woman anchor on a network news program and interviewed Fidel Castro.

Joseph McCarthy died in 1957 at the age of forty-nine. Twenty-five thousand of his followers attended the funeral at St. Mary's Catholic Church in Appleton, along with nineteen Senators and seven Congressmen, many of whom had supported him. Unnoticed by most of the mourners was Bobby Kennedy who flew in privately and sat alone in the church balcony during the service. Roy Cohn was there too, sitting with McCarthy's wife Jean in the family pew, apparently unaware of Kennedy's presence.

After the ceremony, Cohn stood outside the church waiting for a ride to the cemetery where interment would take place. While there, he was noticed by another attendee, Edgeworth Malloy, who had driven up alone from Madison for the occasion. Cohn smiled when he saw the other man and they shook hands.

"Never thought I'd see you here," Cohn said. "Did you come to pay your respects to the Senator?"

"Not exactly," Malloy replied. "To be honest, I just wanted to make sure they put the sonofabitch in the ground at last."

Cohn nodded and looked the other man over. "You're looking good," he said. "You still mad at us? It was a long time ago now."

"I'm doing okay," Malloy said. "Graduated from the University, got a good job, even bought another house to replace the place you lost for me. You could say I'm one of the lucky ones. But you never really get over what McCarthy did and not just to me. A lot of people's lives were ruined. No way to make that go away. At least now he's gone."

"Not really," Cohn replied.

Malloy looked surprised. "No?"

"McCarthy was a man of his time," Cohn said. "But maybe more than that. He wasn't the first and he won't be the last to speak to thousands of people who feel left out and that their government might be acting against their best wishes. People always respond to a man who has the balls to go up against the government, a populist. There were men like this before McCarthy and take my word, there will be more in the future."

"That sounds like a threat." Malloy said. "Are you thinking of finding another senator to work for and maybe making a comeback?"

"Not really," Cohn said. "More like a promise than a threat. Now you take care of yourself, Butch."

Acknowledgements

Scare Tactics is a novel rather than a non-fiction account of the period when a fear of communism spread throughout America. Nevertheless, it involves characters and scenes based on historical figures and events. To aid me in imagining this frightening time, I relied on papers, letters and biographical material, as available, of the main actors at that time.

I am grateful to the librarians at Marquette University for allowing me free rein in the McCarthy papers over two days in 2019. Similarly, I give thanks to the Tufts University library for access to the Edward R. Murrow papers which are collected there. In each case, the staff were cheerful, friendly and eager to help me with my researches. I was impressed and remain thankful for the willingness of those librarians to assist in a project that at that point was less a book than an idea.

The Executive Sessions of the Senate Permanent Subcommittee on Investigations is an invaluable resource for anyone interested in the activities of the McCarthy Committee in 1953-4 and I have relied on the transcripts in these volumes and often quoted them in creating the scenes dealing with the McCarthy Sub-Committee on Investigations in this novel.

Though it was published more than fifteen years ago, David Oshinsky's A *Conspiracy so Immense* is still the best source for information about the inner workings of Joseph McCarthy's mind, though I also found Richard Rovere's *Senator Joe McCarthy* useful as well as *McCarthy and his Enemies* by William F. Buckley and Brent Bozell. For information on the examination of witnesses before the McCarthy Committee, I drew on James A. Wechsler's *The Age of Suspicion* which provides a chilling first-person account of Wechsler's experience as a witness before the Committee.

There is less documentary information available on Roy Cohn, but I found Nicholas Van Hoffman's *Citizen Cohn* crucial in providing a biographical timeline. Perhaps most useful for my purposes was Cohn's own book on the period, *McCarthy*. Tony Kushner's brilliant "Angels in America" was helpful for its imaginative rendering of Cohn's personality and his attitude toward homosexuals.

For information regarding the often exaggerated role of Edward R. Murrow in bringing down McCarthy, I found Joseph E. Persico's *Edward R. Murrow: An American Original* and *The Murrow Boys* by Stanley Cloud and Lynne Olson valuable.

The movement to recall McCarthy has unfortunately mostly been forgotten and is seldom mentioned or even alluded to in most accounts of the period. My primary source for information on the movement and its leader was "Joe Must Go: The Movement to Recall Senator Joseph R. McCarthy" by David P. Thelan and Esther S. Thelan, which appeared in the Wisconsin Magazine of History published by The Wisconsin Historical Society.

Barbara Wright, Dick Blau, Jean E. Milofsky and Jennifer Hoffman all read versions of *Scare Tactics* in manuscript and offered valuable suggestions. As always, I'm grateful for the support of my friends, Frank Gay, Joe Lucas, Josh Johnson, Ronna Wineberg and the late Bob Harding.

THE AUTHOR

David Milofsky has published six novels and a collection of short stories. He has received fellowships for his work from Breadloaf, the MacDowell Colony, and the National Endowment for the Arts. In addition, he has won a Prairie Schooner short fiction award and the Colorado Book Award. He served as editor of *Denver Quarterly* and *Colorado Review* and was the founding editor of the Colorado Prize in Poetry. An Emeritus Professor of English at Colorado State University, he lives in Colorado with his wife Jean.

www.ingramcontent.com/pod-product-compliance
Lightning Source LLC
Chambersburg PA
CBHW061651190726
48289CB00006B/1829